THE
FIRST
GOSPEL

THE
FIRST
GOSPEL

DARRYL NYZNYK

Cross Dove Publishing
CALIFORNIA

First printing 2017

ISBN 978-0-9656513-0-1 (softcover book)
ISBN 978-0-9656513-2-5 (ebook)
LCCN 2016957177

DEDICATION

To the
Ethical System of Love

PROLOGUE

BASED UPON HISTORICAL RECORD
FALL, 943 A.D.

GENERAL JOHN KOURKOUAS crested a rise atop his spirited black stallion. A roiling mass of men and beasts laden with weapons of war stretched far behind him awaiting his command, but he sat calmly, leaning on his saddle's pommel and peering across the valley to the city of Edessa.

The city's stone battlements had repelled Byzantine attacks for more than three hundred years, since Muslims first conquered and began defending it with a ferocity and fervor Christian armies were not able to match. But things had changed.

Nine years earlier Kourkouas had led his troops to their first victory over Muslim forces at Melitene. Since then, one after another Muslim stronghold had fallen to the great general, who destroyed everything in his path as he swept across northern Mesopotamia to reclaim large swaths of land for Christendom. Now he eyed Edessa, the grandest prize of all, for it was the first city in history to declare Christianity its official faith.

Kourkouas leaned toward his second, a burly, battle-scarred captain who sat stoically astride his mount next to the general.

"Let us begin." Kourkouas said softly, but with complete confidence in the inevitability of his purpose.

The captain turned his horse, stood high in its stirrups and motioned sharply over his head. An instant later, the dull blast of war horns echoed their call and eighty thousand troops started their march.

Their coming was not a surprise to anyone in the city, but their sheer numbers were staggering as they swarmed over the rise. Edessa's citizens, Christian and Muslim alike, cowered behind the city's walls, knowing well this force could not be stopped. They'd heard reports of the general's conquests—how he'd overrun higher fortifications and ruthlessly dealt with those who'd resisted him. Not a soul believed the Christian horde could be defeated despite their emir's attempts to convince them otherwise. The only hope for Christians was that their common faith would save them, while Muslims were left to hope for enslavement over tortured death.

Kourkouas directed his massive force to encircle the city, but halted its advance just beyond the range of the city's armaments. As panic spread through Edessa, the general did something that shocked the city's populace to silence. Before a single battle salvo was loosed, he sent an emissary to offer terms to the city's leader.

The emissary told the astonished emir that Edessa would be spared attack and destruction. In addition, General Kourkouas promised to release two hundred Muslim prisoners and pay the ungodly sum of twelve thousand silver pieces, all in exchange for one thing: a thin linen burial cloth upon which existed an image—not made by human hands—of the head and naked body of the crucified lord of Christianity.

After some wrangling, first to cover his shock and then to insure the city's safety, the emir handed over the cloth, and the city and all its inhabitants were spared.

On August 15, 944 A.D. General John Kourkouas and his conquering army returned to Constantinople as heroes. They had restored to the seat of Christianity the holy relic that bore the only true image of Jesus Christ the world has ever seen.

CHAPTER ONE

PRESENT DAY

THREATS WERE NOTHING new to Professor Samuel Rosen. His work at the University of Arizona brought out the fanatics, mostly religious nuts threatening the wrath of God if he didn't cease his work immediately.

University policy required that threats be reported to campus police, who, in turn, would report them to the Tucson Police. Files would be opened, investigations conducted, reports written, and security heightened. But nothing ever came of the threats, and professors simply began to ignore them.

Then, a week ago Professor Rosen received a different kind of threat. The moment he'd heard the voice, he knew it was different.

"Professor Samuel Rosen," the voice started in a deep, almost whispered monotone. "Terminate your research on the Sindon immediately; destroy all evidence of your work, and you will live. Do not, and you will die."

The emeritus professor had been unnerved. The voice's polished, yet deadly timbre and the simplicity of the threat prevented him from grabbing control of the situation.

"What?" he had finally mustered. "Who is this?"

Rosen had listened anxiously to the calm breathing of a man assured of his purpose, and then he'd heard nothing more.

Since the call, the foul words had hung in "repeat" mode in his mind.

...destroy all evidence of your work, and you will live.

He'd heard a rolled "r" and middle-eastern inflection, hadn't he?

Do not, and you will die.

The voice jarred him, even in memory, yet he couldn't do as demanded. He had to preserve his work; it was too important to a world desperate for the truth.

So he'd reported the threat to campus police, and tried to tell them it was something more, something menacing and more deadly than any he'd ever received. Campus police, of course, handled it with as much seriousness as the "over-the-hill, can't-wait-for-retirement" officer who took the report could generate. He had assured Rosen that security would be heightened and the report would be conveyed to the Tucson Police Department.

Rosen had then embarked on a plan to preserve the work he deemed the most important of his life. He spoke to his most trusted colleagues and kept them in-the-loop with e-mails and discussions. He stuffed envelopes to mail with copies of his notes, research, and conclusions as an added precaution. The old professor didn't trust online technology, especially after his experiences with power surges and other esoteric concepts that tended to wipe everything out.

He had nearly completed his preservation plan when he'd gotten the second call just minutes ago.

"You did not believe me, Professor," the voice said flatly. "You did not believe, and your work continues. You will be punished."

That was it. There was no, "I'll give you one more chance," or, "You'd better think about this," or even, "I'm going to slit the tires of your car to show you how serious I am." It was just, "You will be punished."

The professor bypassed campus police this time. He called the Tucson PD directly. After reminding the vexing desk sergeant that they already had an open file and that this was the second of two death threats, and after a crazed shout that this threat was real, the officer finally agreed to send someone over. Rosen didn't wait.

He closed his office door and walked purposefully out of the geosciences building. A manuscript-sized burnt-orange envelope was tucked tightly inside his coat, under his left arm, while his right hand clasped the coat's collar to his throat against the desert chill.

It was an unusually cold evening, the night before the University of Arizona's homecoming football game against the Oregon Ducks. The campus was wild with returning alumni, parties, and rallies. Rosen usually reveled in the festivities and was a favorite of the students, who affectionately dubbed him the "Jewish Leprechaun" because of his small, paunchy stature; cheerful, ruddy face, and animated lecture style. Several students shouted out greetings as he passed them, but he didn't respond. He was single-minded in his march to the off-campus post office, his eyes hooded in concentration, bouncing furtively from face to face in search of one that carried the evil voice.

Rosen made the short trek carrying only one of the seven envelopes he'd been preparing. It was the thinnest of the bunch, containing the least amount of materials, yet it was the only one that was complete. It was intended for someone with whom the professor had not maintained contact. Rosen had no doubt the recipient would be surprised to receive word after so many years, especially the words in this envelope. They would shock the young man. But Rosen was determined; of the seven intended envelope recipients, this one was the most important.

He left the other six envelopes on his desk awaiting final documents that he had trouble retrieving. He intended to go back to try the retrieval process one more time, but he wasn't confident in his computer skills, and he believed he'd have to wait to finish until his assistant came in after tomorrow's game.

Rosen pushed through partying students, paying close attention to facial expressions, body language, and general demeanor of passersby. No stranger seemed interested; none appeared to be tracking him. But he knew the voice was out there somewhere.

He fell in with a group of alumni ambling toward the bars and eateries near the post office. He ducked his already shorter-than-average frame a little lower, and slipped away from the group through the post office doors. Inside, he immediately extracted the envelope, glanced at the addressee's name, whispered an apology, and dropped it into the slot. In moments he was outside again, scurrying back to his office.

As he re-entered his second floor office, the seventy-year-old professor felt a chill despite the heavy coat and heat of exertion from the frantic walk. He pulled the coat tighter and rubbed his arms as he shuffled pensively to the chaos of his desk. He looked down; then, slightly perplexed, he glanced at his worktable stacked haphazardly with papers and books. Without thought, his eyes returned to the mess on his desk. He stared for several seconds before he understood: the other six envelopes were gone. He pushed aside papers, pulled open drawers; panic tightened his chest...and then he heard the voice.

"You are looking for these," it said.

The professor whirled, wide-eyed. A man in black with a stocking cap covering his face emerged from the tiny, adjoining room the professor called his "quiet room." In his right hand the man held the six burnt-orange envelopes.

"You..." Rosen whispered, stunned. He threw a furtive glance at his closed office door and then back at the man, who now strode deliberately toward him.

The man said nothing. He stopped at the corner of the desk, two feet away. The professor had to lean back to stare up at the towering evil.

Rosen wanted to shout. He thought he should run. But he stood frozen as the man laid the envelopes on the desk, and, in a simple, fluid motion, brought his left arm up before the professor. He touched the silenced muzzle of a gun to Rosen's forehead as his other hand lifted the mask from his face. It was a smooth face, unwrinkled and clean-shaven, framed by pitch black hair, and with shockingly steel blue eyes. It was a handsome face that didn't smile, but the lids around the eyes widened with sadistic excitement as the first finger of his gloved hand squeezed the trigger.

CHAPTER TWO

MATHEW CARTER JOINED the throng of rabid fans cheering the Arizona Wildcats' march downfield for the go-ahead touchdown late in the fourth quarter. He was slapping upraised hands of equally inebriated seat neighbors, all of whom screamed from vein-popping red faces after a spectacular, diving catch by JaRon Woodley, the Wildcats' sophomore wide receiver. Woodley had beaten his Oregon Duck defender, and Arizona's quarterback had let loose a wobbly throw that was just beyond the reach of his speedy receiver. At the last second, Woodley dove, stretched full out, and snagged the ball with his fingertips an instant before he crashed to the ground at the Duck's 15-yard line.

The score was tied at 14, and although the Wildcats would have liked to eat up more of the clock before they got so close to the goal line, no one was complaining. Arizona had a first down with just over two minutes remaining in the game.

The game had been a knockdown, drag-out affair, not the type school administrators preferred for a homecoming, when an easy victory would tend to keep the alumni generous. But Matt Carter loved this stuff. He'd followed the Wildcats since graduating from UA ten years ago. He'd fly in at least twice a season to catch games and share memories with his college buddies, and he made sure one of those trips was at homecoming, when everything was a little more insane. Unfortunately, in recent years, his college friends were getting married and having kids, and fewer joined him. This year, Seth Bellow was the only diehard who'd been able to make it, and his seat was on the other end of the stadium. The two had agreed to meet at a local bar after the game.

Matt lived alone in a one-bedroom apartment off an alley in the southern California town of Manhattan Beach. His unit sat atop a garage that he wasn't allowed to use because the owner, who lived in the main house, commandeered the valuable parking space. Matt, like many beach residents, fought for street parking along Manhattan Avenue, some four houses up the alley. His unit was tiny by most standards, but it was big enough for him and an occasional overnight female guest—nothing serious just yet, of course. He had plenty of time for that. He earned a semblance of a living as a waiter at Fonz's, the moderately upscale restaurant in the town's eclectic center, a three-by-six-block area filled with funky shops, eateries, small businesses, and the occasional walk-up office.

Matt had obtained a law degree from the University of San Diego after graduating from Arizona. He passed the California Bar Exam on his first try. He'd even landed a job in the litigation department of a prestigious southern California law firm after graduation. But he realized quickly he hated the practice. He woke up one morning and decided he was through. He walked away, shocking his firm's partners and his law school associates, and devastating his parents. He'd bounced around for a couple years after that, taking odd jobs as a sales rep for various products, those being the only jobs available to an anthropology major with a law degree he didn't want to use.

What Matt found he really liked was the simple, unhurried beach life. So he took the job waiting tables. It allowed him the opportunity to meet people from every walk of life, which, he would often argue, was great for networking for when he might have to leave the beach and "grow up," as his dad was wont to say. Most important, however, it allowed him his indulgences: surfing, beach volleyball, and skimpily clad women. All in all, Matt loved his life…at least that's what he kept telling himself as he grew older and the occasional doubts crept into his mind.

Three plays after Woodley's phenomenal catch, Arizona's offense hadn't done anything but lose six yards in a little under a minute. On fourth down from the Ducks' 21-yard line, Arizona's coaches faced the decision of whether to send the kicking unit onto the field. This part of the team was its weakest—one of the primary reasons the offense found it difficult to score despite the team's high ranking. The Wildcat faithful grew silent as they, like the team's coaches, contemplated going for it on fourth rather than turning the ball over to the kicking team to blow a golden opportunity with a missed 38-yard field goal attempt.

With only seconds remaining before a delay-of-game penalty would be assessed, the field-goal unit sprinted onto the field and readied itself for the kick. But Oregon's coaching staff, knowing the Wildcats weakness, called its final time-out to rattle the kicker into thinking about his kick. After an interminably long two-minute time-out, the lines were finally set. A hush fell over the crowd; the ball was snapped.

The kicker stepped forward, planted his left foot and swung his right at the ball. His plant-foot hit a slick part of the turf and slipped as his kicking leg came forward. He struck the ball awkwardly, sent a wobbly floater in the general direction of the uprights, and crashed heavily to the ground. The ball wafted in slow motion in the now dead silence; it struck the left upright and, after an agonizing bounce, fell through the posts. The referees raised their arms in unison indicating a successful field goal. The hometown crowd erupted. The young kicker was lifted, dazed and confused, by his jubilant teammates and carried off the field to ear splitting screams of victory.

But the game wasn't over.

The high-powered Ducks would get the ball back with just over a minute remaining; plenty of time for their Heisman-candidate quarterback to bring them back.

Matt released his hug of the buxom, braless co-ed next to him as her boyfriend was slapping the upraised hands of his buddies and screaming insanely.

Damn, Matt thought, imagining the co-ed's hug lingering as he began the release. If we can hold this lead, it's going to be great around here tonight.

The Ducks returned the kickoff to their own 42-yard line.

Too close, thought the Wildcat faithful, particularly after the first pass from the great quarterback was caught by his All-American wide receiver at Arizona's forty. By the time the clock had ticked down to 20 seconds remaining, the ball rested on Arizona's five-yard line with a first down for Oregon. The Ducks fans cheered wildly as the Wildcat crowd sat in silence, holding its aggregate breath, eyes bugged out and hands pressed against mouths in fear of the coming Duck touchdown and Wildcat defeat.

Matt joined the rest of the crowd on its feet, all craning to see over hats, #1 foam hand gloves, pennants, and other paraphernalia, hoping that a miracle would stop the drive of the most prolific offense in the country. On first down, Oregon's quarterback, Brett Masters, dropped back and ran out of the pocket crushed by the blitzing Wildcat defense. For a split second he had open field and a straight line look at his best receiver running free across the back of the end zone. He let the ball go in a tight spiral, and, as his receiver's eyes widened and his fingers extended to catch the coming bullet, a body dove out of nowhere. Arizona's middle linebacker, Keanu Maaleva, was tracking Masters. He waited for the ball to leave the quarterback's hand, and then made his desperate lunge. He caught the ball in front of the Duck receiver, hit the ground hard, rolled as the ball bounced in his arms, and then sprang to his feet with the ball gripped firmly in his upraised hand with the interception that won the game for the Wildcats.

The crowd erupted.

Matt again found himself clinging to the firm, cushy body of the co-ed and basking in the glow of drink and anticipation of what lay ahead.

CHAPTER THREE

MATT NEVER RENDEZVOUSED with Seth Bellow.

Immediately after Matt's final clinch with the co-ed, her boyfriend was suddenly interested in her. The euphoria of victory morphed into the excitement of passionate embraces and lip locks, and Matt recognized his cue for a quick exit. He'd started for the bar to meet Seth, but chose a leisurely stroll through Highland Quad since he had some time before they were to meet. He found himself jumping out of the way of excited students hell-bent on insanity and realized, for the first time, that he was more irritated then amused by them. The realization surprised him. As he maneuvered through the quad of science buildings in which he'd spent so much time on campus, he fell into a reflective mood.

Matt had dreamed of being an archeologist after seeing the Indiana Jones movies as a kid. He went to college intending to make his career in the exciting field of the dead and forgotten, anticipating that he'd be a man of adventure, a "field guy" like Indi. It was only after he'd gotten into the upper division studies of his anthropology major that he'd realized Indiana Jones was fantasy. The reality was an academic life of little danger and few earth-shattering discoveries, with most of his time being spent in the classroom, lab, or research library. It wasn't what he'd hoped, but rather than start over completely, he'd stuck with the major, made the decision for law, and the rest was history.

Matt stopped in front of the geo-sciences building, stared up at the four-story brick façade, and recalled his favorite class. It dealt with radio-carbon dating: the science of determining the age of once living objects by calculating the extent to which they have lost their radioactive carbon-14 content. With a half-life of 5730 years, radioactive carbon-14 decays in an organism at a consistent rate from the date of the organism's death. The decay is readily measurable by means of an accelerator mass spectrometer in the use of which the experts at the University of Arizona were widely recognized. Thus, objects from charcoal to wood, and from paper to cloth to bone could be dated to ages as great as 50,000 years.

As a young man, Matt was fascinated by modern science's ability to determine the true age of ancient objects. He figured it would fit well with his chosen field because it would enable him to distinguish between truly ancient artifacts and the fakes that cropped up so often. In fact, it was the University of Arizona's participation in the exposure of one of history's great archaeological hoaxes that convinced Matt to go to that school.

In 1988, as a young boy captivated by the Indiana Jones movies, Matt read about the university's involvement in uncovering the hoax. Arizona was one of three facilities, along with Oxford University in London and the Swiss Federal Institute of Technology in Zurich, to test an object revered by Roman and eastern orthodox Catholics, even while people of other faiths called it a fake. It was the supposed burial cloth of Jesus Christ, known for hundreds of years as the Shroud of Turin. The story was that when the body of the crucified Jesus was taken to the tomb for burial, he was laid on his back on one half of the length of linen, 14 feet long by four feet wide, and the other half was folded and draped over him from his head to his feet. On the third day after the crucifixion and entombment, Jesus supposedly rose from the dead in a burst of light and energy and left the burial cloth behind. His apostles found the cloth on the morning of Jesus' resurrection, opened it up, and saw a full body image, front and back, of their scourged and crucified lord imprinted on it.

Although the history of the linen had been subject to much debate over the centuries, the Catholic faithful believed the cloth was a miracle left to them by Jesus. No other credible explanation of how the image had gotten on the cloth had ever been established, and every test done on it showed it to have come from the area of Jesus's teaching at the time he lived and died. Then came the radiocarbon results of 1988. All three testing facilities came to the same conclusion: despite all other evidence to the contrary, the cloth was created between the years 1260 and 1390 A.D. It could not possibly be 2000 years old and therefore could not be Jesus's burial cloth. It was most likely a painted hoax created during the middle ages.

Even in his youth, Matt understood the enormous impact such a discovery had on the world. It amazed him that so many people could have their entire belief systems affected by such a simple test. The thought of it thrilled him.

When he chose the University of Arizona, one of his hopes was to take a class on carbon dating. Fortunately, he was able to get into the class taught by the Jewish Leprechaun in his sophomore year. He loved Professor Rosen's animated lectures. He was even able to contribute to a demonstration in Rosen's class. When the professor asked if anyone had old letters or other objects in their family histories that they could bring in for testing, Matt raised his hand. His family owned a parchment that was found amongst his grandfather's effects after his death some years before. The parchment contained writing in a language unknown to the family, and no one had any idea how old it was. It was wrapped in linen and sealed in a large plastic bag when Matt brought it to class. Professor Rosen took only a tiny piece of one sheet for testing, but asked if he could copy the others for his records. Matt agreed, of course, and when the test on the tiny piece was complete, it was determined that the parchment dated back to between 920 and 1000 A.D.

Matt shook his head at the memory. It had been a shock that anything so ancient could be in the family. He wondered if the old professor was still around. He decided to look him up the next day if he was in any condition to do so after the evening of partying he anticipated. He turned away from the geo-sciences building toward his meeting with Seth.

Then he heard the scream.

Matt turned sharply toward the building.

Another scream came immediately, this one a cry for help, and, without thinking, Matt ran to the building's double-door entry. He yanked it open and burst into the hall where he stopped to listen. Almost immediately, he heard running footsteps and another plea from above.

"Help!" the voice squeaked as if it had lost its strength. "Help!" it tried to shout as it struggled through sobs.

Matt started up the stairs across the entry hall, taking them two at a time.

"What happened?" he shouted as a young woman appeared at the top landing, long dark hair strewn across eyes wide with fear. Behind him, Matt heard the hurried approach of others.

The girl gripped the handrail with both hands. "He's dead!" she cried. "Help me...please."

"Who?" Matt asked as he reached her at the landing. He placed a steadying hand on her shoulder. "Who's dead?"

"The professor...he's dead," she stammered and pointed behind her. "There's blood," she whimpered, and began to cry.

Wet blood stained the girl's hands and white blouse. Matt guided her gently to sit. He turned as two male students joined him.

"Watch her," he said to the first. "She says a professor is dead up here." He turned to the second student. "Call 911!"

Both men nodded. Matt leapt up to the second floor before he stopped to think about what he was doing. A trail of bloody footprints starting at an office two doors down the hall was clearly visible. His first thought was that he should stick close to the girl and wait for help; he had no idea what he might encounter down the hall. Maybe some crazed gunman waited in the professor's office and Matt would end up his next victim. He'd had several drinks before the game and a half pint flask of vodka during it. Was he thinking clearly?

Behind him, the girl whispered a garbled name. He turned. One student was speaking frantically to the 911 operator as the other tried to calm the girl. She again stated the name, clearer this time.

"Professor Rosen...dead," she stammered. Matt's eyes bulged. "Professor Rosen," she sobbed.

Matt stared at her. The fog of drink and the shock of the victim's name transfixed him. Professor Rosen? Dead? He can't be...I was just thinking about him.

He shook his head, trying to clear it, trying to understand. He continued to stare, dumbfounded, until he realized he had to do something. The stains on the girl were not from her blood. It had to be Rosen's. Maybe he wasn't dead. Maybe he was still alive. Matt started cautiously down the hall.

He heard the sirens just as he reached the door. He leaned back against the wall outside the entry, breathing deeply and steeling himself before he peeked around the jamb, into the office. It was a quick peek—one that revealed nothing to senses addled by alcohol, knowledge of the victim's identity, and fear that danger still lurked in the room. He sucked in a deep breath, this time catching a metallic whiff of blood. He closed his eyes, steadied himself. When he finally opened them again, he did so with new resolve, and he poked his head fully into the opening.

Blood was pooled on the floor to the side and front of the desk. Bloody footprints led from the desk to the door; but he saw no body and no crazed killer. He stepped fully into the opening then, and immediately saw the splatter of blood and detritus across the top of the desk, the floor, and on the wall nearest the doorway.

Matt stepped cautiously over the spatters toward the desk before he finally saw the top of a ravaged head protruding beyond the desk. The head lay in a congealed pool of blood. He covered his nose as he sucked in his breath and held it, and then approached the body.

When he caught his first look at the face, he immediately recognized the wide-eyed rictus of his old professor despite the distortions of a bullet and death. He turned away sharply, squeezing his eyes tightly shut, before he was able to look again. The image was grotesque, but he had to get past it to make sure. He crouched, careful to avoid stepping or kneeling in blood. He reached to the cold throat, felt for a pulse...found none. He pulled back thinking only that he should close the professor's eyes. He reached to do so as police burst into the room behind him.

CHAPTER FOUR

ASSIM RAHMAN WOKE late Saturday morning. He hadn't arrived at the motel until after 10 p.m. the previous evening, and was still so amped he couldn't sleep. He'd considered calling a prostitute from the east side of Tucson, but realized he couldn't do that. No one was to know he was in town, not even the manager of the motel. That's the reason the room was rented by another over the phone, and the key was left under the tattered "welcome" mat at the front door. He couldn't call a prostitute because he would have to kill her when he was satisfied, and that would have raised more questions. So he'd taken a shower, and, as the steam of hot water enveloped him, he'd relieved the tension of his excitement himself.

When he woke in his room's lumpy bed the next morning, he was ashamed that he'd needed relief the night before, when he should have been focused on his work. He knew he was weak, but he also knew he would be forgiven because of what he'd done the previous evening, the work his lord needed of him, the work that brought him excitement because he understood how important it was.

Assim meant "protector" and his last name, Rahman, "most gracious." He'd always been proud of his name, particularly after his purpose had become clear. He was the most gracious protector of the lord, and he was honored to do the work for which he'd been chosen.

He was not a big man, standing slightly less than six feet tall and weighing a sleek one hundred eighty pounds. But he was uncommonly strong, exceedingly coordinated, agile, and very fast. He was a handsome young man with pitch-black hair, deep dark skin, an unusually deep and expressive voice, and eyes that pierced a person to his soul. The steel blue of his eyes was most unusual in a man of his descent. They made him wonder if his ancestry was impure. But that was a question of his early teens, before his parents were killed in the violence of the American attack on Afghanistan. After that, those who raised him in the truth of the lord took him in, and he grew to realize it didn't matter whether he was pure of ancestry. The only thing that mattered was that he use the gifts with which he'd been blessed for the purposes of the lord.

Assim hadn't spent time with the envelopes or the thin folder he'd taken the previous evening except to confirm they were what he sought. He now sat in a wobbly chair at a chipped Formica table and opened the folder. He extracted a creased and crumpled piece of notepaper that bore writing in the old professor's hand. He laid it on the table next to the envelopes, six in total, and he began to read the scratchy writing.

A list of names ran down the page. Next to the names were sloppily formed columns with headings that read "cover letter," "protocol," "research," "conclusions," "parchment," "translation." He read down the list of names slowly, noting that for the last one, a different pen had been used for an address and a "c/o" designation. Someone was added after the list was complete? He checked the names against those on the envelopes and realized he had no corresponding envelope for the added name. He riffled through them again to make sure he hadn't missed one. He hadn't; one was gone. Assim wondered if the professor had simply not gotten to it yet, but then he noticed that checks under two of the six columns had been entered for that name.

Assim pushed back in the unstable chair, frustrated and angry. He had left an envelope behind, or, worse yet, it had been mailed. He couldn't go back to check. He would surely be seen. But he couldn't disappoint the Master. And as he struggled with his rage and need to make things right, he dropped his head. He had only one option. He would have to tell the Master and accept whatever consequence his failure would bring.

He dialed the Master, and, after one ring, he heard the voice he adored.

"It is done," Assim said in a whisper. "The professor will do no more harm."

"That's good," the voice said. "You've done well."

Assim tried to smile, but there was more.

"I recovered only six envelopes; a seventh is missing," he said, understanding fully that the words could mean his death.

After a pause, the Master spoke, his voice even, in control.

"To whom was that envelope to go?"

Assim read the name and address.

"I know this name," the Master said pensively.

There was another pause, as if the Master was searching for something.

"Ah...I know this name," he continued finally with conviction. "He is of no importance, son. We will handle him."

CHAPTER FIVE

HIS EMINENCE, ANDREW Cardinal Metzinger, thumbed his cell phone off and gripped it tightly behind his back. He turned to the window overlooking St. Peter's square, taking in Rome's settling dusk and the darkening dome of the great basilica. The autumn air had turned cold and the people wandering the square this Sunday evening wore coats as they ambled amidst the glow of the cathedral's lights.

Cardinal Metzinger was an enormous man of ample girth and a height approaching six and a half feet. Although large by every definition he was not sloppily so, but rather elegant and fine featured. His voice was rich and deep, and his thick grey hair was always neatly combed, even after the removal of whatever headgear he happened to wear during services and appearances. Although imposing in his bulk, he was a surprisingly warm, genial, and loving man. It was, in fact, his size, coupled with the inviting personality and a dogged work ethic that helped him rise so quickly in the Church hierarchy.

Metzinger was the Cardinal Prefect of the Congregation for the Doctrine of the Faith for the Catholic Church in Rome. His was one of the most powerful positions in the Catholic Church; one, in fact, that the previous pope held immediately before he became pontiff. Metzinger was unique among the heads of the Vatican's congregations because of his relative youth—only 58 years among a fraternity whose average age was at least a decade older—and because he was an American, the first ever to achieve a position of such significance at the Vatican.

The cardinal had worked his way up through the ranks, but gotten a major boost as a result of two events that shook the world. The first was the war in Afghanistan. When the shock of the 9/11 attacks on the United States caused once rational minds to scream for revenge, Metzinger worked for peace, gathering those who would join him and following the troops of vengeance into abandoned Al Qaeda strongholds to care for those displaced by the carnage wrought by both sides. Children were the population that had needed the most help, and that's where he and his aides expended most of their energies. They saved the lives and restored the psyches of thousands of youths while converting many to a new and strangely wonderful faith. His heroic efforts were regarded highly in the Vatican and brought him notoriety in the Church.

Then, Pope John Paul II died in 2005. That brought Metzinger to Rome to join his brethren in electing the next pope. When the choice was his predecessor as head of the Congregation for Catholic Doctrine, Metzinger was picked to replace him. He took to the position with a passion and understanding of the world's needs that surprised many. He believed that the only way to save the world from itself was to indoctrinate it in the love of Christ; and he believed the indoctrination had to start with the world's youth— those who would have the vitality to spread not only Church doctrine but also the core message of love that Christ taught. So sure of his purpose did Metzinger become that he would brook no dissent on any doctrine he came to espouse. He became the Church's leader in defining and spreading that doctrine, as well as protecting it. To him, the only hope for mankind was a youthful clergy properly educated in the words of Christ to advocate for the doctrine and vociferously oppose any who would reject it.

Cardinal Metzinger turned sharply when he heard the hurried steps of his secretary, Archbishop Francesco Cadone, echoing down the long hall to his door.

"Come in Francesco," the Cardinal's rich baritone intoned before the other man knocked.

The secretary was round and florid-faced beneath olive skin. Despite the outside cold, perspiration streamed from his bald pate to his stiff collarino. The shirt itself was wet at the pits and chest.

"Eminence," Francesco stumbled slightly trying to stop for a bow. Metzinger stared at the plump man expectantly.

"Eminence," the secretary blurted again. "The professor has been murdered. The Jew. The Jew from Arizona in America has been murdered, Eminence. Professor Rosen, who desecrated..." he sputtered to a stop as Metzinger dropped his head and looked at the cell phone clutched in his right hand.

"I just heard the news, Francesco," he said, holding the phone out. "It is sad indeed that there continues to be such pain and suffering in this world." He shook his head and plopped down heavily in his leather chair facing sideways across the desk from the secretary. He stared at an ancient painting of some long forgotten churchman on the far wall. "They seek proof when all that is needed is faith," he mumbled wistfully.

"What is that, Eminence?" asked the secretary, who swept the sweat from his brow but only succeeded in changing its course for a few seconds.

Metzinger turned to him, leaned forward, and propped his arms on his desk.

"Perhaps it is our Lord's will that he who goes where he should not will be punished."

Francesco nodded solemnly, the sweat dripping from his face to the carpet.

"We must pray for him Francesco," Metzinger said, "and we must pray for all those who lack the faith to believe without seeing, and venture where they should not."

The secretary nodded vigorously, clasped his hands in front of him, and joined the cardinal in prayer. When it ended, the secretary looked up anxiously, awaiting instruction. Metzinger's head remained bowed for several more seconds. Finally, he lifted it, and looked at his assistant.

"Go now, Francesco; contact our brothers who are preparing the coming journey. Arrange a meeting so that we may discuss what is to come. Perhaps Father Roberts and Cardinal Giordano will now understand the folly of their proposed exhibition."

Francesco nodded sharply, sent a spray of perspiration toward Metzinger's desk, and bowed awkwardly.

"Yes, Eminence," he sputtered, turned, and scurried out of the office.

"Francesco," Metzinger called; the fat secretary turned. "Thank you for your diligence in bringing me the news."

Francesco smiled, thrilled for the compliment.

Cardinal Metzinger watched the secretary walk far down the hall before he swiveled his chair back to his window. He wondered what it would take to end the foolish desire to prove what was already known.

CHAPTER SIX

MATT'S DREAMS OF college nymphs scurrying about in various states of undress, celebrating the victory over the Oregon Ducks never materialized. He spent the rest of Saturday cooped up with investigators, first in the geosciences building, and then, late into the night in the offices of the Tucson Police Department. By the time he was released, his head ached miserably. A hangover was definitely kicking in, but it was the tension surrounding the murder of Professor Rosen that was the worst. He couldn't shake the image of the once lively eyes lifeless amidst the spatters of blood and death.

Before he was taken to the police station, Matt had returned one of Seth's calls, and explained what had happened.

"I don't think they'll need much from me, Seth. I should be out of here in an hour or so. Can we meet then?" Matt asked.

"Are you really up for going out after this?" Seth asked

"I think so. Besides, I could use someone to talk to." Matt grunted a forced laugh. "Hey, there are still parties and women to conquer tonight. It's homecoming."

Seth laughed weakly and said, "Look, it's not going to happen this time, buddy. My plane leaves in less than three hours. I've got to get back to the airport."

"You aren't staying?"

"Naw...I can't. Cybil's got family coming over tomorrow. I promised her I'd be home tonight. I told her I had to see you, Matt. Man, it's been a whole year, and we've barely talked. But I promised her."

Matt's disappointment was loud in his silence.

"We'll do this next year, buddy. See you then?" Seth asked.

"Sure," Matt answered, and they hung up.

As it turned out, Matt wouldn't have made any meeting with Seth. By the time the police were done with him, he was exhausted. He didn't get to his hotel room until after midnight, and he slept hard after downing several Advil. Sunday morning, he returned to the police station for additional questioning and a review of the statement he'd given the previous day.

The Tucson Police Department was located on Stone Avenue at the east side of a group of sterile concrete government buildings clustered in a crude campus-style not far from the University. At 10:40 a.m., after Matt had already waited for more than one frustrating hour, he was finally called. He joined a tall, thin officer at the waist-high security gate, and followed him to the office of Detective Robert Gutierrez. The homicide detective was standing at the side of his desk, talking to a slim, dark-haired girl.

"Detective," the officer with Matt interrupted as they stepped into the open doorway, "I've got Mathew Carter."

Gutierrez glanced up absently. He held a thick hand up for the officer to wait. The girl turned and stared at Matt for several seconds before she turned back to Gutierrez.

Her look carried recognition, yet Matt couldn't place her until he watched her speaking animatedly to the detective. Then it came to him—it was the girl who'd discovered Professor Rosen's body. Gone were the bloodstains, tears, smeared mascara, and drawn look of shock, and in their place were the high-cheeked, soft features of a beauty. She wore tight black jeans and a billowy cotton blouse through which backlight framed her taut silhouette. As she and Gutierrez completed their discussion, the detective extended a hand, touched her lightly on the shoulder, and guided her toward the door.

She eyed Matt as she approached. She stood slightly over five and a half feet tall in flip-flops and walked with a strong confidence belied by the moisture in her caramel brown eyes that seemed to sparkle through the tears.

"Thank you Ms. Melnyk," Detective Gutierrez said. "We'll be in touch as the investigation progresses."

She nodded, but didn't respond as she continued to eye Matt.

"Are you Mathew Carter?" she asked.

Matt's eyes widened. "Yeah. Do you know me?"

"Professor Rosen spoke of you," she answered pointedly.

"Really? When?" Matt's initial excitement at her recognition of him drained.

Detective Gutierrez turned to Matt, suddenly interested in the exchange.

"In his class on carbon dating," she responded. "He said you brought an ancient parchment in for testing. He called it the Carter Parchment. I guess you didn't know. He discussed it in every class he taught; something about a student named Mathew Carter whose family didn't understand the significance of the document they had. It was the oldest document he'd ever tested."

Matt nodded, somewhat abashed, and looked at Gutierrez and then back to the girl before he shrugged. She continued to stare at him, now making him uneasy.

"He mentioned you a few times over the past month," she continued, and Gutierrez gave her a questioning look.

"I didn't even think he remembered me," Matt said.

"In what context did the professor mention Mr. Carter's name over the last month?" Gutierrez interjected.

She turned to him. "He said he wanted to talk to Mr. Carter." She hesitated as she stared at the detective. "He didn't say what it was about, just that he wanted to talk to him."

Matt and the detective shot puzzled looks at each other.

"Did he talk to him?" Gutierrez asked.

The girl smiled for the first time. It was a warm smile, not completely comfortable, but warm and friendly nevertheless. She shook her head.

"I don't know detective; he's right here." She held her hand out toward Matt and looked at him, the smile now directed at him.

Gutierrez nodded. "Of course, I'm sorry," he responded brusquely.

They stood in silence for several seconds before Gutierrez finally turned to the officer with Matt, "Dex, show Ms. Melnyk out please."

She and Matt again exchanged glances before she accompanied the officer away. Matt eyed her down the hall.

"Mr. Carter," Gutierrez stepped aside for Matt to come into his office. When the detective was back in his seat and Matt sat in the one vacated by the girl, Matt motioned over his shoulder.

"Who is she?" he asked.

Gutierrez pushed three sheets of paper toward Matt.

"Her name is Hannah Melnyk. She's a PhD student at the university—in her last year. She was helping Rosen with his work. Why?"

"Just wondering…she's pretty," he said feebly. The detective looked askance at him; Matt continued quickly. "Does she have any idea who killed the professor?"

Gutierrez shook his head.

"We're working on that, Mr. Carter. Right now, I'd like you to read this statement and let me know if it accurately reflects what you remember from yesterday. If it doesn't, I'll have changes made. If it does, I'd like you to sign and date it right," he leaned forward, flipped to the third page and pointed, "here. Also, I'd like you to initial the other two pages, here and here."

Gutierrez leaned back and watched Matt read. He said nothing. Matt was uneasy under his gaze; he had to force himself to focus on the statement.

When he was done, he nodded, signed the last page, and then initialed the first two. The statement, although Matt might have worded some things differently, was accurate. He pushed the papers back to Gutierrez.

"So what's this about a parchment?" Gutierrez asked.

Matt shrugged, confused until he recalled Hannah Melnyk's mention of it. He nodded and responded thoughtfully.

"I was a student in Rosen's carbon dating class about ten…no twelve years ago…my sophomore year. He asked if anyone had any old documents—things over two hundred years old. My family had this parchment we found in my grandfather's attic when he died in the 90's," he looked down at his hands, remembering. "I was a kid then, and thought it was pretty cool because it was wrapped in this really old cloth inside an old plastic bag that was taped shut. My parents talked about getting someone to look at it for us, but they never got around to it. I figured this was a chance to have it looked at."

Gutierrez's look was stony, without comment. Matt moved to his point.

"I brought the parchment into Rosen's class; he copied it, and then took a small corner to date. I was surprised when he came back with the old date."

"What was the date," Gutierrez asked.

"Tenth to early eleventh century; somewhere between 900 and 1000 A.D."

"Do you know what the parchment said?" Gutierrez asked.

"No, it was written in a language none of us understood. My parents wanted to have it translated, but they were concerned about giving it to someone they didn't know. They talked about selling it to a museum, but I begged them to wait because I was all fired up about becoming the next Indiana Jones," he smiled then, a flicker of that old passion playing across his face. "I didn't want them giving something away that might be real valuable until I had a chance to understand it. Over time, especially after my mom got sick, we just forgot about it."

"Do you know where this parchment is?" the detective asked.

"I think it's at my dad's place. Do you think it's important?" Matt cocked his head to the side.

"I don't know…Do you?" Gutierrez asked. Matt shrugged. The detective continued. "Did the professor get in touch with you anytime over the last month or so?"

"No," Matt said.

"Any thoughts on why he would want to call you?"

Matt shook his head.

They sat in silence for several seconds, Gutierrez eyeing Matt, and Matt deep in thought.

"What is it?" Gutierrez asked.

"I can't figure why he would have wanted to talk to me. I haven't heard from him since I graduated, except once…about seven years ago. He left a message at my parents' house. He was asking if I'd had the parchment translated. I returned the call, but got his answering service. I left a message that I hadn't, and asked if he thought there was any need to. I didn't hear from him again."

Both men nodded and stared at each other, each waiting for something more from the other. Finally, Gutierrez stood.

"Thanks for your help, Mr. Carter. I suppose you'll be going home today." Matt nodded; the detective continued. "We'll need to talk again. Don't run off somewhere we can't contact you."

Matt nodded again and stood to leave.

"Mr. Carter," Gutierrez called. "Do you know what a sindon is?"

Matt thought a moment, remembered he'd heard the term somewhere, but had no recollection of when or where. He shook his head.

"We'll be in touch, Mr. Carter."

CHAPTER SEVEN

MATT CAUGHT AN earlier flight than he'd originally planned. All he wanted was to get home. By 3:00 p.m. he was standing in the living room of his tiny apartment viewing the mess he'd left two days earlier. He hadn't seen it as a mess then, but now that was all he saw.

He didn't know what made him see it differently—whether it was the murder of his favorite professor, the fact his friends were no shows at the game, or the memory of Hannah Melnyk. Whatever the reason, the unwashed dishes, overflowing trashcan, unmade bed, and the clothes, towels, and miscellaneous debris strewn about bothered him.

He was tempted to grab a beer, sit out on his cluttered balcony, and get his mind straight. But he found himself cleaning. He emptied the trash, rinsed and stuffed dishes in the washer, straightened his bed, threw dirty clothes into his only closet, and opened windows and the balcony slider to clear the stale air. Only then did he grab the beer and head out to his tiny balcony.

It was a marvelous late afternoon at the beach, with a balmy, late-season Santa Ana wind blowing the unhealthful hot air of the inland empire out over the Pacific.

He eyed the ugly brown haze hanging far out over the ocean and knew, despite its devastating effect on the atmosphere, it would result in a beautiful sunset of blazing oranges and reds. He heard the rhythmic beat of the surf against the shore less than a hundred yards away, and, through a small opening between two Strand mansions, he eyed the speckled white of receding waves against the backdrop of the green-blue Pacific. He breathed deeply, leaned back against the cushioned beach chair, closed his eyes… and saw death.

Professor Rosen's lifeless eyes sprang at him. He jerked forward and shook his head, trying to lose the image. Who could have done it? Rosen was a good guy—the best professor he'd ever had. He had his issues, no doubt; even Matt knew him to be stubborn about things he believed firmly, but he was always accessible and always ready for a laugh, no matter the circumstances. That's why it was so difficult to believe. Who could he have rubbed the wrong way? Matt's mind raced with possibilities, even though he didn't want to think about any of it.

Rosen had been a vocal advocate of fetal stem-cell research. Perhaps it was religious fanatics opposed to the professor's support that killed him.

Matt shook his head sadly and wondered why anyone would oppose the opportunity for medical breakthroughs that could solve untold health issues. He understood the moral fear that people might mine fetuses by getting pregnant just to abort and sell them; but if someone killed the professor for that reason, wouldn't it be contradicting the whole concept of saving life?

Matt sucked down a large gulp of beer and tried again to give his mind a rest. There was nothing he could do about it anyway. What he needed was to calm himself and find his center. He was home in Manhattan Beach, far from murder and investigations. He needed to relax, get his mind off the events of his Arizona trip, and get back into his life. But his thoughts wouldn't let him escape. They moved to Hannah Melnyk, and he smiled briefly until he remembered his first sight of her: the shock, the tears, and the blood.

She must know something, he thought. That's why Gutierrez is staying in touch with her. She worked with the professor. She had to have some idea who the killer was.

Matt tried to leave the thought there. He tried to believe the Tucson police would solve the mystery, and the whole thing would become a sad memory he'd discuss with friends at future homecomings. It was something that happened after the Arizona/Oregon game they all missed. But he couldn't leave it there. The girl wouldn't let him.

He kept thinking about her; the warm eyes sparkling with tears, the deep, dark hair, the confident step. He even remembered her scent, fresh and clean, like honeysuckle; not cloying and perfume-like, but soft, invigorating, and alive, the scent of a most beautiful woman, like none he'd ever known—a woman he needed to see again.

CHAPTER EIGHT

THE SCRAGGLY-BEARDED, leather-faced old man eased down against the ridged trunk of a massive pine, his Remington 700 bolt-action rifle cradled loosely in the crook of his left arm. He'd started carrying the weapon everywhere. There'd been reports of a crusty old bear making a pest of himself about his mountain community. Rangers had dubbed the offending bear "Old One Eye" after he'd lost an eye in a skirmish with another of his kind some years back. Apparently the old fella hadn't followed his brethren into hibernation. As sometimes happened to bears that lived beyond their normal hunting and foraging lifespans, this ancient creature hadn't eaten enough in preparation for his winter sleep. He was now roaming and scavenging among the humans. Things got dicey only two days earlier, when the starving bear approached a young family hiking in the woods and was dissuaded from attacking only because of ferocious challenges by the family's two German shepherds. Rangers had gone to great lengths to warn residents even as they set out to find and tranquilize the bear.

The old man reached absently to scratch behind the ear of his dog, a black lab he called Boone. The dog had been sitting on its haunches next to him at the snow-dusted base of the tree. It now settled onto the ground, and the old man smiled, albeit sadly. He closed his eyes, leaned his head gently against the pine's sharp bark, and sucked in a deep draught of frigid mountain air. He expelled it in a gust of white mist as his mind wandered to the other reason he carried his Remington.

Wasn't it only a week ago, after Samuel Rosen had received a threat from what he described as "some middle eastern punk," that the old man had laughed with his friend? It was nothing new to professors who worked in the sciences. There was always some crackpot wanting them dead. But the old man had heard something else in Samuel's laugh. It hadn't been one of Samuel's open-mouthed, carefree bursts of whimsy. There had been an edge, a tremor of fear, something neither of them had felt since the early years. Samuel was concerned. He made that concern clear to the old man when he'd begged him to beware, for he too was part of the work Samuel was doing.

The old man was Cornelius Crockett—Corny to his friends. He was a retired Professor of Anthropology and Theology from the University of California at Davis. He'd long-since given up academia and moved to his beloved Sierra Nevada Mountains, to a small log cabin he'd built with his wife, Elli, years before. His place was twenty miles northwest of Truckee, close enough to civilization if they needed it, but far enough off the beaten track to be secluded. Seclusion, after all, was a state he and Elli loved for spiritual reflection and understanding. The way they saw things, there was no place like the high Sierra wilderness for communion with God. Their life away from the city gave them the opportunity to pursue the passion they developed as undergraduates in theology at the University of Notre Dame. Even though they received their higher degrees in "money-earning" specialties, he in anthropology, and she in psychology, their work was always influenced by their studies of the human spirit and its relationship with God.

Elli was dead, now. She'd passed away quietly on a crisp, pine-scented spring morning as she sat with Corny on the weather-grayed planks of their cabin's front porch. She'd told him it was her time and that she was ready. He'd known it before she'd said it, but it was nice to hear the words from her beautiful mouth that morning. She'd asked him to carry her out to their love-seat swing, and to sit with her a while. She'd looked up at him as she leaned into his shoulder, her blue eyes twinkling with the love they'd always shared, and, after he bent and kissed her the last time, she smiled, closed her eyes as she snuggled closer, and died. Corny knew she was gone.

But he sat quietly for a time, holding her against the brisk morning air, and he whispered to her that he'd join her soon.

That was three years ago. Although he talked to Elli every day, his time still hadn't come.

Now, with the death of Samuel Rosen, he understood why. Retired professor of anthropology and theology, Cornelius Crockett still had work to do. He had come to believe in Rosen's work and the importance it had for a world in desperate need of hope. For the first time in his life, a life he and his wife had devoted to the study and understanding of the human spirit, his purpose was clear. There were only two problems: the first was to understand exactly how he was supposed to continue Samuel's work, and the second was to stay alive so he could do so. He had no doubt that those who had taken Samuel were coming for him. They knew who he was.

CHAPTER NINE

SUNNY TURNER WAS not a pretty woman. She was a little too tall and thin, and her face had a few too many sharp edges to it. No man would stumble over himself trying to get a second look; yet there was something about her.

She walked with a nonchalant confidence and flashed beguiling smiles with just the right tilt of the head and squint of the eye to make men wonder what she was really about. Once they met her they understood.

Sunny was bright. She was one of the top business writers for the Los Angeles News, a combination of old world media enemies who'd joined forces for survival in the new age. Her insights on things financial and their impact on society were provocative and her flair for the dramatic got people talking. She was very good at what she did, and she knew it. It was that intelligence combined with the unusual tilt of her head and squint in her eye that made her sexy; it drew men to her. But Sunny took it in stride, loving the attention when it came, and relishing the understanding of her unique attraction.

On a clear, cool autumn evening, Sunny sat amidst a throng of suits gathered for the year-end business conference at the Beverly Hills Hotel's Crystal Ballroom. She listened patiently as Los Angeles' mayor droned on about his plans for the city. But she was really there for the keynote speaker: a man named Peter Christian.

Christian's rags to riches story was almost too good to be true, particularly when the riches part of it had elevated him to among the wealthiest men in the world. He was CEO of a business conglomerate with significant interests in every part of the world's economy, and a charismatic figure who had drawn a standing-room-only crowd this evening. They all waited to hear his gospel of economic freedom that would end his country's economic malaise and save the world.

Christian knew the answers to the world's economic woes. He'd known them from the beginning. But no one listened then because there was too much anger, too much finger pointing, too many recriminations, and too much politicking. If only the politicians had gotten out of the way. But they thought they knew the answers, and their politics were just too strong. So Christian sat back and waited for his time. He grew his fortune during the economic devastation, mainly because of military contracts with the same government he lambasted, and he waited for people to come to him. When they finally did, he spoke, and they listened. Now, his answers were getting out, and those who followed him would see how they too could achieve the wealth they all sought.

Sunny Turner wasn't buying it. She'd studied Christian's two and a half decade rise from relative obscurity in mergers and acquisitions with a boutique Wall Street firm to his current position running the behemoth Cornerstone Group. Although they'd grown up in business under the same economic influences and conditions, there was something off about Christian's take. She couldn't put her finger on what it was, but she meant to find out.

Peter Christian stood slightly taller than six feet two inches and weighed in at two hundred pounds of well-toned muscle, agility, speed, and skill, even though he was in his early fifties. He wore his dark brown hair combed straight back, but not slicked fast to his skull. It fell comfortably toward his ears and collar with the occasional stray lock across his forehead being swept back by a casual brush of his powerful hand.

Like every other woman who saw him, Sunny Turner was taken. The possibility of getting the world's most eligible bachelor into her bed was a challenge she relished, and one she would take up after his evening presentation. She had been given the right to an exclusive interview after his talk.

It surprised Sunny that Christian's people had granted her umpteenth request for an interview. She'd written articles strongly challenging the very essence of his rhetoric, and subtly promised her readers more was coming. Yet, his people had stepped up. They knew she wasn't sold, and that's what made Sunny's challenge exciting.

MATT CARTER SAT at a front table, a special guest of Peter Christian. Prior to this evening, Matt had never met Christian, and he had no particular desire to hear him speak. Matt wouldn't even have been at the event, particularly with Rosen's death only five days old, but for a promise he'd made.

Paula Seltzer sat next to Matt. They'd been seeing each other off-and-on for three months, since the warm summer night Matt waited on her and a couple of her friends at Fonz's. The women had spent a lazy day on the beach, drinking, swimming, and sunning themselves into a euphoria of primal passions. By the time they arrived at Fonz's for dinner, their desires were clear. It was a simple matter then for a well-tanned, rugged, and athletic waiter with sparkling green eyes below a thick shock of sun touched brown hair to turn those sparks of passion into an evening of laughs, and an all-night visit by one to his apartment.

Although Paula had been loose and fun during their first meeting, it was quickly apparent that most of that carefree attitude was the result of the day's drink and sun. The real Paula Seltzer was far more intense. She was strong-willed, highly motivated, and aggressive in business as well as bed. Although Matt enjoyed the feral nature of her lovemaking, he could only take so much of it, and he realized only two weeks earlier that he'd had enough. Unfortunately, he'd promised to accompany her to this function before the decision was clear. She'd gone to some trouble, and—as she'd described it— miraculously gotten word the day before that their seats were in front of the dais at which Peter Christian would be speaking.

Christian strode calmly to the lectern after the mayor's address. The crowd applauded thunderously at his introduction.

"Thank you," Christian said as he beamed to all corners of the room, arms outstretched in a call for calm that still invited more applause. He stood thus for several seconds, the smile never wavering until the ovation faded and people took their seats.

Paula was an accountant for Christian's company, but still stared at him wide-eyed. At work she rarely saw him. Yet now she sat in a prominent position. That was all she apparently needed.

As Christian began his remarks, Matt thought about the moments before the evening's speeches began. He'd actually worn a borrowed suit, at Paula's urgent request because they would be sitting at such a conspicuous table. As they approached their seat, Paula pointed "the great Peter Christian" out where he stood less than ten feet away, drink in hand, conversing with early-arriving acolytes.

When Matt and Paula gained their seats, Christian glanced their way and caught Paula's eye. He smiled and, to her astonished pride, he waved. He stepped away from the suits and strode toward Paula, extending his hand.

"Hi Paula," he greeted the beaming woman. "I'm glad you could join us. I may need your help up there if they come at me too hard," he added with feigned fear.

Paula's smile broadened. "You won't need my help, Peter," saying the obvious, as she gripped his hand exuberantly. When she finally released it, he turned to Matt.

"Who's your friend?" he asked.

"This is Mathew Carter. He's a lawyer," she started and then became flustered as she continued. "He works at a restaurant in Manhattan Beach."

Christian's grip was firm, dry, and confident. He smiled.

"Glad you're joining us Matt," he said without missing a beat. "Smart move leaving the practice of law. You learn a helluva lot more about people and this world in the restaurant business."

Although surprised Christian knew he had chosen to leave law, Matt immediately understood the attraction of a leader who didn't talk down to anyone—even a beach guy who waited tables. Matt was impressed with the warm demeanor and the way Christian put him at ease. As Christian spoke, Matt's initial reservations disappeared completely. He found himself listening intently to words that made such simple sense out of the complex issues still affecting the world economy. Matt not only began to understand the man's attraction, he found himself drawn to Christian and his words.

AS PETER CHRISTIAN enthralled the crowd with his animated presentation, Assim Rahman stood stiffly against the back wall of the Crystal Ballroom, watching without expression. Although there had been a time when he, like others in the crowd, was mesmerized by Christian, that time had passed. Now, his feelings were much deeper. He had a powerful, almost overwhelming passion born of a true understanding of good and evil. He had a clear purpose in the battle for the soul of humanity.

CHAPTER TEN

"WALK WITH ME," Peter Christian said.

Sunny recognized the command as an invitation, but intimated surprise, giving him a playful tilt of her head and squint of her eye.

Christian smiled, "I'm sick of these damn conferences. They're so much glam and so little life. Let's get out of here. Do you mind?" He motioned gallantly toward the hotel's entry. Sunny nodded.

Christian's talk had ended an hour earlier, and his groupies were finally gone. It was dark outside with clouds sliding across the moon. The streets of Beverly Hills were wide, well lit, and safe; Sunny didn't mind a walk.

"Are you okay to do this now, Mr. Christian?" Sunny asked. "You must be tired. We could meet in the morning." In truth, she had no interest in putting the discussion off another minute.

Christian nodded and smiled again. Sunny had to admit he didn't look tired or ill used in any way. He was still gorgeous and looked as if his stamina and strength were unlimited—an interesting thought.

"No," he replied. "I'm good to go. But, please call me Peter. We've been bouncing in the same circles long enough for us to use first names, don't you think?"

Sunny agreed, but as they exited and followed the hotel's entry sidewalk to the right, she glanced back to see an enormous man pacing them some fifteen steps behind.

"So who's the muscle?" she asked, jerking her head toward the follower.

Christian glanced casually over his shoulder. "He's a bit distracting, isn't he?"

The follower was unaffected by the sudden attention.

"I guess the best way to describe him is as my bodyguard," Christian sighed.

Sunny shied away in mock surprise. "Peter Christian needs a bodyguard?"

"I never thought it would be necessary, but there are a lot of crazies out there. Walt makes sure they don't get too close. We've been friends for years. He sticks with me." He shrugged.

Sunny was about to make a sarcastic remark, but Christian wanted to move on.

"So, Sunny, where would you like to start?"

She smiled at his discomfort regarding Walt, storing the information away before she held a miniature recorder up to Christian.

"Do you mind?" she asked.

He nodded his consent. She switched it on and held it between them as they turned right onto Glen Way, a narrow, tree lined street that bordered the west boundary of the hotel grounds. Christian walked with his coat open, tie loose, and hands tucked casually into his pant pockets.

"Are you familiar with the movie Wall Street starring Michael Douglas?" she asked.

"Yes." He smiled, knowing what was coming.

"Douglas played a ruthless businessman named Gordon Gecko, who made his fortune buying and ravaging companies." Christian nodded. "Your position that entrepreneurs need freedom from regulation and taxes so they can generate as much money as possible sounded familiar to me. Aren't you simply restating Gecko's 'greed is good' argument?"

Christian gave Sunny a whimsical smile, as if she had found him out. She returned the smile with a challenging squint in her eye.

"I suppose cynics might take that position," he answered lightly. "I don't view it that callously. You must admit it's the pursuit of wealth that motivates people to take risks...to strive for greatness. A society in which people have ambition, motivation, and drive is a society that succeeds, no, thrives. You must admit that."

He turned to her with an imploring look. It made him seem vulnerable. Sunny liked that, but she wasn't ready to agree. She wanted him to work. She shrugged.

He tried again, "It is motivation and drive that produce creativity—and discoveries that are vital to the survival of our society. When people build or manufacture the products that come from these discoveries, they make money, and we all know that when people have money, they're happy."

"I can't argue with that, Peter," Sunny said. "The problem is greed. Doesn't greed make otherwise good people bad?" She pressed. "Doesn't it take the Judeo-Christian ethic of law and love of thy fellow man right out of the equation and start to define life only in terms of money, wealth, and ambition for personal ends alone?"

"There's no question there are bad people out there who can turn something good into something bad," Christian rejoined. "But that doesn't make the thing they abuse inherently bad." He hesitated a moment. "Some may view ambition and pursuit of wealth as the greed you are alluding to. I believe they're wrong."

He stopped and turned to her, withdrew his hands from his pockets, and began gesturing as he continued to speak.

"Greed has a nefarious connotation, so that when people are stamped with that moniker, they are considered evil. But I didn't see any evil in that room tonight; did you?" He continued before she could respond. "I don't view you as evil, yet you and everyone in that room know what makes people happy. It isn't greed in the way the world sees it…but it is wealth. We all know it is the attainment of wealth that enables us to live free of the strictures of this world, the workplace, governments, and this Judeo-Christian ethic you mention."

He was becoming more animated, louder, as if he was once again on the stage. "No one wants to be tied down, imprisoned by these strictures, the bullshit rules that some supposedly do-good government or church wants to impose. The only way to be free is to have money enough to tell them all to go screw themselves."

Sunny pulled back in mock surprise again. A big grin spread across her face. She liked this guy. Make no mistake, there was something about him she needed to tell the world, and she figured it was going to be fun finding it. For now, however, she didn't mind listening to his shtick.

He motioned forward, and said, "So, my position is that the pursuit of wealth is good, and, frankly, anything that stands in the way of that pursuit or creates rules restricting that pursuit is bad."

"Are you suggesting that as long as someone is pursuing wealth, anything she does in that pursuit is okay?" Sunny baited him.

He smiled impishly. "Of course not. Killing or stealing in its pursuit is wrong. C'mon, Sunny, we're not barbarians here, although I will admit that if those acts are necessary to protect what we own or to obtain what is rightfully ours, both would be appropriate."

"Aren't protecting or obtaining what's rightfully ours matters of subjective interpretation? Can't someone say that when he doesn't pay taxes, he's simply protecting what's his and he'd therefore be justified in killing the revenooers," Sunny said with a hillbilly twang, "who try to come after him?"

Christian glanced at her, shaking his head lightly. He head-motioned forward and picked up his pace. She wondered if he was trying to get back to the hotel and end the conversation.

"That's not a bad sentiment," he said, tongue in cheek, but this time without mirth. "Look, the problem is that we have employers who try to hold us down, governments who impose laws that prevent us from succeeding, churches that tell us we're wrong, and media, preachers, and others who try to shame us, all so they can expand their power and control, and have nice little boys and girls giving their hard earned money away in taxes or donations.

"I don't blame them for trying," he continued. "Hell, if I could live with myself, I'd try and take your money for nothing, too. I'd grow fat on your hard work. But that's not me, Sunny. I don't think that's you either. I want to work and keep getting richer just like you and everyone in that room tonight. I don't want anyone telling me I can't do it. I say screw the restrictions of church and state, and let's make our own way."

Sunny stopped and stared at Christian. She actually considered giving him a round of applause. A smile spread slowly across Christian's face.

"If that's greed, then I guess it's good." He shrugged.

Sunny thought he was beautiful. What he said made sense. But there was something wrong, wasn't there? There had to be. His argument was too easy, and he was just too good to be true. She smiled.

"Wow, Peter," she said with a slight chuckle. "That was as impressive as your talk tonight. You've got a gift." It came out a bit too sarcastic.

Christian frowned. He stepped back in line and turned to her.

"You don't agree?" he asked.

"I don't know," she shrugged. He stopped, and she turned sharply with a playful tilt of her head. She said, "I need to give it some th ..." Before she could finish, she lurched sharply to the side, thrown by a terrific force that followed a barely audible thwip.

A second thwip blew Sonny Turner's head open in a spray of blood and brains, and an instant later her body crumpled as Peter Christian reached for her and followed her to the ground. Walt was upon them in an instant, shielding the man and stricken woman and peering into the darkness ahead and to the left. Christian, now covered in blood, knelt next to Sunny. He cradled her as the last of her life streamed to the cold asphalt.

———————

ASSIM RAHMAN STARED at the huddled figures as he clutched the seven-millimeter and tried to discern the effect of his shots. Then, as he heard Christian's bodyguard's call for assistance, he realized he must flee. The young man dismantled his weapon, packed it hurriedly into its case, and scurried from his cover.

CHAPTER ELEVEN

WHAT DID HE say to that reporter?

As Matt clumped down his apartment's rickety wooden steps the next day to fetch his morning newspaper, he tried to remember Peter Christian's exact words. What surprised Matt was that he was hoping to find the quote in the paper. The only reason he even had a paper delivered was because he liked reading sports and comics with the paper on his lap and a cup of coffee in his fist. Even though he was as adept with tech as anyone, he loved reading the "Sports Page." He chuckled thinking his interest in this morning's paper was the previous evening's event. Professor Rosen's death and the haunting Hannah Melnyk occupied most of his thoughts, but the impression that stuck with him from Christian's talk was compelling.

THE REPORTER IDENTIFIED herself as Sunny Turner, from the Los Angeles News. She wasn't particularly attractive until she opened her mouth to speak.

"Mr. Christian," she started, a smirk crawling across her face; she apparently knew something everyone else in the room wanted to know. Christian smiled as if he knew he was stepping into a hornet's nest. "You rail against the establishment, government, religion, and the constraints they impose on free enterprise, yet one of Cornerstone Group's primary income

sources is its contracts with our government? Isn't your company one of the biggest private beneficiaries of the tax dollars collected and the restrictions and policies imposed by this government?"

Christian smiled.

"If you're referring to the support our company provides our troops throughout the world, Ms. Turner, you are absolutely right. In fact, we do the same for other friendly governments around the world. But I don't see that our work in providing technology, infrastructure, security, and the menial tasks of maintaining our troops in war as inconsistent with the position I'm taking here. How do you?"

"Well, sir," the reporter responded, "aren't you either biting the hand that feeds you or being hypocritical in attacking the very government that provides your company such large sums of taxpayer money?"

The crowd sat quietly, all eyes flitting to Christian. He chuckled lightly acknowledging the question's legitimacy.

"It may seem that way, Ms. Turner." He stepped away from the lectern, directing his eyes away from the woman to the large crowd. "But I will say this—my mother didn't raise a dummy. Even I know that the only ones spending money over the past several years with any regularity were our government and other governments around the world. Hell, if Cornerstone wasn't helping our men and women in uniform and making a buck at it, I'm not sure where we would have made that buck. But therein lies the problem. It's because of our government's interference that our country has been in the mess we're just now starting to pull out of. Free enterprise and the gears of capitalism would have weeded out the weak parts, and the strong would have survived nicely. Instead, government interfered, made things worse, and forced itself into having to spend tax dollars to undo its mistakes. I'm happy to say Cornerstone was there to assist, and," he threw a broad smile at the audience before he shrugged lightly, "we made a few bucks along the way."

The crowd laughed lightly as Christian leaned forward and jabbed his forefinger saying, "Just like every one of you wished you had." He joined them in a hardy laugh.

MATT SMILED AT the recollection of how Christian owned the crowd. It was special. He hadn't enjoyed any talk as much as Christian's since his days in Professor Rosen's class.

Shortly after that reporter's question, Christian's remarks ended. As he descended the dais and started back to his seat, he nodded and grinned at Paula and Matt, and it was at that moment that Matt understood something else about the man. He was having fun. He had a purpose in which he believed. He was trying to save the world in his way, and he was preaching that way to anyone who would listen. Everyone now seemed to be listening. That's when the thought of finding a path into Christian's vibrant organization first skittered across Matt's mind. The thought played at the edge of his dreams as he slept, and, now, as he stooped to lift the morning paper, it moved front and center as he anticipated reading about Christian's inspiring talk.

He stood in his tattered robe and bare feet at the base of his steps as he extracted the paper from its plastic protector and unfolded it to the front page. Instead of the news he hoped to see, however, he saw something that shocked him. Emblazoned across the top of the front page was the headline announcing the attempted murder of Peter Christian.

Matt's initial shock turned to fear. The thought that he had, within days, been present at events connected to two ghastly murders was the shock. The fear was that somehow his presence was the point of connection. This sent a shiver through him, but disappeared in a torrent of rationality that his presence was by chance, and that there could not possibly be any connection involving him. Still, the fact remained that two men Matt viewed as significant because of their uncanny abilities to make complex issues simple were the target of an assassin's bullet. And only one, by the intervention of some strange fate, survived as the reporter who had walked with him stepped into the line of fire.

It took Matt the entire morning to reach Paula Seltzer at her Cornerstone office. When they finally spoke, Paula was calm.

"He's okay Matt," she said. "That poor woman is dead though. They said her head was blown off." She hesitated a moment. "You know, she never did treat us very well in her articles…Still, it's sad for her to go that way."

"How about you Paula; you okay?"

"I'm fine. It was crazy here this morning. Some heard it on the way in— others saw it on their computers. Everyone was standing around in shock, but then he came in."

"Christian came into the office?" Matt asked.

"Yeah; it was amazing. He came in smiling and reassuring us. He sent a video blast to the entire company around the world saying he's fine and that we should take a moment of silence in memory of Sunny Turner. He said he wouldn't be here today if she hadn't stepped in the way."

Matt wondered at the sudden turns of fate—at how, just moments before, this reporter had been a celebrated news personality who challenged Peter Christian, and then, suddenly, she was gone.

"Matt, are you still there?" Paula asked.

"Yeah…just thinking about the reporter. I wonder if she had family."

There was silence for several seconds, and, just as Matt was going to continue, Paula spoke again, this time with excitement.

"There's more Matt," she said. "He came to my cubicle. He asked about you."

"What? Why? I mean, what did he say?"

"I had just finished watching his video blast for the tenth time when I looked up and he was standing there. It surprised me. So, I started to babble. He just smiled, raised his hand and asked how you liked his talk. I told you were impressed, and that I'd never seen you so excited about anything other than the beach and volleyball. You don't mind do you?" She finished with a rush.

"No," he stammered. "That's okay. Did he say anything else?"

"He wants me to bring you around the office. He liked you I guess. He said Cornerstone could use smart people who are in the trenches rather than all those business-degree grads who have never lived in the real world. I think he wants to talk to you about a job."

"A job?" Although he'd been thinking it, it made no sense that Christian would suggest something like that. "He doesn't know me, Paula," Matt said.

"He's a great judge of character. He saw something in you Matt, just like I did." She chuckled lightly.

"I hope he didn't see that in me," Matt rejoined.

"No," she laughed. "But he saw something. Are you interested?"

"Sure," he hesitated, crosscurrents running through his brain. He'd never wanted the insanity of big business. Surely he wouldn't really want Christian's mega-business world. But he was intrigued. "Yeah, I guess a talk wouldn't hurt. But it'll have to be after Thanksgiving."

Paula laughed. "I don't think it's anything urgent. We're pretty busy through the holidays, anyway. Now that I think about it, it probably won't be until after the New Year."

The two ended their conversation awkwardly with an unspoken acknowledgement that they wouldn't be seeing each other until after Thanksgiving. Matt was hoping to have ended the relationship sooner, but it would be callous to say something now when she was still shaken over Christian's near-death and had just offered him interesting news. He vowed to address the issue when he returned. Perhaps by then, he'd understand the odd sense of discomfort he had about the amazing opportunity Peter Christian seemed to be offering.

CHAPTER TWELVE

MATT MADE THE decision to attend Professor Rosen's funeral the following Monday before heading up to his father's for Thanksgiving. He'd taken the entire week off work to spend it with his family in the Bay Area. The truth, however, was that he wasn't in any hurry to face his sisters—both more than ten years his senior—and their broods of children, grown-up lives, and way too many questions about his "life at the beach." So the funeral provided him an excuse…not to mention the opportunity to see Hannah again.

On Saturday, after his morning run, Matt checked his landline phone messages. He'd long ago stopped using the landline, but his father never called him on his cell. Thus, on the rare occasions Matt checked the landline, it was because he hadn't heard from his father. There was a message from him.

"Mathew," his father's voice was strong and chipper despite his seventy-seven years and his near complete blindness. "It's your dear ol' dad calling, Wednesday afternoon…ah…early evening. I just wanted to remind you about Thanksgiving. Your sister's plans have changed a bit. They're coming in next Wednesday night. Are you still coming in on Monday?"

Matt's father, Nick, had lost Nell, Matt's mother, four years earlier to a fast moving cancer that shocked the family. Nick's sorrow was deep and biting, but, because of his faith, it had never become dangerous to him. Although he missed Nell terribly, he knew she was at peace, and somehow

56

that soothed him. They'd meet again when it was his time. Until then he would live as Nell would have wanted it.

Nick kept up his health, both physical and mental, with daily walks with his dog Charley and prayer. He spent the rest of his time in his music room, a tiny alcove in the house he'd shared with Nell for fifty years in Larkspur, a bedroom community just north of San Francisco. Music had always been a passion for Nick and Nell, but Nell's death and Nick's blindness made it an obsession.

The blindness had come on Nick slowly, so that by the time he went in for help, his condition was irreversible. Although he could see bright lights and outlines of backlit objects, he couldn't drive, read, watch TV, or do any of the other things that required clear eyesight. But he was a happy man. Despite his losses, he viewed his life with hope and an understanding that God still had a purpose for him.

"Oh, yeah," Nick continued, "one other thing, son. Sheila...you remember the Gordons down the street? Sheila's their granddaughter. Anyway, she brought in my mail today, and I had her read it to me. There's one here for you, son. I didn't open it...don't worry. But it's a good-sized envelope. If you need to know what's in it before you get up here, I could ask Sheila to read it to you. Apparently it's from the University of Arizona, a Professor Rosen, I believe." He hesitated and then seemed to remember he was talking to an answering service. "Isn't he the one who dated your grandfather's old parchment? Anyway, I thought you'd want to know. Give me a call. I'm looking forward to seeing you."

Matt stared at the telephone.

His mind raced with insane possibilities, none of which could take shape as an intelligent thought. Why would Rosen send him something... anything? He hadn't heard from the guy, hell, he hadn't even thought of him other than that one call and the articles on the stem cell thing, since he'd graduated. Now, suddenly, all he was hearing was the professor's name. He shook his head and continued to stare, dumbfounded.

Visions of Hannah flashed before him. They were accompanied by the sound of her voice, "Professor Rosen spoke of you," she'd said. He'd mentioned the old parchment. But why?

"He said he wanted to talk to Mr. Carter," Hannah told Detective Gutierrez. That was surprise enough for Matt, but now an envelope?... What the hell is going on?

Matt dialed his father's number. It rang four times before the ancient answering machine responded.

"Dad, it's Matt. If you're there, please pick up." He waited several seconds, impatiently pacing his tiny apartment. Of course he needed to know what the envelope contained. It had to have something to do with Rosen's death, didn't it? It was just too coincidental otherwise.

"I need you to tell me what's inside the envelope from Professor Rosen," he spoke quickly but tried not to sound too anxious for fear of the impact on his father. "Please call me as soon as you can. Call me on my cell." He then recited the number for the thousandth time to his father. "I'll have my cell phone with me all the time. It's important, Dad."

Matt didn't hear from Nick until he returned from work at 2:30 Sunday morning, and that was in another landline message. Matt gritted his teeth in anger at his father's stubbornness.

"Matt, Dad, here." His father sounded upbeat. "I got your message. I'll try to get Sheila over here after church tomorrow morning to read what's in the envelope. Give me a call after you get back from mass."

Matt shook his head. He hadn't been to mass in years, and his dad knew it. But Nick never failed to dig, particularly since he attributed his life's good fortune to his relationship with Jesus and wished his son would see the light. Matt wondered why Nick always felt he was so lucky, what with the blindness and Mom's death, but he'd given up questioning him. In truth, he was happy his father looked at the bright side of things.

He decided to call his dad the next day.

———

"IS THAT YOU, son?" Nick asked as he lifted the receiver the next day.

"Hi Dad," Matt said, and smiled that his dad guessed correctly.

"I called the Gordons," Nick said. "Unfortunately they're not home today. Probably went to their cabin in Tahoe; should be home tomorrow, though."

"Is there anyone else who can read what's in the envelope, Dad?" Matt asked.

"Uhhhhhh…" Matt could hear his father's thinking on the other end. "I might be able to call Ms. Jacobs over…you remember Ms. Jacobs up the street, don't you Matt?"

"Yes," Matt, frustrated, responded curtly. "Look Dad, can you feel what's inside and describe what you feel?"

"Sure. Give me a minute here," he mumbled, as he struggled to open the envelope.

"Is it a regular envelope or one of the big, orange ones?" Matt asked.

"It's a bigger one…there we go. I've got it open. Let's see here." Nick kept up a running monologue. "Okay now, there are several sheets, let's see, one, two," he whispered a count, "looks like eight sheets of eight and a half by eleven paper, three of 'em feel like bond paper—you know, the thicker letter writing paper—and it feels like one has an embossed letterhead. The others feel like regular copy paper."

Matt nodded, deep in thought. He would have to tell Detective Gutierrez, but he should probably know if it was anything important first. He needed his father to understand the importance of finding out what was on the sheets.

"Dad," Matt's voice was urgent. "Professor Rosen was murdered last weekend." He heard his father's intake of breath. "It happened when I was out there for the homecoming. I really need to know what the papers say so I can tell the detective who's investigating the murder."

"I hear you, son," Nick answered, the lightness now gone from his voice. "I can try to feel the type on the embossed sheet. Maybe he typed it." Nick said, and Matt could hear him fumbling with the papers.

"I'm sure it's from a computer, Dad. You won't feel indentations."

"Yeah, you're right," Nick said. "I should have known that. Look, I'll see if I can get someone to help us here."

"I'm going to Tucson for the professor's funeral on Monday, Dad. I won't be home until Tuesday night. Can you call me as soon as you have help?"

"Sure Matt. I'll get back to you as soon as I find someone."

"Dad, please call on my cell, not the house phone. I'll be gone, and will have the cell with me."

"I understand. I've got your number."

Matt appreciated that his father dropped his sense of whimsy.

"Mathew," Nick interrupted Matt's thought. "Are you okay?"

"Yeah." He hesitated. "Yeah, Dad, I'm good. Thanks. Please get back to me as soon as you can."

"I will, son."

CHAPTER THIRTEEN

THE POOR KNIGHTS of Christ and the Temple of Solomon, better known as the Knights Templar, are believed by some to be the progenitors of the international brotherhood of Freemasons, but there is no historical evidence of that. No reputable historian even pays lip service to the concept that the two organizations had any connection. The existence of the fraternity of pious warriors of the Knights Templar, protectors of the Pope and all things Catholic, ended with the execution of Jacques de Molay, the group's last Grand Master. De Molay and the Knights' Preceptor of Normandy, Geoffrey de Charnay, were burned at the stake on the Ile de la Cite on March 18, 1314 by order of King Phillip the Fair of France, who, prior to the executions, owed considerable sums of money to the Knights. Shockingly, Pope Clement V, Phillip's puppet Pope in Avignon, aided Phillip in his treachery against the Knights. From the day of the execution to this—despite modern writers' efforts to implicate the Templars in every conspiracy and secret society's attempt to discredit some religious belief—the Knights Templar have not existed.

As for the Freemasons, their origins date only to the early eighteenth century without even a hint of the historically romantic connection to the Knights Templar. Although the practice of laborers forming groups for their mutual benefit dates back to the time of the Roman Empire, long before the Templars existed, modern Freemasonry has very little connection even to the early labor groups created for stonemasons. Those groups, referred to as guilds, were formed to provide aid to members, and, more importantly, to confirm the credibility of and distinguish from the imposters, those who actually knew their craft. Most members of the Freemasons don't have the first clue about the craft of masonry.

From their eighteenth century beginnings in Scotland, the Freemasons were a fraternity created to share ideals of freedom from the tyranny of overreaching and oppressive governments and religious institutions. Men joined together in secret, beyond the reach of the eyes and ears of their ruling establishments to resist and to foster rebellion. That's why some of America's founding fathers, including George Washington and Benjamin Franklin, counted themselves members. To be part of an organization with secret handshakes, code words, and distinguishing symbols that provided its members a sense of security from infiltrators during times of revolution was a major boon to the cause.

Peter Christian was a Freemason. He had been the Grand Commander of the brotherhood's Western Jurisdiction for five years before he ascended to a post never before achieved in the history of the organization. Only two months ago, he'd been elected Sovereign Pontiff of Universal Freemasonry. Although Albert Pike, a revered distant predecessor in the Masons, had once claimed that exalted title, there had never been a "Universal Freemasonry," and no such position ever existed. There had always been independent jurisdictions, each with its own Grand Commander. Now, with the wonder of instant communication and the capacity for universal influence, Grand Commanders around the world had made their desires for unity known. And there was no man better to lead them than the charismatic Peter Christian, a powerful business leader and economic philosopher without peer.

To Christian and his brothers, world governments and religious leaders were again trying to take control of peoples' lives. From governments bent on "bailing out" companies they deemed important and dictating health care and basic life-decisions for all, to religious groups espousing rewards in heaven in exchange for total surrender to the dogma of their leaders, the control was growing. To Freemasonry's leaders, this religious and government intrusion meant only one thing: that the pendulum of power and wealth would swing away from the individual to those ponderous institutions. It was therefore the duty of all freethinking, intelligent men of economic means not only to resist the pendulum's swing, but to destroy the pendulum completely.

Christian stood at the window of his tenth floor conference room overlooking his company's latest project: the just completed Masonic Temple, now the largest such lodge in the world. It was built with donations from the Freemasons' expanding membership, first to provide a meeting place worthy of the group's worldwide reach, and second to provide much needed jobs to hundreds of Los Angeles construction workers crushed by the country's economic devastation. Now, the magnificent structure, designed through the collaboration of the world's most renowned architects, rivaled The Walt Disney Concert Hall and the Cathedral of Our Lady of the Angels as the most important architectural wonders of the city.

Behind Christian, his massive bodyguard, Walt, sat stoically eyeing 12 men on a 65-inch computer screen that protruded out of the middle of a mahogany conference table. The men were Freemason Grand Commanders, one each from the Universal's twelve worldwide jurisdictions.

"Peter, please don't misunderstand me!" Albrecht Speer's heavy German accent sharply accentuated the high-pitched anxiety in his voice. "The woman's death is unfortunate, but that bullet was meant for you...if she hadn't stepped into it, you would not be with us, and our cause would be lost."

Speer was a weasel-faced man with an acerbic personality and a high anxiety level despite his 75 years. His thin wisps of white hair were slicked straight back and barely visible against his pallid skin, making his bushy white mustache even more pronounced. Speer was the owner of Europe's largest real estate conglomerate. He was a rich man by anyone's standards, and he ran his company with an iron fist. Most important, however, Speer was Grand Commander of the European Union Universal's northern jurisdiction. His current anxiety stemmed from his reference to Sunny Turner as "that bitch who had never been a friend."

James McGinnis, a large florid faced Scotsman leaned toward his computer monitor. His face replaced Speer's in the speaker window. He was

Grand Commander of the United Kingdom's Universal and the President and CEO of Europe's second largest commercial banking institution.

"He's right Peter," McGinnis said, his booming voice surprising everyone by supporting a man with whom he usually disagreed. "We should, of course, be careful about using Albrecht's reference to Ms. Turner, even though she was a problem. You've done well expressing sympathy for a woman who wasn't your friend. It's now time for us to go on the offensive. Let her rest in peace, but let us use this to our advantage."

"What do you propose, Mr. McGinnis?" Christian asked with a hint of sarcasm.

McGinnis' eyes widened at the formality. He hesitated, and then continued with a degree of caution.

"We've been inundated with e-mails, tweets, and every other form of contact from well-wishers expressing shock and thanks for your survival. Virtually every one of our chapters has experienced a surge in interest. Shouldn't we use this to advance our cause?"

"Yes!" Speer blasted, his face suddenly looming in the speaker screen. "Let's call out the ones who are responsible! We know it's the damn Church! They hate us because we do our business without bowing down to them, and they hate us because we're Masons. They can't stand that we have a leader as influential as their pope. Hell, the whole world knows they're behind it; it's all over the talk shows."

"Gentlemen, I appreciate your passion," Christian said in a calm, almost fatherly tone despite the fact that most of the men were his elders. "But we can't go off half-cocked and start a battle yet. It'll do no good to engage the Church and its billion half-assed followers." He chuckled and several faces on the screen smiled. "Let's keep our heads about us, and let this thing run its course. The truth will come out soon enough."

The Masons and the Catholic Church had been engaged in battle since the beginning of the brotherhood. The Church had at one point issued rules prohibiting Catholics from joining the fraternity, and while it stopped short of claiming that it was Satanic, some Church leaders condemned Freemasonry as an organization that has "led or assisted" the "partisans of evil." For their part, the Freemasons regarded traditional Christian faiths as allied to old world standards of inhumanity with the intent of maintaining the status quo against the growth of the independent human spirit.

"The media's running with this. They've picked up on the Catholic attacks against us. They're quoting Church leaders who came out against me being honored with your vote as the leader of this great fraternity." Christian placed his fingertips lightly atop the table and nodded. "The Church is afraid, and the media knows it. Let the story have its legs. Refrain from comment and they'll do our work for us."

Heads nodded and smiles returned to the faces of the Grand Commanders.

"Look gentlemen, let's break for now. We all have important things to get back to. We'll keep an eye on things, and reconvene next week. For now, I need time to think."

Each man signed off understanding the trauma with which Christian must certainly be dealing. No one doubted the attempt on his life had shaken him. None of the brothers would have blamed him if he'd said he was through and gone about his own business without any further regard for the cause to which they had all ascribed. Yet, every one of them knew that wasn't Peter Christian. He'd never give up. He just needed time.

Christian sat quietly after the call. He knew there would be a time for bravado and overt action. This was not that time.

"Walt, get the Warden on the line for me," he instructed pensively.

The big man nodded.

CHAPTER FOURTEEN

CARDINAL METZINGER SOMETIMES envied fanatical Muslims. They didn't have to deal with questions of faith. They simply forced belief as they saw it. If a person had doubts, he'd be maimed or killed; if he considered changing his faith, he'd be maimed or killed; if he chose to skip prayers or violate some other rule, he'd be maimed or killed. There were no philosophical discussions of right or wrong, and never a question about whether God actually existed. Either a person believed and followed the rules or he'd lose a finger, a hand, or a head. It was that simple.

Metzinger knew, of course, his envy was ridiculous. He didn't approve of the barbarity. The cardinal didn't want to force belief. The foundation of faith in Christ was choice. God imbued man with a free will to choose. To force a man to believe would take away that free will.

Still, after yet another grueling battle over Church doctrine, he sometimes resented free will and the continuous battle to influence it.

Wouldn't it make our task of saving souls much easier Lord if you simply appeared before a packed house at Yankee Stadium and broadcast the truth of your divinity to the world? he'd wonder. *Imagine how the world would be if no one could ever again deny your truth.*

But before the thought ever fully formed, he'd stop himself. Hadn't Jesus told his disciples that if they walked into a town to preach his love and no one welcomed them, they were to turn away, shake the dust from their sandals, and not look back? The whole point was choice. In his love of man,

God gave him the ultimate choice: to choose the path for his eternal soul. It was up to people like Metzinger, those who understood the truth and believed so strongly in their mission, to guide the flock to the correct path.

Cardinal Metzinger sighed. He and his brethren were engaged in a war. The ultimate prize was the soul of humankind. Arrayed against them were the worldly temptations of money, power, and earthly possessions. Metzinger knew the enemy well, and, unfortunately, the enemy was winning.

How easy it had become for the rich and powerful to turn man's dreams of eternal peace into a fantasy of money. Business leaders preached their gospel of wealth and its pursuit unshackled by moral compunction or any belief beyond an individual's freedom to do as he felt. Worse yet, those business leaders and organizations were revered while men of faith were ridiculed. That Freemason Peter Christian could draw a bigger crowd than any church leader save the Pope astounded Metzinger. But he saw what was happening. Like Moses when he came down from the mountain and found his people worshipping the golden calf, Metzinger saw the people's folly. While he might not be able to force belief, he could do whatever was necessary to remove the obstacles. He could help make the road smooth and wide so all people could find their way along the proper path. And if, along the way, some were lost for the cause, so be it. Metzinger would do whatever he had to do.

CHAPTER FIFTEEN

THE DOMED TOWERS of St. Augustine Cathedral stood majestic against the clear blue Arizona sky. It was a magnificent Monday morning with a temperature in the high 70's and an atmosphere of crystal clarity—a morning fit for the funeral of Professor Samuel Rosen.

Matt arrived early, but found the only parking still available was in a lot across Stone Avenue. The street was jammed with police vehicles and media vans bearing call letters of local stations and national networks. Obviously, the old professor's renown was far greater than Matt imagined. As Matt joined the crowd moving toward the cathedral's double-door entry, he caught snippets of speculation on the motive behind the murder. Redneck fanatics angry at the professor's "liberal" stand on climate change? Religious zealots enraged over the professor's position on fetal stem-cell research? Opinions abounded, but no clear answers existed.

When Matt stepped inside the cathedral, his eyes were immediately drawn to the enormous statute of the risen Christ hanging above the altar. It depicted a fully robed figure with arms outstretched in welcome instead of the typical half-naked figure of a man hanging in excruciating pain. This image exuded warmth, calm, and quiet peace despite the hum of the large crowd.

Seating was scarce despite the cathedral's capacity for twelve hundred fifty guests. Matt grabbed the first end seat he could some three rows from the back. He immediately started looking for Hannah, but it was impossible to distinguish the back of one dark haired head from another. In fact, the only person he was able to distinguish was one that stared at him as his eyes made their sweep.

Detective Gutierrez's large, square, mustached face stuck out in the sea of heads. When he caught Matt's eye, he motioned a greeting. Matt smiled awkwardly. Their eyes held for several seconds before Matt pulled away and continued his search for Hannah. He didn't see the detective whisper to the plainclothes officer next to him and then push himself out of his seat. Nor did Matt notice, until Gutierrez was almost on top of him, that the detective was approaching.

"I'm glad you came to town, Mr. Carter," Gutierrez spoke softly while extending a meaty hand.

Matt took the hand and looked up at the black eyes and heavy brow. The detective crouched down in the aisle next to him. People, still searching for seats, maneuvered around the beefy body, but the detective paid them no mind. Matt pushed back into his pew, uncomfortable with the man's closeness.

"I'd like you to come by the office tomorrow morning. Will you still be in town?" Gutierrez asked in a whispered, gravelly voice.

"Yeah. My flight isn't 'til five."

"Good, can I send someone by to pick you up?"

Matt shot him a look of surprise.

"You mean a police car?"

Gutierrez nodded.

Matt shook his head, "I don't need an escort. I'll be there. Is there something specific you want to talk about?"

"No," Gutierrez hesitated long enough to make him wonder. "Just a few things I need to clarify. I was going to call you, but thought you might show up here."

Matt nodded and eyed the detective.

"Yeah…well sure, I can drop by. I have something I wanted to talk to you about anyway." He immediately regretted the words.

Gutierrez arched his heavy brows. "What did you want to discuss?" he asked.

"It can wait till tomorrow." Matt tried to sound matter-of-fact. Even though Matt was frustrated that his father hadn't gotten back to him about Rosen's envelope, he had intended to tell the detective about it. But, he was uneasy. He thought it was because the burly cop was so close to him in the crowded church. But he wasn't sure. "What time should I come by?" he asked.

Gutierrez smiled. "Ten o'clock?"

Matt nodded, and the detective struggled to his feet, wincing with the effort. Finally erect, he smiled and placed a firm hand on Matt's shoulder.

"See you tomorrow."

Matt watched the detective lumber back to his seat.

THE CEREMONY BEGAN shortly after Gutierrez left Matt. It was a Catholic mass – something that felt so natural to Matt from his childhood that he didn't give the matter much thought, until the presiding bishop got to his homily. Then it hit him. The Jewish Leprechaun was having a Catholic funeral.

Matt looked about the church and noticed yarmulkes sprinkled throughout the crowd; he saw heads turning, exchanging expressions, some confused, some angry. Matt focused on the bishop.

"Samuel didn't view his action as a conversion," the bishop was saying. "He never cast away the faith and traditions into which he was born and raised. No, like our Lord Jesus Christ and his followers, Samuel embraced his Jewish faith even unto his dying day. He viewed his move to Catholicism as an extension of his great faith rather than an abandonment of it. He came to believe in the word of Christ as that of the God his family had worshipped through its Judaism. He was moved to believe, like the great disciple Paul himself, that Christ was the savior for whom the Jews had waited throughout their history."

The bishop hesitated and eyed the standing-room-only crowd.

"Brothers and sisters, Samuel Rosen was not a Jew or a Catholic. He was, just like each of us here today, a child of God. He didn't want to judge those who believed differently from him, and he didn't want to try to force his beliefs on anyone else. Simply put, Samuel came to a realization: from which he could not run, from which he could not hide. He came to believe with all his heart and all his mind and all his soul that Jesus Christ is the Lord of all. Although I cannot describe his precise journey to that understanding, I can tell you his belief was real. Let us not then judge our brother and the decision he made, rather let us..."

As the bishop droned on, Matt's eyes wandered again, this time to the expressions of disbelief on the faces of those who'd known the professor's position on religion. He was a scientist who'd followed the cultural traditions of his Jewish faith because that was how he'd been raised. But he'd never put much store in the spirituality of religion. In fact, his classes often included joking references to true believers. Had he really become one of them?

CHAPTER SIXTEEN

ROSEN'S INTERMENT WAS at Holy Hope Cemetery in a grave over which would eventually stand a monument bearing a Crucifix atop a Star of David. Some heads shook as the bishop was joined by a rabbi for the final prayers and incantations. The graveside ceremony was relatively short, and it wasn't until late during the wake in a University gathering hall that Matt and Hannah Melnyk finally bumped into each other.

They'd made eye contact several times, but had been unable to talk. Mourners, who knew she was Rosen's graduate assistant, surrounded her continuously seeking details of Professor Rosen's "conversion." As the day wore on, Matt lost sight of her and gave up hope of talking to her.

"Mr. Carter." Matt whirled. "It's nice to see you could make it," Hannah said.

"Ms. Melnyk," he stammered. "Yes, the professor...the professor was a good guy." He looked past her, awkwardly searching for words.

She nodded, but said nothing.

"Please, call me Matt," he finally blurted. "When you say Mr. Carter, I feel like you're talking to my father or something."

She chuckled, "I'm Hannah." She extended a tiny hand and smile in new greeting.

He took the hand, smiled confidently for the first time in her presence, and began to feel at ease. He gestured toward a nearby table. They settled into folding chairs.

"I've been wanting to ask you a question since our meeting at the police station," he said. "Do you have any idea why Rosen wanted to get in touch with me?"

She glanced down, considering her answer. Finally, she looked at Matt again.

"Yes," she said. "It was the parchment. That's all he talked about whenever your name came up." She eyed him. "Why do you ask?"

"A package, well, an envelope arrived at my dad's house from the professor a few days ago. He must have sent it just before he died."

"What was in it?"

"I don't know. My dad is blind. He didn't have anyone handy to read it to me. I've been waiting to hear back from him. I just thought since you worked with Rosen, you might know what was in it."

She shook her head, her brow furrowing in thought.

"I really don't, Matt. He never mentioned what was in the parchment, so I don't know what it related to…except," she hesitated, a thought taking hold.

"What is it?" Matt asked.

"I was just thinking that he mentioned your name around the time of the first threat a week or so before the murder. That's when he first said he needed to talk to you about the parchment…something about needing to make sure it was safe."

"Safe? From what?"

"I don't know. Maybe he thought it had something to do with the threat," she said slowly, still thinking carefully as she talked. Then, she looked him squarely in the eyes, "You know, he was concerned about some tests he was running and research he was doing. He must have believed your parchment related to his research."

"Do you know what he was working on?"

"That's the same question that detective has been hammering me about," she said disdainfully.

"Gutierrez?" Matt asked.

"Yes," she chuckled sarcastically, "Detective Gutierrez. His goons marched into the lab and confiscated all the computers and files that had anything to do with the professor's work." She looked down at her fisted hands, deliberately relaxing them on the tablecloth. "I understand their need to gather evidence. The problem is they took everything, even my personal notes and files. I'd already copied and delivered everything to them a day or two earlier. They were so heavy handed about it, like I was the enemy or something." She shook her head. "I don't trust him."

Matt remembered his own uneasiness with Gutierrez in church.

"Did they say what they were looking for?" he asked.

"No. Just came in and took it all."

"Do you know what the threats were about? Did they have anything to do with his stand on fetal stem-cell research or anything like that?"

"No," Hannah said softly, her eyes flitting furtively about the room. "That's what the press is talking about, but he hasn't been involved in that for a while. It was nothing like that." She paused, as if steeling herself. "It was the Sindon. They wanted him to stop working on it."

Matt's ears caught the word the detective had mentioned.

"Gutierrez asked me if I knew what a Sindon was. I didn't. Do you?" he asked.

She eyed him quizzically.

"It's the shroud," she said as if it were obvious. "The burial cloth of Jesus Christ. Professor Rosen was doing tests on it."

Matt was taken aback.

"The Shroud of Turin?" he asked.

She nodded.

"What was he doing with the Shroud? It's a fake. His own lab determined that back in, hell, I don't know, the late 80's or so. The carbon dating proved it. Why would he be working on that?"

Hannah stared hard at him. Her eyes made another sweep of the room. Finally, she leaned over the table and spoke in a whisper.

"The carbon dates were wrong."

CHAPTER SEVENTEEN

ASSIM RAHMAN STOOD beneath the skeletal limbs of the massive oak, now completely denuded by the season's turn to late autumn. The moonlit shadows of those limbs danced about his firmly rooted silhouette as he eyed the house in which Mathew Carter was raised.

The street was quiet, just as he had expected at 10:30 at night. He'd driven through the neighborhood the last two evenings learning the roads in and out, and that few people ventured outside after dinner. Even late dog-walkers were now ensconced snuggly inside their homes watching whatever inane product their televisions offered.

Assim smiled at the stupidity. How could they all be so content when the very fabric of their existences was being torn out from under them? They didn't understand, either out of complacency or, more likely, a real lack of intelligence. Assim knew exactly what would happen if not for people like him and the Master. They'd wake up one day wondering what had happened, how they'd been imprisoned, how they'd let someone do this to them.

The Master understood it clearly. He knew what was coming if the people didn't accept the truth. He knew the exact nature of the prison in which these people would find themselves if they didn't stand up. They might still be alive, but they would all be dead…a living dead that would be worse than death itself.

Together, Assim and the Master were taking steps. They would destroy the prison, but not in one fell swoop. No one would believe if the truth were revealed in a single overt event. It would have to come over time—subtly. Small, but very important steps would have to be taken so people would come to the truth on their own. On this night, yet another of those small steps was at hand.

Assim crossed the deserted street confidently. Although this step didn't seem significant, the Master assured him it was more important than anyone could know. To Assim the relative importance of a task rarely fazed him, for if the instruction came from the Master, it was important. The unusual thing about this task however, was that the Master had imposed a restriction upon him. Assim nodded his assent to the restriction, but he wondered what he would do if he had no choice.

Fortunately, the Master anticipated his concern.

"Son," the Master had said, "use your judgment in this matter."

———————

NICK CARTER DOZED in his music room. His head rested softly against the cushion of the recliner while his left arm hung lazily over the side, above the head of Charley, the German Shepherd Nick referred to as his eyes. The dog lay quietly, dutifully awaiting his master's need.

Nick listened to the exhilarating sounds of Dvorak's Slavonic Dances. They took him on a journey of adventure with their wild runs, rich cadences, and enchanting calls to love amidst the turbulence and danger of the Ukrainian steppes. He smiled with the memory of Nell in her younger years, dancing lightly to the songs of her Ukrainian youth, when he'd come to town like a marauding Cossack and stolen her heart.

Nick woke from his trance when he felt Charley's head come up suddenly to his hand. He scratched the dog, felt a quiver of tension, and realized Charley was standing. Nick leaned toward the dog.

"What's up, Charley?" he whispered. "Relax, buddy; we're almost done here."

But Charley didn't relax. In fact, the tension became more apparent as Nick stroked the animal's back and felt his hairs bristle.

"What is it, boy?" Nick pushed the recliner's footrest closed and came forward. He turned toward the door, open to the hall. He heard nothing, but Charley had. Nick reached for the sound control and reduced it to nothing. He then directed his ear to the doorway.

Charley whined.

"Okay, boy," Nick said, his stomach churning. He stood, took Charley's handgrip, and followed the dog to the door. Charley began to growl. As they gained the hall, Nick turned toward the front door. He could make out dim outside light through the open doorway. In the center of that light, at the hall's entry table, stood a shadowed figure.

"Who are you?" Nick demanded.

Charley growled murderously and strained at his grip. When Nick received no response, he released the dog. Charley shot away from him. The shadow's left arm swept out in a defensive motion as the dog leapt at it. The shadow cried out and staggered back; but at the same time it swung its right arm at the dog in a powerful underhand arc. Charley screamed.

The dog's cry was horrifying and continuous. Nick strained to discern what was happening, but all he could sense were Charley's plaintive cries. He took a stumbling step forward until the human figure stepped again into the backlight and raised his arm. Nick saw a glint of light off something in the figure's hand. Nick stopped.

"Help!" he screamed.

He couldn't move. But he could shout, and he did so again and again, until the shadow moved. He stopped shouting and heard an angry grunt, as the shadow turned and, with a mighty heave, kicked Charley. The poor beast yelped again before the figure fled into the street's dim light.

ASSIM CRADLED HIS bloodied left arm. What a disaster. He'd found the envelope sitting in plain view on the hall table. He could have simply run out, but he'd confronted the attacking dog and the envelope had been torn in the battle. He'd held it firmly and, he believed, kept it mostly intact. But he couldn't check on it now as lights of neighboring houses were coming on in response to the old man's pleas for help.

Assim shoved the long knife with which he'd dispatched the dog, into the sheath at his belt, and he ran to his rental car. He needed to get out of the neighborhood before the neighbors knew what was happening or the police arrived.

The pain in his arm was excruciating. The dog had clamped down quickly, and as Assim instinctively shoved the arm far back in the beast's mouth, the dog released, re-gripped, and pulled away in a tearing motion that gashed him.

Assim was red with rage that he hadn't brought his gun. He should have killed the old man and the dog with the silenced weapon. But he'd heard the Master. The restriction had not been a request.

"Don't kill this one," the Master had instructed. "It will be best that it look like a burglary. To have another professional death to draw the authorities will complicate our ultimate task."

So Assim hadn't carried a gun with him. What he hadn't counted on was the strength and savagery of the dog.

He heard the sirens, but not until he was back on the freeway, heading south on the 101 for the city. He would have to tend to his wound before it became infected, but first he had to move far enough away that there could be no connection.

CHAPTER EIGHTEEN

"WE'VE BEEN THROUGH this, Eminence," said a flustered Father Aaron Roberts, pastor of the Cathedral of Our Lady of the Angels in Los Angeles. He'd flown to Rome as the American Catholic Church's point man on the topic of discussion, and feared his trip would end in disaster.

At 44, Father Roberts looked years younger and still exuded the energy and passion that were hallmarks of his work when he was first ordained. With deep brown eyes and sun-bleached brown hair swept loosely back, he was accustomed to infatuated attention from women in his parish, but he was largely oblivious to it. His looks were simply a part of him, like a finger or a toe, and that was the end of it. Teaching the word of Christ and working to change the hearts of those who were lost were the things that mattered to him. That was the reason he was flustered as he sat in a Vatican conference room at a table with eight others.

Cardinal Metzinger presided over the assembly with his secretary, Francesco, to his immediate right obsequiously scribbling down every word he said. If not for Cardinal Antonio Giordano, Archbishop of Turin and successor "Custodian" of the famous shroud, Father Roberts would already have been dismissed.

Giordano leaned his short round frame forward and propped his forearms on the table. "Please, Father Roberts, go through it once again." He nodded encouragingly.

Roberts scanned the other faces before turning back to Metzinger.

"We've spent the last three years working out the security issues. For two years, we've been promoting the Shroud's journey to the United States. America's Catholic community, which I must add has been sorely tested by our church's scandals, waits breathlessly for its arrival. Its flight to California is in less than one week. Everything is in motion. We cannot stop now."

Roberts glanced at Giordano, who again nodded. When Roberts' eyes moved to the others, all men of importance at the Vatican, he sensed no additional support. In fact, he could sense no emotion one way or the other. All eyes flicked to Metzinger.

"I understand your frustration, Father," Metzinger said patronizingly. "You and our brother, the Archbishop of Los Angeles, as well as the other American bishops have planned long and hard for this exhibition. It would be a shame to disappoint these good men and the flocks they shepherd. But it simply is not safe."

Roberts glared at Metzinger. The cardinal had been opposed to a worldwide Shroud exhibition from the beginning. He'd fought hard before the Holy Father himself to have the matter tabled, but he'd lost. Now he acted as if he were arriving at his conclusion anew.

"Why not leave the Shroud as it has been since its discovery in Lirey so many centuries ago? Those who wish to see the cloth can take their pilgrimages to Turin. There is no need to subject this most precious of our Lord's gifts to the risk of travel."

"The successful exhibitions of the Dead Sea Scrolls and the Tomb of Tutankhamen brought those artifacts to the masses," Roberts retorted hotly. "Do we not want to make the Shroud accessible to all, or just to the rich who can travel to Turin, or those who already believe?"

"Things have changed," Metzinger said, anger creeping into his tone. "The murder of the Professor from Arizona has changed everything."

Father Roberts started to speak, but a sharp look from Metzinger quieted him.

"It was because of the professor's tests of the holy relic that he was killed." Metzinger glared at the younger priest, still angry at the betrayal that had gotten a piece of the Shroud into the professor's hands in the first place. His eyes moved to the others as he calmed himself. He spread his arms, pleading for their understanding.

"We all know the truth, gentlemen. Had this professor left matters as they were, he would be alive today. If we do not take the initiative now, there will be more deaths. We don't know which way this professor's work was going, but we do know it would have offended someone, as it apparently did. There are those who would kill to prevent the truth about the Shroud from being known, whether that truth is that it is real or that it is a fake. The Church cannot be responsible for what might come." Metzinger's eyes bored into the others, his face reddening as if he could will them into acceptance of his position.

Cardinal Giordano cleared his throat. "Brother," he started and eyed Metzinger, his younger counterpart. "Our Lord was never shy of a challenge. He was not afraid to throw the greedy moneychangers out of the temple, and he was never afraid to stand up to those powerful forces that opposed him. Neither should we be afraid."

Metzinger leaned forward to respond, but Giordano lifted his hand, "Please brother, let me finish my thought lest I forget. We old men find it difficult to remember where we are headed."

A smile came to everyone's lips, even Metzinger's. Giordano might be old, but they all knew him to be as sharp a political operative as ever.

"What we have brothers," he turned to eye everyone at the table, "is the opportunity to evangelize the world. We know the Lord provided this gift for a purpose. Those who see it and truly understand what it is will have no choice but to believe that Christ is Lord. We cannot back down now." He turned to Metzinger. "I cannot support your desires here, my friend, because I believe firmly in the course upon which we have embarked, and I must respectfully assert to the Holy Father that it is the proper course."

Metzinger regarded him steadily. Neither one smiled.

"One last thing, if I may, Eminence," Father Roberts interjected. Metzinger sighed. "This is our opportunity. I believe the image on this linen is the very sign we have always sought. It is our Lord's 'Yankee Stadium moment,' where He tells the world who He is, and the world will have no choice but to believe."

"And what if it isn't real?" Metzinger demanded. "We know what happened when the carbon test established a date no earlier than 1260. The damage of that finding was so great that even now we are having difficulty trying to win back the souls we lost." He hesitated and calmed himself before he continued. "Is it not better to teach and encourage faith? Why must we have a sign? Why must we have proof?" He asked the questions with such passion, no one at the table would have guessed that his words contradicted his own oft-dreamed desires.

"I agree we should need no sign," Giordano started again. "But when our Lord has provided one, we ought not hide it. Our duty is to exhibit that sign, to give the world its benefit, to help the world understand its significance, and to provide all people the opportunity to know the peace we know."

Silence descended upon the table. They all knew a sign from God would dramatically change the state of the world. Yet they were afraid they might be wrong— all, that is, except Father Aaron Roberts.

"The truth, Eminence, is that the Shroud is real. It is not a fake. It's time we stood together and acknowledged it."

Metzinger saw the nodding heads and understood. He would have no support trying to convince the Holy Father to cancel the exhibition. Yet he knew they were wrong. A second scientific finding that the Shroud was a fake could be catastrophic to the Church, particularly in a world already doubting the existence of God.

But what concerned Metzinger even more were the bloody conflicts with other faiths that would ensue from a new carbon finding that the Shroud was real.

CHAPTER NINETEEN

CORNY CROCKETT CONSIDERED his reflection. He fingered the scraggly beard he'd been cultivating since Elli's death. It was something he'd wanted as far back as the late 60's when his students paraded into his classes garbed in motley tie-dye and stripes, with hair that protruded from every part of every body. He'd refrained back then because he was just starting and didn't have the presence of mind to understand that his example of the "proper" university professor meant nothing. Over the ensuing years, every time he tried to grow a beard, it had been so sparse and patchy that he'd given up. Elli never objected to the look, saying only that it itched her when they made love. For Corny, that and the reality that he hated how sketchy it was, had been enough. It was only after Elli was gone and no one was around to take notice that he decided he'd make a real effort to grow a beard. As he stared at his reflection again, cocking his head this way and that to find the best angle from which to view his masterpiece, he realized there was no "best angle," and what he viewed was no "masterpiece."

With the sagging flesh of his red-rimmed eyes, even the still rich brown of the orbs couldn't make him look anything but old and haggard—something that might seem natural for a man approaching his seventy-seventh year. But he wasn't old, even though the years and his mirror told him otherwise. He was still ripcord strong, quick and agile as any man twenty years his junior. Mountain life, with its harsh winters and hike-filled summers, had taken care of that for him—the same way it had for Elli; and, but for that damn cancer, she'd still be with him, strong as ever.

Seeing the age that streaked his face above the patchy whiskers brought him down, made him feel old, and just plain sucked the passion right out of him. He had to get it back, and he had to do it now. The beard had to go. So he set to work, and after only fifteen minutes, three years of growth was gone and he found the soft white skin of the lower half of his face. It formed an interesting contrast to the weather-beaten upper half, but it also brought life to him. He felt strong again, and he had to be strong because they were coming for him.

Corny knew he was on their target list. He wasn't afraid to die because that would bring him together with Elli. Yet he had work to do, not just for Samuel and Elli, but for a world that had to know the truth. And he'd be damned if he was going to let some punks kill him the way they did Samuel, before he did what needed to be done.

He'd deal with the threat he knew was coming, and then he'd finish Samuel's work.

CHAPTER TWENTY

HANNAH WOKE FROM a dead sleep to a pounding at her apartment door. She could hear neighbors stirring angrily through the paper-thin walls. She rolled out of bed, threw on a tattered robe, and staggered, dazed, to her door.

"Hey, shut the fu…" she heard one neighbor shout, and then stop as if he'd seen what was making the noise and thought better of his epithet.

"Hold on," Hannah said. She reached for the chain. "Who is it?"

"Ms. Melnyk? It's the police. Please open the door."

Her surprise brought her immediately out of her half-consciousness. She tightened the belt of her robe, slid the chain out, and opened the door.

"What's happened?" she asked as officer Kraben, the same man who'd led the team that confiscated the items from the lab, stepped toward her with his badge held high.

"Ms. Melnyk, we have a warrant to search your home." He brandished a folded piece of paper. "Will you step aside and permit us to proceed?"

"What?" she started. "What do you guys want?"

No one answered. Her eyes darted from Kraben to the three officers behind him.

"Will you step aside, Ms. Melnyk?"

Hannah was shocked, flustered, and angry. She couldn't develop a straight thought, so she started to move aside. She stopped suddenly, however, when Kraben jammed the paper into his pocket, and started to push past her.

"Just a minute," she said. "Let me see that." She pointed to the paper.

Kraben hesitated, then handed her the document. He stepped past her with the other three officers at his heels. Still bleary-eyed and not sure what she was looking for, she discerned only that they were here to search for and take all computers, backup storage equipment, and all other electronics and files that could have anything to do with projects upon which Professor Samuel Rosen was working.

"Wait, damn it," she finally shouted as she lifted her eyes from the warrant and spotted Kraben and one of the officers disappearing into her bedroom. She scampered after them.

"None of this is the professor's or the school's. This is my personal stuff," she said, and turned to Kraben's cohort, who had lifted her laptop from the desk and was bending over to unplug it. "You can't have that," she shouted, and grabbed the computer, bumping the officer. He stumbled off balance, but caught himself before he fell. He turned to her.

"Don't interfere, Ms. Melnyk," Officer Kraben stepped forward menacingly. "If you interfere, you will be arrested. Now, return the computer to Officer Douglas."

Hannah stared at Kraben, her eyes filling with tears, powerless and frustrated. The officer was unfazed. She held the laptop with both hands, slightly behind her and away from both officers. Their eyes locked in the standoff, each waiting for the other to buckle. No one saw Hannah extract and palm the flash-drive before finally, slowly, bringing the computer forward and handing it to the officer.

A smug smile turned Kraben's lips. "Thank you, Ms. Mel…"

Hannah whirled away from him and stormed out of the room. She clasped her hands in front of her and tucked the flash-drive into the waistband of her underwear, beneath her robe.

———————

BY THE TIME Matt finally stepped into Gutierrez' office Tuesday morning, it was nearly 11:00. The detective was riffling through papers when he glanced up and motioned Matt to sit. He deliberately straightened the materials in front of him and didn't say a word until he'd pushed the stack aside and folded his hands atop his desk.

"Thanks for coming in," he said perfunctorily.

Matt nodded, angry to again have waited for almost an hour.

"You had some questions?" Matt said brusquely. The wait coupled with the discussion of Gutierrez's jackboot tactics with Hannah at the wake had affected him.

"Yeah," Gutierrez responded, eyeing him quizzically. "I want to know if you've found the parchment."

"What?" Matt started, then collected himself. "Are you talking about my grandfather's old document?"

"I am," the detective responded flatly.

"Was I supposed to be looking for it? I thought it wasn't important. I mean, I recall you asking me about it, and I asked you if it was important, and you said you didn't know."

"Mr. Carter, perhaps I didn't make myself clear in our last meeting. It appears Professor Rosen was interested in you at the time he was killed. The only connection we discussed other than that he was your professor many years ago was this parchment that he called the…" he glanced to the pile of papers he'd set aside, "the Carter Parchment. Do you recall that?" he asked patronizingly.

"Sure." Matt nodded.

"Good. It seems obvious the parchment is somehow connected to the professor's death. Do you have it or not?"

"Like I said last time, Detective," he responded icily, "I believe my father has it somewhere. The last time we talked, you didn't seem interested in it."

Gutierrez's eyes flashed anger. Matt held his gaze, knowing he had rights the detective would not abuse in his office. He needed Gutierrez to understand he would not be intimidated.

Gutierrez finally nodded and leaned back in his chair. He eyed Matt, and then smiled. "You're correct, of course," he started with a lighter tone. "I'm sorry, Matt…do you mind if I call you Matt?"

Matt shrugged.

"I'm on edge over this damn case," Gutierrez continued. "He was a great professor and we don't have much yet; I'm just trying to figure this out." Matt nodded. "Look, I think your grandfather's parchment might be important. Do you think you can locate it?"

"I don't know, Detective," Matt responded calmly. "I haven't been home for a while. I'll ask my dad if he knows where it is when I'm home for Thanksgiving."

"Could you call him now?" Gutierrez asked.

"I've been trying to reach him for several days. I tried just before I left the hotel this morning. He won't answer the phone." Matt shrugged. "That's not unusual. He goes by his own schedule and rules. It'll do no good to call him. I'll check when I go there for Thanksgiving."

"That would be great. Can you call me as soon as you know?" Gutierrez leaned forward and handed Matt a card on which he'd written a number. "That's my cell number. You can reach me at any time over the long weekend. It's important."

Matt took the card and nodded, "I'll see what I can find."

"Good," Gutierrez said. "Now, I believe you had something you wanted to talk about?"

Matt shook his head. "No, I..." he eyed Gutierrez warily. "I was just going to ask you how the investigation was going, if you had any idea who killed the professor. But I guess I just got the answer."

"Yeah, we're on it but, nothing yet," Gutierrez said. "You'll check on the parchment and get back to me?"

Matt nodded. He couldn't believe he'd just lied to a cop investigating a murder.

CHAPTER TWENTY-ONE

MATT STEPPED OUT of the police station into another beautiful autumn day. He decided to walk to his lunch date with Hannah to clear his thoughts. Although it was a long hike to the Frog & Firkin, a hamburger joint near campus, he had enough time before the noon meeting.

Matt was mystified by his decision to hold information back. He might have argued that he didn't know for sure the envelope was from Rosen until he saw it himself or had someone read it to him. What point was there in saying anything until he knew the real facts? Good argument, but it was bullshit. The truth was that he was uneasy about Gutierrez. The cop's overbearing attitude coupled with Hannah's distrust just didn't feel right. He wanted to go slowly until he could think through his uneasiness about the man.

The other thing that weighed heavy on Matt was the reason the professor was killed. Hannah stated that the original threat had nothing to do with Matt's suspicions of possible motives. Instead, it was related to work the professor was doing on the Sindon…the cloth Matt knew as the Shroud of Turin.

"The carbon dates were wrong," she'd said.

In Rosen's class, when the Shroud was considered it was as a case study, one of the first that had world renown. Although quacks that claimed the tests were wrong had been mentioned, there was never any serious discussion of their position.

Three of the top labs in the world had tested pieces of the cloth. Each came to the same conclusion. How could they have been wrong?

At the wake, Hannah had explained that about a year and a half ago Professor Rosen had returned from a trip to Italy, and was all fired up. He'd had a package she later learned contained a small piece of the cloth. She'd never learned whether he'd stolen it or if it had been given to him. But he laid out a very specific protocol for cleaning and preparing it for the test and then methodically chronicled the actual process. He performed a range of tests, which took months, and ended with the Accelerator Mass Spectrometer. The results had come down just two weeks ago. Since then he'd been holed up reviewing notes and preparing a presentation he was to make in Los Angeles sometime around Christmas.

Matt questioned her about the test results.

"I had to help him get into the computer occasionally," she'd said, smiling at the memory. "He was impatient about spending time mastering the computer when he had so much else on his mind. He was quirky that way." She'd eyed Matt sadly.

"Anyway," Hannah had continued, "when I helped him with the computer, I caught glimpses of his work, but he didn't want me to get more involved, particularly after the first threat came down. He said it was better that I not know specifics."

"So you don't know what he found," Matt said.

"Not specifically." Hannah had said. "He definitely believed the original tests were wrong, though. I don't know why. But he actually danced around the lab, shouting that they'd made a mistake."

Matt arrived at the Frog & Firkin ahead of schedule. He tried to calm his mind by sipping an iced tea while he waited for Hannah. When she finally pulled her hybrid into a parking space across the street and stepped out, he smiled and waved. Hannah stared at him for several seconds, as if she didn't know whether to join him. Finally, as Matt dropped his hand bewildered, she forced a smile, closed her door, and stepped across the street.

Although still taken with her beauty, Matt was no longer nonplussed in her presence. As she approached him, however, he was again uneasy. He could see confusion on her brow and a weight seemed to stoop her bearing. Her smile wasn't real.

"Morning Hannah," he said lightly as he pulled out a chair. She smiled but cast her eyes down. She took her time dropping her keychain into her purse and then deliberately positioned the purse beneath her chair. Matt couldn't help but notice the key-chain's large, blue, hard-plastic handgrip that bore sharp, pointed knuckles at three locations. Hannah obviously carried it for protection. She maneuvered her chair to the table, one hand opening the menu awkwardly while the other rested on her lap.

"You okay?" Matt asked.

"I'm good," she said without looking up.

"Hannah, what's the matter?"

She hesitated. A tear escaped from one eye. She wiped it away quickly.

"What's wrong?" Matt's voice was urgent. He leaned forward and reached for her hand.

She pulled away, wiped her eyes, one with an open hand and the other with the closed fist that had been resting on her lap.

"They came to my place this morning," she said flatly. Her eyes were fixed on Matt, both hands back in her lap.

"Who?" Matt asked. "Who came to your place?"

"Gutierrez's goons; this morning, first thing. They took everything, all my notes, computers, electronics…everything." Her tone was resigned.

"What the hell are they looking for?" Matt asked.

"I don't know," she sighed, defeated. They stared at each other for several seconds without words. Finally, Hannah shook her head, "I don't trust them, Matt. There's something wrong. They're trying to get everything."

"They're cops," he echoed the previous evening's excuse, but he now was confused, too. "They have to have everything, don't they? That's their job. They can't know what's important until they see it all."

"They had everything. They had it from the lab," she rejoined. "I had nothing that was relevant to the professor, other than my backup notes. They had the original files. I gave them all of it in the beginning, before they raided the lab. I copied everything from Rosen's computer and handed it over."

Matt couldn't understand why the detective was taking such a hostile approach.

"How did your meeting go with Gutierrez?" she asked without emotion.

"I didn't tell him about the envelope," Matt said. An action that had seemed crazy at the time now made a bit more sense.

She smiled weakly, nodding approval.

"Do you have anything left of your work or the professor's?" Matt asked.

After a brief hesitation, she searched his eyes. She glanced around as she lifted her fisted hand to the table. She opened it slowly, palm up.

Matt's eyes moved from the flash-drive in her hand to her face. He shrugged.

"Professor Rosen left this in an envelope addressed to me in a book I'd left in his office. I went back on Tuesday and asked one of the officers if I could pick up my book; it was for one of my classes. He didn't even open it; just handed it to me when I pointed it out on the professor's shelf. I didn't see the envelope until Sunday night when I was using the book. It was taped to one of the end pages."

"What's on it?" Matt asked.

"I only got a chance to see the beginning," she started, hesitated, and then, knowing she had gone too far to consider further caution, she continued, "I don't know if it's everything, but it looks like his work on the Shroud."

CHAPTER TWENTY-TWO

HANNAH DROPPED MATT at the police station to retrieve his car. Their separation was awkward with each acknowledging they'd stay in touch and compare notes over the next weeks. They offered each other a "happy Thanksgiving" and shook hands with half-smiles, and, finally, a quick hug that Matt appreciated despite its clumsiness.

As Matt stepped toward his rental, Hannah eyed him. Matt turned back.

"The offer's real, Hannah," he said, trying to sound natural. "There's no obligation; it's just so you can get away, have something different for a few days." He shrugged. "Hop on a plane tomorrow. I'll pick you up at the airport. Thanksgiving's fun at my dad's house—loud with my sisters' kids and all, but it's fun."

The offer was first made at lunch. Hannah's family lived in Canada and didn't celebrate the American holiday.

"You need to get away from here," Matt had said. "Why don't you join us, get a good home-cooked meal…well, I don't know how good it'll be with my dad cooking, but at least it'll be home-cooked." They'd laughed.

"Thanks Matt," she'd said. "I appreciate it, but I think I'll stick around here. I need to find a computer, spend some time with the flash-drive, try to understand what's going on."

He nodded and wondered if she was getting herself into something best left to the police. But he didn't press her.

At the police lot, Matt smiled with the second offer.

"Thanks," she said again, this time, nodding and smiling before she continued. "I'll let you know."

Matt was surprised. She'd obviously given the matter some thought and now it wasn't a definite "no." He knew the chances were remote, but she'd opened the door.

"Good," he said. "I hope you come."

MATT CHECKED HIS cell messages while he waited for the boarding call. There was nothing from his dad. While that didn't surprise him, he clenched his back teeth in frustration. Nick knew how important the envelope was. Maybe there was something wrong with him. Maybe he was losing it.

Matt tried not to think his father's mind might be deserting him. He'd been ashamed over the whole attorney thing, and for that reason had avoided both his parents for a time. He regretted it when his mother died and vowed he'd have more contact with Nick. Unfortunately, his life didn't play out that way and contacts had been sporadic. Was it possible the old man had lost more than Matt realized?

Matt shook his head. He'd be "home" in a few hours. He'd see for himself what was in the envelope and how his dad was doing.

He did notice several calls from Paula Seltzer. Although he didn't feel like talking to her, it would take his mind off his dad. Paula picked up after the second ring.

"Mathew, thank God you called back," she almost shouted. "Where are you?"

"Hi Paula," Matt responded sarcastically.

"Oh, hello Matt; I'm sorry. I've just been trying to get in touch with you since yesterday morning."

"I'm in Tucson; you know that—my professor's funeral."

"Yeah…" she said absently. "So, you're coming home soon?"

"I'm heading up to my dad's for Thanksgiving. We talked about this. What's going on?"

"Peter...Mr. Christian wants to see you," she stammered.

"I know," he said calmly, but confused. "We discussed that too. We agreed a meeting could wait till after the holidays."

"I was wrong Matt," she blurted. "He came into my office yesterday morning and asked when you'd be coming in. When I told him it would be after the New Year, he wasn't happy."

There was silence for several seconds as Matt tried to understand what the hell was going on. "I've never seen him that way, Matt. He was really upset—didn't yell, but the look in his eyes was scary. He wants to see you."

Matt chuckled and shook his head.

"I can't see him until I get back home. I'm heading to my d...."

"Can't you fly in tonight, see him tomorrow, and then head up to your father's?" she pleaded.

"No!" he declared. "I'm boarding in a few minutes. I'm not going to change my plans. I'll see him when I get back next week. It's only a few days."

No response. Matt could hear Paula breathing—hyperventilating.

"Are you okay?" he asked.

No immediate response; finally her breathing slowed enough to respond.

"Yes, I'm fine, Matt. Next week should work. I'll tell him you'll be here on Monday?"

"Sure. Fine. Monday."

When the call ended, Matt tried to get his head around Paula's anxiety, as well as Peter Christian's urgency to meet with him. It made no sense. He brooded about it, wondering at the unusual events of the past week and a half. Could they be connected? Finally, he shook his head, smiled at the absurdity, and picked up a discarded newspaper to take his mind off it all. He'd worry about Christian on Monday. Meanwhile, he'd head up to his father's and see what Professor Rosen's envelope held.

MATT CHECKED HIS messages again after landing in San Francisco. Hannah had called. He returned the call.

"Matt?" she said lightly.

"Hi, is everything okay?"

"Yeah, it's good. I was just thinking that if you meant it when you invited me to join your family for Thanksgiving…I…I would like that. If it's okay. It would be nice to get away."

Matt was shocked.

"Sure," he said a little too excitedly. "You're welcome to join us. We'd be happy to have you. When can you come in?"

"Is tomorrow afternoon okay? There's a plane that arrives at 5:30?"

"I'll pick you up then."

As he stepped outside to hail a cab, Matt wondered at the unusual turns of life. He couldn't understand most of it any more than the next person, and he certainly couldn't make any sense of the murder of Professor Rosen or the interest Peter Christian had in him. What he did understand was that Hannah Melnyk was a person of great interest to him, and she had just said she would be joining him and his family for the Thanksgiving weekend. That was a good turn.

CHAPTER TWENTY-THREE

HALF A WORLD away, Stanley Cavendish woke with a start. Flora, his wife of fifty years, a light sleeper under the best of circumstances, woke with him.

"What is it, Stanley?" she whispered.

"Flora, I'm sorry," he said as he threw his legs over the side of the bed and sat at its edge. He turned to her, "I didn't mean to wake you. I...I'm okay...I need a cup of milk, that's all."

Flora pushed herself up on an elbow. "I'll get it for you. You stay here, Stanley. You need the rest." She grabbed her covers, but was stopped short by her husband.

"Flora," he started too sharply. He calmed himself. "Please Flora, I need to move around a bit. I'm okay...really."

He shambled out of the bedroom, head bowed, as if the real reason for his waking was a bad dream and he was just tired. He didn't want to worry Flora.

Poor Stanley, Flora would think, still thinking about his students after years of retirement; and so concerned about the turmoil in our world. He takes it all so personally. He simply cannot rest.

But Stanley wasn't as lethargic as the appearance he projected for his wife. He was anxiously alert, his ears attuned for the sounds that had woken him.

Flora's concerns however, were well founded. Stanley's restlessness had intensified in the years since his retirement from teaching the classics at Oxford University. He'd abandoned his lifelong study of his specialty in favor of an obsession over what he'd grown to believe was an insurmountable problem of Muslim extremism.

Just yesterday, Stanley had read of young, jobless Muslim men marching in London, shouting and carrying placards calling for "death to Europe," the overthrow of its governments, and the replacement of European laws with Sharia law.

The hypocrisy of these people was beyond Stanley. How could they partake of the largesse of the western democracies, while trying to destroy them? Where was the sense of honor and love of neighbor that was so important to the world in which he'd grown up? Was it really gone? Was the world really bent on destroying itself in the hedonism and narcissism that destroyed the ancient societies? That's what Stanley was beginning to believe. In fact, had it not been for his work with an old colleague in recent years, Stanley might have given up all hope.

Five years ago, Stanley had translated an ancient document for his good friend, Samuel Rosen. It was an exciting project because of the document's age and the archaic Greek in which it was written. The fact that it was a personal letter from the hand of a Byzantine knight was intriguing as well, but its full significance was lost on him until Samuel explained that he intended to retest the subject of the letter. It had taken Samuel years to obtain what he needed for the retest. It was during those years that the two friends discussed the wonders the results could bring to a world crumbling under the weight of apostasy to any truth beyond the power of money, selfish indulgence, and fanaticism. It was also during those years that Stanley regained hope.

Now, however, with the murder of his friend, his hope was shattered.

Stanley moved through the kitchen of his mid-sized Tudor cottage—a country home along the banks of the River Cherwell, isolated far from the bustle of English society that was scaring him.

He didn't switch on lights as he strode lightly toward the front door and peeked through its curtained sidelight. He didn't have a perfect view of the tiny outbuilding that had been his office for years, but he immediately caught an unmistakable splash of white light through a window.

Damn, he thought, dropping his head and pulling away from the glass. What could anyone want from my old shed?

He again peeked through the glass, thought about calling the police, but decided that the intruders were just a group of young hooligans out on the prowl. Several of his distant neighbors had reported minor acts of vandalism over the past weeks; obviously it was now his and Flora's turn. The best thing would be to switch on the outside lights and step out onto his porch, cricket bat in hand, shouting epithets like a lunatic. That would scare them off.

He grabbed the meter-long, flat paneled wood bat from the umbrella basket behind the door. He quietly unlocked the door, flipped the light switch, and pulled the door open while shouting, "Who goes?" with a gruff anger uncharacteristic of him.

He knew instantly he'd made a mistake.

The light in the outbuilding wasn't extinguished. He didn't hear cries of fear or scurrying footsteps. In fact, he neither saw nor heard anything that would indicate concern young vandals had been interrupted.

Instead, Stanley Cavendish sensed a presence. A young man was standing on the opposite side of the glass through which he'd looked seconds before. Stanley turned sharply, bat poised, stomach lurching.

"Stanley?" he heard Flora shout. "What is it?"

He turned.

The young man stepped into him, driving a heavy blade deep into Stanley's stomach, twisting and working the haft to tear Stanley's insides to shreds. At the same time, the young man threw his other arm around Stanley's shoulders and held him close so the blade could not be dislodged. Stanley screamed.

Flora screamed.

As Stanley slumped to the wood boards of the porch, the young man released him and turned to Flora. She screamed hysterically, eyes wide with terror. The young man stepped into the foyer; Flora continued to shriek as she stared at the crumpled body of her husband. The young man withdrew a handgun from his belt, stepped up to Flora, and placed the weapon's muzzle against her temple. She stopped screaming, flicked her eyes to the man, and saw his smile before he pulled the trigger.

Stanley heard the gun's explosion, and knew his life was over. As he lay dying in the expanding pool of his own blood, his hands clasped tightly to the hole in his abdomen, he saw the second intruder, the one whose flashlight had given him away in Stanley's shed. He walked nonchalantly up the steps carrying two large petrol cans, one in each hand.

"Drag the old man in here Ali," the killer instructed.

"He's still alive, brother," Ali responded. When the other didn't answer, Ali said, "Hassan, he is alive still. Should I finish him?"

"Drag him here. He'll be dead soon enough."

Stanley recognized their Arabic dialect. He understood their words.

Ali grabbed Stanley's heels and dragged him into the cottage. Stanley could see flames licking up from the outbuilding as his consciousness began to fade.

He tried to speak—to say something that would make them understand they didn't need to do this, that there was still hope of unity, that they could all live in peace. But the words wouldn't come.

Stanley Cavendish gave up his last breath before his body was placed next to Flora's. He didn't suffer the agony of seeing his dead wife, and he didn't suffer the physical pain of the fire that consumed his cottage on the banks of the river Cherwell.

CHAPTER TWENTY-FOUR

"THEIR BLOOD WILL be on your hands."

The words of the Ayatollah Hussein Chalaby, a Shiite religious leader, rang in Cardinal Metzinger's ears long after he hung up the phone. Chalaby had been calling the cardinal for two years, ever since the first public announcement of the Shroud's tour. Today his tone had been considerably more strident.

"The Muslim world will not stand for it," Chalaby had said. "There can be only one reason for this tour, particularly at a time of such turmoil. It can only be for the purpose of converting people around the world to your faith."

Even though Metzinger had never approved of the tour, it had fallen to him to mollify the Ayatollah and others who expressed concern.

"Evangelization is the purpose Mr. Chalaby, just as your own followers look to convert people to your faith. However, it is my belief that this will have no greater impact than did the tours of King Tut's remains or the Dead Sea Scrolls. Like them, the exhibition will be of historical importance, and, for most people, nothing more than a curiosity."

That had been the essence of Metzinger's message from the beginning. But as time passed and the truth about the conspiracy among Turin's Cardinal Giordano, America's Father Roberts, and the Jewish professor from Arizona became clear, he began to understand his message was wrong. If things proceeded as the conspirators hoped, true evangelization would be the result. And although Metzinger would welcome the resulting conversions, he dreaded the violent backlash that was likely from hardline leaders of other religions, like Chalaby, who would see their flocks questioning, and even leaving, those faiths.

"It is yet another attempt by the Zionist/Christian west to marginalize Muslims," continued the Ayatollah. "If people believe the cloth is what you Christians claim it to be, the natural conclusion is that it was formed through the divine resurrection of your Jesus, a man we know is not divine, but only a prophet. We cannot permit these wrong conclusions. The exhibition must be stopped."

"Unfortunately, that is beyond my ability to influence. You know of my efforts. Barring some catastrophic event, the tour will proceed. But the mere exhibition should have little effect on the issue of the cloth's legitimacy. Right now, the world only knows that the carbon dating proves it a fraud." Metzinger knew all other scientific evidence contradicted the carbon dating but since that was the only evidence of which the general public was aware, without refutation of the carbon test, the worldview of the cloth would not change, and there would be no reason for the Ayatollah to be concerned.

"And what of efforts to retest the cloth, efforts to refute the carbon test? What if they change the original conclusions? If these results are presented on a world stage through America's insidious media, this world will change."

"No such tests are being conducted," Metzinger responded tightly.

"That is not the information we have," said Chalaby.

Metzinger bit down hard. Why should he care what this man, who openly supported the destruction of Israel and all Christian nations, thought? They were at war. What more could these fanatics do that they were not already doing?

The cardinal tried to control his anger. He couldn't ignore the man's concerns. That would only further inflame him and never bring the peace the world desperately needed. Deep down, Metzinger knew the only road to victory was through small steps. The "Yankee Stadium moment" Metzinger often longed for, would only create panic among those who followed Chalaby and his ilk. Panic would bring the war to an immediate cataclysm from which the world might never recover. The only real path to Christ's peace was through the painstaking process of spreading the word through acts of kindness and love, and only then would good people see the truth. The opposition would crumble from within.

"The tests of which you heard no longer exist," he said resentfully, not wanting to kowtow to his adversary but knowing it was the only way. "They ended with the death of the American professor. There are no others."

"What proof do we have? Are there not others with whom he worked?" demanded Chalaby.

"You have my word, Mr. Chalaby, and that is all you will have," Metzinger responded caustically. "The tour will proceed, but there will be nothing that will remove the taint of the carbon dating from the cloth."

"I hope you are right, Mr. Metzinger. A mistake in this regard will result in untold deaths. Men, women, and children around the world will suffer. Their blood will be on your hands."

"Damn," Metzinger cursed as he slammed his phone into its cradle. He seethed at the effrontery of the Ayatollah's threat. But almost as much, his anger was directed at the conspirators. "Damn," he said again, "your stupidity may yet bring us down, Giordano."

IT WAS SIX months earlier that Cardinal Metzinger learned of the duplicity of Turin's Bishop Giordano and Father Aaron Roberts.

The process of getting the Shroud's tour approved and securely implemented had been long and arduous for Giordano and Roberts, not the least because of Metzinger's continuous attempts to derail it. But they had other problems right from the beginning.

The last non-Church owner of the Shroud was the deposed Italian King Umberto II of Savoy. Upon his death in 1983, Umberto's will gave ownership of the cloth to Pope John Paul II and his successors, but the bequest was accompanied by a restriction: that the Shroud never leave the city of Turin. That prohibition was the reason no world exhibition was ever seriously considered and the main reason Cardinal Metzinger thought the proposal had no chance. But Giordano and Roberts were prepared. They persuaded the people of Turin, through their elected leaders, to let the cloth leave the city temporarily. As "third party beneficiaries," in legal parlance, of Umberto's restriction, they could override it. Before Metzinger knew it, a deal was made with a promise that fifty percent of all net proceeds of the tour would go into the city's coffers, and city leaders believed future tourist dollars would pour into Turin as the world came to know the Shroud.

As a result of the agreement, all that was left for Metzinger to argue about was the security of the most holy relic. There had been several attempts to destroy the Shroud over the centuries with the most recent being on April 11, 1997 when an arsonist set the High Altar of the Shroud's cathedral ablaze. As Turin's XXI fire brigade burst into the cathedral, it found itself engulfed in a chaos of smoke, flame, and raining debris. Fireman Mario Trematore acted quickly. He attacked the Shroud's two-inch thick glass display with a sledgehammer, barely making a dent in it until others joined him. With the fire raging around them, the team finally broke through the glass and Trematore hauled the Shroud's heavy aluminum casket to safety.

Security in the reconstructed cathedral was now impregnable. Metzinger argued that a traveling exhibition could never adequately protect the Shroud. Again, however, the team of Giordano and Roberts were prepared. They convinced the Holy Father that security could and would be as unassailable as that in the cathedral.

So the tour was set. But the final act in the conspiracy of Giordano and Roberts shocked Metzinger.

"Is it true?" Metzinger demanded over the telephone the day he learned of it. "Is this professor in Arizona testing the cloth again?"

Giordano hesitated. "It is. His tests will be completed soon."

"Is he testing the remnant?" Metzinger referred to the tiny remaining portion of the cloth from which the pieces that were originally carbon dated were cut. Giordano's predecessor had preserved it at the cathedral. "That piece is as tainted as the others. It will provide no different result."

"The remnant remains in place, Eminence," Giordano answered. "I provided the professor with a new piece."

"You what?" Metzinger shouted.

"Father Roberts and I cut a piece from the field and gave it to the professor for a new carbon test," Giordano answered firmly. "We have done what the Lord demanded of us, Eminence. There will be no argument with the results this time."

"And you have a direct line to our Lord?" Metzinger was beside himself. "You have cut a piece from our church's most holy relic without discussion with your superiors, without even considering a request of the Holy Father?"

"Yes," Giordano answered flatly. "To process such a request would have taken too long. We had to act when the professor met with us. We had no choice."

Metzinger didn't know whether to continue shouting at a man obviously unmoved by his rage. He was stunned not only by Giordano's action but by his lack of remorse.

Giordano prayed silently as Metzinger boiled on his end.

"This will not pass, Giordano!" Metzinger finally growled and hung up. But it did.

There was no way to remedy the situation. After considering every alternative—including demanding the return of the piece from Professor Rosen—Metzinger, in private discussion with an equally irate Pope, realized the only choice was to let the matter rest. To make anything of it would invite frenzied media attacks on the Church for its cowardice in facing the truth about the relic. The resulting damage would be incalculable.

Metzinger brooded for a time and had only recently found the peace he needed to once again deal with the problem. Everyone knew there was no going back. The fallout, however, would have to be contained. Action would have to be taken, and if some poor soul were to lose his life to avoid the cataclysm Metzinger envisioned, it would have to be so.

CHAPTER TWENTY-FIVE

THOSE CALLING WITH congratulations said that Peter Christian's performance the previous evening had been stunning, pointed, and unmatched by the others. In a live, prime-time broadcast, with highlights shown around the world, Christian had deftly handled a panel of religious leaders—one each from the Catholic, Jewish, and Evangelical Christian faiths—two U.S. Representatives and one U.S. Senator from the Fed's Finance Committee, and two other business leaders. The topic had been: *Which way America? Is Capitalism the Answer?*

The sides in the debate were predictable. The three business leaders, one representative, and the senator were staunch supporters of unregulated capitalism, particularly in light of the years of economic malaise the world had experienced as a result of entitlements, higher taxes, and stifling government controls and intervention. The religious leaders and one representative were on the opposite side. Although all members of the panel had their say, the real fireworks came down to the two most eloquent and charismatic speakers: Peter Christian and the Catholic priest, Father Aaron Roberts.

By most accounts, the non-regulation forces won the evening with the bulk of the credit going to Christian and his always "camera-ready" skills. But Christian knew better. He may have won a resounding victory in the minds of those who were already blind to the opposing side's arguments, but to people of intelligence, Peter Christian had made a mistake. It was only one mistake in a carefully crafted argument that clearly held the higher ground, but it was a mistake that could prove troubling.

"WITHOUT REGULATION," RABBI Ariel Goldberg started angrily as he sat forward and glared at the pro-capitalism panelists, "the unbridled capitalism of which all of you speak," he waved his hand at them, "leads only to pain and suffering. Look at the bank and lending frauds that almost brought down the world economy, look at the exploitation of children and the poor around the world, blood diamonds, oil wars, the denuding of forests, environmental destruction, and the reality that only the rich prosper while the poor and middle classes toil away on hopes and dreams that can never be realized. And why is that? Because of the manipulation of markets by the rich who rule their societies unfettered by common decency or effective governmental regulation."

As the rabbi nodded firmly, a few in the audience applauded loudly. But the silence from the others in the massive auditorium overwhelmed them, making their cheers tinny and trite.

John Patrick, CBS's national anchor and the moderator for the evening, looked to the pro-capitalists for response. Peter Christian caught his eye with a slight gesture. Patrick nodded, and Christian stood.

"I'd like to respond if I may," he said as he stepped away from his colleagues, and stood to the side, facing the crowd. The cameras focused on him.

"I will admit that bad people take even the best of systems and try to manipulate them wrongfully—fraudulently, if you will," he corrected himself with a quick nod to the rabbi. "For these, there are laws. There are laws against theft and fraud in any civilized society, and the authorities responsible for enforcing those laws must do so." He shrugged as if that was a given. Then, after a pause, he extended a forefinger to the crowd and raised his voice, "But that doesn't justify the strangulation of a system that has provided such enormous benefits to our world."

He paused, glared over the assemblage, and continued, "It doesn't give any government, religious organization, or other institution the right to restrict and control the hard working people who created the greatest nation the world has ever known. Our forefathers knew, as every single one of us know, that capitalism, wealth, and money are the great equalizers. They are the things that make us free. Societies that control their economies also control their people in every other respect. They control speech and thought, and ultimately those societies fail."

He held the audience's eyes for several seconds before continuing.

"Look at the former Soviet Union, the great experiment of equality and entitlement—the great power that failed miserably. That society couldn't succeed because there was no incentive to do anything more than meet basic survival requirements of their five-year plans. Socialism sounds nice, but guess what folks? It doesn't work! Soviet society failed. Even China has recognized the folly in control and restriction of its economy. They have opened their arms to capitalism and they are the fastest growing economy in the world.

"The truth, folks, is that the democratic capitalistic system upon which this country was formed is the only system that works. There are no viable alternatives."

The applause was immediate and overpowering. It thundered through the auditorium and was accompanied by a standing ovation that made Christian smile humbly and bow his head before turning to his seat. But he stopped short as the ovation ended abruptly. He glanced toward his opponents and saw Father Roberts stepping away from his chair with the same theatrics Christian had employed moments before. The priest was holding both hands above his head, motioning for quiet. Christian turned to him.

Father Roberts wore a tight-lipped smile and shook his head until there was silence. He eyed the crowd with his hands raised, palms up, in a beseeching gesture.

"There is not one amongst us who longs for Communism. Despite Mr. Christian's eloquence and his masterful ability to turn words to his cause, none of us believe capitalism is evil or that we should have an artificially controlled society. That is thinking straight out of the dark ages."

The priest paused to let his words sink in.

"Our issues are not with capitalism, but rather with the type of unregulated capitalism that seems to be spreading around the world. Like any good thing, capitalism will be abused if its only purpose is the pursuit of money and wealth. Without restraints, either internal or societal, the pursuit and achievement of material goals will cause people to use any," he drew the word out and raised his voice, *"means necessary to achieve them. Don't you see?"* He glanced at Christian and then back to the crowd, *"Our world has become mean-spirited. We are ravaged by war, filled with hatred, fearful of everything and everyone, and sickened by anxiety over things we can't even define without therapy. We fear we won't measure up, that we won't 'keep up with the Joneses,' that our kids might not get the same opportunity as our neighbors', that if we don't maintain the intensity and achieve the 'golden calf,' we'll be left behind. We actually fear that if we don't make lots of money, our lives will have been for naught, our very existences meaningless."*

He stopped to refocus.

"I'm not saying capitalism is evil. All I'm saying is that without controls, the pursuit of its goals can lead to only one place..." he paused again to build anticipation, but the pause opened a door for Peter Christian.

"Yes, Father, it will lead to one place." He stepped forward looking directly at Roberts. *"Capitalism's pursuit of wealth will lead to happiness, for in that pursuit there is accomplishment, creativity, imagination, and a belief in and hope for a future."* He turned to the audience, *"As I stated earlier, there are bad people in this world, but we already have laws to control them, and ultimately they are controlled. In those cases where damage is done because of the evil deeds, a society based on the freedom of capitalism will come out stronger, with greater hope for the future, and a real belief that every single person can achieve the goals he sets for himself."*

He turned back to Roberts, *"The pursuit of capitalism's goals will indeed lead to one place, Father. It will lead to the happiness every single one of us deserves."*

As some in the crowd began to applaud, Father Roberts interrupted tersely.

"I did not relinquish the floor, Mr. Christian. I sat patiently to hear you out, and only stood when you had finished. I would appreciate the same courtesy from you."

A stunned silence fell over the crowd. To this point, the discussion had been absurdly polite. But the priest was angry. Christian was noticeably nonplussed. They glared at each other until Christian finally gathered himself, bowed slightly, and deferred with a wave, offering Roberts the crowd and a tight smile. The priest turned back to the crowd.

"With due respect to Mr. Christian and his companions on this panel, I disagree with their assessment. Rather than the enrichment of our world, the uncontrolled, selfish," he emphasized the word and glanced at Christian before looking back out at the crowd, "pursuit of wealth will lead to our destruction. It will lead to the rampant cheating we see in our schools because of the false belief that all is fair in the quest for financial success. It will lead to despair for the vast majority who will never achieve their dreams of wealth. And it will lead to the depression that comes from the realization that the moneyed life they dreamed of is no more satisfying than the life they already had."

He turned to Christian. "There is a better way, Mr. Christian. There is the way of God. It is the way of love, where every person replaces the golden calf with the wonder of faith and eternal life. Our Lord spoke of love, not money; he spoke of giving, not taking, and he spoke of looking out for your fellow man instead of 'every man for himself.'"

He turned back to the audience.

"It is the love of God and our fellow man that makes this life worth living, and it is that love and only that love that will protect us against the greed and hatred engendered by the uncontrolled pursuit of the capitalist goal."

Christian was livid, but realized he had to respond with the confidence that was expected of him.

"May I, Father?" he asked sarcastically.

Roberts turned to him and nodded grimly.

"You say this god will protect us—that some ephemeral concept of love will carry us through and make us happy." He shook his head with a smug smile. "I think you are naïve. Our media overflows with news of catastrophes that *plague our planet: the natural disasters, the brutality of man, the randomness of disease, and the chaos of our world. What god would permit such things?*

"The reality is that belief in a god and pursuit of some hereafter might actually be dangerous! Look at Waco and Jonestown, the Jihadists, and, historically, at human sacrifice in the name of god. Hell, look at your own church's Spanish Inquisition, the Crusades, and numerous other examples of what comes from the belief you champion. It's a horrible mistake to put your faith in a magical hereafter, because, by doing so, you forget the now. People don't create, produce, or consume when their heads are in the clouds, because there's no point in it. Such belief destroys human motivation to achieve the better things of this life, the life we actually live."

Father Roberts' look softened as Christian turned to him. It threw Christian off balance. He grew angrier.

"Look, Father," he spat with bitter emphasis. "There is no god. You know it, we all know it." He swept the audience with his arm. "It's been this way throughout history. Every time the individual starts to gain freedom, they," pointing at Roberts, "try to retake control by preaching fear of some angry god.

"Folks, we're on our own down here. We've got to make our own way. There's no benevolent old man sitting up on some heavenly throne. We need to fill our own stomachs and put roofs over our heads. It's up to each and every one..."

He stopped dead. A voice of caution thundered through his head. Though barely discernible through the glare of television lights, he caught the shocked stares of the audience. Blood surged to his neck and face. He'd gone too far. He wanted to say more, to explain, but he knew it would be suicide. He stood slack-jawed, desperately trying to find his way back. He searched for words, but none came. He dropped his head, embarrassed, but knowing he needed to recover. For several interminable seconds during which the crowd moved from stunned silence to awkward rustles and more shifting of seats, he gathered himself. Finally, he looked up and forced his winning smile to his face. All eyes focused on him.

"There's only one way to get this economy on track," he started slowly, with authority. "We all know what's needed. We can argue the merits of different philosophies forever, and get nowhere. What we know, without equivocation, is that capitalism, the very system that made this country great, is teetering because of people who want to regulate and control it and each and every one of us. We don't need control. We need to let our system work and tell those who would stop it to get out of the way. If we do, our time, your time," he waved his pointing hand over the audience, "will see prosperity like no other time in human history. All of you will achieve your wildest dreams and live the life you want instead of the life someone tells you to live."

He nodded, swiveling his head over the crowd, standing tall, again in charge.

"Let's fight for the freedom we deserve, folks. That's the only system that works."

The crowd was silent until Christian turned to his seat. Then slowly, sporadic applause began. Soon it spread, and the initially subdued response grew to resounding applause until the moderator finally broke in.

"Thank you for your time tonight, panelists. That will end the discussion …"

Peter Christian painted a smile on his face and accepted handshakes of congratulations from his co-panelists. But he wasn't happy.

CHAPTER TWENTY-SIX

HANNAH SENSED SOMETHING was wrong the minute Matt greeted her at the airport. He sported a plastic smile, spoke without interest, and avoided eye contact as he pulled into traffic, turning to look back or focusing frequently on the rear-view mirror instead.

She began to think she'd made a mistake. She'd convinced herself he was a good guy—perhaps someone she could trust. Yet suddenly he was distant and unresponsive.

"What's wrong, Matt?" she asked. "Should I not have come?"

"No!" he started. "No, Hannah, I'm glad you came."

She said nothing, instead continuing to stare at him as he occupied himself with freeway traffic. Finally, he nodded.

"I'm sorry. Something happened at my dad's house. I don't know what's going on. It doesn't make sense."

"What happened?" She paused as Matt took a deep breath. "Maybe I can help, Matt."

"Somebody broke into my dad's house while I was in Arizona for the funeral."

Hannah flinched.

Matt noticed her reaction. "My dad's okay. He wasn't hurt, but the guy stabbed Charley, his seeing-eye dog. Charley attacked the intruder, bit him we think, and the guy stabbed him, and then he ran."

"Is the dog okay?" Hannah asked.

"He was hurt pretty badly, but he's been stitched up and looks like he's mending."

"Thank God for that, and that your dad wasn't hurt. Did the burglar get anything?"

"That's the problem. He only took one thing. He went right to the hall table where my dad stacks his mail. He went through the pile and took only one piece, the envelope from Professor Rosen."

Hannah was taken aback. "Are you sure? That couldn't have been all he came for, could it?"

"That's what I thought. My dad and the police inventoried the entire house. Nothing else was missing. He came for Rosen's package."

"How would he have known about it?" Hannah rejoined.

"I don't know. The only ones who knew about it were my dad, a neighbor high school girl, me and…" he hesitated, "you."

Hannah pushed back against the car door. "I didn't tell anyone, Matt!" she exclaimed. "I haven't spoken to anyone about any of this."

"I know," Matt said. "I wondered about it, but I knew. We couldn't figure out how they learned about it. The police called the next morning and said they'd have to come by and pick up the rest of the mail. They wanted to check for fingerprints."

"Did your dad turn the mail over?" Hannah asked.

"No, not everything." Matt shook his head. "When my dad was describing the contents of the envelope to me over the phone the other day, he took the first page of the professor's letter out. He didn't replace it. When he went through the mail after the burglary, he realized he still had the first page, so, he put it aside for me.

"The cop's call about fingerprints didn't make sense to my dad. He wondered why there'd be prints on the mail when they found none anywhere else. So Dad thought about holding the first page of Rosen's letter back from the cop. It struck him that since Rosen's envelope was the only thing missing, maybe the cop was coming back for the only piece that wasn't in the envelope. Dad went to the neighbor's house to make a copy of the professor's first page. He put the original back in the stack of mail. Sure enough, when the investigator left, the only paper he took from the stack was the professor's first page. He knew what he wanted."

"The cop can't be involved in Rosen's murder, can he, Matt?" Hannah asked.

"I don't know, but someone tipped this guy off that the envelope was missing one sheet of paper. There's something going on here that's much bigger than any of us are thinking," Matt said.

"What does the first page say?" Hannah stammered, shocked by the weight of the possibility that the San Francisco police could be involved in Rosen's death.

Matt reached into his jacket pocket and extracted a twice-folded sheet of paper. He handed it to Hannah.

Re: The Carter Parchment

Dear Mathew;

This letter will, no doubt, come as a surprise to you, first because it has been so many years since we've had any contact, and second, because of its content. I must apologize, at the outset, for not calling you back after your response to my call some seven years ago. Although there was no legitimate reason for my failure, the truth is that I was so immersed in a new project that I simply neglected the courtesy of a return call once I had your answer. In addition, I didn't, at that time, fully understand the significance of that with which I was dealing. Please bear with me in this missive, Mathew, as I explain the reasons for this contact. But, before I get to those, I must ask that you protect the ancient parchment you once brought into my class for dating. I have learned of its great importance and it is essential that it remain safe. There are interests in this world that want it destroyed. You must not permit that.

As you will recall, when we tested your parchment, it was the oldest written document I had ever dated. Since then, I

*have not been associated with any older documents. Yours,
then, has always held a very special place in my heart. Over
the years, I have often referred to it in my classes and, in fact,
christened it the "Carter Parchment."*

*When I phoned your parents' home seven years ago, I had
just retired from my position as a full time professor. I had
decided, as part of my continuing quest for new*

...And that was it. Hannah turned to Matt, deeply confused.

———————

THE MASTER WASN'T happy that Assim Rahman had not gotten the
entire letter. The Master was trying to control his anger, but Assim felt it.
He had let the Master down. He was prepared to die for his failure. He
would have preferred to do something, anything, to make it right, but,
if the Master wished it, he would take his life immediately. The Master's
silence tore at him. He held his breath as the Master spoke.

"If he has learned what was on the first page, he will not bring the
parchment to us." Assim breathed again, realizing there might still be
purpose for him. "He will not know who to trust. He will try to hide it. You
must go there. Follow him to the place where it is hidden. You must take
this thing from him. Bring it to me, and together we will destroy it."

Assim closed his eyes and nodded.

CHAPTER TWENTY-SEVEN

THANKSGIVING DAWNED BRIGHT on Corny Crockett's knoll. His cabin sat atop a rise that fell off at easy grades on all sides. To the southwest from his porch he saw the crystal waters of Independence Lake. Pines, firs, and beeches of the Sierras described a haphazard quilt of motley greens laced sporadically by touches of overnight snow. The air bit Corny's lungs, and wisps of vapor escaped with every exhalation as he stood on the porch surveying his domain.

He appreciated the weight of the Remington clasped tightly in his right hand, as he hugged himself against the cold and waited for Boone to complete his morning business around the perimeter of the knoll. When the dog finally ambled up the porch steps, his tail pumping excitedly, Corny smiled.

"Thanks buddy," he said. "It's great to see a happy face right now."

Before re-entering the cabin, Corny pressed tightly against the inside curve one of the porch columns and took one last look into the woods. When he neither sensed nor saw anything, he followed the dog inside. He bolted the door, poured himself a bowl of granola with strawberries and skim milk, and made his way to the spiral staircase that led up to his viewing room.

It was a room he'd always envisioned—even during his youth. He'd built it as a tree house, enclosed against the elements, rising through the roof of the cabin. It sported furnishings fashioned by him and Elli out of fallen logs and wilderness debris. It was his writing room, his and Elli's playroom, their room-above-it-all; now it was his watchtower.

The room commanded a 360-degree view of the forest and every approach to the knoll. Corny had been sleeping there since he'd heard about Samuel's murder. He'd kept a lookout, assisted by the motion detector floodlights he'd installed outside years earlier to ward off night intruders, human and wild. He'd rarely used the floods, remembering only one especially dry summer when the bear population had been particularly worrisome. The sudden glare kept the thirst and hunger-crazed animals away. Now, however, he kept the detectors fully active. Once activated, they provided an umbrella of light to the rim of the forest on all sides.

Corny's biggest problem was that he had to find time to sleep. The motion detectors were so sensitive that any creature wandering inside the forest's perimeter would trip the system. Thus, the lights tended to be on most of the night. So Corny had to find his sleeping times during daylight hours. He kept himself as alert as possible at night. Luckily, Corny had one impregnable line of defense. Boone could sense intruders from distances unimaginable to human faculties, and whether the animal dozed or was wide awake, his senses were always alert.

As Boone lay quietly at the foot of the staircase this morning, Corny ate his breakfast and stared into the distance.

"Let's get it over with, you sons of bitches," he growled. Boone lifted his head and glanced up the staircase, waving his tail lazily before again settling down and drifting off into his morning nap.

CHAPTER TWENTY-EIGHT

"YOU SHOULD GIVE it to that cop," said Matt's brother-in-law, Dexter, the always practical accountant husband of his second sister, Christine. "This is too big for us, Matt. You've got a family to think about."

A sumptuous and surprisingly tasty dinner (surprising because Nick had been the main architect of the meal) had been served. The feast of turkey, Mom's stuffing, Ukrainian cabbage rolls called holopchi, vegetables, salads, gravies, cranberries, and yams was just ending, and dessert and coffee were on the table. When the kids excused themselves—the older ones for the late football game and the younger for their computer games— the talk turned serious. Christine questioned Matt about what he intended to do.

"I'm not sure, Chris," Matt said. "I guess I need to get that parchment from the safe deposit box tomorrow, but then I don't know."

That's when Dexter stepped in. They'd all read the first page of Rosen's letter. Matt and Hannah expressed their beliefs that the professor's murder and subsequent events had something to do with the Shroud of Turin. Although Matt's sisters understood the Shroud to be a cloth that purportedly bore the facial image of Jesus but was believed to be a fake, neither they nor their husbands could conjure any meaningful connection between the cloth and the professor's death. All they understood was that someone was desperate enough to put their father in mortal danger. No one wanted any part of whatever the professor's plan had been. They wanted it to go away. The best way was for Matt to turn the ancient parchment over to the Arizona police.

"You're right," Matt said to Dexter. He bowed his head and stared at his hands. "It just frosts me, you know. That was Gigi's parchment, something he'd hidden away and protected all his life. Hell, it's been hidden and protected by our ancestors for a thousand years. Are we just supposed to turn it over to some cop who's probably part of this thing anyway?"

"Yes," Dexter asserted without hesitation. "You should call this guy, right now. Call and tell him you'll bring it to him as soon as you pick it up tomorrow. Maybe he'll call off the guy who broke into the house."

Heads nodded support. Matt glanced at Hannah who eyed him sadly, clearly understanding his dilemma.

"C'mon Matt, there's no other choice here," said Alison, Matt's older sister. She turned to her father. "Tell him Dad. Tell him he should give it up."

Nick leaned forward. All eyes turned to him.

"I hear your concerns, all of you. Lord knows, I was scared to death with this guy in the house, and poor Charley will be dealing with his wounds for a while. But I don't like being bullied. And I didn't like how that investigator barged in here, going through my mail with a hidden agenda. There's more going on here than we know. I think Matt should go with his gut."

"Dad," Christine interrupted, exasperated. "This isn't Matt's decision. That parchment belongs to all of us. We should decide this to protect the family."

Nick waited patiently for his daughter to finish.

"You're right of course, Christine. The parchment is a family heirloom and as such, it's up to all of us to decide its fate. But, as we've all discussed, there's something bigger than the parchment here, and the decision isn't as simple as a vote."

As Christine and Alison began to interrupt, Nick raised a hand.

"Please, let me finish. Your brother has been called upon by someone he deeply respected. If, as Matt and Hannah believe, the parchment has something to do with the Shroud, it could indeed be much bigger even than the professor's life. For him it certainly was. He died for it."

Everyone was silent. Matt felt the weight of his professor's request.

"I've seen the Shroud," Nick continued calmly. "Your mother and I had the good fortune of traveling to Turin many years ago, before my eyesight disappeared. It's real. There is no doubt in my mind. It is the actual burial cloth of Jesus Christ and bears, not just the face, but the image of the entire body, front and back, of our crucified Lord. For years, people have been trying to make light of the cloth; some have even tried to destroy it. But the truth is, if this cloth really is what it purports to be, that means Jesus left it for us, all of us, so that we may see and believe. If your grandfather's parchment can shed light on this gift from God, perhaps we should all be interested in its protection." As voices rose, he raised both hands until everyone settled down again.

"This is Matt's decision," he continued firmly. "He's been entrusted with it for some reason. None of us know why. Perhaps it's God's wish. Whether it is or not, however, it is for Matt to decide." He turned to his son.

"I'll stand with you, Mathew, whichever way you go," he said. "For what it's worth, I don't think we're in any danger right now because the parchment isn't here. I think whoever wants it knows that."

As other voices again rose in protest, Nick raised his own voice. "I've thought a lot about this, everyone. That guy could easily have killed Charley and me the other day. He didn't because all he wanted was the package. How did he know we even had it? I don't know; maybe something in the professor's papers told them he'd sent it here; maybe someone is listening in on our phone conversations; maybe the Arizona cop and our local investigators are bad. Whatever the explanation, what strikes me is that all they want is the parchment. I don't think we're in danger here at the house. And, I don't think we should give it to them."

He smiled broadly knowing his final comment would elicit argument—and it did.

LATER, DEXTER, STILL confused and angry, joined the older kids and Alison's equally perplexed husband for the second half of the football game. While Matt and Hannah were completing the dinner cleanup, Christine and Alison sat with Nick in the dining room where they talked in hushed tones over coffee.

As Hannah was drying the last of the wine glasses Matt had washed, he eyed her with a touch of melancholy, wishing they'd met under different circumstances. When she turned to him, she smiled.

"I think we need to look at the flash drive, Hannah." Matt whispered. She'd told him she'd brought it with her. "Maybe there's something there that can help us understand what's so important about the parchment. Maybe it has the translation."

"I'll get it," Hannah said and walked to the bedroom for her purse. Matt asked Dexter for his laptop. Dex reluctantly handed it over.

Hannah joined Matt on the back deck. The large, weather-bleached redwood deck overlooked the quarter-acre back yard— overgrown now with mature trees and shrubs, but magnificent in its wildness. They sat comfortably together, something in the family meal and the seamlessness with which Hannah had melded into the fabric of the family having put them both at ease.

Matt booted the computer up and passed it to Hannah to plug in the flash-drive. The first thing that came up was a message from Rosen; one Hannah had already seen, but wanted Matt to peruse. It read:

"Hannah;

If you are reading this, I am either dead or in some other way unable to communicate. It is important that you do not try to do anything with the materials you find here other than to contact the men listed below. These men have played important roles in my research and in the conclusions I have reached on the Sindon. They have copies of everything and will know what to do when you turn over this flash-drive, which contains my report in its entirety and my final conclusions. I have e-mailed this to each of them and I intend to snail-mail these materials as well. However, since I don't trust that either method will result in receipt of the materials, I ask you to make contact and delivery. I apologize for having to put you through this, but you are my only hope if the most recent threat against me is as real as I believe it to be. As always, I am grateful for your assistance over the last two years. Thank you for this last service. May God bless us all."

A list of names followed:

— Bowler, John, Professor, Harvard University, Cambridge, Mass.
— Cavendish, Stanley, Emeritus Professor, Oxford University, England
— Crockett, Cornelius, Emeritus Professor, University of California, Davis
— Glauser, Willkie, Professor, Federal Institute of Technology, Zurich
— Kosar, Raymond, Professor, University of California, Los Angeles
— Moreau, Jean Pierre, Professor, Paris Institute of Technology

Each name was accompanied by an e-mail address.

"He knew the threat was real." Matt shook his head. "Why didn't he just give them what they wanted?"

"Knowledge was too important to him, Matt. Threats emboldened him. Kind of like you, it seems." Hannah smiled.

Matt nodded acknowledgment, then waved at the screen.

"Let's see if there's anything about the parchment."

Hannah scrolled to the next batch of material. She moved slowly enough to comprehend what she was seeing. Matt was barely able to follow the complex figures, equations, and data.

"Are you seeing anything about the parchment?" he asked, frustrated.

Hannah shook her head.

"Nothing yet; this is scientific data and analysis. It looks like the professor gathered together a lot of existing tests and facts, organized it in some fashion, and then...wait..." Matt looked over Hannah's shoulder as she slowed down for new text and then more equations.

"Sorry Matt. This is the professor's work now," she said. "It looks like he's repeating some of the tests that were done by others. I can't say for sure. I'll need to spend some time with this." She stopped the cursor and turned to him.

"That has to wait, Hannah. We need to see if he mentions the parchment. If it's so important, he's got to talk about it, doesn't he?"

Hannah nodded and turned back to the screen. They watched the tide of data roll past, Matt conscious of Hannah's proximity even as he struggled to understand what he was seeing. Finally, Hannah turned away from the screen, bleary-eyed. "Nothing; I don't see anything, do you?"

Matt shook his head. He leaned back heavily in his chair, propped his elbows atop the armrests, and stared into the distance. Hannah went back to the screen and scrolled to the end.

Suddenly Matt sat forward.

"Let's go back to the beginning. The professor knew this thing was coming down on him. He asked you to deliver this information to these other guys, right? They know something, don't they?"

Hannah nodded and took the screen back to the beginning.

They leaned in and reread the Rosen's opening message.

The understanding that they had to contact these men came in a rush. That Hannah would carry out Rosen's wishes was a foregone conclusion, but it was the realization that they already had knowledge of Rosen's work and the possibility that they could guide Matt and Hannah that moved Matt. He motioned his desire to take over at the computer. Hannah moved aside. Matt minimized the information from the flash drive and went immediately to the Internet.

"We should get their numbers and call them," he said.

As he waited for the search engine to boot up, Hannah said, "It's late Matt, and it's Thanksgiving. We're not going to get anyone tonight."

"Let's at least track down their numbers and call first thing in the morning. These guys are probably the only ones who have a clue about what's happening. One of them must know about the parchment."

It didn't take long for them to realize they would not be contacting any of these men.

Matt Googled the first name in the alphabetical listing. The first reference that sprang to the screen was to an article dated two days after Rosen's murder. It started:

"John Bowler, world renowned professor of the antiquities at Harvard University, was killed last night in a single car collision. Professor Bowler's Toyota Prius was traveling at an extremely high speed, according to Boston police detective, Jack Reynolds, when it slammed head-on into a telephone pole. Bowler was not wearing a seat belt, and his body was thrown forward, breaking the steering wheel and sending him through the windshield to his death. Although investigators at the scene said the professor's body and the car reeked of alcohol, this reporter has learned that Bowler did not drink.

'John hasn't touched a drop of alcohol in the last twenty years,' Helen Bowler, wife of the deceased, shouted through hysterical tears.

Investigators are ..."

The shock was complete. Matt and Hannah glanced at each other but said nothing, each fearing to voice the obvious.

"Check the next one," Hannah whispered.

They pulled up the name of Stanley Cavendish of Oxford University in England. They immediately found that he too was dead—killed just a day after Bowler in what Scotland Yard termed "another random act of thievery and brutality" by thugs who had been terrorizing the English countryside for weeks. Although investigators acknowledged that the murder of Professor Cavendish and his wife exceeded previous acts in the area with its barbarity, they nevertheless believed they were dealing with the same group of "heartless savages" and they vowed to put an end to the "criminal rampage."

Matt fingered the keyboard through the remaining names. He and Hannah did not speak except in whispered, terse instructional phrases to "go back" or "wait," as they read of the un-natural deaths of UCLA professor Raymond Kosar and Paris professor Jean Pierre Moreau.

Kosar died the weekend after Rosen in a freak surfing accident at the Wedge in Newport Beach where he had gone night surfing, alone! Although an accomplished surfer, Kosar knew better than to tackle the Wedge alone at night, yet he was found the next morning, his body grotesquely battered atop shoreline boulders with a broken neck reported as the cause of death. On the same day, on the other side of the world, the athletic Moreau died in a fall from the roof of his house where he was getting a jump on the Christmas season and putting his lights up early.

Of the six names on Professor Rosen's list, there were two for whom death had not yet been announced on the web. The first was Willkie Glauser, the nuclear physicist from the Federal Institute of Technology in Zurich, and the second was the retired professor of theology and anthropology from the University of California at Davis: Cornelius Crockett.

Despite the shock at the unfolding tragedy, Matt realized their only hope of understanding anything and perhaps saving his family's heirloom, was to contact one of these two. He moved back to his e-mail and composed a terse plea to both men. It read:

Gentlemen;

My name is Mathew Carter. I am a former student of Professor Samuel Rosen. My family owns the parchment Professor Rosen referred to as the 'Carter Parchment.' You and several others were identified as people with understanding of the parchment's importance and knowledge of its translation. The others on the professor's list are dead. If you are able, please tell me how I may contact you to discuss the parchment and the professor's research. Clearly this is a matter of great importance. It looks like it is also a matter of life and death. Please contact me immediately.

He signed off leaving his cell phone number.

CHAPTER TWENTY-NINE

CORNY WOKE WITH a start. His first move was mechanical: an eye-flick to the clock atop his driftwood desk. The digital display read 3:00 a.m. He was slouched in a half-sitting position in his worn leather chair. His left leg was stretched in front of him, his knee hyper-extended with his heel resting on the floor. The right leg was bent in the normal sitting position. His rifle lay across his lap grasped loosely at the barrel in his left hand. The watchtower was blanketed by shadows cast by the same stark moon Matt and Hannah had been sitting under only a few hours earlier. It now hid from Corny behind the lone black cloud scudding across the night sky.

Corny shook his head groggily, confused and in pain as he tried to move from his awkward position and recapture a sound. He couldn't remember anything specific, only that something woke him, and it didn't feel right. He stopped fighting the pain, deciding instead to hold position and allow his brain to catch up to him.

And suddenly he knew. He'd slept for several hours without interruption. That hadn't happened since he'd activated the floodlights. It simply wasn't possible for a night to pass without something tripping the sensitive system. Yet it hadn't been tripped for at least four hours by Corny's quick reckoning. Then he heard the sound, distinctive and startling.

It was a sharp screech, like a rubber sole catching on metal treads. It came from the spiral staircase leading up to his tower. Corny's eyes bulged. He jerked awake and tried to stand, but the pain of a cramped leg shot through him. He fell back into the chair, leather and springs creaking loudly. An instant later he heard footsteps scurrying up the staircase before they suddenly stopped. He glanced, bug-eyed and numb, at the hole that gave access to his room. The wide-spaced metal handrail provided the only obstruction of his view, but it did not block the sight of the barrel of an enormous handgun rising through the hole in the clutch of a gloved hand. Corny's brain screamed for immediate action.

He tried frantically to grip and turn the rifle but managed only to grab its muzzle in both hands. He staggered up with the rifle slung back over his shoulder just as a masked head followed the handgun through the hole. An instant later a bright flash and monstrous explosion sent a searing pain through Corny's right leg, just as it launched him from the chair. Corny held his scream and swung the rifle's butt at the rising figure as he crashed to the ground in a heap of stabbing pain. The polished hard-wood of the rifle's stock caught the assassin's head with a sickening crunch and the full force of Corny's swing. The figure grunted. The gun fell from his hand as his body slammed against the rail and disappeared down the hole. An instant later, Corny heard the thud of the body, a grunted exhalation, and cracking bones.

Corny lay on his side, the pain of the gunshot wound unbearable; yet he knew instinctively he couldn't think about it. He needed to act. He started to pull himself along the floor to the opening through which his attacker had fallen. He immediately thought better of it however, as he realized he had no idea what awaited him below. He pushed back, up and against one of his desk's tree-trunk legs. He gripped his rifle tightly, his finger pressed ready at the trigger. He tried to calm himself but a quick glance at the growing stain of blood oozing out of the thigh wound brought nausea which clawed at him as sweat beaded on his face and arms. He closed his eyes against the unsteadiness, struggled for deep breathes, and forced himself into the calm he needed to survive. Finally, after seconds that seemed eternities, his breathing began to slow. He looked again at his leg. He unhooked his belt, removed it, wrapped it around his thigh, and pulled tightly above the wound as he gritted his teeth against the pain. He then leaned back heavily as the blood flow slowed. He tried not to move the leg for fear the pain would send him into unconsciousness. He had to think.

Boone sprang to his mind. What happened to his watchdog? Did Corny miss a warning? Did the assassin do something to Boone without Corny hearing? Was Boone dying while Corny wondered if anyone else was in the house or if the one who shot him was coming to?

Corny focused his hearing. He leaned toward the floor opening and listened, but heard nothing. He wondered again if he should poke his head into the opening but sensed that would be folly. Yet he couldn't just sit there, not knowing, wondering, and ultimately dying from blood loss or infection. He pushed himself up again into a full sitting position against the desk's leg and called to his dog.

Boone responded immediately. But the response was weak. It was a whimper followed by a yelp and a dragging sound, as if the dog was pulling itself along the wood floor. When the dragging stopped, there was silence for several seconds and then a deep biting growl followed by a sharp screech of human pain.

"Sonuvabitch!" screamed a startled voice. "Damn," was followed by what sounded like a struggle and more growling from Boone. Then Corny heard the thwip of a silenced gun and the thud of a bullet striking wood. More growling, struggling. Corny had to act.

He fell forward to the opening, throwing caution aside, and looked down the stairwell. The body of his would-be assassin hung with a knee curled grotesquely around a metal spindle, his head on the ground, contorted awkwardly from his broken neck. Corny pushed down further into the hole, his rifle in front of him until he could see through the moon-cast light that Boone had the lower portion of another man's leg gripped in his teeth. The man staggered backward toward Corny as Boone held tight. An instant later, Corny heard another "thwip" and then a yelp from Boone as the dog released its hold in a torrent of cries. The man stumbled backward, into Corny's view.

Corny was hanging into the opening, his elbows braced atop a stair tread. He scrambled for leverage and tried to maneuver the rifle for a shot. But the man looked up too soon. His black eyes widened, and a smirk bent his mouth as he raised his weapon, took aim, and fired at the exact instant Corny squeezed his trigger.

CHAPTER THIRTY

"I'M GOING TO give it to Gutierrez," Matt said as he backed his father's SUV out of the garage and down the driveway, Hannah sitting silently in the passenger seat. His sisters and brothers-in-law had spoken to him this morning, and the plea was the same: to give it up for the family's safety.

Matt's natural instinct was to fight. Yet, they were right. This was way over his head. He hadn't passed on to his family the information of the deaths of men listed in Rosen's memorandum. He didn't tell anyone that he and Hannah had sent e-mails pleading for acknowledgement of life from two men, or that they'd received no response. Matt was convinced they were also gone, and it was glaringly obvious that any hope he might have had for allies was gone with them.

"Whatever these guys are after," Matt said to Hannah, "they're not going to quit. It doesn't make sense to me, Hannah, but I can't put the family in jeopardy. I'd sure like to know what that damn parchment says. What's so important about it? I guess we'll never know though; I've got to give it up."

Hannah frowned. "I know. None of us signed up for this."

"Damn!" he whispered, and they rode the rest of the way in silence.

The First Bank of Larkspur was a community bank of which Nick and Nell Carter were charter members. One of the perks of charter membership was a free safe deposit box in town. It was that box, Nick believed, that housed the infamous parchment.

Traffic was heavy, as the Black Friday sales seemed to bring out the world. Despite thick clouds, the promise of rain, and biting cold, Larkspur's downtown streets were teeming with shoppers. The street and sidewalk in front of the bank were no exception as Matt and Hannah donned down jackets, and wended their way through the masses after parking in the lot behind the bank. Matt carried an empty leather folder under his arm.

"Are you okay to do this?" Hannah asked as they approached the entrance.

"Yeah; we have no choice. If it's here, I'll call Gutierrez and tell him I've got it, and that I'll deliver it Monday. Hopefully that'll get him to call off the hounds."

Hannah took Matt's arm, and accompanied him up three steps to the bank's entrance, eyes absently panning passersby. As they reached the door, Hannah held back an instant. Matt turned.

"Something wrong?" he asked.

"No," she answered pensively. "I thought I recognized someone." She glanced up and down the sidewalk. "Guess not."

The bank was busy. Each of the teller windows had a line of twenty people. Although Matt had been in the bank to sign documents after Nell's death, he had no recollection of which desk he should approach. So he chose the first one at which no customer sat. He motioned Hannah to join him and started toward a young man riveted to his computer screen. Hannah held back.

"You go Matt," she said. "I'll wait here. This is about your family's private things."

Matt started to protest but Hannah smiled.

"Give me the keys and I'll go wait in the car. Don't worry about me; I'll be okay. You get the parchment."

Matt handed her the keys and turned toward the young man.

MATT HELD HIS breath as he removed the metal box from the wall and carried it to a tiny, private, closet-like room. He sat in the only chair—a straight back, no frills, dark-wood affair that he pulled up to a table of similar design. He placed the box atop the table and had a silly moment of expectation, imagining he was some pirate about to pry open a treasure chest, before he came back to himself and the gravity of his situation. He lifted the lid.

A large plastic zip-lock bag was the only item in the box. Inside the bag was the linen cloth he remembered from the first time he came upon the parchment. It was yellowed and wrinkled from a time even before his grandfather's stewardship of the ancient document, which he assumed was still wrapped inside.

Matt wasn't sure what he was expecting to find in the box, but he was surprised to see that the only item his parents thought valuable enough to protect was his grandfather's heirloom. There were no old coins, no jewelry, baseball cards, or other collectibles. There was only the nondescript bag and the wrinkled yellow cloth that concealed an old document. He smiled lightly at the irony that this was the only item of value his family had, and he was going to give it away.

Matt gently fingered the plastic bag. He felt the firm strength of the cardboard backing that had protected the parchment even before his parents transferred it to the zip-lock bag. He wondered again what could possibly be so important that people were willing to kill for the contents. He couldn't even imagine an answer. Finally, he lifted the bag and pulled it open. He reached inside, lightly gripped the cardboard-firmed cloth and slid it out of the bag. He laid it on the table, hesitated only a second, and then pulled back the folds of the thin linen.

Before him lay three wrinkled, dark mustard colored sheets with uneven edges, slightly torn and frayed, but otherwise intact. He took the tip of the first sheet between his thumb and forefinger and immediately recalled the rough, seemingly brittle, yet surprisingly supple skin from the first time he'd seen it. It sent a new shiver of discovery through him.

To hold something that someone over one thousand years before had held again excited Matt. It was enervating to think that someone had sat down and put a quill to the animal skin that became this parchment, and then had written words that were so important even to this day. The knowledge that this document contained the thoughts of an ancient time coupled with his sense of ownership produced a sudden need in Matt to protect it. But his rational mind won out. If he was going to protect his family, there was no option.

He gingerly refolded the linen over the sheets, slipped the contents back into the bag and re-sealed it. He then laid it flat inside his leather folder, and left the room.

MATT GUESSED HANNAH was waiting in the parking lot when he didn't see her as he stepped onto the bank's stoop. He tucked the folder under his arm, zipped his jacket to the collar, and stuffed his hands into his pockets. He then walked down the steps, and turned north toward the parking lot. He took less than a half dozen steps before he heard a voice so deep and breathless that it almost slipped past him until it caught suddenly and forced a shock of fear to skitter up his spine.

"I will take the folder, Mr. Carter."

Matt's first reaction was to stop and turn, but as he started to do so, a body bumped him firmly from behind, and he felt the pressure of hard metal against his lower back.

"Walk, Mr. Carter," the voice commanded. "Do not turn. Remove the folder from under your arm and hand it back to me without turning."

Matt's mind was numb. Although he heard the words and was able to continue walking, it was only because the bump and pressure of the metal object had propelled him forward. He couldn't formulate the thought necessary to obey the command nor could he maintain his forward motion. He again stopped and was again bumped, this time with a force that caused him to lurch sharply forward, stumble off balance, and turn sideways. Mechanically, despite the warning, he turned his head and caught steel blue eyes.

"Move!" the voice commanded with a promise that death would follow if not obeyed.

In an instant of slow motion clarity, Matt became aware of passersby glancing at them, the two now suddenly facing each other, one glaring with deadly menace and the other staring in stupefied ignorance at the coat pocket that held the gun.

It was in that instant that Hannah appeared.

She came up from behind the voice. Matt watched her raise the hard plastic knuckles of her key chain, and in a single, savage, downward thrust, drive the sharp bottom knuckle into the man's arm. He screamed. Hannah then brought the knuckle up sharply and slammed the upper point into his chin. The man lurched backward, his damaged arm bleeding through his jacket and rising to his chest in a protective motion, while his other arm pin-wheeled for balance.

Matt's shock was broken; his senses came roaring back. Hannah grabbed his arm.

"C'mon Matt!" she screamed and tugged.

But Matt struck out, driving his lower shin between the off-balance man's legs and up into his exposed groin. The connection forced a gust of air and a hoarse scream from the man as he doubled over and grabbed at the wounded area.

"Matt, please!" Hannah screamed again.

But Matt didn't stop. He stepped to the man, who, although bent over and reeling in agony, had lifted his head and was glaring murderously at Matt. Matt swung his right arm up at the face and his tightly clenched fist hammered into the upturned jaw. The man's eyes rolled up and he flew backward, crashing to the ground unconscious. Matt stood over his enemy as blood pooled beneath the man's head where it had struck a stone planter. Adrenalin raced through him. He kicked the prone figure viciously in the side.

"You sonuvabitch!" he shouted. "Leave us alone!"

"Mathew!" Hannah's shouts finally broke through his haze. "We've got to get away from here."

Matt glared at the unconscious attacker, fear and hatred battling in a blast of adrenalin. Finally, he bent, grabbed the gun lying in the man's open palm, and followed Hannah away from the gawking crowd.

CHAPTER THIRTY-ONE

CARDINAL METZINGER'S THANKSGIVING passed with little notice. The Vatican had no interest in the American holiday, and he'd long ago given up trying to contrive a celebration when no one around him understood a thing about it. Besides, he had more important things on his mind.

The letter from the Holy Father had arrived that very morning. The exhibition of the Shroud of Turin would proceed as planned. Metzinger had failed to persuade the Pope, and now he was left to safeguard the relic the best he could.

So Metzinger spent Thanksgiving Day confirming his travel plans. He was coordinating a Christmas visit with family in Southern California with the start of the Shroud's tour. He instructed his personal emissary in Turin to ensure that security for the packing and shipping of the Shroud was proceeding in accordance with the protocol the Vatican's vaunted security forces had laid out. He and the Shroud would be leaving together the following afternoon. He had little else to do then but pack and think.

Toward the end of the day, he dropped heavily into a chair in his apartment's living room. He stared out his sixth floor window over the city of Rome, and prayed for the safety of the Shroud; but thoughts of responsibility to a world in need of direction overtook him.

Offbeat religious concepts were spreading in an again expanding world economy. They were part of a roaring tide of narcissism and selfishness against which no force could stand, and in its path, Christ's simple message of love was being lost. From the sudden new popularity of atheism—almost a religion of its own—to the surge in followers of the ancient beliefs of Gnosticism and the Oneness of the human spirit, it seemed to Metzinger that the devil was winning the battle for the soul of humanity.

Gnosticism was sneaking into the mainstream through the popularity of books and movies like The DaVinci Code, written in the guise of "historical" fiction. Characters that professed "special knowledge" from "long lost gnostic gospels" argued the Gnostic case that only a select few of Jesus' followers knew the key to eternal life, because they had been given this "special knowledge" by Jesus himself. Their duty was to reveal this knowledge only to those "select" few who were capable of understanding it, while the common man continued to be subjugated to the will of some "church." After all, the simpleton could never understand the real key to enlightenment and eternal life. Among the select who were supposedly given this special knowledge were Judas, the betrayer of Jesus, and Mary Magdalene, the alleged wife of Christ and mother of his supposed heirs.

Metzinger couldn't understand the painful need of individuals to separate themselves from others by accepting complex structures of enlightenment through which only they could attain joy, while simple folk wallowed in the eternal suffering of their ignorance and the flames of hell.

Couldn't they see that Christ's message was simple because salvation was for everyone? No all-powerful, all-loving god would create a world in which only a few bearing some secret knowledge could attain eternal life. Yet people persisted in their pursuit of secrets and in the divisiveness, partisanship, and hatred that pursuit bred.

And then there were those who believed in the "Oneness" of the human spirit—that there were no individual souls, but rather one universal soul of which all things were a part. There was no god in this system, only a god-spirit that included all. Thus, everyone was god because everyone was part of the god-spirit. Everyone then had the right to create his own morality because if he was god, who could question him? How absurd, Metzinger thought, for men to think this world could survive with each person setting his own morality.

As for the atheists, Metzinger had no tolerance. Bastardized interpretations of Charles Darwin's theories of evolution and survival of the fittest led them to believe happiness could only be attained through winning and stocking up of material possessions. Yet most who attained material wealth realized too late the emptiness of their belief. And despite Darwin's strong belief in God and statements that it was not inconsistent for a person to believe in God and evolution, the atheists persisted.

Metzinger understood the drive for man to identify purpose, to find meaning, to pursue a life course of risk and excitement, and ultimately to seek success in this world by acquisition of wealth and station. But he also knew the emptiness of these goals. That's why so many sought solace in "secret" teachings, longing to feel special.

Few gave thought to the simple words of salvation. They were too busy, and on those rare occasions when they could give such thought, they believed there had to be more to attaining eternal happiness than just loving God and your neighbor.

Metzinger's job was to help teach the simplicity of life's mysteries. It was the only hope for humankind. The process would be long and arduous, made more so by the difficulties that would accompany the Shroud's tour. But he would stand fast, fight to prevent the devastating fallout from the tour, and help guide the world away from the forces of evil that would pursue the Shroud on its journey.

CHAPTER THIRTY-TWO

NEITHER MATT NOR Hannah spoke. They stared at the blur of a world racing past them. Despite the chill, perspiration beaded on Matt's forehead and ran into his eyes. He flicked it away before he re-gripped the wheel and continued his forward focus. Adrenalin still surged through him, but he noticed nothing except the road they traveled out of Larkspur.

It wasn't until they'd transitioned from the 101 to the John McCarthy Bridge over San Rafael Bay that Matt's breathing started to settle.

"Where are we going?" Hannah finally whispered, shock still clutching her throat.

Matt bobbed his head, trying to respond.

"I don't know," he finally stammered. "I don't know," he repeated. "We've got to get away."

Again there were no words for several minutes as Matt maneuvered the SUV across the final span of the bridge and through the growing traffic of highway 580 into the blue collar, harbor industrial enclave of Richmond.

"We have to call the police," Hannah said.

"We can't." Matt shook his head. "The police are involved. How could he have known we'd be there? It's got to be the police." He dropped his head. "I don't know. I don't get what's going on. We've got to think this through."

His eyes scanned the roadway for a place to stop; somewhere he could think without fear of someone seeing them. He glanced at road signs and chose the nearest cut-off, swerved through traffic, and exited at Hoffman

Blvd. The SUV descended the ramp into the desolate harbor industrial complex, devoid of activity this Thanksgiving Friday, and pulled into the first empty lot. Matt pulled behind the rectangular concrete tilt-up at the front of the lot, hidden now from casual sight from the freeway and frontage road.

He turned off the motor and dropped his head back against the headrest. He closed his eyes and breathed deeply. Hannah stared ahead, bewildered, her eyes moist with tears she struggled to restrain. Matt rolled his head toward her and saw the same fear in her that gripped him. The sight softened his edge. He sought words to break the silence.

"How did you know him?" he asked softly.

She hesitated, lost for a moment before she understood and turned to him.

"I'd seen him before. When we were walking up the steps to the bank, I caught a glimpse of someone who looked familiar." He nodded his recollection. "I couldn't see him when I looked again, and I couldn't place him, but it came to me inside the bank. He was on campus, Matt, a few times, hanging around the geo-sciences building. I noticed him because of those eyes. Did you see the eyes?"

Matt nodded.

Hannah trembled.

"They're so evil. When I left you in the bank, I walked to the car and then came around the other side of the building. That's when I saw him again. He was waiting out front, standing next to a tree and watching the bank. When you came out, he went after you." Hannah dropped her head and whispered, "He's got to be the one who killed the professor."

"He's probably the guy who broke into my dad's house," Matt said. "Did you see how his arm bled after you hit him? You must have hit the spot where Charley bit him."

They were silent again. Matt reached into his pocket for his phone.

"Look Hannah, I've got to call and let my family know what happened." He pulled up his dad's number.

"They can track it," Hannah said.

Matt hesitated, but touched "call."

"I've got to let them know we're okay," he said. "I'll be quick."

Nick answered at the second ring.

"Dad, it's Matt. I wanted to let you know what happened at the bank..."

"Mathew, we're watching it on TV. News of the attack interrupted the football game. Was that you? Are you okay?"

"It was. We're okay."

"Where are you? Are you coming home?"

"Dad, we can't. I...I can't tell you where we are. I don't trust the police." Matt paused. "We're okay, Dad. We need to stay away for a while, so we don't put any of you in danger. We need to lay low and figure this out."

"Mathew, this is too much." Nick hesitated. "Your sisters are right, son. We need to go to the police, even if we don't give them the parchment. We can't believe the police are all bad, son. We need help."

"They're involved, Dad. That's the only way whoever these people are could know what we're doing." Matt hesitated again. "Did they pick up the guy who attacked us? He's the one who broke into your house, and probably killed professor Rosen."

"No, he disappeared. Witnesses said he came to, bleeding badly. He ran off before the police arrived."

Silence for several seconds.

"There's more, son," Nick said. "The police have put out a description of my car, and they're putting together a composite of you, Hannah, and this other guy. They're looking for you. Come home, son," Nick pleaded.

"Did they get our license number?"

"No license number was mentioned on the news, but they're still talking to witnesses."

"I can't come home, Dad. This doesn't make sense. We need to figure it out. I'll be out of touch for a while. They can probably trace these calls. I've got to go." He ended the call abruptly.

Hannah looked at him.

"The police are looking for us," Matt mumbled, shocked at the reality that they were now fugitives. "They have a description of the car. They're putting together sketches of us."

Matt shook his head, absently fingering the reset button at the bottom of the phone. As his mind wandered, the application icons came up on the screen. Just to the right and slightly above the e-mail icon appeared the number "1." For several seconds, the notation's meaning didn't register in the awkward, almost hopeless silence.

Then suddenly he sat up. He pushed the icon; up popped a message line indicating something had come in.

"What is it?" Hannah asked.

"I've got something here from Crockett—Cornelius Crockett—one of the guys on Rosen's list. He answered our e-mail."

He read the e-mail so quickly he barely understood it. Hannah waited expectantly. Matt reread it aloud.

"It's dated yesterday at 11:05 p.m.," after the Carter household was down for the night. "It reads, 'I am alive and well for the moment. I was Samuel Rosen's close friend, and I did assist him in various ways on his research. I remember your name as the owner of the parchment that launched our dear friend on his mission. We need to talk right away. I fear our good friend's death will not be the last until your parchment is safe. Please call me or come to see me at the address below. We have no time to delay.'"

It was type-signed by "Cornelius 'Corny' Crockett." Matt read the phone number and address to Hannah who transcribed them onto a scratch paper from the SUV's glove box. Matt went immediately to the phone function and entered Professor Crockett's number while Hannah Google-mapped the address. Matt held his breath and waited for Crockett to pick up.

"Hello..." came an answer to the fourth ring.

"Profes..." Matt started only to be interrupted by the remainder of the message.

"...You've reached Corny and Elli Crockett's number. Please leave your message."

"Professor Crockett, this is Mathew Carter. I e-mailed you last night about Professor Rosen and my family's parchment. I need to talk to you as soon as possible, sir. Please call me." He recited his cell phone number. "Things are out of control here, Professor. Please call me right away. Thank you."

"He didn't answer." Matt stated the obvious. He rubbed his forehead and stared anxiously at his phone hoping for a ring. "Damn," he finally said as he glanced up and surveyed the stark surroundings of the parking lot and the industrial community in which it sat. "We can't just wait here."

"I've got directions," Hannah said, holding up her phone.

Matt turned and smiled anxiously.

"It's a five-hour drive," Hannah said. "It's 1:00 now, we should be there by about 6:00 or 6:30."

Matt reached for her phone, read the route, and handed it back to her. "It's past Sacramento, north of Tahoe." He eyed Hannah. "We have to do this, right? We can't just go to the police?"

She nodded. "We have to do this."

CHAPTER THIRTY-THREE

PETER CHRISTIAN STOOD, legs slightly spread, arms clasped loosely behind his back. He watched with amusement as Paula Seltzer stopped at his front door, turned, and glanced at him in his half-clothed majesty before she joined his driver for the ride home. As the massive steel-wrapped door of his Bel Air mansion closed behind Paula, Christian's smile broadened.

"She's afraid of me," he thought aloud, a statement of fact of which he was well pleased. Anyone viewing the young woman's carriage as she slunk away from him, arms clutching her bag to her breast, would have sensed something submissive in her. Only those who knew the confident woman of substance and strength would have recognized the complete turn in her bearing. None would have been able to attribute the turn to fear for none had ever seen fear in her. But Peter Christian knew it was fear—something in which he had considerable experience.

Christian mulled over Paula's journey from infatuation to the fear he'd instilled during their intimate time together, and ultimately to the worship that would evolve from that fear. She was his for as long as he needed her, but his need now was minimal. He would soon cast her away to fend for herself in the befuddled worship to which she would cling.

It was two days earlier, just after noon, that he'd approached Paula. He was still smarting from his mistake in front of the national media the previous evening, and had already turned down several offers to join Thanksgiving celebrations. But the bile that surged in him as a result of

Father Robert's manipulation of him in front of the world audience needed a release. He cast his eyes on Paula at the last minute. It didn't hurt, of course, that she might prove useful with information. So he invited her to his private Thanksgiving dinner. She'd accepted without hesitation, readily abandoning family plans.

Christian had been angry when he'd first heard Paula's friend wouldn't see him until after Thanksgiving. He'd calmed as events unfolded in a way that his problem would be resolved without him ever having to waste time with the young man. Still, it wouldn't hurt to have more information about him delivered by a woman of Paula's obvious talents.

"He's not much into causes," she'd told Christian at the sumptuous dinner table set on the patio of his one-acre back yard. They dined alone, save for the service by Walt, amidst the tranquil scents of Bel Air's pines and eucalyptus. It was a million miles from the chaos of Los Angeles, yet smack in the middle of it, a secluded island of multi-million dollar homes above the hubbub of life of the common man. The evening was balmy and the setting, adjacent to a pool that looked like a forest pond with tiny falls cascading into it, was mystical.

"Actually," she said with a slight, wine-induced chuckle, "Matt's not into much of anything except the beach, volleyball, and women."

"They seem like honorable pursuits to me," Christian said with his infectious laugh. He leaned forward on elbows that straddled his plate. "So, he's not interested in coming in to talk about joining the company?"

"No, Peter, not that at all," Paula responded quickly. "It's not that he's not interested. In fact, the sense I have is that he's very interested…maybe for the first time in his life, in the concept of working in a real job. The problem is that I came on a little too strong when I finally reached him. He doesn't do well with pressure. He likes to slow things down. A real job is something new to his thinking. He'll be in Monday. He's good about keeping his promises."

"You like him," he said.

"Yeah, he's fun," she offered. "But I'll be honest with you. I'm more into men with a little more motivation." She smiled coquettishly and took another sip of red.

They ate dessert quietly and continued to consume substantial quantities of Christian's fine wine, before they made their final commitment to swimming naked and rolling into the wild, almost frenzied sex that took them through the night. More surprising to Christian than Paula's sexual appetite was her acceptance of the exuberance with which he liked to play. And all was perfect from Paula's perspective until early afternoon on Friday, when something cracked in Christian and his exuberance turned to violence.

The day started slowly; it was late-morning by the time Paula woke. Christian was not in bed; probably in the gym downstairs, Paula thought. So she rose and went out for a mid-morning swim—just the thing to get her juices flowing again. She couldn't believe her luck and wanted to be at her best when Peter returned. But by the time Peter joined her darkness had descended upon him. It cloaked his face as he ordered her out of the water for lunch.

What Paula didn't know was that Peter had received two phone calls, each of which had made his blood boil.

The first came just as he started his treadmill workout.

"We have no news from either of them, Peter," the voice on the other end said. So accustomed was he to hearing, "it's done," that the statement didn't register. It was only after he asked the caller to repeat it that he understood. He glanced at his watch and quickly calculated that it should have been done hours ago.

"What do you intend to do about it?" Christian asked curtly, picking up the pace on the treadmill.

"We're trying to track down our closest operatives to get up there and find out what happened. The soonest anyone can be there is late tomorrow."

"How about our boy?" Christian asked.

"We haven't..." the voice started and then hesitated. "We haven't spoken to him yet, Peter. We've got him on another project."

"It will be done shortly. Send him up there when he reports in. He's a damn sight closer than a day and a half." Peter jabbed the treadmill's buttons to bring it up to a run. "Anything else?" he asked, his voice coming in short bursts.

"No..." the voice trailed off.

"Good! Get it done!" He ended the call and placed the phone back into its cradle. He clenched his jaw and increased his pace to a sprint long before he would normally have done so. He hated failure. But he had to control himself. It was a critical time that required calm thinking.

It wasn't until he had completed his workout almost two hours later that he received the second call. Perspiration ran streams down his bare chest and back. He was breathing heavily, preparing to jump into the shower before re-joining his houseguest. He glanced at his phone and recognized the code.

"Is it done?" he asked without preamble.

There was a hesitation before the low, whispered voice responded. It sounded shaken, without its normal force and conviction.

"I…have failed," it said.

Christian didn't respond. He waited, his anger rising.

"She came out of nowhere, cut my arm, and then he attacked. My head struck a planter. I lost consciousness."

"Where are they?"

"Gone. I don't know."

"Where are you?"

"Hiding…the police…I woke and ran before the police came. There was much blood."

Christian said nothing. He seethed, but tried to control it.

"I've failed you again…Ma…" the voice started.

"No," Christian interrupted with forced calm. He was surprised that such a reliable product had failed a second time. Hot anger competed with reason for his emotions. "It will not stop us. I will handle it. Can you come home?"

"I need help."

"Tell me where you are, I'll send someone."

Christian took the name and location of the seedy San Francisco motel. The darkness of his mood tempted him to send an assassin, but he still needed the asset. There was one task remaining—one only he, of all the others in Christian's employ, could perform.

Moments later Peter Christian sat across from Paula Seltzer. She was garbed in a white terry-towel robe secured loosely to tantalizingly reveal her bounty. They sat at a round glass table that had replaced the dinner table of the previous evening. Despite the beautiful day and his guest's inviting appearance, Christian seethed.

"I want him here, Paula," he growled under brow-hooded eyes.

Paula was taken aback. She looked at Peter questioningly, not wanting to respond for fear of what reaction a response would elicit.

"I want Mathew Carter here, now," he demanded, the darkness growing.

"I…" She clutched the robe tightly to her. "I won't be able to get him here till Monday," she stammered. "I'm sorr…"

He slammed a powerful fist on the table's top. The glass shattered and sent their lunch crashing to the deck with chunks of glass. He stood, towering and menacing. Paula cowered. Christian stepped to her, grabbed an arm, and yanked her to her feet. He tore at the robe. It fell away easily. She stared in shock at the demonic fire that burned in his eyes. She struggled feebly as he lifted her over a shoulder. Her struggles intensified, legs kicking, fists pounding, yet he seemed not to notice. In seconds he'd pushed through the sliders into his bedroom and had her sprawled across the bed, her eyes wide with fear. He descended upon her and ravished her in a flurry of violent control and angry thrusts. When he was spent, he rolled off and lay on his back, breathing heavily. Paula scrambled away from him to the upper corner of the bed. She pulled a sheet up to her throat, stared in horror, and trembled. Several minutes later, he spoke calmly.

"Walt will take you home."

She nodded, fear etched on her brow.

"Go on, now," he said with a nod, still calm. "Get yourself cleaned up and ready. I'll tell Walt to bring the car around."

She was ready in minutes. She moved quickly through the cavernous house to the enormous foyer where he waited, dressed only in his sweat-soaked workout shorts.

"Don't let me down, Paula," he said as she stumbled past him. "I want Mathew Carter in my office on Monday."

She nodded, saying nothing. She barely breathed as she turned at the door to make sure he wasn't following.

When the door closed behind her, Peter Christian smiled.

CHAPTER THIRTY-FOUR

BY 6:30 P.M., THE sun had become a smudge on the western horizon. In the Sierra foothills north of Lake Tahoe, where walls of birches, pines, and firs stood sentinel astride Highway 89, not even that smudge was apparent. Night had taken the day.

Matt and Hannah had been following Google map directions for five and a half hours. They'd driven warily through Sacramento to the old mining town of Truckee on the northern edge of Lake Tahoe. After a fill-up and quick bite, which they paid for in cash, they turned onto the divided two-lane country road known as Highway 89 in search of the Sage Hen Road cutoff. Drizzles that had started just west of Sacramento had given way to showers by the time they reached Truckee, and the blackening clouds that hung thick over 89 promised a massive storm to come.

Matt and Hannah began to doubt the sanity of their venture, particularly since Sage Hen Road was nowhere to be found. It had to be no more than a minor cut in the forest by the looks of the occasional marked path they'd seen along the route. They had probably already missed it and certainly wouldn't find it in the dark, particularly since the phone's GPS was no longer working in the remote foothills. Matt slowed the vehicle to a crawl, he and Hannah peering at the forest out the side windows, as the car's thumping wipers struggled unsuccessfully to clear the now pouring rain from the windshield. Frustrated and nervous, they rounded yet another bend, and finally saw a dim light.

As they drew closer, they were able to discern the silhouette of a squat log structure, barely visible against the forest backdrop. The yellow light struggled through grime-marred windows partially covered by signs that defined the structure as a market. In front of the market, caught at the edges of the light's glow, stood two 1950's style gas pumps, ancient and weather-beaten, each atop its own gouged and pitted concrete rise. Matt pulled the SUV onto the gravel apron in front and stopped. The market was called "Grants" according to the splintered, barely legible sign that overhung the door.

Matt and Hannah pulled their jackets tight around themselves before they stepped out into the wet, frigid air, and ran, hunched against the cold, to the closed, weather-pitted pine front door. Matt tried the door with a gentle push. It swung open easily to the tinkle of an overhead bell. He stepped aside for Hannah to precede him.

They were immediately struck by the interior's warmth as the door creaked closed with a hollow thwack. In the cramped confines stood rows of foodstuffs and sundry displays separated by narrow aisles, arranged in no immediately discernible order. To their left, past two metal-wire carousels, one containing comic books and the other greeting cards, was a battered cabinet and counter-top behind which stood the store's clerk.

"Hi folks," said the thin, wiry man, who wore the facial ravages of an old man, but stood erect with the fitness of a hardscrabble mountain life. On the counter to the man's right sat an antique finger-key cash register. One arm was draped casually over the top of the register while the other rested on the counter. His greeting was pleasant. "Can I help you with anythin'?"

"It's cold out there," Matt offered with a relieved smile as he shivered away the last of the outside chill.

The man nodded. "Yup, gonna get worse I imagine. We'll be gettin' snow soon enough. We got a biggun' comin'. How can I help you?"

"We're lost," Matt said. "We're looking for Sage Hen Road. Are we close?"

"Not far," the man answered. "You headin' up to Independence?"

"Yes, do you know how to get there?"

"Sure, I got me a girl up there. It'll be rough in the dark if this is your first time." He shook his head. "It's not the best of roads in the daytime. At night, it'll be tricky, particularly with weather." He eyed them curiously, a half smile turning his lips.

Matt nodded, smiling at the thought of this guy's "girl."

"You lookin' for somethin' in particular up at the lake?" the man asked.

"Actually, we're trying to find Cornelius Crockett's place. Do you know him?"

The man's smile and casual demeanor disappeared. He stood up straight, took a half step back, and eyed Matt suspiciously before he looked past him to Hannah.

Matt turned to Hannah, surprised. She smiled, softly touched his arm and stepped to the counter.

"Do you know the professor?" she asked.

"I might," he said guardedly, his eyes flitting back and forth from the beautiful young woman to the young man. "You students of his'n?"

"No," Hannah answered with a smile, trying to regain the man's initial ease. "He invited us up to see him. We're having a heck of a time finding our way."

"If you ain't his students, what's yer business with 'im?"

"It's something personal, sir," Hannah answered. The man's face hardened. "Honestly, I don't think Corny wants anyone to know his business on this matter." She used the nickname, hoping it would elicit some softening in the man. It did. He nodded, eyed Matt, and then went back to Hannah.

"You have anythin' that shows yer invited?" He asked hopefully.

She glanced at Matt and nodded encouragement. He understood and pulled out his cell phone. "I do, sir. Let me show you." He pulled up Corny's saved e-mail and reread it quickly. He didn't want to show the entire e-mail but he had no choice if they were going to get his help. He turned the screen to the man. "He sent this last night."

The man, surrounded by his old-world existence, looked at Matt for a moment and then at the screen. He pulled it closer and read the Corny's message. He nodded, but continued to stare at Matt's screen until he could make up his mind what to do.

"Have you called him on this 'ere machine?"

"We've called several times. We've left messages but haven't heard back. We're concerned that maybe something's wrong," confessed Matt.

"Naw," the man started, shaking his head and seemingly more comfortable. "Naw, taint it a-tall. Sometimes these cell phones jest don't work up here, particularly in weather. He don't answer his land line or I'd call 'im right now." He stared hard at them before finally nodding and saying, "I can direct you, I guess."

He reached under the counter and pulled out a faded and wrinkled old map. He pointed out their current location, described distances, landmarks, and timing, and slowly described the route to "the perfessor's house." Apparently they were only about fifty yards shy of Sage Hen Road, but then a good five miles over what the man described as "wild forest roads" to Corny's place. "You'll be ridin' over some pretty uneven track. It'll be chockfulla rocks most places and you'll probably be crossin' a few streams…not over 'em…through 'em if they ain't froze over yet. If you go real slow, you should be okay…unless the snow gets to fallin' too heavy." Matt listened carefully as Hannah entered the directions into her phone.

Matt smiled nervously. He wouldn't have been overly concerned if the drive was during daylight hours, as he had done some off-road driving in his past. Rivers, streams, rocks and uneven surfaces were what made such adventures exciting. Now, however, he sought no adventure. He wanted information, and he would have preferred that the last five miles of their journey could be easier.

"Thank you, sir," Matt said. "We appreciate this." He hesitated. "Why were you so concerned about giving us directions, if you don't mind my asking? Do the people living up here have problems with visitors?"

The man shook his head, dropped his eyes for a moment and then answered.

"Naw. For the most part, they don't get many. It's pretty remote and until the State's Nature Conservancy took the lake over, no one even knew the place existed. It's jest," he hesitated again, "A few days ago, two fellas was here asking for directions to ol' Corny's house, jest like you two. They was from the city, too. I give 'em to 'em, but felt real bad about it afterwards. Tried to call Corny but didn't get no answer. They jest didn't look right to me is all. Guess I shoulda gone up there an' checked on the perfessor. Ain't had the time, I guess. You'll check on 'im won't ya?"

"We will," Hannah answered. "Thanks for your help, sir. We'll tell Corny you said hi."

"Name's Gus. Corny knows me. Comes in to buy his needs here. Tell 'im Gus sends his regards."

As Matt and Hannah stepped out of the market's warmth, a chill greater than the weather went with them.

CHAPTER THIRTY-FIVE

BY THE TIME their headlights found the cabin-shaped mailbox bearing the name "Crockett", another hour and a half had elapsed. A long gravel drive cut up a slope and disappeared into a thicket of pines and firs above. Matt and Hannah fought headaches brought on by five miles navigating through icy streamlets, around large rocks strewn over rutted, uneven dirt-packed roads, in pitch-black darkness. When they finally arrived, they breathed easier.

"I guess we go up," Matt said and maneuvered the SUV's high beams up the slope. He pushed the accelerator and followed the beams up toward the tree line.

At the tree line, the vehicle negotiated a sharp left turn within the thicket. Faint moonlight appeared ahead. Within another few seconds, after a slight jog to the right, the tree barricade ended and they found themselves atop a plateau cleared except for a cabin some thirty yards ahead of them. Matt jammed on the brakes. The car skidded on loose gravel, crunching rock until it stopped, its headlight beams now directed slightly to the right of the structure. As his eyes ran over the clearing, he tried to maintain calm, but a lump of dread began working its way up his gullet.

"No lights," he whispered.

They sat for several seconds trying to muster the courage to take the next step.

"I'm going to get closer," Matt finally said, eyes again scouring the clearing. He pushed his foot down slowly to right the direction of the SUV until the vehicle's beams splashed against the backside of the cabin and what appeared to be an attached garage. They saw nothing else except for scattered flurries of snow that had replaced the rain. There was no light, no movement, and no sign of life. Matt again leaned lightly on the accelerator, this time directing the car past the garage, ten feet to the right of the house. From this vantage they could see the cabin's west-facing wall and windows, and, beyond them, the posts, spindles and rails of a wrap-around porch. He doused the headlights, but continued idling the engine as their eyesight adjusted to the darkness.

"What now?" whispered Hannah.

Matt reached under his seat and withdrew the handgun he had taken from the attacker in Larkspur. He had no clue what make or model the gun was. It looked like the guns he remembered from the war movies he'd watched as a kid—like a German Luger, except that it had a slide. He turned to Hannah.

"Can you look in the glove box? My parents always carried a small flashlight."

Hannah found a nine-inch penlight. She turned its head to produce a white beam, and handed it to Matt.

"Okay, I've got to go out there and see if he's here," he whispered. "You okay to wait in the car? I think it'll be safer here."

"I'm coming with you," she answered tightly. "I'm not staying here alone."

Matt nodded, turned off the car, directed the gun's business end awkwardly toward the house, and pulled the door handle open with his other hand. Hannah stepped out on her side, did a quick survey of the clearing in the sweep of the flashlight beam while the car was still between her and the house, and then joined Matt.

They walked slowly, in clear view of anyone who might be watching from the cabin, yet they crouched, as if that made a difference. Neither had a clue how they were supposed to handle this situation. Still, it wasn't until they'd inched themselves, backs plastered against the west wall, past windows that revealed nothing in the interior's black shadows, to just beyond the front of the porch, that they stopped.

They'd caught whiffs of an unusual stench the moment they stepped out of the SUV, but its full force didn't hit them until Matt's beam swept across two bodies lying like pavers on either side of the rough, foot-beaten path from the cabin's front steps to the woods on the south side of the plateau. Although they'd experienced the horror of Samuel Rosen's brutal death, they were not even remotely prepared for the sight of two new bodies painted in the vampire white of their hand torch, or for the reek of blood and decay that accosted them.

Hannah pressed hard against Matt's shoulder even as Matt pushed back, subconsciously trying to distance himself from the macabre scene. Hannah's closeness had no impact except to prevent him from pushing completely away. His only sensation was fear—exactly what he felt coursing through Hannah as she held a death-grip of his arm. Matt shifted the gun awkwardly to his left hand and pointed at the bodies.

With Hannah clinging, Matt stepped away from the porch, into the yard, toward the bodies. Something crunched sharply beneath his step. He glanced down and caught a flash of his light off glass. He redirected his light above his head and noticed two empty outlets that had once held outdoor bulbs. His beam then followed the roofline away from him to two other pairs of outlets, empty also, save for jagged reminders of what once occupied them.

They inched away from the porch, shying away from the bodies even as they approached them, as if they were circling them to arrive from a different angle. Matt trained the gun on the dead while Hannah stared silently at the eerie tableau. Finally, they stood at the feet of the two bodies, light quavering over them.

What neither Matt nor Hannah noticed was that they had stopped breathing. The frigid air no longer existed for them; all they sensed was death: its grisly sight, its abominable stench, and its complete horror. Once again it had been thrust upon them—into their lives—into their very souls.

They could make out no facial features of one corpse whose head looked to have been completely blown away. As for the other, with his neck and head so badly twisted, it seemed that he was but a mannequin thrown in a heap out the door of some dress studio. Matt shook his head, perhaps to clear it—or maybe to remind himself this was real. In so doing, the beam of his light rose and danced across the front of the house where he noticed something strange. His mind at first had difficulty registering what he was looking at, but then, suddenly, he knew. And in that instant of recognition he understood he was too late to do anything about it. A rifle barrel was poking through the slightly ajar front door, aimed directly at him.

CHAPTER THIRTY-SIX

THE ASSASSIN'S BULLET had pinged off an iron spindle, glanced off Corny's left temple, and embedded itself in the wall over his left shoulder. In the same instant, the killer's malevolent grin had disappeared in a spray of blood and facial structure as Corny's projectile hit the point of his nose and exploded.

The recoil unbalanced Corny, throwing him down the spiral staircase headfirst. He bounced awkwardly and out of control down metal treads as he dropped his rifle, reached out frantically and finally grabbed a passing spindle before it became a full fall. His legs swung out wildly, hammered against another spindle and came to rest below him, against the calves of the other assassin who lay upended with his head lolling crazily on the floor at the end of his broken neck. Corny stared into the macabre, moonlit death scene as he fought off the growing nausea of shock and the excruciating pain in his wounded leg. He struggled to a seat on a metal tread, closed his eyes and tried to breathe deeply. His mind raced with the sure knowledge that his ordeal wasn't over, but instead was just beginning. For the time being however, he had to gather himself, to prepare for the next attack. It wasn't until he was again breathing calmly that fear's vice-grip on his brain began to loosen and he remembered his best friend.

"Boone," he called as he slid gingerly from one tread to the next, trying to protect his throbbing leg. There was no response. When he reached the bottom tread, the first assassin motionless next to him, Corny tried to pull himself to his feet. Pain shot up from the wound and sent him sprawling backward. Perspiration ran beneath his clothing. He gritted his teeth and clenched his body to fight the pain and maintain consciousness. After a time, he finally slid to the floor in a sitting position, his wounded leg extended. He dragged himself across the wood planks in search of his dog.

"Boone," he called again. This time he heard a soft whimper.

Corny pulled himself around furniture, past the death detritus of the second assassin, and finally to Boone. The dog lay on his side, his fur matted with blood as he whimpered a greeting and feebly lifted his tail.

"Take it easy buddy," Corny soothed. He stroked Boone's head with one hand while his other gently probed the body. He found three wounds, the first in the lower rear left leg, which appeared to be broken, the second, the most dangerous it appeared from the large amount of blood that had flowed from it, was just to the left of the ridge of Boone's back, some six inches behind the base of the dog's neck. This was undoubtedly from the bullet fired as the assassin fought Boone off an instant before he turned and met his fate to Corny's shot. The third wound appeared to be that bullet's exit wound at Boone's lower left abdomen.

Corny had much to do to contend with his own wounds, determine what to do with the mess in his home, and most importantly, to protect against what he knew would be another attack as soon as the assassins' employer realized they were not reporting in. But his first priority was to do everything he could to save his best friend's life.

By the time the sun rose some three and a half hours later, Boone's wounds were medicated and wrapped, as was Corny's left temple. His right leg was splinted and wrapped from the thigh down. He'd managed to get water into Boone and himself, and he'd crafted a crutch from an old kitchen broom. Then, he rested. He sat on the floor, back against the wall below the front window, Boone's head cradled lightly in his lap, his reloaded rifle again gripped tightly next to him. His exhaustion was complete from the hours of exertion and blood loss. He closed his eyes "for just a few minutes," but the minutes ended up turning into hours.

When he finally woke shortly after noon, Corny's first thought was to call the police. He had such trouble leveraging himself into a standing position that he again dragged himself along the floor to his landline and lifted the receiver. He waited for a dial tone but realized he wasn't going to get one. The lines had been cut. He considered climbing the spiral staircase to retrieve his cell phone in the hope he'd have reception, a hit and miss proposition at the best of times; but he weighed the danger of attempting the climb on a leg he could barely manage on flat ground, and decided against it.

He couldn't drive down the hill because his right leg was incapable. Besides, it would take hours, even if he only went to Gus' place and called the police from there. He couldn't leave Boone for hours and there was no way Boone could travel. Not yet, anyway. Corny considered seeking aid from Independence Lake neighbors, but similar issues existed. They were so remote to his cabin that he ran as good a chance of spending hours checking the few cabins reasonably near him and finding no one in residence as he did of finding any help. But the question was moot anyway as he could neither drive nor hobble on foot anywhere just now.

Corny wasn't going to be getting any help soon. He had food, water, and medical supplies sufficient to hold out against a siege for at least two weeks. All he had to do was survive until he was able to get up to his loft to his cell phone, assuming it would work, or until Boone was ready to travel. In either case, he figured if he could hold out for a couple days, he'd be in better shape.

Something with which Corny had to deal immediately were the dead bodies. The cabin's heated interior was starting the decay process even as he sat wondering what he was going to do. He couldn't let the bodies stay inside, as they would become as hazardous to his health as any assassin's bullet.

He could drag the bodies outside and bury them, but he didn't believe he had the strength to dig; and that's when the new thought struck him. He recalled stories of the American West where "bad guys," killed by a town's sheriff, were put on display as a warning to others that this was what awaited them if they didn't toe the line of the law. That's what he would do to these two. He'd lay them out so those who came after would see them. But that wasn't the only reason. He knew the stench of death would draw the feral creatures of the forest. His hope was that it would draw something big enough to create some havoc just as new assailants happened upon the scene. Perhaps it might even draw Old One Eye, the starving bear that had been marauding local homesteads. There were wolves too, and other creatures that might give city folk some pause. Any one of them could affect the odds of Corny's survival.

So Corny stripped the bodies of their weapons and reload cartridges, dragged them onto his porch, and rolled them down the steps. He followed them to the ground by butt-sliding down the steps, and then he shifted to a standing position once he reached the bottom. This time the leg, splinted and secure, held him with tolerable pain. He used his makeshift crutch for balance and managed to drag each of the bodies about fifteen feet away from the steps. He positioned them astride the beaten path that led into the woods and, with his remaining strength, beat his retreat back to the relative safety of his cabin.

The retired professor of theology and anthropology spent the rest of the day between bouts of rest cleaning the spattered remains of death from the room, tending to his and Boone's wounds, and trying to get food into them. It wasn't until after the sun had disappeared behind clouds and the rain was turning to snow that he had the first inkling the next attack was upon him.

Boone heard it first. The slight jerk of his head and a barely audible "yipp" woke Corny to the sound of tire-churned gravel. He maintained his sitting position next to Boone, his hand lightly stroking the dog, as he looked to the window of the bedroom nearest him along the west wall. He immediately saw the glow of head lights splayed across the glass.

"Shhh," he whispered and pushed himself away from the dog. "Keep still Boone. I'll see who this is." He pulled himself up to his feet, positioned the crutch under one arm, clutched the rifle in the other, and felt the weight of the assassin's handgun tucked into the waistband of his jeans. He hobbled into the front bedroom—to the window, pulled back the sheer curtain slightly, and caught the shadows of two figures, at least one carrying a weapon and flashlight, as they melded into the darkness next to the cabin.

Corny pulled back into the room's darkness as one shaded head pushed up slowly to look inside. After several seconds, the head dropped back below the sill, and the two figures proceeded past the window. Corny hopped out of the room using furniture and walls for support lest the crutch make a noise that would give him away. He moved quickly to the door, pulled it slightly open, and peered through the crack as the intruders followed their light to the two bodies. He lifted his rifle to the opening, leaned lightly against his crutch and waited for them to step into his line of fire. They obliged all too easily.

When he could see them clearly in the growing white of their own hand torch, he took aim. But in the split second between his decision to squeeze the trigger and the physical act, he faltered. He wondered, nonsensically, why the new assassins appeared glued together, as if they were trying to provide him the easiest possible target. Why were they so intent on the two bodies when it would be clear to any killer that if there was danger anywhere, it was from within? The bodies, after all, were dead and would be of no interest to someone coming for him. Corny watched with growing interest as the two figures continued to gawk at the bodies, seemingly without thought to their own safety. The leading figure finally raised his head and then the flashlight toward the front door. His left hand continued to clutch a handgun pointed down at the dead bodies.

"Well, are you going to stand there staring," Corny finally shouted, "or are you going to come in out of the snow and help an old man?"

CHAPTER THIRTY-SEVEN

"WILLKIE GLAUSER'S DEAD." Corny said in response to Matt's question about the last of the men on Professor Rosen's list. "His body was found at the bottom of a ravine… 'skiing accident.'" He drew quotes in the air. "That was no more an accident than those two bastards out there." He jerked his head outside.

Corny sat at the end of an old, beaten leather couch. His right leg was propped atop pillows and took up the rest of the couch. Hannah and Matt sat in matching faded, blue-denim barrel chairs pulled close to a finely crafted driftwood coffee table, all within the corona of light and heat from the large, stone fireplace.

Behind Corny's couch stood the spiral staircase, and beyond that a kitchen and small dining nook, both of which bore old west décor with modern appliances. At the back of kitchen was a door to the garage.

It had taken Hannah nearly a half hour after they'd warily entered the cabin to convince Corny to let her inspect his wounds. Although lack of light made it difficult to ascertain seepage stains, the cabin's putrid smell told her something wasn't right. Thankfully, although the wounds needed fresh bandages, the smell had not come from them. Nor had it come from Boone, who rested comfortably on blankets arranged by Matt. The odor wasn't of any wounds. It was of death, of the blood and decay that clung to walls and furnishings even after they opened doors and windows to the frigid night and Matt lit the fire to combat the cold. They spoke little for a while except of the need to call the police and ambulances only to realize they had no service in the remote area. When Matt suggested they pack Corny and Boone into the SUV and take them to safety, Corny said simply that Boone couldn't travel, and, more significantly, the now heavily falling snow would make it impossible to get out, particularly at night.

When Corny and Boone finally rested comfortably, Matt retrieved the folder containing the parchment from his car. He then closed the cabin to the elements, either because the odor was gone or they had been sufficiently desensitized to it. Only then did they speak of the things that brought them together. Matt held his folder close as he explained how they'd come to Corny. Corny explained the bodies arranged as frozen dinners for the forest scavengers outside his cabin. When Matt mentioned his e-mail to Willkie Glauser, Corny described his friend's death.

The old professor, lean and leathery, dropped a hand to his wounded thigh, un-splinted by Hannah because there was no break. He rubbed it gingerly and tried to flex the knee against the pain that clawed at him in sporadic waves. He grimaced until the wave dissipated; then he eyed his companions, doubt playing across his face.

"I shouldn't have invited you up here," he said. "I knew they'd come for me. I…I guess I felt Samuel's work couldn't die with me."

Matt and Hannah nodded but offered the old man no reassurance, their doubts and confusion holding the greater power over their minds.

Corny finally eyed the folder Matt clutched.

"Is that it?"

"Yes, it's the parchment."

"May I see it?" Corny extended a hand.

Matt stared at the old man for a time before he finally undid the folder's hasp, opened it slowly, and laid it on the coffee table, pushing it to Corny. The old man leaned forward, touched the plastic bag gingerly and stared at the yellowed cloth that covered the parchment. He leaned back, eyes fixed on the bag.

"This is what started Samuel's journey, you know?" He raised his eyes, chuckled mirthlessly. "It gave him his life's final purpose. I suppose it gave all of us who went along with him that purpose."

Corny again glanced at the bag, nodding and sighing with weariness.

He motioned to Matt's handgun on the table. "Do you know how to use that thing?"

"No." Matt's voice came out as a hoarse croak. Corny reached for the gun.

"I'll show you." He removed and checked the gun's clip, re-inserted it and held the weapon up for both to see. "You pull back on this," he noted the slide Matt had noticed but didn't use in the car, "and then you point, and squeeze."

Corny looked at his visitors. The dazed looks told him he wasn't connecting.

"Are you with me? Can you do this?" he asked, his voice rising to jar them out of their trances.

Hannah nodded solemnly.

Matt turned, stared absently for a moment, and then reached for the gun. Corny released the hammer and handed it to him. Matt gripped it tightly, anger suddenly surging to replace the blank stare. He pointed away from the table, pulled back viciously on the slide, and turned his glare on Corny.

"We can do this!"

"Good!" Corny returned Matt's bellicose tone. "One of us will have to be awake at all times." He paused to listen to the banshee wail of the wind's increasing force. "It sounds like the storm might be setting in for a while. It'll make it difficult for anyone to get up here. I suspect we've got some time, but we can't be too careful. We'll take turns keeping watch." The old man maneuvered himself to the edge of the couch. "Can you help me to that bed?" he asked, pointing into the front bedroom.

"Wait," Matt whispered as he fingered the gun. "Wait a minute." His voice strengthened, his look sharpened. "What the hell are you talking about? We can't sleep. We were almost killed today, there are two dead bodies out there, at least a half dozen more around the world, apparently you're next on someone's list...or maybe we are. You want to go to bed?"

Corny didn't respond for several seconds. He nodded, understanding their needs, but also understanding that if he didn't rest, if they all didn't get some rest, they would not survive the coming ordeal. He finally spoke softly.

"I'm exhausted, son. I haven't had any real sleep since three this morning, and before that, I hadn't slept for a week. I can barely see straight, my head and leg are killing me. I can see that you two are played out too. This will hold till morning. What we all need is rest, to regain our strength. Please, help me to that bed."

"Look, professor, Corny, I can't sleep yet," Hannah rejoined quickly, before Matt's frustration exploded into anger. "My mind is racing. We need something. Is there anything you can tell us or give us? Anything that will help us understand?"

Corny hesitated, eyed them thoughtfully, and then glanced again at the parchment bag. He pointed at it.

"Do you know what it says?"

"No..." Matt answered, hopeful. "That's the reason for all of this, isn't it? You said it yourself just a minute ago. It's why we're here." He glanced at Hannah who nodded her support.

"The truth is that it's only the beginning," Corny said. "But it's a good place to start. The translation is on my laptop upstairs. If you get it," he pointed to the spiral staircase, "I'll find it so you can read it. We'll discuss it tomorrow morning."

When Matt returned, he plugged in the power cord, started the computer, and turned it to Corny. Corny rubbed his weary eyes and waited for it to boot up. Finally, he clicked on a folder titled "Rosen," ran quickly through the files, and clicked on one titled "Carter Parchment." He scrolled past photocopies of the parchment and finally came to the translation.

"Here it is. But first, give me a hand to the bedroom."

Matt stood, eyes glued to the computer, desperate for its knowledge, but understanding of the old man's need. He helped Corny to his feet. The old man leaned against him, heavy despite his lean frame. Matt braced him and followed Hannah into the bedroom. They laid him on the bed, propped his leg up on a pillow and threw a blanket over him. Corny whispered some last thoughts.

"Your parchment turned our friend, Matt. We need to complete his journey."

Matt nodded.

"Go; wake me in three hours," Corny said. "I'll take the next watch."

MATT SAT IN front of the screen, opening an aisle of sight for Hannah who sat to his left. They were desperate to understand the document that had overturned their worlds.

The screen had "Translation of the Carter Parchment" centered in bold print. Without preamble, the translation started. Matt's grandfather's parchment, a document that, according to the most advanced testing methods available to the modern world, was 1100 years old, read:

To Phillip, my son;

It has been three years since I left you in your mother's arms. I continue to write you so that when you come of age, you may know your father and the duty to which he has committed. I have previously written of my travels in the service of our Lord and Savior, Jesus Christ, of the conquests in his name, through which we have freed holy lands and peoples living under the yolk of the Saracen, and of the duty you may likewise undertake when you reach manhood. I now write to describe a duty far nobler even than conquest in His name.

For many years, I have heard of the Cloth of Edessa. It is said that the king of Edessa during the time our Lord walked this earth, was stricken with leprosy. Now this king, named Abgar, had heard of the healings performed by our Lord, and, believing Jesus to be the Son of God, he sent an emissary to ask if our Lord would come to his kingdom and cure him. Jesus was so moved by the faith of a man who had never met him that he bid the emissary return with a message that He would send His own emissary to the king after his work in Jerusalem was complete. After our Lord's resurrection, His emissary did go to Abgar and cure him by simply holding up a linen cloth bearing our Lord's image upon it. Since Abgar's cure, the cloth has been revered, yet few outside Edessa have beheld it in the three hundred years since the Saracen took the kingdom. Some believed the cloth bore only our Lord's facial image, others the image of His entire crucified body. We now know the truth.

Upon reaching Edessa in our march across Mesopotamia, I, as commander of general Kourkouas's first troop, was enlisted to accompany our priest into the city to ensure that Edessa's emir hand over the real cloth rather than the fake he had first sent out of the city. It was upon this errand that I first witnessed the true nature of the cloth. Although I did not see the entire image, I saw that it bore much more than our Lord's face. I was blessed to touch the blood of our Lord's suffering from the crown of thorns and with that touch there came over me a profound peace. I knew I was in the presence of a gift from God.

During the long journey back to Constantinople to return the treasure to the heart of Christendom, I was given the task of protecting the cloth, which was carefully folded and sealed in a gold casket. Upon our arrival only two days ago, there was great joy and celebration in the city for word had preceded us of what we carried. But it was not until yesterday, as I sat on a dais with other commanders in the cathedral of Hagia Sophia that the full import of what we had done struck me.

The Archdeacon Gregory Referendarius, a tall, thin man with a powerful voice, conducted the mass in which the Cloth of Edessa was unveiled. In his sermon, he spoke forcefully but his words had little effect in the sight of the cloth, which mesmerized the assemblage. Yet, knowing it will be his words that will forever be remembered, I must relate that they did not do justice to the sight that met our eyes and touched our souls as the cloth was unfurled to its full 9 cubit length.

The archdeacon spoke of the facial image of our Lord and noted the blood and sweat that appear on the cloth, but he paid little attention to the rest of the image. Although he spoke of the form on the cloth, the only clear reference that the image contained more than our Lord's face was when he mentioned on two occasions that blood and liquid from the wound at our Lord's side also appeared.

The truth, my son, is that the cloth bears the true, full-body image of our crucified Lord, impressed upon the cloth by the power of his resurrection. I have participated in the rescue of this holy relic, and although the image of our Lord's suffering brings tears to the eyes of all who see it, my tears are those of joy at the wondrous gift He has left us as a true remembrance of His saving grace and the eternal life it brings. It is indeed the First Gospel of the good news of our Lord's glorious resurrection and ascension.

The duty I now know to be nobler than conquest in His name is to protect and spread this gospel and the peace it brings.

Take care of your mother until my return. She is, like you my son, in my thoughts all my days, and I long for the time when I will be with you.

Your Father
Andre Chartier,
Knight Commander of Emperor Romanus I
In the Service of Our Lord, Jesus Christ

CHAPTER THIRTY-EIGHT

"THEY CAN'T GET out, Peter. If our guys can't get in, they sure as hell can't get out."

Roland Barker spoke from his office in San Francisco. Barker was President of Archer Zanger Company, third largest investment banking conglomerate in the United States. He'd also replaced Peter Christian as Grand Commander of the Freemason's Western U.S. Jurisdiction after Christian became Sovereign Pontiff. Barker relished his exalted position in the brotherhood, for he was one of the true believers engaged in a battle for the survival of their way of life.

Barker followed Christian's lead and agreed with him on most matters relating to their cause, but he found it difficult to completely grasp his friend's current obsession.

"Where are our guys?" Christian asked icily.

"In Truckee; holed up in a motel until the storm blows over. It's bad up there, Peter."

"I don't give a shit how bad it is. We pay these guys too much to worry about that. We don't need excuses from them. I want the job done!"

Barker bristled. He was not accustomed to being spoken to as an underling. Yet he knew Christian's words were correct. Barker, in fact, spoke similar words when addressing the vast number of people under his control. He didn't care about excuses. There weren't any legitimate ones anyway. A person either got the job done or was terminated. That's it. No reason to consider alternatives.

"I'm with you Peter. I'll get it done," he said, even as the niggling question of its relevance played at the back of his mind.

Christian hung up with his own doubts. It was likely Carter and the bitch had no clue what they were dealing with. The reality is that he could probably talk Carter out of the parchment and that would be the end of it. The problem was Cornelius Crockett, the old bastard who knew too much. He wasn't certain Carter and the girl had made it to Crockett's cabin. His people had tracked the girl's cell phone, but that tracking ended just northeast of Truckee.

Christian had no clue whether Crockett was still alive. What he did know was that if the old professor had an opportunity to explain the importance of Rosen's work, the chances of it getting out multiplied. He needed to stop them, and, in truth, there was no harm in killing them—just three inconsequential lives taken to protect a system that worked just the way Christian and his friends needed it to work.

If Christian were ever to voice the other reason he wanted them dead, he would have to admit he was just damn agitated. They were minor players, little people who shouldn't even be an issue. Yet their knack for evading his attempts to get rid of the parchment was galling him.

Cornelius Crockett, Mathew Carter, and Hannah Melnyk were in his way. He wanted them gone. Then he could focus on the last step that would put this mess behind him and his brethren for good.

CHAPTER THIRTY-NINE

THE STORM EXPLODED after Corny went to bed. Winds surged out of the northeast spewing ice pellets and snow against the cabin walls in a rhythmic staccato of nature's rage. The fury was shocking at first, as if some otherworld force was intent on destroying the tiny cabin. But, as the intensity persisted unabated, the old professor slept soundly, and the cabin withstood the onslaught with the fire's blaze continuing to warm from the fireplace, the shock dissipated. Matt and Hannah focused on trying to understand the words in the parchment.

The first thing that struck Matt was the name of the knight who had written the letter to his son. It was a pre-Americanized version of his family name. His grandfather had regaled Matt and his sisters with stories of ancestors who'd been knights. His sisters had been entranced with stories of romance and chivalry, of maidens saved from evil lords, and life lived happily ever after. To Matt, they'd been stories of the courage of men on noble quests; but he hadn't thought of them in years.

Yet beyond the recognition of his great ancestor's name, nothing took hold in Matt or Hannah's minds. While the immediate significance of the parchment's carbon date might have been obvious to well-rested minds, both simply stumbled past the date until exhaustion finally took them and they fell asleep, never waking Corny for his watch, and sleeping through theirs.

The next morning, Matt woke to Boone's snuffling in his face. He was slouched in the old recliner next to the fireplace. His initial reaction was surprise at the wet nose and pleading brown eyes propped inches from his own. But understanding came quickly as he scanned the room and remembered that he was trapped in a nightmare that was real. He closed his eyes to gather himself for the battle that was yet to come, and when he opened them again, the dog waited patiently.

"How you feelin' Boone?" he whispered. The dog's tail slowly swept the pine floor. "Much better I guess. Wish I could say the same."

The dog stared.

"I guess you have to go out," Matt continued. He stretched the awkward kinks out of his body and pushed down the recliner's leg rest.

He sat for several seconds rubbing the sleep from his face before he looked up and saw Hannah's still slumbering figure on the couch. Her face was turned to him, its perfect contours caught between the shadows and flickering light of the fading fire and a new day. He shook his head, transfixed for several seconds with conflicting thoughts of hope and fear, until Boone laid his chin on Matt's thigh and broke the trance. He smiled, scratched the dog behind the ear, and stood.

"It's nice to see you moving around buddy." The dog pushed itself up gingerly onto all fours. "C'mon, let's get you outside."

Matt placed new logs onto the fireplace's dying embers, waited until one caught, and then led the limping dog to the front door. As he opened it, a surge of frigid air blasted into the room. He pushed the door back to a crack through which he peeked and was accosted by a scene of surreal beauty.

An unblemished white canvas was draped mid-shin high in the yard beyond the porch. The stark blanket covered the professor's would-be assassins and cleared all evidence of the previous day's macabre events. The evil had magically disappeared in a sparkling reflection of intense light from a sun now rising in a cloudless crystal blue sky. At the distant tree line, hoarfrost spun webs of refracted light that danced beneath the trees' swaying branches. Matt had never seen such white brilliance, nor had he ever experienced such complete silence, as if the world had died. There was not even a hint of sound from a once raging wind or any of the forest's winter creatures.

Matt slid through the opening, into the doorframe and looked to his right. A massive snowdrift spilled through the porch rail's wooden spindles and over the railing, onto the deck to a height that reached Matt's waist. From that point, the snow tapered down to about one-foot high in front of the door, and then to a thin carpet at the rail to Matt's left.

He held himself tightly against the cold as misty vapors rose with each exhalation, staring at a scene few had ever witnessed until he could take the cold no longer. He reached for his down jacket and the professor's gloves that hung on the hook next to the door. He slipped them on, rubbed warmth into his arms and hands, and then glanced down at Boone whose nose protruded through the opening.

"Let's figure out how to get you out there, boy."

A snow shovel was propped against the exterior cabin wall to his left. He eyed the task of digging a path for the dog with little excitement. It was something his beach and occasional snow skiing lifestyle hadn't prepared him for. But the sudden pressure of Boone's body against his leg moved Matt to his task.

"Okay buddy, I'll see what I can do."

Matt began shoveling. Within seconds he'd opened a path directly in front of the door. He coaxed Boone into the space and closed the door behind them before he dug an opening to his left, toward the south rail. The dog limped that way to relieve himself as Matt started down the steps and into the yard. He quickly got the hang of his work and found he relished it. He lost himself in the physicality of it, and the horror of the past days seemed to drift away. Trickles of moisture ran down his spine and forehead, and adrenalin coursed through him with the excitement of the work. It wasn't until the cabin door opened and Hannah smiled at him that he came back to the moment.

"Wow," she said jokingly. "You get to work early, don't you?"

"Wasn't my choice," he said and pointed at Boone. "He needed to go."

They eyed each other for several seconds, wistful silence the only communication.

"You okay?" Matt finally asked. "Did you sleep?"

She nodded.

"Is he awake?" Matt asked, motioning beyond her.

She nodded again. "For a while now. He told me how to make his special brand of scrambled eggs." She laughed. "He throws everything in. I hope you're hungry."

Matt's stomach rumbled on cue. He started toward the steps. "Is he okay?"

She shrugged. "He's a tough old guy. I think he's going to be fine."

Matt eyed her hopefully as he ascended the steps.

"He's anxious to talk to us, Matt," she said.

———

"WE DON'T GET it." Matt shrugged. "We read the translation a half dozen times, and didn't see anything that would make it dangerous."

Corny nodded, dropping his eyes to his steaming mug of coffee. He'd slept soundly and awoken refreshed, albeit still in pain and moving gingerly.

"The parchment was the start of Samuel's journey to death," Corny sighed. "He had the copy you allowed him to make, translated by Stanley Cavendish—our friend from Oxford—several years ago. Samuel had been using the dating of the parchment as a teaching tool for a few years when students started asking him what the parchment said. That's when he contacted Stan and sent him a copy. Stan was an expert in ancient Greek, the language of literacy during the middle ages, and apparently the language of your parchment." Corny nodded to Matt.

"Well, because of Stan's workload at the time, it took him several months to complete the translation." He leaned forward to make his next point. "As soon as Samuel saw it, his world, and ours, changed."

"Why?" Matt asked testily. "I don't see anything that would change anyone's mind about whether the Shroud was real."

Corny nodded, glanced down at his cup, seeking a starting point. Finally, he looked up again.

"Your parchment was dated by the same method used on the Shroud." Matt and Hannah nodded. "The parchment's test resulted in a date of between 900 and 1000 A.D. The Shroud's date, you'll recall, was 250 to 500 years later. Assuming the parchment was referring to the Shroud, one of the dates had to be wrong. Samuel believed he knew which one it was, but he felt compelled to dig deeper."

Corny glanced from Matt to Hannah inviting a response. They nodded, but said nothing. He continued.

"All experts on carbon dating were aware of attempts by 'Shroud-freaks' to discredit the carbon dating of the cloth. Samuel understood the best argument they'd come up with was potentially legitimate—enough to be considered anyway. However, it would require another test with a new piece of the cloth for comparison. You see the argument was that the original piece tested was tainted.

"In January of 1988, the eight centimeters by one centimeter piece that was cut from the cloth was taken from the lower left hand corner of the foot end of the cloth's frontal image. That small piece was then cut in half with one half then being cut into three, one for each of the laboratories performing the carbon tests. The tested pieces were tiny." He spread his thumb and forefinger about a quarter inch apart.

"The remaining half was left in Turin and is kept at the Shroud's cathedral to this day. Each of the labs chosen for the carbon test, one in Zurich, one in Oxford, and the third at Samuel's school in Arizona, tested their respective pieces and came to the same conclusion: the cloth was manufactured sometime between 1260 and 1390 A.D. It therefore could not possibly have been the cloth in which the crucified Christ was buried around 30 A.D."

"So where was the supposed taint?" asked Hannah.

Corny leaned forward to strike a conspiratorial pose but grimaced with the pain in his leg. Leaning back again, he winced, rubbed the leg, and finally looked up. He caught a deep breath and continued.

"It turns out there were several arguments posited, but the one Shroud believers seemed to put the most stock in was that the cloth was repaired several times during its history, and that the piece tested came from one of these repair sites. Apparently, in the centuries after Christ's resurrection, the cloth was unfolded and handled for exhibition thousands of times. When so handled, it was gripped at its edges," he lifted an open napkin from the table and gripped it with closed fists at its edges to illustrate, "so people could see the image in the center of the cloth. Over those centuries, those edges naturally became frayed, thus necessitating repairs to prevent the unraveling of the entire cloth. The cloth was repaired several times by interweaving new linen into those frayed edges. The tiny piece that was tested in 1988 was made up of thirteenth or fourteenth century linen from those repairs."

"Okay," Matt started, holding his hand up to slow Corny down. "So Professor Rosen knows of the 'taint' argument but doesn't think enough of it to do anything until he receives the translation of my parchment?"

Corny nodded.

"Why? If he's so concerned about it after he reads the parchment, why didn't he pursue it before?"

"Even though the argument of taint was a possibility, carbon date experts were never given credible evidence that would suggest the test results needed to be revisited. They viewed the possibility as so remote that it was a move of desperation by true believers rather than anything that should really be considered. The parchment changed things for Samuel. You see, your parchment was the first credible evidence he'd seen that suggested the cloth existed prior to the dates determined in the carbon test."

"Wait, didn't Professor Rosen consider the possibility that the parchment referred to something totally different—something other than the Shroud?" Matt asked.

Corny nodded. "Sure he did, but that wasn't Samuel's issue when he read the translation. Whether the parchment referred to the Shroud was irrelevant. He was more concerned about the integrity of the original tests. What he had in front of him was a writing he knew he'd dated properly, which potentially supported an argument that the carbon date for the Shroud was wrong. His first interest then was to see if there was any other evidence that could suggest the same. So he dug deeper, not to prove the Shroud was the burial cloth of Christ, but rather to determine if the argument that the carbon test was wrong had any merit. He started a search of historical records to see if there was anything that would lead a reasonable person to believe the original test was wrong. His intent was to put that question to bed, and then, if he was so inclined, to determine if there was any other explanation for the cloth to which the parchment referred."

Corny winced again as he adjusted his position.

"What he found was that the Shroud's carbon date was wrong," he whispered, as if the entire affair was still a mystery. "But, more importantly, he learned this linen was the actual burial cloth of Jesus Christ…and the image upon it could only have come from a burst of intense light and energy that accompanied the man's resurrection from the dead, searing his image onto the cloth."

CHAPTER FORTY

ARTHUR CANTWELL, OPINION writer for the Wall Street Journal's Weekend Edition, came down hard on Peter Christian. Cantwell wasn't what anyone would refer to as a religious person. In fact, he was a dyed-in-the-wool agnostic capitalist. But he knew a story when he saw one. His senses were attuned to controversy, particularly controversy that would sell his paper. Christian had given him a tremendous opening in front of a national television audience the previous Wednesday. He wasn't going to let it slip away.

The thing Art Cantwell didn't expect as he finished the piece that flowed so easily from him was that he would believe what he wrote.

"Peter Christian: 'There is no God.'"

It was an incredible moment; a moment of surreal theater: the incomparable Peter Christian, one of the world's leading voices on matters financial, raised his hands and shouted at a worldwide audience that there is no God…and he nearly started a fight with a priest in the process. It appears Christian has suddenly appointed himself the clearinghouse for religious and spiritual belief in this country. Are we really ready to let that pass?

Shame on Mr. Christian for losing his legendary cool and succumbing to the lure of hubris, stepping away from his platform in an attempt to influence society on matters of which he has no expertise. We hoped he was better than that.

Perhaps we business-minded capitalists should start paying heed to those who speak from the pulpit lest our society revert back to the financial class and caste systems that existed during the dark ages. These were times of extreme blue blood, upper crust disregard of anything and anyone below their inherited station. These were times of hatred among the classes, when a middle class that might propel a society forward was not even a consideration. These were times of dysfunction and suffering, yet it appears we face them again.

Perhaps Christian has opened our eyes to the true result of his philosophy—a society where money is god and nothing else matters, whether it be the understanding of those less fortunate or compassion for the needs of common society. Is that really how we want our society to define itself?

"SON OF A bitch!" Peter Christian threw down the Wall Street Journal. His people had assured him they'd spun the story away from the "god thing." Clearly they hadn't considered that the Wall Street Journal, the bastion of capitalism, needed spinning and would be the one to deliver the blow.

Peter Christian feared no person; he feared no institution; he feared no god. He was master of a world he created by the sweat of his brow and the superiority of his intellect. His acolytes loved or feared him because of the power, wealth, and influence he wielded; they loved or feared him because of the strength and composure he exhibited; and they loved or feared him because they knew that he could make or destroy them—any of them...all of them.

No one would openly challenge him.

Yet Arthur Cantwell of the Wall Street Journal had done just that. He'd chosen to go his own way, and Christian's first response was anger—that of boiling blood and thirst for vengeance. But, as rational thought took hold, he knew the worst thing he could do was to lash out.

Who would care if he said there was no god?

Priests, rabbis, and other clerics who made their livings spewing their faiths would complain, but who in the real world would give a damn? Most people didn't follow any real faith anyway. Sure, the majority of Americans "believed" in some superior being—a god if you will—but very few really practiced a faith, and those who did rarely took it beyond their periodic "Sabbath" observances. Certainly, no one of any means and intellect gave it credible consideration. Despite the fact that one of the requirements of the Freemasons was that members acknowledge a belief in a supreme being, none of his brothers took it beyond the mere acknowledgement. That, in fact, was the reason for their great success. None was shackled by the ludicrous demands of religious faith.

When Peter Christian became a Mason, he acknowledged the belief the brotherhood's rules required. After all, he'd faked such belief his entire youth, until the day his oppressively demanding religious mother died when he was in high school. She'd been a passenger of his drunken father, and in one fell swoop, he'd lost them both. Shockingly, even to him, his most intense feeling was of relief, at least in the case of his mother. As for his father, he felt sadness for a life wasted in the hell of a horrifically restrictive household, and he vowed it would never happen to him.

As with all other Masons, Peter was never required to name the divinity in which he believed. Had he been required to do so, he would most likely have taken the stance of the fraternity's most renowned leader, the man whose statue graces Judiciary Square in Washington D.C. to this day.

Albert Pike, a Freemason sovereign grand commander from an earlier age, the one who first tried to take on the mantel of Supreme Pontiff, expressed his belief that it was Lucifer, "the Light-Bearer and Son of the Morning," who should perhaps be revered. And why not, Peter Christian thought, since none who followed Lucifer worried about the restrictive rules of faith. The real light was in the unrestricted pursuit of a man's goals, not in the controlled and tortured struggle to achieve some fanciful belief in an afterlife with wings and harps. That was the whole point of the Freemasons.

To be free to think and act as one felt rather than to pay homage to rules and restrictions of some man-made government or religion interested only in its own survival. Lucifer would applaud those who eschewed rules. He would stand with those who pursued their greatness untethered.

Had Peter Christian been required to name his supreme being, it would have been Lucifer. But the naming had never been demanded.

Christian's truth was that there was no such thing as a supreme being. He knew it. He was an atheist, but not of the old order—one who sat passively scoffing at the idiots who wasted their time imagining "the next life" while they struggled through this one. He was of the modern thinkers, the "new secularists," who understood action had to be taken.

The old order believed the concept of "God" would eventually disappear from an advanced society because growing prosperity, wealth, and station would eliminate the psychological "need" for a god. Once a person reached a level of pecuniary well-being, he would no longer need the mythical father in the sky. He'd achieve his goals on his own.

American history exemplified the inexorable march from immersion in faith by masses struggling for survival during the early days of the country, to the occasional church visits and "never talk about religion" attitude of the modern day. There was no question that the wealth, fame, and power of the individual in America had reached heights never before seen in history.

Peter Christian knew that growth of individual power and fortune was directly and inversely related to the crumbling of a religious mindset. When people focused on a promise of an afterlife in exchange for compassion, giving, and love of one's neighbor in this life, they moved away from the material world, and the engines that drove wealth and power suffered. On the other hand, as people moved further from the belief in the hereafter, they inevitably moved to beliefs in the "now" and the satisfaction of their immediate desires. That was the world in which Christian and his cohorts thrived.

The old-order atheists' vision of a society without religion was coming to pass. The problem was that it was happening too slowly, and waiting for the inevitable was not an option. Peter Christian needed to speed the process, particularly in light of the new challenge: the recruitment of scientists to the cause of a god.

The world never had proof of a god's existence or of an afterlife. "Faith" had always been simply that: a belief in something no one could prove. Clearly if some god appeared and announced his existence, proof would exist. But that had never happened. People of faith, to the extent any still existed, relied on ancient writings. These were woefully inadequate in preventing the society's move to secularism, especially in the face of the modern world's many distractions. And until Professor Samuel Rosen's work came to Peter Christian's attention, only subtle efforts were required to continue pushing secularism's agenda forward. Rosen's work changed that.

The destruction of the professor and his work was a necessary step in the process of secularization. It was that simple. And for those who chose to challenge the process, as Arthur Cantwell had blatantly done, there would be consequences.

CHAPTER FORTY-ONE

CARDINAL ANDREW METZINGER, resplendent in his robes of office, stood over the corpse of an old man, the top of his head gone in spatters of blood and detritus spread as far as the eye could see. At Metzinger's feet lay a weapon—a massive handgun—with which the evil deed had been done. He turned, eyes wide with fear, soul tortured…and there, in the near distance lay another body, another old man, next to a woman, their bodies charred beyond recognition, yet Metzinger recognized them; and then closer, another body, at the steps of his parents' home; and others, hundreds, thousands of others spread across the continents, across the globe. He turned away…away from the death…away from the suffering. But he could not escape them, and then he saw the cloth, a thin linen bearing the image of his Lord, but it was aflame—burning to ash as his left hand clutched the torch that destroyed it.

Cardinal Metzinger bolted awake, tangled in bedclothes soaked by the sweat of fear and anxiety. His air came in strangled gasps as his eyes darted around the room. But all he saw were shadows cast by furniture and the sporadic movement of air-blown curtains in the moonlit night. It took long moments, but slowly he calmed himself and his breathing came easier. And he began to wonder. Was it he who would bring the world to its destruction? Would it be because of his failure to stop those who had betrayed him and the Holy Father? Could he yet do something to prevent it?

Metzinger turned to the clock on his bed stand. It read 3:45 a.m. He closed his eyes, nodded weakly, collecting himself further and acknowledging that his journey was only a few short hours away.

He threw his legs over the side of the bed and dropped his head into his still moist palms. Wouldn't it be better, he found himself thinking, if the Shroud had never existed? Wouldn't it be best if it had been destroyed?

"Lord, please guide me in this troubled time," he whispered as he stood. "Please show me the path you need me to take."

He turned, stood next to the bed for an instant, and then dropped to his knees. He lifted his eyes to the crucifix hanging on the wall, and he began to pray.

CHAPTER FORTY-TWO

THE FRIGID EARLY morning gave way to an afternoon of steady sun arcing through a cloudless sky. They'd talked the entire morning, and now Corny stood at the kitchen window gazing over the sun speckled snow.

"The main highway should be open, Matt. They're working the side roads, now, I'd guess. I expect Sage Hen will be navigable sometime tonight at the latest."

Matt nodded pensively, thoughts of their discussion and the trials he and Hannah still had to face running through his head. He turned to Corny.

"That's good," he said. "That means we can get you and Boone out of here, to the hospital in Truckee before anyone else comes."

"No," Corny said softly. "You and Hannah need to move at first light tomorrow. Boone and I will stay here. If no one knows we spoke, they won't come after you. We'll hold them and at least give you a fighting chance of getting your parchment to Father Roberts in L.A."

Corny's reasoning was sound, as far as that went. The obvious problem was the likely result if Corny stayed behind.

"Let's just go straight to the police. We can get to them in Sacramento."

"You really think our friends haven't gotten to them already. They were able to get to the police in Tucson and San Francisco. No." Corny shook his head. "You've got to get your parchment to safety with the priest, before we talk to any police."

Corny had made up his mind. He eyed Matt as he leaned on his makeshift crutch.

"You should clear a path from my garage down to the road, Matt. Take my ATV and work off some of your youthful energy. Make sure the blade's sitting at a 45-degree angle toward the downslope."

Matt nodded grimly. He wouldn't give up his attempts to cajole Corny into joining them in their escape, but whether he could convince him or not, the path would have to be cleared. He set to the task: first shoveling his own SUV out of the snow, starting the vehicle after several attempts, and then clearing the gravel driveway using Corny's ATV to push the hardening snow off the path, through the trees, and down the slope.

While he worked, Matt tried to get his mind around the facts and images they'd discussed continuously since breakfast.

That Matt's parchment was the catalyst for Professor Rosen's search for the truth about the Shroud was undeniable. It set him on a seven-year quest leading to findings that would have shocked the professor had a colleague made them instead of him. Rosen found historical evidence of a cloth having characteristics similar to the Shroud dating back long before the carbon dates. He also found records of the cloth having been repaired several times. The problem was that none of the scientists responsible for the carbon dating had ever looked at that evidence. If they had, they most certainly would have questioned their carbon results and dug deeper.

The historical record existed long before anyone had ever heard of the Carter Parchment. Byzantine General John Kourkouas had indeed returned the Cloth of Edessa, as it was then known, to Constantinople. In celebration thereof, the Archdeacon Gregory Referendarius had conducted a mass in which he described the blood and figure of the crucified Christ on the cloth, all as related in the parchment. And although historians viewed King Abgar's cure as legend, historical evidence in writings, icons, and artifacts establish the Shroud's existence to at least the sixth century, with legally probative evidence taking it back to the time of the crucifixion and alleged resurrection of Christ.

Furthermore, Rosen learned that every test on the Shroud performed by noted scientists in their respective fields established that the cloth came from the area around Jerusalem during the time of Christ, and was indeed a burial cloth bearing the image of a man crucified in the manner of Christ's crucifixion as related in the biblical gospels. In fact, the only test that told a different story was the carbon test.

Rosen became convinced the carbon test was wrong. So he made it his duty to find a way to get to the true date, which he believed would corroborate every single other piece of credible evidence: that the cloth was indeed from the time of Christ. That's when he went after acquiring a new piece from the previously untouched field of the cloth.

"He somehow managed to get that new piece." Corny shook his head with a half-smile of respect.

"But even if he got another piece," Matt questioned, "and he proved the cloth was older than the carbon results, it's just a cloth with a picture on it, isn't it? There've got to be millions of pictures, icons, paintings, and other representations of Christ dating back to the beginning of the Christian era. What's so important about this image that someone would want to kill for it?"

"That's the point isn't it, Matt?" Corny nodded. "If it was a mere painting or some other form of human art, Samuel wouldn't have risked his life to continue his studies of it. After he reviewed all the evidence, he concluded that the image could only have come from some cosmic or divine event."

Matt and Hannah shook their heads doubtfully and stared at Corny.

Corny grabbed a manila file from a stack on the floor next to him. He extracted two large cardboard backed photographs and pushed the first one in front of Matt and Hannah.

"This is a photograph of the Shroud as it can be seen by the naked eye," he said.

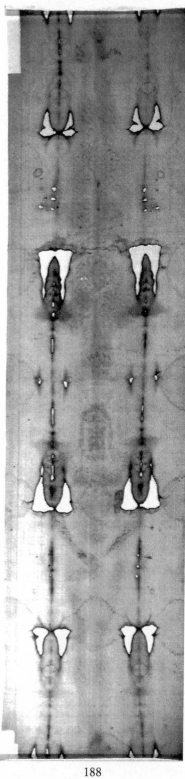

Photographic image of the Shroud of Turin

They glanced at the sepia colored photographic image but found it hard to make anything of it other than a number of brown splotches and the faint outlines of a man. They looked at Corny. He then slid the second photograph in front of them.

"This is a copy of the photographic negative of the cloth," he said. Hannah and Matt stared at the second photo. Corny continued. "This was a negative that came from a photo taken on May 28, 1898 by Italian photographer, Secondo Pia. Pia was commissioned to take the first-ever official photograph of the Shroud. After snapping his photo, he scurried back to his darkroom to develop the plates. As the process was unfolding in the negative that would be used to create the Shroud's photograph, a shocking thing appeared. The negative image actually depicted a positive image of the entire body, front and back, of the man on the cloth.

"Please look closely at the negative image," Corny said, pointing again. "Note how clear the features and elements are as compared to the actual photo." Corny took a deep breath. "What do you see?"

Matt and Hannah's expressions of idle curiosity morphed quickly, first to surprise, and then to recognition. Hannah looked up first.

"I see a man," she whispered. "A man at peace, it seems; but a man who has suffered terrible pain."

Corny nodded.

"This is no mere artist's rendering of what someone hoped Christ looked like," Corny said. "This is the actual full body, front and back image of Jesus Christ before anyone ever knew anything about photography."

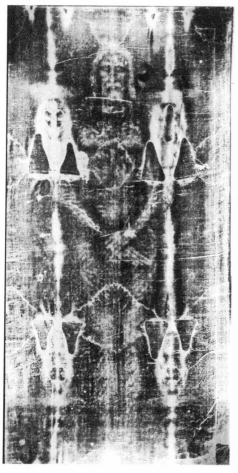

Negative of
photographic
image of the
Shroud of Turin

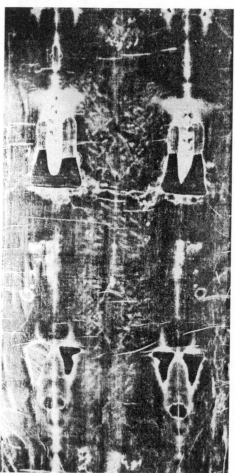

CHAPTER FORTY-THREE

"HE WAS JUST under six feet tall," Corny said. "He weighed approximately one hundred seventy pounds. Although he was lean, you can see he was well-muscled—fit, even by today's standards. But, as you were also able to discern, Hannah, he suffered mightily." Corny leaned forward to scrutinize the backside negative image. "Look," he said pointing. "You see these marks that look like barbell stripes on his back, buttocks, and legs?" They nodded. "There are over one hundred of these, some extending onto his chest, stomach, and the front of his legs. These are from the scourging the soldiers administered to him with something they called a flagrum."

As Hannah and Matt looked up quizzically, he explained.

"It was a Roman whip that had three leather tails or straps," he hesitated as he began scanning through something on his computer. He found an image, and turned it toward them.

What they saw was a fearsome looking apparatus with three long leather straps sticking out of a thick leather-wrapped handle. At the end of each strap was an inch-long dumbbell-shaped metal pellet tied in the middle and weighted for debilitating impact.

"This poor man was stripped naked, forced to stand shackled to a post, and whipped mercilessly thirty to forty times. The savagery of his torturers can be seen clearly in these marks where the metal dumbbells struck and tore flesh, leaving behind these dark pressure and puncture wounds."

Matt and Hannah grimaced as they viewed the painful results of each stroke.

"Now look at his face," Corny said. "Do you see the swelling of the nose, cheeks and eye? These are from beatings after his arrest and again after the scourging."

"And these," pointing to stains on the cloth at the forehead and hairline on the frontal image and on the hair on the backside image. "This is blood from the crown of thorns. The Roman soldiers didn't just place a simple circlet bearing a few thorns on his head. The bleeding was extensive. The 'crown' was really a group of branches laced together in a thick ball with an opening in the center. Each branch bore long spiky thorns that were driven into his flesh until his blood flowed." He hesitated a second, then whispered, "The pain must have been unbearable."

He stopped and leaned back, wiping moisture from his eyes. Finally, he leaned forward again, a tortured frown on his face.

"Far worse was yet to come for this poor man. If you look closely, you can see abrasions at his knees, shoulders, arms, his entire body. But the worst of it comes from the crucifixion itself. We can see blood flows on the back of his visible wrist and the top of his forearms. At his feet, the blood flow is from wounds at the sides of his ankles.

"The soldiers laid him on a wooden cross; then they used heavy mallets to drive six-inch metal spikes through the flesh and bone of each of his wrists. After that they positioned his feet on either side of the down-post and hammered these huge spikes through the bones on the sides of each ankle, and into the post.

Corny tried to gather himself. He pointed to a stain—white on the negative image; dark on the positive image—appearing at the figure's side just below the right breast.

"Finally, as if they hadn't done enough, we see blood from a wound created by the spear a soldier thrust into him as he hung crucified."

Corny sat back quietly, spent. Hannah and Matt continued to closely view the photographs, each lost in their own thoughts of the horrific suffering endured by the man depicted on the cloth. Matt shook his head.

"This is...unbelievable," he stammered softly. "I...I never understood the brutality."

Corny nodded. "Yes. And the worst part...the worst thing is that this poor man knew before his torture began that it was going to happen. Every wound. Every stroke. Every spike. He knew it, and he accepted that he would suffer it."

CHAPTER FORTY-FOUR

"IT'S CLEAR TO the lake," the brutish man grunted eyeing his three companions from beneath a heavy black brow. "They say Sage Hen Road is passable, but it should be avoided until noon tomorrow. This warming will make it less dangerous." A thick-lipped smile turned his face. "We go now."

The man was called George. He and his partners were of Arabic descent, specifically recruited because of that descent. Their American names were chosen only for superficial cover. Anyone seeing George, Fred, Herman, and Lou Brown, "American brothers" on a ski trip to Lake Tahoe, would know they weren't what they purported to be. That was the point.

They'd been recruited and trained as assassins specifically because of the way they looked and spoke. That potential witnesses would label them "Muslim fanatics," and that blame for deeds attributed to them would be cast on those viewed as evil by much of the world, was what their employer wanted.

The four men had little difficulty with any of this. Their pay was beyond their wildest dreams, and they knew American prejudice would prevent even the most conscientious witness from giving any meaningful description of them. By the time any witness had finished describing "fanatical Muslims" to the authorities, they'd have already disappeared back into their lives, and no one would be the wiser.

"Why does it have to be snow?" grumbled Lou, the oldest and stoutest of the four. He stared out the motel window at the neon lit remains of the day. "I hate this shit."

"What the hell do you have to worry about, fat boy?" laughed Fred, tall and needle thin. "At least you have some meat on you to keep you warm. I," he motioned theatrically to his body, "have nothing but muscle, and muscle will not keep me warm."

Herman grunted a short laugh as George eyed Lou.

"We should wait till tomorrow, as the report suggests," Lou said, ignoring Fred's quip. He turned away from the glass, his heavy jowls sagging into a scowl. "There is no hurry. If they are up there now, they will be there in the morning. I don't trust weather we don't know, especially at night."

George nodded. He then spoke with grave deference to Lou. "I understand your concern, brother. I like this weather no more than you. But we will not wait. In the morning, chances of detection increase, and another storm is coming. We move now and we will return before morning."

George lifted his Glock .357 Sig from the table and tucked it into the back of his pants. He scanned the other three.

"We go now!"

CHAPTER FORTY-FIVE

MATT LEANED AGAINST the post absently staring at the moon high in the eastern sky. The evening air bit at his lungs and exposed skin, but he felt no discomfort. A hot shower and hardy meal of Corny's pot roast had eased his tension and provided the nourishment to think clearly. The warmth he now felt came not only from his flannel, denim, and down, but from a surprising new understanding taking hold of his consciousness.

"How could Rosen conclude the image came from some burst of energy? How could anyone prove that? How does he know someone didn't paint the image?" Matt had fired these at Corny in a final attempt at devil's advocacy.

"The main argument against the Shroud's authenticity is that the image was painted," Corny said. "And although one prominent, now deceased, microscopic analyst believed paint appears on the cloth, he never saw or touched the cloth. The vast majority of evidence establishes that there is no paint or other human coloring-medium anywhere on it. Tests by numerous experts who have seen and touched the cloth reflect that there is no such medium and that what appears to be blood on the cloth is indeed so." Corny eyed his companions and raised a forefinger. "But put the issue of scientific tests aside and let your own senses and sensibilities guide you to the truth."

He pointed at the two photos.

"What we have here is a perfectly depicted three-dimensional image. Look how lifelike it is. Now, recall your studies of history. Never, at any time between the dawn of man and the time of Leonardo da Vinci in the late 1400's, did any artist even come close to painting the perfect human dimensions that appear on the Shroud. And, even with the great artists like Da Vinci, none ever captured the living reality that you see on the Shroud. No one in the 1300's or earlier could have painted something as remarkably lifelike as the image we see of the man on the Shroud."

He paused to let his point sink in.

"But don't stop there. Remember," pointing to the sepia colored image of the man, "Photography involving a negative didn't even exist until the early 1800's. No one of any repute has ever suggested that anyone from the Middle Ages had even an inkling of an understanding of a 'negative' image. Yet you can see with your own eyes that a negative image of a man is what appears on the cloth."

Corny shook his head as his hand rested lightly on the photograph.

"No Matt, despite the naysayers, this image was not created by man's hand. There is no paint or other artist's material anywhere on the Shroud, nor was there the knowledge, understanding, or skill available to anyone in the Middle Ages to create such a wonder. Truth be told, there is no such knowledge, understanding, or skill in existence today that would enable anyone to duplicate the Shroud."

Corny sat back as Matt and Hannah looked up. Again Corny shook his head.

"Science can tell us much about the physical world. It can tell us much about the Shroud. What it can't tell us is how the image of the crucified man we three have viewed today appears on the cloth. Samuel determined, through his scientific and deductive reasoning, that the only way the perfectly proportioned, three-dimensional image of this man could have gotten on the cloth was through a burst of energy from the being of the crucified man; a burst that seared the image onto only the topmost fibers of the cloth. There is not even a hint of the image bleeding through to fibers below the top fibers. Our friend concluded it could only have happened at the instant of this man's divine resurrection from the dead."

Matt didn't hear anyone exit the cabin behind him.

"Matt?" Hannah said and lightly touched his arm folded in front of him as he leaned against the post.

Matt jumped, startled.

"Oh, I'm sorry. I didn't mean to scare you," Hannah said. She stepped back.

Matt shook his head and smiled.

"I must have been off in some other world," he said lightly. "Something that seems to be happening a lot lately."

"Are you okay?" she asked.

"Yeah, under the circumstances I guess." He turned to her. The only light was the yellow filtering through the gauze curtains of the cabin and the bright white of the moon reflecting off grounded snow. He spoke softly.

"It's amazing isn't it? I never gave any of this much thought. I guess I just felt it wasn't real…like something from The Lord of the Rings or something."

Hannah nodded.

"Did you ever think about this—not the Shroud maybe, but about God, and, well, about God having anything to do with our lives?"

Hannah nodded again. "I'm Catholic, Matt. I was raised Catholic. My family's pretty strong that way, and I, well, I've always had a personal relationship with Christ." She shrugged. "Despite all the insanity we've been dealing with, my belief gives me hope."

"My family's Catholic, too. I suppose you could see that in my dad," he laughed awkwardly. Matt looked wistfully into the moonlit shadows; he rested his hands on the rail.

"So what are you thinking?" Hannah asked.

"I guess…it's real," Matt shook his head, dropped his eyes to his hands. "It's real. I can't come up with any other answer. The Shroud's the real deal; I know it is. It's…it's like he left us this gift, something that people would talk about, something maybe that would make us understand the truth if we'd only stop and think about it. This cloth actually touched him, Hannah. It… it covered Christ's body. It's real," he finally repeated in a whisper.

He looked at her sheepishly as if he might be going crazy. She nodded and smiled, the moon dancing in her eyes.

"I know," she said. "I've seen a lot of relics, ancient documents, artifacts, and archaeological finds, but I've never seen anything like this. All those others are so clearly man-made, almost childlike in their simplicity and lack of fine skill, and then we get this…this perfectly delivered, photographic…" she shrugged thoughtfully, "…image of a man who lived 2000 years ago. There's something special here, Matt."

Hannah hugged herself against the cold, wisps of mist puffing from her mouth.

Matt turned to her. He caught a faint whiff of soap and shampoo. Though not the fragrance that had intoxicated him when they'd met outside Captain Gutierrez's office, the waves of warmth from her closeness carried her scent to his brain.

"Are you cold?" he whispered.

She nodded slightly.

"Do you want to go in?" he asked.

She shook her head.

He reached for her cautiously, his eyes searching hers for permission. She didn't hesitate. She stepped into him; he pulled her against him, the warmth of the two bodies suddenly mingling. Shivers ran up Matt's spine.

"We've got to protect it, Hannah," Matt stammered hoarsely. He felt her head turn up against his chest. He looked down. She pushed away slightly, her eyes locked on his.

Matt bent to her, pulled her to him, kissed her lightly, and then more intensely as her mouth opened to him and they melted into each other.

Matt's head swam with the excitement of her; his body reacted immediately.

They crushed each other in grips of ravenous desperation for several seconds until a sudden, deep-throated roar startled them out of their clinch.

They turned and caught the shadow of a man skittering through the trees at the forest's edge and they knew their killers had arrived.

CHAPTER FORTY-SIX

"SHIT!" CURSED LOU Brown for the thousandth time, as he trudged through knee-deep snow at the edge of the wood. His boxy frame and lead-heavy legs made his progress slow and ponderous, the main reason his lighter brother, Fred, was tasked with getting around to the front of the cabin.

Lou leaned against the thick trunk of an old oak to catch his breath before he would have to make his move across the clearing, past the SUV to the side of the cabin. A warm yellow glow beckoned him from somewhere beyond the room closest to his vantage. It reached to the window nearest him, but died at the gauze curtain. Sporadic human shadows flitted through that distant light making it clear that at least one person was in the house.

Lou marked his partner's progress through the wood's edge toward the front of the cabin. He dropped his head and gritted his teeth after he caught Fred's lanky silhouette prancing gingerly through the trees.

"Son of a bitch," he thought. "They're going to see you."

He followed Fred's progress until he disappeared into a thick stand of pines without obvious detection before he began to breathe easy again. He then checked his watch, noting that they had five minutes before they were to make their coordinated assault on the front of the cabin. He glanced back to the cleared gravel drive up which they had come moments before. At the bottom of that drive, George and Herman waited to cut off any escape attempt. Lou wondered absently why George hadn't sent the younger Herman up the trail through the snow. Probably because they knew Lou was the best of them in a close quarters skirmish, assuming, of course, his heavy body could survive the trek up to the cabin.

Lou took another quick sweep of the structure to assure himself there was no readily identifiable rear entry to the house. Other than the garage, there was none. If their intended victims were able to make it out the garage, they wouldn't get far with George and Herman waiting below. Lou took one more deep breath before he started across the snow-covered clearing to the side of the cabin.

———————

FRED MOVED LIGHTLY through the trees, smirking at the thought of his heavy compatriot's discomfort. Fred didn't care for the snow anymore than Lou, but he wasn't letting the man know that. In fact, he wanted to make Lou think he had no problem with it. It wasn't that he didn't like Lou, nor did he have any particular interest in showing him up. In fact, he liked the man, perhaps more than his other two companions. Lou was, after all, a generally friendly guy, and he was definitely a good man to have on your side in a tight spot.

Lou would be where he was supposed to be, and never falter for any reason. More important, if things got dicey, there was no one better than the old veteran to come up with ways to turn things around. So, it wasn't that Fred had any desire to humiliate Lou; it was more a fact of who Fred was. He was handsome, nimble, a comic at appropriate times, and he was damn good at what he did. A little fun helped make his business less stressful, particularly since he was able to put the fun aside when the time for performance arrived.

As Fred maneuvered through the thicket of pines in front of the cabin, the time for performance came. The silly smile disappeared. He crouched behind a thick trunk and peered toward the cabin. He caught the shadowed figures of two people standing close together to the far side of the porch. They were silhouetted against a moon that was too bright for him to make an undetected run to the cabin. He glanced back toward Lou's position and saw his partner emerge from concealment and run in a crouch to the cabin's west wall.

Good, he thought. He'll catch them before they have a chance to get inside.

And then he heard movement behind him.

———————

OLD ONE EYE had caught the scent. It had been clinging to the air for some time. Although it was faint now, he still had it. It was the scent of death; and it was the scent of food. For a creature starving because he was too old to keep up and too weak to fight his feral brethren, the smell of death was welcome. All he had to do was find its source before it was too late.

Old One Eye first caught the scent the day before. He'd tried to follow it then but the savage storm made it difficult. The scent seemed to come and go as the wind and snow swirled. But he'd caught it again as the day warmed. And he'd followed it to this point. It was out there somewhere. He hunkered down on his haunches to catch his breath and try to discern what danger lay between him and the meal he knew was close. But so crazed with hunger had he become, that danger really played little part in his instincts. He was exhausted. He should be with others of his ilk, lying in hibernation, his natural state at this time of year, but he couldn't. He needed to eat, and he needed it now.

As his head hung low and he gasped for air, he caught another scent. It was human, a living human. Under normal circumstances, he would have moved away, wary of the evil creature his kind had come to fear. But his hunger was too great for him to be wary, his instinct for survival too overpowering for him to fear. Old One Eye knew only that his meal was in jeopardy. He lifted his head, sniffed the air, and saw movement. A human suddenly stepped into his path, within his reach.

Old One Eye stood. He roared.

———————

FRED TURNED SHARPLY, stunned by the ferocious roar. A clawed paw swiped toward him.

He screamed as the paw caught him across his upper left arm, throwing him several feet against a tree and to the ground. He bounced up quickly, his stomach churning, his rifle no longer in his grasp; blood was running from his arm and head. He stared as the creature fell forward and started for him. Fred ran, dodging trees, but knew he was too slow. He thought only of escape, yet this nimble athlete was quickly overtaken.

He screamed for help as the bear caught his legs. He flew headlong to the ground, his shoulder smashing into a tree trunk, horrific pain and sudden dizziness shooting through him. He rolled to his back, his mouth wide with yet another scream, but the bear was upon him. A clawed swipe took Fred's left eye and crushed his nose, and a moment later the bitter breath of his death filled his nose as teeth sank into his throat.

LOU HEARD FRED'S screams. His eyes bugged out with a fear he'd never experienced. He heard another roar, another scream, and then no more. He saw only shadows in the woods, but the sound of branches breaking (or was it bones?) told him his partner was gone. He leveled his AR-15 automatic rifle at the woods and glared into the moonlit darkness. He stood still, waiting for whatever had taken Fred. But nothing came. All he heard were branches breaking in bizarre rhythm, and then he smelled the metallic scent of blood and death wafting on an icy breeze from the woods.

CHAPTER FORTY-SEVEN

"THEY'RE HERE!" MATT shouted as he and Hannah burst into the room, slammed the door, and threw the deadbolt.

"I saw," Corny whispered, limping out of the bedroom, his rifle gripped tightly. "One's outside." He pointed behind him.

"We heard something else out there," Hannah said.

Corny nodded. Boone stood alert, nose and ears rigid.

"It's a bear," Corny said with a tight smirk. "Old One Eye showed up after all. Messed up their little surprise."

Matt and Hannah watched wide-eyed and frozen in place as Corny moved behind the protection of the couch.

"You'd better move, now!" Corny exhorted. "They're coming!"

Matt's shock was complete. He'd understood they were in danger. But that understanding was academic. This was real—real guns with real and imminent death coming with them.

"Move, you two!" Corny shouted.

Clarity came in a rush. Matt yanked the handgun from his waistband and grabbed the folder containing the parchment in one motion. He ran with Hannah past the bedroom door, caught a peek of a shadowed figure moving briskly outside the window, and joined Corny behind the couch. Corny knelt with his head and shoulders above the couch's back, his rifle trained on the door. Matt and Hannah eyed the back of the cabin, searching for an escape. And then they heard the squawk of a hand-held radio where they'd seen the shadow seconds before.

LOU PRESSED HIS back against the cabin wall at the porch. He peeked around the corner. Whoever was out there seconds before was gone. Surprise was no longer possible.

He grabbed his hand-held, pressed his connection and whispered frantically.

"Mahmoud!" He used George's given name. "Something has happened to Omar. He is no longer with us."

"What are you doing Lou? This is GEORGE!" he shouted angrily.

"George," Lou whispered vehemently. "Fred is dead! There is some creature in the woods. It has taken him."

Silence for several seconds.

"What are you talking about?" George asked.

"We were ready. I heard a roar and Fred's screams, and then I heard his bones…his bones! They were breaking. There is something in the woods. I am alone here."

Silence again.

"Are you able to proceed?"

Lou's breath came in tight gasps as he stared toward the trees, his back mashed to the cabin wall.

"Are you able to proceed, Lou?" George demanded.

Lou's gaze moved to the hand-held and then moved back to the woods. He tried to calm himself.

"Lou! Are you there?"

Lou closed his eyes, pressed his head against the wall, and came back to himself. This is what he did. He didn't need Fred. He didn't need anyone. This is why he was hired.

"Lou?"

"I'm here," he answered hoarsely. "I will do this!"

"We're coming up!" George shouted. "Get ready at the front door."

OLD ONE EYE hunched over his feast, filling his long-empty body with nourishment and paying little attention to anything else. Yet he noticed movement near the human structure. He lifted his blood soaked snout and eyed the creature that moved cautiously to the front of the structure. Was it coming for his food? Old One Eye pushed himself up higher on his front paws and watched the creature. It moved along the part of the structure nearest the wood, but made no move toward Old One Eye and his meal.

When the bear sensed no threat, he dropped back to his meal. But, when the explosion jarred him seconds later, and the smoke that spewed from it accosted his nostrils, Old One Eye stood, gripped his meal in his powerful jaw, and dragged it to a place where he could complete it uninterrupted.

THE EXPLOSION BLASTED the door off its hinges. Its sonic wave threw Boone and drove the couch backward into Corny, Matt, and Hannah; it knocked them to the floor where they sprawled as the acrid smells of c-4 and charred wood curled on clouds of black smoke toward them. Out of the smoke came a broad, squat man firing an automatic weapon, its spray shattering the room and thumping through the back of the couch.

Matt and Hannah cowered face down on the floor covering their heads, waiting for the onslaught to end, sensing it wouldn't, but having no idea what to do. Corny scrabbled to the inside edge of the couch for a view of the man; but the smoke was impenetrably thick and the gunfire intense. Matt and Hannah held their positions as wood, couch-foam, and other debris peppered them.

The ear splitting firing rhythm continued uninterrupted for several seconds until it suddenly stopped, the man ejected his ammunition clip, jammed a new one in place, and started again, moving closer as he continued his attack. But something changed with the second clip. While the firing continued, its trajectory had lengthened. After covering the entire front part of the room upon his entry, the gunman was now directing his fire to the kitchen, beyond the couch.

Matt glanced up, both hands still atop his head, handgun clutched tightly in his right, leather folder beneath him. He squinted through smoke-tears until a heavy boot thudded directly in front of his face. His eyes followed the boot up the thick leg and into the mist of the powerful body and gas-masked face that loomed above him. Again the firing stopped, the mask glanced at Matt, now frozen as the man ejected his clip, and, in one agonizing motion, jammed another in place while swinging his weapon at Matt.

The explosion, so close to Matt's ears was deafening, but the pain he expected did not come. Instead, the heavy boot flew up as a spray of blood struck Matt, and the assassin flew backward in a heap of gurgling chaos with the force of Corny's weapon.

Sudden silence.

Several seconds passed without sound or movement of any kind, only the quiet, exacerbated by the numbness in Matt's ears.

He turned his head and pushed himself up on an elbow. Corny lay still on his back at the far end of the couch, breathing heavily, his rifle resting across his stomach. Between them, Hannah removed her hands from atop her head and lifted it to catch Matt's inquiring eye. She nodded.

"Is everyone okay?" Corny whispered.

Matt sat up, back to the couch, the gun still gripped tightly in his hand. He nodded and helped Hannah to a sitting position.

"Is that it?" Matt whispered. "Is it over?"

Corny pushed himself up and shook his head. He put a finger to his lips for quiet. The sound came seconds later, a churning of tires on gravel, and they knew it had just begun.

CHAPTER FORTY-EIGHT

"DID HE GO in?" George wondered aloud. The explosion answered his question, and it was immediately confirmed by the staccato gunfire that roared louder as he drove the SUV up the gravel track to Corny's plateau.

By the time they reached the top, a matter of less than two minutes since his conversation with Lou, the gunfire had stopped. It ended with one sharp report, so out of place amid the continuous fire of Lou's automatic. Was it his handgun used to kill the last of the survivors? Or was it Lou's death shot?

George brought the SUV to a skidding broadside halt behind Matt's vehicle next to the cabin. Without a word, he and Herman leapt from the vehicle in crouches. George pointed Herman to the garage while he ran to the cabin's west wall and toward the front. The scent of c-4 mixed with the heavy metallic smell of fired weapons and hints of blood filled the air. At the porch, he peeked around the corner, and heard a voice. It wasn't Lou's.

"C'MON CORNY," MATT whispered desperately. He'd gained enough of his senses to understand they needed to move. They'd been lucky so far; the luck wouldn't hold if they stayed behind the couch. He struggled to help Corny to his feet, but the old man saw his dog.

"Boone!" he shouted, his voice an agonizing wail that carried through the open door and into the night. Matt and Hannah ducked, their eyes scanning the lingering smoke haze. Boone lay on his side, ten feet back from where he'd stood just before the explosion's concussion sent him sprawling.

Corny limped to his friend and fell to the floor next to him. The dog didn't lift its head. Its tail moved only slightly. Corny pressed his ear to Boone's side, heard a faint heartbeat, and felt the rise and fall of his shallow, struggling breathing.

"Corny, let's go!" Matt tugged at the old man's shirt. "We've got to get out of here."

"I'm not leaving Boone," he shouted, now sitting up, back to the dog, repositioning his rifle for action. "I'll hold them here. Take Hannah and go through the garage." He sat with his legs apart facing the door with Boone's body behind him.

"Damnit, Corny!" shouted Matt. "This isn't a game some hero's going to win! We need to move...now!" He turned to Hannah. "Can you help him? I'll carry Boone."

Corny resisted Hannah, but only until Matt lifted the dog and scurried to the garage access door at the back of the cabin. He pulled the door open and peered into the darkness, lit only faintly by light flickering from the main cabin.

"Corny," Matt shouted. "Where's the key to your car?"

"On the nail, same ring as the ATV."

Matt grabbed it and ran to Corny's powerful 4X4 SUV. He yanked open the back door and laid Boone gently on the seat. Then he heard the shot.

Hannah screamed as she spun through the door, falling hard against the back of the vehicle. Corny stumbled, but caught himself at the doorjamb. Another shot tore through the wall at the jamb. Corny turned, directed his rifle's muzzle back into the house and squeezed off several rounds, sending their assailant diving for cover.

Matt jumped to Hannah's side.

"My arm," she winced, gritting her teeth.

Corny loosed a final shot, and then stepped back behind a cabinet. His shot was answered by several in quick succession. Hannah tried to rise, but dizziness took her; she fell against Matt. He caught her, lifted and pushed her into the back seat next to Boone.

"I'll get you out of here! Hold on!" Matt exclaimed.

He slammed the door, opened the front door and jumped behind the wheel, stuffing the key into the ignition and turning it in one motion. The vehicle roared to life.

"Corny, let's go!" he shouted.

Corny turned as a shout came from the man in the room. He glanced back and saw the man hustle outside. Corny fired off another round and then turned and limped spastically to the passenger side of his vehicle. He pulled himself into the car.

"He's heading outside, Matt. It sounds like there's another one with him."

Corny slammed the door, Matt shifted frantically into drive and gunned the SUV past the ATV and through the heavy garage door. As he emerged through splintered wood and cascading hardware into ghostly moonlight, a body dove out of his way. Just beyond, another man leveled a handgun at him at a dead run. Matt swerved sharply to the right sending a shower of gravel at the approaching assassin; at the same instant, his side-window sprung spaghetti cracks and he felt a sharp nick at his neck. He crouched lower over the wheel, his stomach churning in desperate anticipation of a bullet to the head, and he floored the pedal. The back wheels spun wildly without purchase for eternal seconds before they finally bit and the car lurched forward to the driveway and down the hill.

Corny glanced at Boone and then Hannah, who fumbled for her seat belt as the car jounced over the rutted hard-packed road. An instant later he saw headlights at the top of the drive.

"They're on us, Matt! Turn left as soon as you hit the bottom."

Matt stomped on the break and turned the wheel as the SUV skidded down the last few feet of the driveway, slid into the snow embankment, and careened into the street before it stabilized.

"That way," Corny instructed, pointing toward the lake, the direction from which they had come the night before.

Corny directed Matt carefully, controlling his voice to calm Matt while keeping an eye on headlights from the rear and road conditions ahead. As usual, there were no other vehicles on the road this late. He considered the various routes back to Sage Hen Road's access to Highway 89, deciding that taking Sage Hen itself would leave them too wide open for other potential allies of their attackers. He chose the quickest, albeit most treacherous route, one their followers couldn't possibly know. If there was a chance to put distance between them and their pursuers before they hit the most difficult areas, they'd be able to handle it better than the assassins with Corny's knowledge of the road. The major unknown was whether the entire track was clear of snow.

CHAPTER FORTY-NINE

CORNY'S PLAN WORKED perfectly...for a time.

After almost five miles of hairpin turns, crashing through deep ruts, around rock, tree, and snow obstructions, Matt's rigid concentration faltered. It was only for an instant, but it was enough to send the SUV skidding sideways through a patch of ice into a massive oak. The driver side door took the impact but held as the stump of a low branch crashed through the side glass behind Matt's bent-forward body. The car died with the impact.

Matt tried the ignition immediately. Corny anxiously scanned the road for approaching lights; he saw none.

Matt turned the key several times, pumping the gas pedal in the process, before he realized the car was still in drive. He frantically jammed the stick into park and tried the key again. While the engine turned over, the smell of gas wafted into the cabin. He continued to turn the key, desperately demanding that the car start. Corny put a firm hand on Matt's arm.

"It's flooded, son. Leave it. Let's get out of the car," Corny said, trying to remain calm. "We're almost at the 89 junction. You can run there, to Grant's Market. Somebody should be there, hopefully Gus. You can get us some help. Help us out of the car and up into the woods there," he said, head motioning off the road.

"I'm not leaving you here!" Matt yelled. "Hannah and Boone are shot, you're limping. You'll freeze out there."

"If they're coming," Corny motioned over his shoulder, "they'll be coming hard. We're blocking their path. The likelihood is they'll plow into us. If we're in the car, we'll be worse off. Help us get behind the trees. I've got my rifle," Corny said, and patted the weapon on his lap. "I can do some damage until you get help. If we've lost them and they don't come, we'll wait a few minutes until we can start the car; we'll join you at Grant's."

Matt eyed the professor. He glanced back at Hannah who gritted a smile through her searing pain. She held her left arm tightly. She nodded. Matt turned back to Corny and handed him the keys. He followed Corny out his door and then opened the back of the SUV to pull out blankets before he went to the back passenger door. He draped a blanket over Boone, lifted him gently and followed Corny into the snow-shrouded woods, just off the road. He then went back for Hannah.

"You okay?" he asked as she gingerly slid toward him.

She nodded.

"I'm a little dizzy, loss of blood, I guess. But it looks like it's stopped."

Matt peeled back the top of Hannah's jacket at her left arm. It looked like the bullet had penetrated meat and muscle in her upper arm, but whatever pressure Hannah had been applying had staunched the blood flow.

"I think it'll be okay," he said. "Let me get you out of here."

As he trudged with her in his arms to Corny's redoubt behind a tree, she clung to him, warm against his body.

"I'm so sorry about this Hannah," he whispered.

She gripped him harder and whispered, "Get us out of here, Matt."

He laid Hannah in a sitting position on a blanket next to Boone and crouched with Corny to hear directions to the highway some 500 yards away. Within seconds however the engine-whine and crunch of gears of a fast approaching vehicle jarred them.

———

"THERE!" SHOUTED GEORGE pointing as they rounded another treacherous curve and their high beams picked up Corny's vehicle directly in their path. Herman slammed on the brakes but his back wheels locked and threw the vehicle into an icy skid past Corny's SUV headlong into a massive boulder just to the right of the road. George's seat belt caught him and held as the air bag deployed and saved his life. Herman wasn't as lucky. While his air bag deployed, his head was already crashing through the windshield. The bag simply lifted him to the roof before it deflated and dropped his broken body over the wheel.

George sat for a moment, catching his breath, shaking his head. He turned to his partner, nodded slowly.

"I told you to put your seat belt on, you dumb son-of-a-bitch."

He peeled himself away from his deflated air bag and out of his seat belt's embrace before pushing open his door and rolling out of the car. He crouched low behind the vehicle, eyes focused on the other vehicle. In the reflected light of his SUV's headlight, he was able to make out footprints heading into the woods. He stood slowly, keeping a sharp eye out for his prey, and he smiled. Let them try to take me, he thought. It will give them away.

He moved away from the car, eyes glued hard to the shadow shrouded woods. He saw the explosion an instant before he heard it.

———————

"I'VE GOT HIM," Corny said, drawing a bead through the thick trees. He followed the sidelong movement of the assassin and squeezed the trigger at the exact instant the barrel moved in line with a tree. The bullet glanced off the trunk, taking bark into the leaves and brush beyond.

The response was immediate. The assassin loosed a burst of automatic fire toward the sound and light of Corny's shot. One bullet caught Corny's bandaged temple and sent him sprawling backward. Others tore harmlessly through foliage. Corny fell unconscious across Boone. Hannah screamed and another burst followed.

Matt and Hannah cowered. They imagined the assassin running at them behind his curtain of withering fire. As the firing stopped—again to reload—Matt glanced at Hannah. She lay in a fetal position next to Corny, both helpless.

Matt rolled away from them and onto his feet. He began to run, crouched low as he heard the click of the new clip being jammed into the weapon. And then came the fire. It cut leaves and branches, and thudded into tree trunks and earth. Matt dove behind a fallen log. He heard the ragged breathing of his pursuer running up the rise toward him.

Matt had never fired a weapon. He'd never imagined having to do so. Yet he had no other course. If he lay still, he might survive, but Hannah, Corny, and Boone would surely die. He drew the gun, pulled back the slide with an audible metal zing, and he stood.

The assassin was upon him, eyes wide, smile broad. He swung his weapon at Matt. But Matt fired first, at point blank range. The assassin flew backward, glancing off a tree, and fell to his back. He slid down the rise to the road, his finger twitching tightly on the trigger of his automatic weapon as it fired off another burst into the air.

Matt stood for a moment, watching the body slide and bump to a stop. He stepped over the log, beyond fear. All he understood was that this asshole needed to be dead, or none of them would survive. He stepped gingerly down the slope to the assassin's feet. The man lay on his back staring wide-eyed into the sky, struggling for air through a gaping hole in his throat.

CHAPTER FIFTY

CARDINAL METZINGER STARED out the window of the Vatican chartered Alitalia Airlines Boeing 737. Black clouds churned to the north, jagged spears of lightening sliced curtains of black rain that swept the earth below; yet over the Los Angeles basin, not a drop fell.

A hazy film hung over the basin, which spread like a carpet of concrete and steel, cut by endless bands of highway. Only the vast Pacific Ocean glistening to the west, and the snow-capped San Gabriel Mountains to the east broke the relentless sprawl. To some, the sight conjured images of immense opportunity with myriad chances to make it "big;" to others, it was the perfect example of urban decadence and progress gone wild. To Cardinal Metzinger, it was an almost overwhelming challenge to guide the lost masses of disparate people to a new understanding of peace and happiness through the Lord. And despite his excitement to see his home and family, he could not escape a deep sense of foreboding.

Metzinger was to head the Shroud's tour of his home country. With him came other prelates and their assistants, Italian journalists, Church officials from the Shroud's hometown of Turin, and members of the Vatican's own Swiss Guard whose mission was to protect the Church's most holy relic at any cost. With these came hopes that the exhibition would bring the splintering American faction of the Church back to the fold, and then loose the innate zeal and creativity that only independent Americans seemed to have, to spread Christ's message to the world. Yet all Metzinger could imagine was failure.

The underbelly of the Vatican transport had been specially reinforced at the request of the Holy See as additional protection for its precious cargo. The international terminal at LAX was shut down to all air and ground traffic for the two-hour periods on either side of the transport's arrival. Security on the ground was impregnable, all at enormous cost to the Church, as well as the American and Italian governments, with the agreement that all such contributions would be reimbursed out of first proceeds of the exhibition.

Metzinger and the other passengers disembarked on the open tarmac. They were met by a contingency of Church, government, and business luminaries, along with privately hired security forces that immediately fell into position at the direction of the Swiss Guard. American television crews were permitted for only ten minutes of the debarkation and initial greetings. Security forces then whisked the cameras back to the terminal, behind barriers that blocked views of the tarmac. No shots were permitted of the Shroud's removal from the plane's hold, and cell phones and other photographic devices were confiscated even from the dignitaries present to welcome the delegation.

After cameras were removed, the private security forces joined the Swiss Guard in removing the twenty-foot long by five-foot wide by four-foot tall titanium crate that encased the steel and glass coffin containing the Shroud of Turin. The container weighed several tons, but was maneuvered easily on wheels out of the plane's hold and into an armored transport, which was to be escorted in procession by heavily armed security to the holy relic's first stop at the Cathedral of Our Lady of the Angels. There the Shroud would be guarded until the next day when it would be unveiled before a crowd of the city's finest. Los Angeles Archbishop Roberto Parra would have the honor of conducting the first mass for the Shroud on American soil. The next day it would be transported to the Los Angeles County Museum of Natural History, where it would be exhibited as part of a painstakingly produced historical display for the first 60 days of its stay in the United States. After Los Angeles, the entire production would move to San Francisco, and then ten more cities east over the next 14 months before crossing the Atlantic for its European tour and home.

"Eminence," Father Aaron Roberts greeted Metzinger. He could barely contain his excitement, smiling broadly and taking the Cardinal's meaty hand with a slight bow. Despite his attempt at the proper level of respect, his eyes and attention flitted to the deplaning titanium housing of the Shroud. "We're all excited for this day," he chortled.

"No doubt," Metzinger responded brusquely and glanced past Roberts. "The archbishop is not with us this morning?"

"He awaits us at the Cathedral, Eminence," rejoined the priest. "He has a terrific dinner planned, and wanted to make sure all was in order." Not related by the priest was the archbishop's desire to theatrically welcome the delegation and the holy relic on his terms within his jurisdiction. It was the Shroud's first appearance on American soil, and the head of the largest archdiocese in the country would be recognized for his significant role in such an historic event. Cardinal Metzinger nodded, sadly understanding the egos among his brethren, not unlike his own for many years. He then caught Father Roberts' trancelike smile as he stole another look at the Shroud's encasement.

The cardinal had to admit that if the church had more men and women with Roberts's intelligence, selflessness, and passion to evangelize, the world would be a far better place. Despite Roberts's complicity in the betrayal by the Shroud's keeper, he silently applauded the young man for pursuing his vocation with such passion.

Metzinger directed his attention up the line of greeters past Roberts. He immediately spied an enormous man, even larger than himself, about halfway up the line. The man stood rooted firmly behind another man, whom—with a jolt of surprise—Metzinger recognized. He averted his gaze to focus on those who extended hands before he reached their position. Finally, he stood before them.

"Welcome, Eminence," Peter Christian said with a smile, as he took the cardinal's hand in a firm grip.

Metzinger returned a curt smile. He knew the man well by reputation, and then more recently as a result of his television debate with Father Roberts. The cardinal was surprised at the confidence and seeming warmth of the man's grip. Yet, as Christian's smile broadened, Metzinger felt a heaviness in his heart, as if a dark cloud had passed over him. He pulled his hand away.

"Thank you, Mr. Christian," he said tersely.

"I think you'll be very pleased with the security my company will be providing your treasure during its stay in our country," Christian said, his eyes glued to Metzinger's.

"Yes, we hope so," Metzinger stammered, trying to hold his smile.

Christian's eyes shifted to Roberts. His smile didn't waver.

"Father," Christian nodded to the priest.

"Good day, Mr. Christian," Roberts responded casually. "It's nice of you to join us." Roberts eyed the man with a half-smile that made Christian's smile falter, but only for a second.

Metzinger moved mechanically through the rest of the line, glancing back several times at Christian who stood quietly staring after him.

"Why did we choose his company for security?" the Cardinal asked after he sat next to Roberts in the back of the limousine. "He is not a friend of the Church, Aaron. You, more than anyone, know that."

"Cornerstone's bid was accepted long before our debate, Eminence," Roberts responded defensively as he eyed Christian through the tinted window at Metzinger's shoulder. "He owns America's foremost private security company with a sterling reputation. Their plan has been reviewed and modified by our own Swiss Guard numerous times. The guard is in charge of implementing the plan. Mr. Christian has given control over his security people to the guard...reluctantly I might add; but he has done it nevertheless. Everything will be fine."

The priest nodded his reassurance before he turned his attention to the itinerary on his lap. Metzinger turned back to the window and prayed that the young priest was correct.

"THE GIRL AND the old man are in the Sacramento Police Department's protective custody," Roland Barker reported hurriedly.

Christian slouched against the back seat of his bulletproof Mercedes limousine, legs spread wide, eyes glaring ahead. He didn't respond.

"They've recovered five bodies so far." Barker rushed in to fill the silence. "We don't have identities on any of them, yet."

"No reports from our guys?" Christian asked curtly.

"No, nothing yet, Peter. We have no word."

"What about our people with the Sacramento P.D.?"

"We've got two. Neither is part of the force investigating the Lake Independence Incident, as they're referring to it. They're trying to get information, but all they've gotten so far is that Carter is not with the old man and the girl. They're both badly shaken; a lot of tension and fear according to what our guys have been able to gather."

Christian needed to know if they'd located the parchment but knew it would be an exercise in futility to ask. Barker understood what he was after. If he or any of his people had it, it would have been the first thing he mentioned.

"One other thing, Peter. We've tried to track Carter's cell phone. It's not operational. He's either out of range, or he's dead. He definitely isn't with the girl and old man."

"Okay," Christian said. "Okay, Roland. That's good. Stay on it. We need confirmation on Carter."

"I'll stay in touch."

Christian thumbed his phone off, glanced at the vehicle's rear view mirror and caught Walt's eyes. Christian nodded.

"Let's get this over with."

Walt set his course for the Cathedral of Our Lady of the Angels.

CHAPTER FIFTY-ONE

MATT WOKE WITH a start, jolted by an explosion of thunder that reverberated through his sleep. It took several seconds for nature's throat clearing to dissolve into eerie silence, leaving in its wake the promise of another storm. Matt pushed up from the bench of Gus's battered pickup. He rubbed his face, felt stubble at his unshaved jaw, and glanced into the mirror at his bloodshot eyes and dark pouches beneath them. He shook his head with sad understanding that none of his ordeal had been a dream.

He'd left the assassin dead at the edge of the roadway. He'd stood silently as the killer gave up his last breath in a gurgle and spray of blood through the hole in his throat. Matt had then turned and let his still surging adrenalin drive him up the rise to Hannah. She'd cradled Corny's head in her lap and spoken soothingly to him. Although conscious, Corny was dazed and in need of medical care, blood streaming from a head wound. Hannah had looked up at Matt.

"He's dead," Matt mumbled, motioning down the slope. They stared at each other, stunned. Matt whispered, "I'm going to try to start the car...get us out of here." Hannah nodded numbly.

The vehicle started on the first turn, the flooded engine having sat long enough to clear the lines. Matt maneuvered it away from the branch stump sticking through the driver window before he loaded Corny, Hannah, and Boone inside. He arrived at Grant's Market minutes later. Gus was manning the register. He jumped to their aid, getting them stabilized within the warmth of his store before he picked up his phone to call the police.

"Wait, Gus," Corny pleaded through gritted teeth. "We're…we're okay here for a few minutes. We've got to think this through."

Matt, Hannah, and Gus resisted Corny until they understood his reasoning. The parchment had to get into the hands of the priest in Los Angeles, Corny explained. Although he didn't believe the local police were connected in any way to the attempts on their lives or the parchment, he knew what their arrival would entail. Undoubtedly word would filter back to those who'd hired the assassins, and he had no doubt the parchment would be lost in the ensuing investigation. If it were lost, Samuel Rosen's work was also lost. His death and all that they had been through would have been for naught.

"We've got to finish this thing, Matt," Corny begged. "Get it to Father Roberts. He'll keep it safe. We'll deal with the police after you leave."

Matt nodded, but turned to Hannah. He couldn't leave her. In his dazed thinking, he felt she wouldn't be safe if he wasn't there to protect her. Hannah smiled wearily.

"You have to go, Matt. We'll be okay with Gus." She motioned to the wiry man who nodded, his eyes squinted in focused concentration. He was energized, poised for action, his behind-the-counter shotgun gripped loosely in the crook of his left elbow.

"You do as they say now, Matt. They'll be safe here with me." He nodded sharply affirming the absolute truth of his statement.

After Matt's neck was cleaned and bandaged where the assassin's bullet and broken glass had grazed him, Hannah and Gus escorted him to Gus's ancient, battered pickup.

"You best take my cell phone and credit card too, Matt," Gus said over his protests. "Ain't no one knows 'bout me. You should be able to get down without being tracked if you use my things. There ain't much room on the card, so just use it for gas." He then reached into his jacket pocket and extracted some cash. "You use this for anything else you need. I've got a hundred and fifty bucks here." Matt shook his head, but Gus insisted. "I know you ain't got much cash, and you can't use your own card. Corny's good for this. You go on now and be safe."

Matt accepted the money and nodded his thanks. "I'll get it all back to you, Gus."

"I know you will, son. Go on now. Get this done."

Matt turned to Hannah. Gus took his cue to leave them alone. "You all right?" he asked, lightly touching her arms.

She nodded, wincing at the touch to her wound. "I'm good," she said, nodding and looking up into his eyes. Her voice dropped to just above a whisper. "You be careful out there, Matt. Don't use your cell phone." Matt nodded. "Please don't take any risks," Hannah continued. "If they find you, just hand the parchment over. Don't fight them. Please be safe."

"I'll be okay," he whispered.

Hannah took the lapels of his coat in her good hand and pulled him close. She pushed herself up on her toes and kissed him firmly. Matt reached for her, pulled her to him tightly only to have her wince again. He loosened his grip and smiled awkwardly.

"I'll come back for you as soon as I deliver it," he said. He turned and pulled himself up into the old pickup.

Hannah stood alone, hugging herself against the cold and watching Gus's truck disappear into the night.

THE DRIVE OUT of the mountains into California's central valley was agonizing. The intense concentration required to navigate the pitch-black mountain roads while watching warily for new assassins at every turn was cause enough for Matt's headache, at least until he reached Truckee. From there he was somewhat more comfortable with the road and the probability that no one knew about Gus' truck. But that's when his soul's pain began.

Matt had killed a man. He'd fired a gun and put a bullet through a man's throat. He'd stood over him, watched him die, helpless to do anything, but, more importantly, having no interest in aiding a human being gasping for his last breath with eyes bulging in fear.

Matt's rational mind argued that he had no choice, that if he hadn't squeezed the trigger, he would have been the one lying dead, and his assassin would have walked away without so much as a backward glance. But he kept seeing the protruding eyes, the black orbs in gleaming white frames streaked with red and rimmed with the moisture of tears. He kept seeing the shock of the man's knowledge of his death and the fear that came with that knowledge. And he kept seeing the plea, always the plea, that Matt save him.

Matt agonized as he drove, accompanied only by sporadic taillights and headlights that reminded him of those horrified eyes, until finally he grew numb—numb to the dead man, numb to the part he had played in the death, and numb to his humanity. He grew numb until weariness finally overtook him.

When Matt could barely keep his eyes open, he exited Highway 5 at a road marked "119 West." He pulled off the one lane road onto a dirt flat behind a rusted oil derrick that bobbed lazily on the arid outskirts of the city of Taft. There he slept until the monstrous thunderclap woke him. The storm it heralded came from the north, whence he had come. It promised more snow in the mountains and a rain downpour for the denizens of Southern California's lower reaches. He had to get through the Tejon Pass at the highest point of the Grapevine—the road that joined the central valley to Southern California—before the new storm closed off his escape.

CHAPTER FIFTY-TWO

MATT REACHED THE Grapevine's peak of 4160 feet just north of Gorman ahead of the storm. He sped past bloated mountains of hardened snow pushed to the side of the highway after the previous storm, and breathed easier knowing he'd made it through the pass before the roadway could be closed. Now, as tiny flakes fell in soft swirls, he picked up the train of thought that had occupied him since he woke.

"Who are these people?" Matt had asked Corny as they sat down to dinner before the attack. "Who'd kill to hide the truth about the Shroud? Why is it so important?"

Corny leaned back and braced his palms at the edge of the table.

"I asked Samuel the same question, Matt," he started thoughtfully. "We talked about it after the first threat and couldn't come to an answer. My first thought was anti-Christians, of course—Al-Qaeda or another fanatical Muslim group. And it could certainly be that. Those two frozen fellas outside," he waved in the direction of the two assassins he'd dragged outside, "sure look like Muslim fanatics. But I don't think that's who's behind this.

"They're running around too freely here," Corny continued. "Someone is helping them. We know Muslim terrorists, or anyone even smelling like they might be terrorists, have the CIA, Homeland Security, and every other government agency following every step they take. They wouldn't be able to do this without someone powerful helping them. To me, that means someone with exceptional capability in the United States."

"What about the Catholic Church?" asked Matt. He hesitated as Hannah gave him a puzzled look. He shrugged. "They seem to be everyone's favorite villain. Besides, if the Church were interested in the truth about the Shroud, wouldn't they just authorize formal tests and be done with it? Why would Professor Rosen have had such trouble getting a new piece to test? Maybe they're trying to cover something up. The Church has the size and influence to pull something like this off."

Corny nodded thoughtfully. "The Church hierarchy definitely doesn't want its members' faith to turn on the Shroud's credibility. I could see them fearing new test results that might be negative again.

"And there's another possible argument implicating the Church," he continued. "Some theorize the Church purposely provided a tainted piece of cloth for testing because they wanted a negative finding on the Shroud. These people argue that because there are blood flows on the Shroud, the man whose image appears there couldn't have died on the cross. If he had died, blood would have stopped flowing, and no such flows would have appeared on the cloth. The ramifications of that would be devastating to Christianity because Christ's death, resurrection, and ascension form the foundation of all Christian faiths. If he didn't die on the cross, then his resurrection and ascension couldn't have occurred."

"What about that argument?" Hannah asked.

"Weak." Corny shook his head. "Scientific evidence is clear that blood does flow for a time after death. More important, even long after normal blood flow stops, blood that is caught in the body will leak out of wounds as a body is moved. Common sense tells us that. The thought the Church might want to suppress the authenticity of the Shroud because of fear that Christ survived his gruesome torture and crucifixion is bunk, particularly since there's no evidence anywhere that he survived.

"No," Corny continued, "Samuel didn't believe the Church was behind this. Neither do I. If the Shroud were proven false, the Church is no worse off than it already is. If, on the other hand, as Samuel's tests confirmed, the cloth is the burial shroud of the crucified and resurrected Christ, the Church's evangelization efforts would get a major boost. Someone else is pulling the strings."

"Who?" asked Matt.

"Think about it. Who benefits from a finding that the cloth is real?" Corny asked.

"The Catholic Church and every other Christian faith," Hannah answered. "It's strong evidence that Jesus Christ rose from the dead, and… that he's God."

Corny nodded. "Now who is hurt by a finding that the cloth is real?"

"Other faiths that don't believe in Christ," Matt answered.

"Yes, but who else? Let's consider others. If we don't believe it's Muslim fanatics who are doing this without the help of someone powerful in this country, who is helping them? Who stands to be hurt if the Shroud is the real deal?"

"I suppose atheists might have some interest," Matt offered.

Hannah shook her head doubtfully.

"I've never heard of atheists trying to force their non-belief on anyone," she said. "They're passive non-believers, not active obstructionists."

"I have to differ with you on that, Hannah," Corny interjected. "Haven't you noticed how vocal and aggressive atheists have become? In Santa Monica, an atheist got the right to erect an angry atheist display next to a Nativity crèche at Christmas and ultimately forced the city to end a decades-long tradition of permitting the beautiful Nativity display during the Christmas season. Then there's the YMCA; they actually changed their name to the "Y" in order to take references to "Christian" out of the name because it was harder for politically correct businesses to donate if "Christ" was in the name. Christmas celebrations are now "holiday" celebrations. You see it everywhere. Atheism and its counterpart "Political Correctness" are having their way in our society, and Christians have been too passive to stand up and resist. Your passive atheists have turned the corner, Hannah. They even go by a different name. They call themselves secularists."

"But would they kill to hide the truth about the Shroud?"

"I don't know…probably not for the most part. There might be some nuts out there that would, but my suspicion is that the people involved in what's going on here have motivation beyond mere atheism, even if their atheism is the new aggressive kind. Let's consider a larger view for a moment."

Hannah and Matt shrugged.

"How about government...not a particular government, but the larger generic concept of 'government,'" Corny suggested. "Would 'government' be hurt by a finding that the Shroud is real and that Christ might actually be God?"

"My guess is no," Matt started. "Governments typically like constituencies that believe in a god that tends to keep people in line; it makes them follow the law because of the fear of retribution in the afterlife."

"That's my feeling as well," Corny responded. "Who else then? The military establishment, the business establishment, others?"

"Both of those certainly," Hannah rejoined. "I can see the military being wary of a god who teaches love and selflessness. They might take the position that a society that believes strongly in a god like Jesus is a society that will resist war. Unfortunately, history seems to contradict that. It seems like just the opposite is true in supposedly God-fearing countries."

Matt sat quietly, trying to capture a thought. Corny and Hannah turned to him when he finally leaned forward.

"I can see where the business establishment would resist a true belief in God, particularly in one like Jesus Christ," he said. "I mean, if people take Christ's words to heart—'Love God ... and Love they neighbor as thyself'— it's arguable people would be less interested in the things of this world; we'd still spend for basic living, but the frivolous things, the things we all spend so much on, would tend to lose their luster." He hesitated a moment. "If the world really, truly believed that God exists and that the real reward for a good life is in heaven, wouldn't it change the whole consumption focus?"

Hannah and Corny nodded.

"Sure," said Hannah. "Maybe you'd get a lot more human focus on helping the poor and sick; maybe even a lot more sharing and a lot less of the 'me first' attitude."

"We might stop chasing the golden calf and find happiness in the knowledge of heaven," Corny said softly.

"But, like Hannah said with the military establishment," Matt rejoined, "history hasn't borne that out. We've all just gotten better at trying to get rich and spending everything we have."

"Yes," Corny said. "But consider this; until the Shroud, the world never had tangible evidence of God's existence. Sure, people claim to have witnessed miracles, spoken to God, and seen heaven through 'near-death' experiences. But never has anyone presented scientifically substantiated evidence of these claims. In the past, if one chose to believe, the choice was one of faith alone. We all know how weak faith can be; the minute a person suffers a setback, he will blame everyone but himself. He'll even blame his faith. On the other hand, the minute a person experiences a great victory or fortune, God-faith disappears in the glow of that victory and fortune, replaced by a new faith in that person's greatness. There has never been hard evidence of the existence of God, until now...until this very moment in human history.

"So who is doing this?" Corny eyed them closely. "If the world really, truly believes Jesus Christ is God, and that the only real reward for a life well-lived is a place in God's kingdom of heaven, I think the world changes dramatically. The obsession for things ends. Doesn't pursuit of fame and fortune end? Like Matt said, spending on the pointless wealth of this world ends, doesn't it?"

They nodded thoughtfully.

"We can argue forever about whether business interests would really suffer and the pursuit of the golden calf would diminish, but it doesn't matter what we argue. It only matters that some in the business establishment believe that would be the result of a true belief in God. I think those who want to destroy your parchment, Matt, are from the business establishment. They are the ones who believe business interests should be free to do as they see fit in their pursuit of the almighty buck. They don't believe in regulations, restrictions, or controls of their inalienable right to make as much money as they can. They don't like a god of peace who preaches love, giving, and the existence of an afterlife. They don't like it because they believe the only life is one where they win the most on this earth simply because they're better than the rest; and they don't win unless everyone is in the game to be beaten.

"We need to look to the business establishment." He nodded slowly. "It's there we'll find our killers."

CHAPTER FIFTY-THREE

THE CATHEDRAL OF Our Lady of the Angels consumes one square block of downtown Los Angeles. Bordered on its north by the Hollywood Freeway, drivers are graced with views of a cross atop the cathedral's soaring corner tower, an alcove protrusion bearing the image of Our Lady of Guadalupe, and windows bearing ethereal images of angels.

The cathedral's most prominent feature is a fifty-foot concrete cross "lantern," which adorns the entry courtyard's wall of the structure. At night, alabaster windows built to frame the massive cross are illuminated to display the cross's image far to the east in the cathedral's call to the faithful.

Matt approached the cathedral from the west. He took the Hill Street exit and tried to enter the underground parking structure there. A bored guard demanded a special access pass, which Matt didn't have. That surprised Matt—special passes to access a church parking structure on a Sunday made no sense.

It was 2:00 p.m.; traffic was light; so Matt drove away from the cathedral and found off-site parking in a lot two blocks away. The short walk to the Shepherd's Gate, the main entrance to the cathedral grounds off Temple Street, took him only a few minutes, but it was then that he found another surprise. A locked iron gate barred access to the grounds. The church was closed.

CARDINAL METZINGER STEPPED out of the apartment provided for him in the rectory on the cathedral grounds. Archbishop Roberto Parra, a short round man with a powerful voice, had greeted Metzinger with a perfunctory bow, kiss of the hand, and booming welcome, but it was clear his real interest was in the Shroud. He left it to Father Roberts to escort the Vatican entourage to their quarters, while he personally accompanied the titanium container holding the holy relic through the underground maze of corridors that provided secure access to the cathedral.

The closing of the cathedral to Sunday worshippers bit at Metzinger. He was the first to appreciate the intense security for the Shroud. From the metal detectors, to guards with weapons prominently displayed at every point the eye could touch, it was imposing. Yet closing God's house on the Sabbath didn't seem right. Metzinger wanted to believe that the Lord would protect His gift to the world as He had throughout its two-thousand-year odyssey to this place. But neither Metzinger nor anyone associated with this latest leg of the journey had faith strong enough to let it go. So, despite the niggling sadness over the cathedral's closing, the cardinal understood.

The cardinal was dressed in standard non-ceremonial priest apparel, only the white collarino interrupting the black ensemble of coat, shirt, pants and footwear. He felt a chill and crossed his arms tightly over his chest as he glanced to the cloudy sky before his eyes drifted across the wide plaza to the cathedral. Before him rose the cross "lantern," the alabaster windows protected behind tinted glass starting some 50 feet above the ground and reaching to a height of one hundred feet. The cathedral's smooth concrete-block façade was a rich salmon in color, and its lines were elegant in their simplicity with nary a square corner anywhere to be seen. Metzinger turned right and smiled at the sense of peace the grounds evoked, excepting the black-garbed guards strutting about. He shook his head and turned left for a quick glance down the steps to the Shepherd's Gate entry before he turned back and started across the plaza.

It didn't click for Metzinger that someone was waving and shouting to him from the locked gate until his third step. He stepped back and stared. He saw a man in light shadow through the gate.

"One of our Lord's children," he thought. "As upset as I that he can't come in."

Cardinal Metzinger started down the steps. The man calling to him came into clearer focus. He was a young man, badly used, it seemed from his haggard appearance, and seemingly in need as the guard tried to muscle him away from the gate.

———————

THE GUARDS, LOCKED gate, and metal detectors gave Matt the impression of a prison entry rather than the prayerful grounds of a Catholic cathedral. He saw people moving about inside the enclosure on the upper plaza, but they looked to be guards with black uniforms, protective vests, and weapons at the ready, like the beefy character who stood just inside the gate, feet spread, hands clasped in front of him, and a rifle strapped over his shoulder, muzzle up at his back.

"What's going on?" Matt asked.

"It's closed," the guard responded curtly.

"I can see that. I'm just wondering why."

The man shook his head.

"I've got business with Father Roberts," Matt said when he realized nothing more was coming from the guard. "He's the pastor here. Can you let me in?"

"Sorry, no one comes in."

Matt eyed the guard, seeking another tack when the guard's walkie-talkie squawked to life at his belt. The guard didn't react.

"Hey, can you call someone on your phone there?" Matt pointed. "Can you get in touch with Father Roberts? This is urgent." The guard shook his head. Matt continued. "I don't have to come in. I have to give him something." He lifted the leather folder for the guard to see. "That's all. It's really important. Could you call and get him to come to the gate?"

The guard took a step forward and extended a hand.

"Leave it with me. I'll get it to him."

Matt pulled away.

"I can't do that. I've got to give it to him personally. Please, can you call your boss and see if he can get Father Roberts? I'll wait here. Please, it's urgent."

The guard shook his head.

"Step away from the gate and move on. You'll have to give it to him some other time." The guard now stood at the gate. He was a bit shorter than Matt, but considerably bulkier.

Matt took the bars of the gate in his hands. He glared at the guard, challenging him, before he looked past him, frantically searching for anyone who wasn't carrying a weapon.

"Move away from the gate, sir!" the guard commanded.

Matt craned for a view...anyone. He saw a priest emerge from a building in the upper plaza. The priest stopped for a minute, crossed his arms over his chest and peered across the plaza.

"I said move away from the gate!" the guard growled.

Matt released his grip, moved to the side.

"Father!" he shouted and waved. "Father! Please, may I talk to you? Father!"

The guard jammed his arms through the gate's iron grill and grabbed for Matt, but Matt stepped nimbly away.

"Damn!" the guard cursed.

"Father!" Matt shouted again. The priest turned. "Father, I need to talk to you."

The guard moved in front of Matt and reached through the iron bars again; again narrowly missing him. The guard pulled his arms back through the bars and unslung his rifle.

Matt held his hands up and backed away as the guard trained the muzzle on him.

"Get outta here!" he ordered.

"Hold on there," came the voice of the priest Matt had beckoned.

The guard turned sharply to see the massive shape of Cardinal Metzinger towering over him. He stepped back slowly. Metzinger turned to Matt.

"What do you need, my boy?" he asked.

"I need to see Father Roberts. Are you Father Roberts?"

"No," Metzinger answered.

"But, you know him, right?"

"Father Roberts is occupied at the moment," Metzinger said. "Can I help you?"

Matt frowned, frustrated.

"Look Father, this is urgent. I have something he needs. I can't tell you what it is. But it's urgent, a matter of life and death. Please can you talk to him and see if he'll come to the gate?"

Metzinger eyed Matt warily before he finally nodded.

"Yes, I'll talk to him. Whom shall I say is calling?"

"He doesn't know me, Father. Tell him I have something here from Professor Samuel Rosen."

CHAPTER FIFTY-FOUR

THE PROFESSOR'S NAME rocked the big priest. He stopped short, stared, mouth slightly agape, as Matt raised the leather folder for him to see.

"What is your name?" the priest asked, barely above a whisper.

"Mathew Carter."

The priest nodded, his brow creased in concentration. Finally, he instructed the guard to open the gate. The guard protested loudly, but the priest stood his ground, finally growing agitated when the guard attempted to contact his commander over his hand-held.

"I am Cardinal Andrew Metzinger, keeper of the Shroud while it is on American soil. I am the one who employs you here today, sir," the priest growled and took a menacing step toward the guard. "I demand that you open the gate immediately and permit this young man access."

The guard hesitated another moment, glanced about the grounds for help, and finally shrugged. He unlocked the gate.

"Come with me," Metzinger said to Matt. "I'll take you to Father Roberts."

Matt's immediate question was about the cardinal's mention of the Shroud. What did he mean that he was the Shroud's keeper on American soil? But he was unable to ask the question. The two marched up steps to the plaza level, Matt almost running to keep pace with the larger man's strides. No words were spoken until they passed through the cathedral's massive sculpted-bronze entry doors and up the interior ramp of the structure's south ambulatory, a fifteen-foot wide corridor that mirrored a similar corridor on the cathedral's north side, both of which flanked the nave, the church's main body. They turned right into a short, narrow aisle between high concrete block walls before Metzinger spoke.

"Father Roberts will be in here."

As they emerged into the massive nave, Matt was struck by the modern architectural touches, nothing like the medieval churches he'd seen on trips to Italy and France. Where the ornately dark interiors of the European structures marked them as ancient citadels of a seemingly morose faith, the Cathedral of Our Lady of the Angels evoked hope in the airy lightness of its modern turns, high ceilings, hanging pyramidal light fixtures, and finely crafted tapestries bearing the images of saints along the side-walls. The nave sloped downward from the back to the sanctuary in which sat a massive stone altar in front of a ground-mounted crucifix. Above the sanctuary, the alabaster windows that gave shape to the exterior cross were visible. Next to the windows rose the 6000 pipes of the cathedral's organ.

The Cathedral provided seating for 3000 people. Approximately 200 clerics and business luminaries sat or stood about the first four rows of pews immediately in front of the altar. They conversed softly as workmen busied themselves at the back of the sanctuary making adjustments to a magnificent vermillion velvet cloth draped over a long credenza. Attached to the wall above the credenza were two horizontally mounted life-size photographic images of the Shroud of Turin.

"Is the Shroud here?" Matt whispered anxiously.

"It is," Metzinger answered curtly. "Isn't that why you're here?" The big man eyed him, as Matt stood transfixed by the distant images of the Shroud.

"Yes," Matt stammered. "I guess it is."

Metzinger turned back toward the sanctuary.

Matt's mind raced. Had Corny mentioned a tour of the Shroud? He had a vague recollection of reading about a world tour like the one for the Dead Sea Scrolls, but it wasn't something he had any memorable interest in. As he thought about it now, Corny did mention it when he spoke of Father Roberts, but it had been in passing, and for some reason, the mention hadn't stuck. Yet it made sense. The sudden and extreme interest in his parchment and the timing of the murders spoke of more than the simple testing of the Shroud by Rosen. The immediacy of the attacks had to be related to the tour. Someone was afraid. But who? Matt struggled to get his head around it until he was interrupted by the cardinal's jab at his arm.

"There he is."

He pointed at a young priest standing in the center aisle near the front of the church. Roberts was looking their way. Metzinger waved him over as he and Matt maneuvered between pews to the center aisle.

PETER CHRISTIAN STOOD at the end of the third pew surrounded by suited men and women, all of whom jockeyed for a moment with him. Walt stood well back of the pod surrounding his boss. He leaned against a wall along the north side of the nave, interested only in Christian's safety.

Christian caught a glimpse of Cardinal Metzinger looming large on the opposite side of the nave as he emerged from the side aisle. He noticed that a bedraggled young man accompanied the cardinal, but he paid little attention until he saw Father Roberts walking toward them. That's when something familiar struck him. He waved Walt forward, excused himself from the press of his fans, and stepped away to speak quietly. Before he could say a word, however, the young man appeared to recognize him and started to raise a hand in greeting. Father Roberts arrived at that instant and the young man's attention was diverted.

"Do you recognize him?" Christian asked as Roberts and the young man shook hands.

Walt squinted and shook his head "no."

"Find out who he is," Christian instructed.

"I HAVE THE parchment," Matt said without preamble, when Roberts stepped up to him. He wished only to put the whole matter behind him. "I have the original."

Roberts' eyes widened. He turned, quickly perused the pews, glanced back at Metzinger, and then nodded sharply.

"Follow me. I have a place we can talk."

The priest escorted them up the aisle to the back of the church, then right to the north ambulatory, and down a flight of marble steps to a small, private chapel on the crypt/mausoleum level of the cathedral. He sat in a pew, inviting Matt and Metzinger to join him. Matt sat in the same pew turning slightly to face Roberts, and the big cardinal sat in the one immediately behind. Both clerics eyed the folder Matt held.

"Eminence," Roberts said to the cardinal. "This is Professor Samuel Rosen's former student, the one whose parchment set the professor on his course with the Shroud."

"I understand that, Father. It is also the parchment, I believe, that led to the professor's murder, and to the murder of others," Metzinger responded tightly.

Roberts nodded, grim reserve restraining his retort.

The three were silent for several seconds; Matt's head swiveling from one to the other, anticipating something more.

"I have the original here," he finally repeated, lifting the folder. "I need to leave it with you."

Roberts pushed back slightly, eyeing Matt quizzically.

"Why leave it with me?" the priest finally asked.

Matt hesitated, pulled the folder back.

"I guess I'm not sure…maybe I should take it to the police. But, I…I guess I really don't know if I can trust them. To be honest, I'm not sure whom to trust. There seem to be a lot of people who want to get this; to destroy it, I think. I can't let that happen…Cornelius Crockett," he hesitated to gauge recognition. "A friend of Professor Rosen's? He said it would be safe with you."

He hesitated again, exhausted, not thinking straight.

"It will be safe with you, won't it, Father?" he asked, clutching the folder tightly.

Roberts hesitated before he nodded tentatively. Slowly he reached for the folder.

"May I see it?" he asked softly.

Matt placed it on the pew seat between them, stared at the priest before he turned the hasp toward him. Roberts reached down, unsnapped and opened it. All eyes watched him gently finger the zip-lock bag containing the parchment.

"Please explain how you came to me," Roberts said, his head still bowed to the bag.

Metzinger and Roberts sat quietly as Matt related the events of the past two weeks. He spoke of his long ago relationship with Professor Rosen, of the discovery of the body, and of the deaths and attacks that led him to the cathedral. He spoke of the emotions and fears that had bedeviled him, and he spoke of the need for safety for his family heirloom. When Matt was finished, Roberts glanced at Metzinger, who stared at Matt as if some revelation had struck him. Roberts turned back to Matt.

"We will protect it, Mr. Carter. We will keep it with the Shroud here at the cathedral, and then we will find a safe place for it when the Shroud moves. Will you be okay?" he asked.

"I don't know. Yeah...I guess," Matt stammered. "I really don't have a clue where all this goes. I need some sleep." He nodded wearily. "I'll be fine."

They sat a while longer exchanging contact information. Matt was surprised by the big cardinal's willingness to provide his information. He'd seen the deference with which Roberts dealt with the big man, and from his own upbringing, Matt understood the Church's hierarchy well enough to know where a cardinal fit. The surprise was that he would give his private cell phone information to someone with whom he had no relationship and of whom he had no information. Yet he took out a personal card, wrote his cell number on the back and handed it to Matt.

"Go home and rest, Mr. Carter," Roberts said. "We'll care for this until you want it back."

As they emerged from the chapel and made their way to the steps, Matt caught a fleeting glimpse of a large body slipping out of sight ahead of them. But the sighting was there and gone before he could formulate a clear thought of whether a person had really been there. Neither of his companions seemed to notice.

"Thank you for coming to us, Mr. Carter," Roberts said as they reached the top step. "Please allow me to show you out."

"I'm okay," Matt shrugged. "I'll find my way."

Matt shook hands, his mind flitting to a slight daze, as if it couldn't accept that the strain and anxiety of the past days were over. He glanced absently toward the nave, whence he heard a low chanting.

"Is the Shroud in there?" Matt asked.

"It is," Roberts answered. "The Archbishop is blessing it to start the tour. It appears the ceremony has started. Would you like to join us?"

"Will the real Shroud be on display?"

"Not today," Roberts said. "We're having a special mass tomorrow at noon. It will be out of its case and displayed then. Would you like to join us?"

"I would. Will they let me in?"

"I'll leave word at the gate."

"If you have any problems, Mr. Carter, call me," Metzinger interjected. "Father Roberts will be extremely busy tomorrow."

"Thanks," Matt said. "I appreciate that."

He turned and started down the hall.

"Thank you again, Mr. Carter," Roberts called after him.

Matt waved over his head without turning. They watched him far down the hall without discussion.

"Shall we step in for the blessing, Eminence?" Roberts finally asked, bowing and offering the lead to his superior.

"You go, Father," Metzinger said. "I need a few minutes."

As the priest stepped into the nave, Metzinger continued to stare after Matt. Thoughts of the young man's harrowing story mingled with his own fears about the safety of the Church's most holy relic. He bowed his head and prayed.

CHAPTER FIFTY-FIVE

WALT WAITED FOR Archbishop Parra to turn away from the congregants and make his way to the casket of the Shroud before he approached Peter Christian.

"They called him Mr. Carter," he whispered.

"What?" Christian turned sharply, the unvoiced question racing through his mind. "Carter." He whispered the name as the brief visual of Matt with Roberts and Metzinger came into clear focus. "Son of a bitch!" he hissed.

His anxiety drew quick attention, so he said nothing for a time, eyes forward, deep in thought as the Archbishop droned blessings over the cloth's casket. Finally, Christian stood as quietly as his persona would permit. Dozens of eyes flicked his way. He strode out the side access into the north ambulatory with Walt at his heels.

"Where did he go?" Christian asked.

Walt pointed to the exit. Christian glared in that direction, the muscles of his jaw working angrily. He spoke without turning.

"Bring him to me. We'll take care of this ourselves."

The big man reached for his cell phone and jogged toward the exit. Christian watched for several seconds before he turned and glanced up the hall. His eye caught movement—something in shadow far up the corridor. He back-stepped for a better view, but saw no one…until he walked into the nave and saw Cardinal Metzinger settling into a seat in the back row.

WHEN FATHER ROBERTS left Cardinal Metzinger in the north ambulatory, Metzinger feared for Mathew Carter's life even as he wondered at the young man's commitment. It wasn't clear that Carter had made a conscious commitment to the things about which he'd spoken. He'd appeared spent—exhausted and unsure of what he was doing. But something had happened to him. It was as if a commitment had overtaken him without his full understanding. Metzinger bowed his head to recall Carter's words.

"I intended to give the parchment to the police the day we went to the bank. That was Friday…two days ago," Matt said and shook his head, surprised it had only been two days. "I had concerns about the police, but I'd made the decision to turn it over to protect the family. Then, after the attack, I was pissed." He glanced awkwardly at Metzinger, who nodded for him to continue. "I was angry."

"I understand, but what about now?" Roberts asked. "Why don't we call the Los Angeles Police and turn it over to them? Why bring it to us?"

Matt smiled wearily.

"I guess I'm hooked now, Father," he said.

"What do you mean?"

Matt eyed each man in his turn, sizing him up for trust.

"You know…it's real," he said hesitantly. "The Shroud? It's not a fake. It wasn't painted by medieval artists who had no understanding of human dimension and definitely knew nothing about photo negatives. It's negative is a real photo image of a man." He slid forward to the front of his chair, shook his head, and balled his right fist atop his thigh.

"But it's not just a photo…do you understand that? It's the image of Jesus Christ, the only true image of him in existence. It depicts how he was brutalized—scourged, crowned with thorns, and hung with metal spikes through his wrists and ankles." His eyes bored into the holy men, hoping they could understand as he now did. Finally, he dropped his head and whispered, "He suffered all of this…for us."

Matt lifted his head slowly.

"I don't know," he continued wearily. "I'm sorry about that. I suppose I'm preaching to the choir, but I was zapped, Father. I don't understand it all. I suppose I don't understand any of it. I'm tired; scared, I guess; dazed a bit, but I do know I can't just let this parchment go. I can't let it fall into the wrong hands and just disappear. Jesus left us the cloth for a reason. I don't know what it is, but it's something. My grandfather's parchment is important to understanding the truth about the Shroud. I can't let it go… especially after Professor Rosen died for it."

Metzinger was moved. And now he was ashamed. Mathew Carter understood little about the world of the "Church," or the politics of "religion," or the relevance of "dogma," yet he had a faith that put all those who knew such things to shame. In simple words, the young man made Metzinger realize how weak he'd been in his fear of the Shroud's exhibition; how he'd fallen prey to the egotistical belief that he alone knew the way of Christ's gospel and what mankind really needed.

And now the meaning of his dream came to him. Whether it was his brain trying to show him the truth, or it was a message from the Lord himself, he realized he was complicit in the murder of Samuel Rosen, because he could not see past his own dogmatic fear of the professor's work. And it was that fear that would inevitably lead him into complicity in the destruction of the Holy Shroud of Jesus Christ.

Moisture welled in Cardinal Metzinger's eyes as he prayed for forgiveness even as he thanked God for his new understanding. He prayed for guidance, he prayed his thanks for young Carter's passionate understanding, and he prayed for the life of Mathew Carter.

CHAPTER FIFTY-SIX

THE PIERCING SHRILL finally woke Matt. He'd heard it several times since he'd passed out, exhausted. Each time, it was muffled, distant, too far for his mind to grasp. This time it woke him. He rolled from his position crossways on the bed to the nightstand. He plucked the landline receiver out of its cradle.

"Hello," he mumbled.

"Mathew! Oh, Mathew!" Paula Seltzer's voice was frantic. "Mathew, are you there?"

"I'm here," he croaked hoarsely.

"Thank God," she said. "Oh, thank God," she repeated. "Matt, where have you been? I've been calling since Friday. I've called…"

"Paula," he stammered groggily, pressing his free hand to his face. When she continued yammering, Matt raised his voice. "Paula, wait! I'm here." He pulled himself to a sitting position at the edge of his bed. "What's the matter?"

"I've been trying to reach you, to remind you about your meeting tomorrow morning," she said.

The daze with which he'd left the two clerics at the cathedral clung to him the entire drive home. He'd wanted to make some calls as soon as he got home, but he needed a few minutes' rest first. Two hours later, Paula's call woke him.

Matt dropped his head, trying to focus.

"What meeting?" he asked.

"The meeting with Peter? Peter Christian is expecting you tomorrow morning."

He shook his head and rubbed his face again.

"I can't make it tomo…"

"You have to!" Paula shouted. "Matt, please, you have to. I told Peter you would be there. Please!"

Matt shook his head, tried to think.

"Matt," Paula started again. "Matt, it's my job if you don't show," she pleaded. "Please Matt, do this for me. Even if you don't want the job, please come in tomorrow morning."

Matt closed his eyes, dropped his head into his hand.

"Matt?" Paula entreated.

"I'm here."

"Will you come in?" Her voice cracked.

Matt rocked his head back, eyes to the ceiling. He blew out a sigh and nodded.

"Yeah, I'll be there. What time?"

"Early? What's good for you?"

"Ten?"

"Can you make it earlier? Peter is leaving before noon. He's got a meeting out of town. Can you be in at nine?"

"I'll be there at 9:30," he said, angry and unwilling to completely give in.

"That's great, Matt. Thanks. I'll tell him."

MATT COULDN'T UNDERSTAND where everything fit. Hadn't he nearly been killed? Hadn't he killed someone? What the hell was he doing agreeing to meet with Peter Christian when he hadn't even put the shock of recent days into perspective? Was it supposed to be that simple? One minute someone is trying to kill you, and the next minute you're back to normal as if none of it happened; did that make any sense? Shouldn't he take time to figure things out? But the bigger question working its way through his addled brain was whether his life could ever be back to normal. Hadn't something life changing occurred?

Matt glanced around his room as if it was foreign to him. What was he doing? Paula's anxiety thundered at him, forcing its way through his concerns for Hannah and Corny. Yet, though Paula's needs were real to her, the only thing that made sense was the safety of his friends. He needed to talk to them; to tell them he was safe, and that their ordeal was over. That, at least, was within the context of the last several days. That was consistent with his dazed reality.

Hannah answered her cell at the second ring.

"Hannah, it's Matt. Are you okay?"

"Matt, where are you?"

"I'm home, in Manhattan Beach. I met the priest and gave him the parchment. What about you and Corny?"

"We're okay. My arm's sore, but the bullet didn't do any major damage. Corny's having some trouble though; the last bullet left something in his skull. They removed it and are keeping a close eye on him. I haven't been able to see him."

"Is he going to be okay?"

"The doctors are saying he'll recover. They're keeping him sedated and monitored. But they're talking as if he'll be all right."

Matt hesitated.

"Matt?" Hannah called.

"I'm here. Give Corny my best when he wakes, will you?"

"I will."

"Have you talked to the police?" Matt asked tentatively.

"Yes, but not 'til today. Gus called them after you left. Ambulances and paramedics arrived pretty quickly. You might have heard them," she said, hesitating before continuing when Matt didn't respond. "They stabilized us and rushed us to the hospital without asking anything. The police spent most of their time with Gus last night, and," she hesitated again, "with the bodies. I didn't talk to them until late this morning. They haven't talked to Corny."

Silence for several seconds.

"Are you okay?" Hannah asked. "Did you have any trouble?"

"I'm good," Matt responded hesitantly. "No, no real trouble. I think it went okay. The priest took the parchment. I think that's the end of it." He was trying to convince himself.

"The police want to talk to you, Matt," Hannah said softly.

He nodded.

"I figured they would. Did you have trouble with them? About me or the parchment?" His voice hinted distrust of the police.

"They were upset that they didn't know about you until today; surprised at first; then they were angry, I think, at Gus for not mentioning you. They wanted your information, but I didn't get the impression they knew anything about the parchment or were involved in any way.

"But this afternoon two other guys came to see me. They were, I guess agitated is a good word. They weren't part of the group we originally saw. These were plain-clothes guys, detectives or something. They wanted to know where you were. They acted as if I hadn't spoken to their associates."

"Did they ask about the parchment?" Matt asked.

"No, but they bothered me. They left a few hours ago. I think they're working with whoever wants the parchment. It wasn't anything specific, Matt, I just felt it."

Matt's initial thoughts were that even if they were "the enemy," he didn't have the parchment anymore, so none of them had anything to worry about. Hannah's voice was tight, however.

"What are you going to do?" she asked.

"I don't know," Matt sighed. "I don't know what I'm supposed to do. Maybe I should call the Sacramento Police, explain everything. I have to get Gus' stuff back to him and get my dad's car. I'm going to come back up there." He hesitated a moment. "How about you? Are they keeping you in the hospital?"

"Matt, can you hear me?" Hannah asked.

"Hannah, I'm here," Matt answered. "Can you hear me?"

"I hear you now. My charge is almost gone; I've got to go Matt...try to find a cord somewhere."

Matt wanted to say something more. Every part of him desperately wanted to pursue the relationship he believed they had started. He didn't want to deal with Paula Seltzer, but he had an obligation. He wanted to deal with Hannah, but he didn't know where to go. He didn't know how to say good-bye. Hannah broke the awkward silence.

"I'm going to head home tomorrow or Tuesday morning, Matt." She hesitated, conflicted herself. "Will you come see me when this is over?"

"Yes," he stammered hoarsely. "Definitely," he said with conviction. "I don't want to end what we might have going, Hannah."

Silence.

"Hannah," he called. "Can you hear me?"

There was no response.

———————

MATT SPOKE TO his father with a lighter tone, telling him everything was okay and that the parchment was safe, but skipping the more troubling events of the past days until they could speak face to face. He asked Nick to call Matt's sisters and let them know everything was okay.

Matt convinced himself he had nothing further to worry about as he showered, shaved, and changed to go out for dinner and a beer. He walked to El Sombrero, a Mexican restaurant a few blocks north of his apartment, actually refreshed and believing that the fears with which he'd lived for the last several days were behind him.

248

CHAPTER FIFTY-SEVEN

THE BURRITO REGULAR, shredded beef and refried beans wrapped in a flour tortilla, was just what Matt needed. The food filled a large void, and the beer eased his mind; but he limited himself to one brew; he still needed to get himself into focus. He left the eatery a little before seven-thirty.

The evening was cool, the sky surprisingly clear with only intermittent patches of cloud wafting across the moon. The storm that seemed so powerful that morning made a sharp turn east just after it dropped into the Los Angeles basin. Only the northernmost part of the enormous county experienced any rainfall.

Matt jammed his hands into his jacket pockets and bowed his head in thought. He understood the Sacramento cops' annoyance that he'd left a crime scene, but Hannah's suspicions of the plain-clothes detectives bothered him. He couldn't put them into his "safety" perspective. While lost in such thoughts as he walked home, he didn't notice two shadowed figures standing two blocks ahead of him at the top of his alley. Nor did he see them move down the alley toward his apartment. He had no clue anyone was at his door until he reached the alley and started down it himself. He glanced up, convinced his next move would be to call the Sacramento Police, and then he saw them.

He stopped in full view of the men if either had turned to look up the alley. His mind didn't click that something was wrong until the man at the bottom of his steps started to turn. Matt leapt back to the curb and slid into the shadow of the corner house, a two story, zero-lot-line structure with a front door opening directly onto the sidewalk. He pressed his back into the front wall and held his breath, his heart pounding.

He waited, fear rooting him, his head, back, and hands crushed against sharp stucco, his eyes bugged to his right desperately waiting…

No one came. Nothing. Dead silence. Not even a sound from the few cars that rolled by. Darkness surrounded him, the only light being the streetlight funnel that pointed directly at him. But no one appeared to notice him.

After several tortured seconds, Matt tried to breathe, shallowly at first, so no one would hear him. Finally, he began to hear sounds again. First the auto traffic, and then the ocean—the roar of waves slapping wet sand less than a hundred yards away. He closed his eyes, forced himself to relax. Slowly, warily, he pushed himself to his right, scraping against stucco, and poked an eye around the corner.

One man stood in the dim light of the landing at the top of his stairs. He was thin, scarecrow-like in a long black duster that hung on him, as if from a hanger. He was knocking at Matt's door.

The other man, bulky in shadow, wearing the same dark overcoat, stood with one foot on the bottom step, his head tilted up, watching the man above. Beyond him Matt made out the hulk of a large, dark car parked lengthwise across the garage doors below his apartment.

When no one answered the thin man's knocks, he reached for the doorknob and tried to turn it. It was locked. He let go of the knob, cupped his hands around his eyes and leaned against the door's glass. After several seconds peering through curtained shadows, he turned to his partner, shrugged, and said something Matt couldn't hear. It caused the lower man to glance over his shoulder, up the alley. Matt pulled back again. After a few seconds, he heard a sharp crash and tinkle of glass. He leaned right and watched the thin man reach into his apartment to unlock his door.

"Matt?" came a voice from behind him. "Is that…"

The man at the bottom step turned sharply. Matt jerked back, scraping stucco, fear staggering him. He stared, eyes bugged wide. His neighbor, the owner of the house into which he was pressed, stopped short. They stared at each other until Matt lifted a finger to his lips. He flashed a look right and then back to his neighbor.

"There's someone after me, Bill," he whispered frantically. "I've got to get outta here." He glanced back and then bolted past Bill to Gus's truck less than a half block away. He grabbed the tailgate as he ran by and used it to turn himself behind it. He crouched, breath coming in gasps. He peeked around the truck.

The bulky man reached the top of the alley at a lumbering jog, his right hand in front of him gripping what appeared to be a handgun. The man turned toward Matt's direction just as Bill was turning away. The bulky man jammed the weapon into the shadow of his thigh.

"Hey, Nat," Bill shouted at his front door. He turned to the bulky man.

"Hi," he said lightly, as if he'd been drinking. "Did I disturb you? Sorry about that. I lost my keys; calling my roommate." He began patting his pockets in search of the keys.

The bulky man stared past Bill, sweeping the street. His features were in shadow from Matt's vantage, but there was no mistaking the powerful, boxy body.

"Do you know Mathew Carter?" the man finally asked Bill, his voice deep, guttural, without emotion.

"Sure," Bill responded, turning slightly toward the man while continuing to search his pockets. "Aw, here they are," he said, and pulled a ring out of his jacket. He grinned. "Guess I had them all along."

"Have you seen him?"

"Matt?" Bill asked as he stuffed the key into the door. "Sure, he's my neighbor. I see him all the time."

The man stepped closer, now filling the space between them and exposing his face to the light of Bill's overhead bulb. The face, like the body, was boxy—as if carved haphazardly from a block of wood—and heavy browed, drawn, and liberally creased. It bore no emotion except for the deadly glare of two dark eyes just inches from Bill's face.

"Have you seen him today?" the bulky man growled.

Bill stood taller than his interrogator and his athlete's body carried a bulk and strength that might have been able to contend with him, but he stepped back.

"Who's asking?" Bill asked, the lightness now gone from his voice.

The bulky man reached into his coat, extracted what appeared to be a badge, and said, "Police. We need to talk to him. Have you seen him today?"

"No." Bill shook his head. "He went home for Thanksgiving. I haven't seen him since last week."

The man glared at Bill.

"Hey," came a voice from the bulky man's partner, who had just reached the top of the alley.

The bulky man turned. His partner waved him over. The bulky man eyed Bill for an instant before he stepped to his partner. Bill turned the key, entered his unit, and glanced furtively toward Matt before he closed and locked his door.

"HE'S HERE, HOUND," the thin man said. "Somewhere in town. He just ate at a place called El Sombrero. It's up that way." He pointed.

Hound stuffed his gun inside his overcoat. He and the thin man started in Matt's direction. Matt maneuvered to the street-side of the truck, still crouching behind its mass.

"Did he use his card?" Hound asked.

"Yeah," laughed the thin man. "The dumb sonuvabitch used his credit card. I just got the call." He held up his cell phone. "The shower stall in his apartment was wet. He showered before he went out to eat."

As they moved out of Matt's hearing range, Matt jerked open Gus's truck's door and jumped into the cab. He glanced in the rear-view mirror and saw the thin man stop, turn thoughtfully, and then move back toward Matt. Matt dropped down in the seat, eyes glued to the passenger window, hand poised at the door handle. When no face appeared at the passenger window, he lifted his head to see the thin man turning down his alley. Matt waited several seconds, breathing heavily, before he turned the key. The ancient vehicle coughed hesitantly and then roared to life much louder than Matt's hyper-tuned senses recalled. He waited again, holding his breath. When neither man appeared, Matt backed the truck up and pulled away from the curb into the traffic lane. As he approached his alley, a cone of light shot out into the street. Matt hunched forward over the wheel as the pick-up lumbered past the thin man's black BMW.

In his rearview mirror, Matt saw the Beamer turn left, make a U-turn a block away, and then pull into the space he'd just vacated.

CHAPTER FIFTY-EIGHT

CARDINAL METZINGER FELT it immediately. Even from the back of the nave, he felt the evil. It wasn't just the smirk Christian directed at him when he'd re-entered the nave. And it wasn't the fact the industrialist had sent his man jogging out the north ambulatory earlier.

What he felt as Peter Christian assumed his seat near the altar was a foreboding, as if a great darkness was coming. It was what he'd felt when Christian shook his hand at the airport, and it was what he felt each time he looked at Christian. The man whose company was responsible for the security of the Church's most holy relic bore an aura of darkness that no secular mind could imagine. Yet to Metzinger it was clear.

The cardinal let down the kneeler, pulled himself forward to his knees and began to pray. He closed his eyes and begged for wisdom to understand the message he believed the Lord was trying to convey. When the blessing of the Shroud by Archbishop Parra was complete and the small crowd of luminaries began to file out of the church, Metzinger didn't rise. He continued to pray, head bowed, eyes closed, until he felt a touch on the shoulder. When he looked up, Peter Christian stood before him smiling.

"I hope you enjoy your stay in our great city, Cardinal. Perhaps we'll have an opportunity to talk before you leave," Christian said.

Metzinger stayed on his knees. He leaned back against the bench and eyed Christian warily.

"Will we see you for the unveiling at tomorrow's mass?" Metzinger asked.

"No. I have to go out of town. But you'll be here for a while, won't you?"

Metzinger nodded.

"Then we'll meet again," Christian chirped as he smiled and walked away.

Cardinal Andrew Metzinger slept fitfully that night. And in the morning, during his prayers, he finally understood. The facts came together in a rush, and he knew Christian's man had set out after the young man whose parchment had already been the cause of so many deaths.

Cardinal Metzinger tried to reach Mathew Carter on his cell phone but received no answer. He tried the young man's home phone as well, but reached only his answering service. He had no idea what he would have said had Carter answered. All he knew was that he was afraid for Carter's life.

CHAPTER FIFTY-NINE

MATT DROVE TO Torrance, fifteen minutes away from his apartment in search of a place to hunker down for the night. He registered under Gus's name at a Residence Inn, and paid with Gus's cash.

He tried again to understand.

If the two men were cops come to question him about the deaths at Lake Independence, why break into his apartment? Why did the bulky guy draw his gun? If they wanted to talk, all they had to do was call. On the other hand, he had run, hadn't he? He left the scene of a multiple homicide. It made sense they were cautious.

But Matt knew better. As Hannah had known when she'd talked to the "detectives," these were not ordinary cops, if they were cops at all. They were after the parchment. They, whoever "they" were, believed he still had it; or even worse, they didn't care.

He tried Hannah's cell phone several times, hoping to compare descriptions of the "detectives;" but he didn't connect, remembering soon enough that her battery had been spent only a short time before. He wrestled with thoughts of where else to turn, but realized he had no options.

For the first time during his ordeal, Matt was alone.

He tried to sleep, to refresh himself, but dozed fitfully with dreams of chaos and death. When he woke fully clothed to a morning darkened again by storm clouds, the clock on his bed-stand read 9:00 a.m.

He sat up groggily, rubbing his face and temples to sooth a throbbing headache. He felt like he was missing something, but was unable to click on it until suddenly Paula's desperate pleas came back to him.

"Shit!" He jumped out of his clothes, into a quick shower, back into the same clothes, and ran out the door. In the hotel's office, he grabbed the remnants of a continental breakfast, and checked out. He was in Gus's truck heading downtown by 9:25…no chance of making the 9:30 appointment. He used Gus's phone to call Paula.

When she didn't answer her cell, he left a message and called the office directly. The receptionist put him through.

"Don't tell me you're not coming, Mathew," were the first words out of her mouth.

"I'll be a few minutes late. I'll be there," Matt responded. He wanted to shout he wasn't coming, but he didn't want to deal with her response. All he wanted was to get the meeting out of the way and then determine his next step.

THE DREARY MORNING started much earlier for Assim Rahman. This was the day for which the steely-eyed Afghan had been waiting. It was the day that would make up for past failures.

Assim had slept soundly. He wasn't haunted by dreams, nor was his mind in conflict. The task before him was the one for which he'd been born, for it was the one the Master had given him. He, Assim Rahman, "the most gracious protector" of his lord's will, was the only one capable of performing it. He clearly understood that, and he understood how important it was.

He did not eat after he woke. His last meal was the hardy repast of traditional Afghan dishes he'd eaten the previous evening. The meal reminded him of those of his youth, before the war, before the Master saved his life. He was grateful for the Master's thoughtfulness in having such food delivered to his door. After the meal, he went inside himself to make final preparations for the moment that would soon be upon him.

As he dressed in the morning, he stared at his changing image in the room's full-length mirror. First, after a cleansing shower, he eyed his naked physique, the finely muscled, dark-skinned body, perfect in the drab morning light; a testament to the regimen of nutrition and exercise the Master had given him. The only blemish was recent—another testament, this one to the failure for which he had come to grips only through the Master's soothing promise that his redemption would come this day. Wrapped around the top of his shaved head was a white gauze bandage covering the gash acquired during his encounter with Mathew Carter. Already he was forgiven, but it was a reminder, if one were needed, that this day he would not fail.

When he finally donned his uniform, he did so slowly. Meticulously. Deliberately. He first pulled on engineered boxer briefs and a short-sleeved base-layer under-shirt. He stopped then to view the ripcord musculature that was more pronounced in the skintight underwear. He smiled, acknowledging the perfection the Master had crafted. Then he stepped into cargo trousers and lifted the vest that came next.

The vest had been manufactured for defense, lightweight and bulletproof. For Assim, it had been remade into a weapon—a bomb of horrific destructive capability with a control mechanism wired under his right armpit down the inside of his arm to a detonation device within immediate grasp at his wrist. His vest was no thicker than the bulletproof version; there was no other recognizable difference, particularly after he slipped on the long sleeved shirt, jacket, and outer utility vest that completed the outfit. On his feet he wore thick-soled boots tied to the ankles with the bottoms of each pant leg tucked neatly inside. Atop his head, large enough to cover the white bandage, he wore a cap pulled low to just above his ears. Every part of the uniform was deep black in color except for the red side-panel stripe under each arm of the jacket and the white lettered "Cornerstone Security" on its back.

He nodded as he stared at himself. He was at peace, knowing this was his time. He would fulfill his destiny, serve the Master, and enjoy the eternal life for which he had always longed. He needed only one thing more before he set to his final task. Thankfully, he had the time yet to seek it.

CHAPTER SIXTY

"DAMNIT!" PETER CHRISTIAN cursed and thumbed his cell phone off. He shook his head and pushed up out of his chair. Walt stood, but Christian held out a hand.

"No Walt, I'll go alone. I don't want to mess with his head; he's got something against you." Christian shrugged. "I'll take care of it. Wait here in case Carter shows. Make sure the Hound and Sprigs are ready when we need them."

Walt nodded and dropped back into the leather couch in Christian's spacious office. He lifted his cell phone to his ear.

Christian glanced at his watch. It read 10:15, long past Carter's appointed time. Christian wondered if he'd show, despite Paula Seltzer's anxious assurance that he'd called only moments before. He chuckled lightly at the ridiculous efforts to which he'd gone to get to Carter, even raging at Walt's henchmen, Hound and Sprigs, for losing Carter the previous evening. But then he'd arrived at the office this morning and Paula had reminded him that Carter was coming in of his own volition. Christian could barely contain his excitement.

Christian stepped out his side door to a private elevator, accessible only by use of his or Walt's handprints. The elevator shaft bottomed at his personal parking space on the garage level below street grade. He would meet Assim Rahman there.

The young Afghan was an unusually useful part of Christian's vast empire. None except for Christian's closest associates knew about him. Like Walt, the young man's loyalty was unquestioned. Unlike Walt, that loyalty was also a weakness.

To the steely-eyed killer, Christian was the father he'd lost in the war, and he was much more. Like other "expendables" Christian had rescued from the ravages of wars around the world, this young man was vulnerable to the suggestion of Christian's powerful influence. Assim had been steeped in his own family's religious beliefs before the war. In the isolation of the intense training Christian demanded of all his "expendables," Christian strategically bestowed fatherly affection on Assim, and it was only a matter of time before the boy came to revere him and, in so doing, accept Christian's truth that a reward greater than any he could imagine awaited Assim in death. He would sit at the right hand of Lucifer, the "morning star" and "bringer of light," if he simply obeyed the Master. Assim Rahman understood this without question, because Peter Christian, the Master, had taught him this. The fact Peter Christian didn't believe a word of it didn't matter. Assim Rahman believed it all.

He was prepared to die this day. But the young Afghan was still of this life, and he needed to see the object of his earthly adoration one last time. And so Christian reluctantly agreed to break the most sacred of his rules: never to meet his expendables at any place where a chance encounter could tie them to him. He'd agreed because he'd felt a weakness in his protégé when they'd spoken. He'd agreed because Assim Rahman could not slip; he could not doubt; for it was a task like today's for which he'd been groomed. If he needed this final boost, Christian would give it to him.

The elevator doors opened at his private parking space. Christian stepped out to the sight of the magnificently clad figure of Assim Rahman, bowing slightly at the waist, hands clasped loosely in front of him. Christian glanced about the garage. Satisfied no bystander was near, he greeted the young man with a powerful hug.

CHAPTER SIXTY-ONE

"DAMN," MATT CURSED as he hit another bottleneck on the Harbor Freeway. Although late enough that most of the commuting traffic was gone, the stop-and-go drive was a hassle, added to in no small part by the rain that started after Matt left the Residence Inn. It wasn't heavy yet, but the slick roads made for a difficult drive, and the darkening clouds promised a downpour.

Matt was more than 45 minutes late by the time he reached Cornerstone's garage. He snatched his parking ticket and began his search for a space. Finding nothing on the first floor, he directed Gus's truck down the ramp to the second level anticipating a trip to the bottom level when he spotted a car backing out of a space. He stopped and waited, impatiently thrumming his fingers on the steering wheel. As the tiny Prius completed its exit and headed past Matt, he pulled the ancient truck into the compact space; too small under normal circumstances, but Matt didn't have time to worry about it.

He squeezed out of the cab, stepped to the back of the truck and spied a sign directing him down to the nearest elevator. Near the bottom of the ramp, he noticed two figures standing a short distance to the left of the elevators. One was dressed in the "Cornerstone Security" uniform he'd seen at the Cathedral the previous day. His back was to Matt shielding the second man from view until the first went down to a knee and bowed his head. The second man stepped out of shadow and laid a hand atop the kneeling man's shoulder at the very instant he looked up at Matt. Matt recognized him immediately. He smiled and began to raise a hand to Peter Christian.

Christian's eyes suddenly bulged wide.

Matt dropped his hand just as the kneeling man turned. Matt recognized him, too. The last time Matt saw him was when the man lay unconscious at his feet, blood seeping from a head wound.

Matt's face dropped…stunned. He didn't move until the kneeling man leapt to his feet and started toward him at a run.

Shock rooted Matt, but only for an instant as the sixty-foot distance between them closed rapidly. He turned to sprint up the ramp, fear running with him. His stomach lurched and his senses screamed for him to push harder; he felt as if he were running in place, struggling to gain traction. He hunched his shoulders and strained for speed, anticipating with every step that it would be his last. Eternal seconds passed before he reached Gus's truck and felt as if he was finally picking up speed. But he could distinctly hear the killer's breathing. It prickled Matt's ears, yet he dared not turn. As Matt reached the first floor turn toward the exit, he felt a hand; it tried to grip, but fell away, and Matt spurted forward, heart pounding in his ears.

"Son!" Peter Christian shouted, his voice echoing loudly in the garage. "Come back."

Matt didn't realize his pursuit had stopped. He ran wildly, each second anticipating a bullet in the back of the head. But Assim Rahman had stopped. He glared after Matt, and then turned back to the Master.

CHAPTER SIXTY-TWO

MATT COULDN'T STOP; he couldn't breathe; he couldn't think except of escape. He pushed himself, pounding faster till he passed the guard gate and sloshed into pouring rain outside. He bolted across the street, through congested traffic and blaring horns, and barreled into a motley crowd of rain-splattered pedestrians. He jostled, bumped, and thrashed through umbrella wielding suits, swearing city workers, and homeless folks seeking shelter before he finally turned. He saw no pursuit.

He moved past the corner crowd and turned to look again. His breathing was ragged, his thoughts scattered. He craned over the crowd toward the garage entrance, the rain now matting his hair and running down his face. He saw no one. He tried to catch his breath, stepped away from the crowd toward the curb, and craned another look; no one from the garage. His eyes slid toward the front of the Cornerstone Building, and he saw two familiar forms exit the doors at a run and turn his way.

The sight of the bulky "detective" and his thin companion rocked Matt. The thin one smiled, lifted a hand-held device to his mouth and joined his partner in pursuit of Matt.

Matt ran without thought, driven by fear. He ran over cracked sidewalks, through city-project barriers, and past harried pedestrians scampering for shelter from the rain. Each time he stopped to see if he'd lost his pursuit, the thin one was there, losing some ground, but still doggedly there. Matt ran into street-front stores only to be cast out by proprietors disinterested in a soaking, homeless vagabond, as they immediately pegged him. Each time he re-emerged, the thin one was closer, unflagging in his methodical pursuit.

He tried to lose himself in larger retail establishments, but eyes followed him and guided his pursuer who flashed a badge that everyone duly respected. Finally, after charging out of the warmth of a bank, Matt sprinted back into rain clogged traffic, slipping on wet concrete, skinning exposed flesh, and crashing through people scurrying about. He tried no other stores. With every ounce of energy and strength, he ran, all the while knowing his only chance was to use his youthful strength to outpace his pursuit before he again sought shelter. And then he came to the construction site.

The chain link fence was locked, the view beyond obscured by a thick green nylon-mesh screen. He glanced up and down the street and pulled himself up and over the fence. He landed in mud, quickly assessed the dangers of muck and debris, and scampered past rain soaked equipment into the structure's open first floor. He stopped in darkness, well back in the structure, breath rasping, and waited for his eyes to adjust. When he was able to discern makeshift wooden stairs a few feet away, he took them, running up as far as they went, ultimately to the fourth floor, where they ended and gave way to exterior lifts for access to the higher levels. He stayed put, finding a place to hide in the lee of conjoined girders, a place from which he could view the street.

———————

"WE LOST 'IM," shouted the thin man into his phone. His voice came in gasps. "It's pouring out here."

Christian glared at his cell, his clenched jaw twitching angrily. He glanced at his watch—10:45—nearly a half-hour since Carter had seen him with the Afghan.

"Where are you?" he demanded.

"Not sure, Mr. Christian. He's taken us all over the place. I lost him in an alley. When I got to the end, he was gone."

"Where's the Hound?"

"Lost him a while ba…wait, sir, here he comes. He's here."

Walt stepped into the room holding a sheet of paper aloft and nodding to Christian.

"Wait a minute," Christian instructed over the phone. He turned to Walt. "What do you have?"

"We've got him," Walt grinned. "He's in a building not far from here. It's under construction, shut down today because of the weather."

Christian raised a hand, palm up, asking how Walt knew.

"He called in twice this morning. Paula Seltzer's phone had the number recorded. It's not his phone, but we've tracked it. We're controlling it now. We've got him."

Christian nodded, quickly planning his next move as the excitement of the hunt surged.

"Stay where you are, Sprigs," he instructed. "He's close. Keep an eye out. Walt and I will pick you and the Hound up in ten minutes."

"Yes, sir," was the discomfited response.

"Peter, you don't have to go. I'll take care of it," Walt offered.

Christian shook his head. His eyes narrowed and bored through Walt.

"I'm not missing this. I want this son of a bitch in front of me," he growled. "Let's go."

CHAPTER SIXTY-THREE

"LOOK TO THE business establishment," Corny had said. "It's there you'll find our killers."

Matt shivered. He pushed deeper into the corner girders and pulled his legs up, knees and upper thighs tight against his chest. His shelter protected him from the rain but not the icy wind blowing through the skeletal steel framing and his drenched clothing.

Peter Christian? Was it Christian all along? Was he behind all of it: Professor Rosen's murder; the others; the attack on Corny; the pursuit of the parchment? And even as he asked it, Matt knew. Not only could it have been Christian, there was no doubt. Matt saw him with his attacker: the man with the steel-blue eyes who had accosted Matt in Larkspur; the one who had broken into his father's home and stabbed his dog; the man who had probably killed Rosen. And Christian had been so desperate to interview Matt—a nobody by anyone's account—at the very time it became clear that his family's parchment was a threat. It was Peter Christian all along.

Corny had said it was a person of business who so feared the truth about the Shroud and the man whose image appears on it that he would kill to conceal it. He so feared the possibility that people would understand that truth, and in so understanding it, follow it to a life far different from the life of petty consumption in which Peter Christian and his ilk thrived. Of course it was Christian...and others like him. They were the ones who would be king, but only if the true king were forgotten. And it was their purpose to make the world forget.

With Matt's realization, however, hopelessness suddenly overcame him. He dropped his head to his knees. How could he contend with Christian's power and influence? How could anyone? If Christian wanted the parchment, he would get it. Neither Matt nor any other person, not even the Church, could stop him. Maybe if he just gave it to him, it would be over. Maybe it would end the insanity.

Matt shook his head. He'd angered a powerful ego. He'd frustrated a man who did not tolerate frustration. And Matt had seen too much. It was too late to go back.

Matt eyed the street for the hundredth time. The occasional pedestrian scurried for cover, but no one glanced his way. They were out there somewhere, though; he knew that. They would be everywhere until the threat they perceived was gone, and it would never be gone until they'd dealt with Matt and his parchment. Tears came suddenly to Matt's eyes. He had no answer, nowhere to turn.

He tried to push himself to his feet, to do anything that might give him hope, but his muscles cramped and he fell back, catching himself only by slamming against steel. He flexed his legs, stretched them against the pain and finally stood. He stepped away from the girders, hugged himself against the shivers, and walked in tiny circles, stretching and bending to relieve the kinks; but his mind wouldn't let go. It drifted from fear to despair and back again, as he searched for a way out. Finally, he looked skyward, cold, scared, lost, and alone, and for the first time in his memory, he began to pray.

"Jesus," he begged in a tortured whisper, his mind reaching for the man on the Shroud. "Please help me."

In a moment of sudden clarity, he remembered Gus's cell phone, and hope filled him. He pulled it out of the back pocket and flipped it open. No light appeared on its face. A stab of new fear pierced him as he realized the rain might have destroyed it. He pulled it closer and leaned into a shaft of dull sunlight. A tiny prick of light from the phone made him breathe easier.

He dialed Hannah's number, hoping she'd recharged her cell. He heard a ring, but it was garbled; and then it disappeared completely.

Matt thought of the police. But what of the influence Peter Christian would undoubtedly have? Then he thought of the priests—Roberts and Metzinger. He reached into the same pant pocket and withdrew a sopping wet card on which the cardinal's number had run but was still legible. He tried it, but got nothing.

He closed the phone, stared at it. Had he given himself away? Were they monitoring Gus's phone? Was it possible they had Gus's number?

He glanced at the street; again saw no one. The rain had stopped, but water ran everywhere. He finally nodded, suddenly knowing his only option was to leave his shelter and find his way to the police, whatever the consequences.

And then he heard them.

CHAPTER SIXTY-FOUR

THE CRACK OF a weight splintering wood was followed by a scream and angry curses. Matt jumped, turned in a crouch, his heart in his throat. He held his breath, trying to be invisible, but a shadow emerged from behind a girder twenty paces away and he knew he'd been seen. It came toward him.

"Can you be any louder, you idiot?" A voice whispered harshly from downstairs.

"Get up here, you fools," ordered the voice of the shadowed figure before him. "He's here."

Matt turned, frantic, seeking an escape.

"Are you going to jump?" the shadow asked, not threatening except in its calm. "It would save us a lot of trouble."

The shadow stepped into a tiny shaft of sunlight, which had made its way through the clouds.

Matt recognized the shadow—the massive man to whom Peter Christian had spoken at the cathedral.

"Give us what we want, first. Then you can jump," the man said.

Matt stared wide-eyed, unable to respond...unable even to think.

Two other figures reached the floor and stepped out of the shadows. The first was the thin man who'd been chasing him and the second was his burly partner, a heavy limp apparent as he leaned forward, his left paw gripping his bloodstained upper thigh.

"Hound, invite our friend to move away from the ledge, will you," the first man instructed. "Bring him here where we can talk."

"I'm bleeding bad, damnit," Hound growled. "I fell through the damn floor down there. I need a minute, Walt."

Walt glared at him, and then flicked his look to the thin man, as Hound plopped down atop a large padlocked wooden box. The thin man stepped toward Matt.

Where Matt's first, distant impression of the man had been scarecrow thin and brittle, he realized immediately he'd been mistaken. The man's dark suit, soaked tight from the rain, displayed a muscled, wiry frame.

Matt stepped back, raising his hands pleadingly, his head swiveling back and forth.

"C'mon, I don't know what this is about. I'm not trying to hurt anyone," he pleaded. "I'm not trying to hurt Peter Christian. I was hoping to get a job with the guy for God's sake."

The thin man stopped as Matt neared the floor's edge.

"Job?" Walt chuckled. "We have a job for you Mr. Carter; one that'll make Mr. Christian very happy."

He nodded to the thin man.

"Encourage our friend to join us, Mr. Sprigs."

Sprigs stepped toward Matt, whose heels now rested on the steel floor beam, precariously close to the edge. Sprigs reached, took Matt's upper arm in a strong grip, and tugged. Matt didn't budge. He stared at Sprigs, eyes wide, paralyzed with fear.

"Let's go you sonuvabitch. We're not asking," Sprigs snarled and tugged angrily.

Matt instinctively pulled away, yanking Sprigs toward him, off balance. Sprigs' right shoe slipped from the wet wood floor to the steel beam and into air; he lost his grip of Matt in his attempt to find balance. An instant later, he reached for Matt again, this time in a desperate grab to right himself. But Matt jerked away causing one of his own feet to slip on the wet steel. Matt's motion turned him face out over the ledge, his arms pin-wheeling as Mr. Sprigs' body followed his foot into the air beyond the beam. Matt righted himself in the instant he saw Sprigs' eyes and mouth form enormous holes of shock as he tumbled over the edge to the construction equipment and debris four stories below. A scream ended abruptly with a sickening crunch of breaking bone as Sprigs struck bottom.

Matt turned sharply.

Hound let out an enraged shout as he leapt to his feet, ignoring the pain from his wounded thigh. He withdrew a massive handgun and leveled it at Matt.

"Hound!" shouted Walt. "Wait! We need to talk."

"He just killed Sprigsy!" Hound bellowed. "This sonuvabitch is dead!"

"Hound!" Walt withdrew his own silenced weapon, and aimed it at the bulky man's head. "I need to talk to him."

The heat of Hound's rage surged off him. He turned, eyed the silenced barrel directed at his forehead, and slowly backed down. He turned back to Matt, glared murderously, and limped to him.

"All right you piece of shit," he growled. "You get your ass over here now, or so help me, I'll make this real painful for you." He pointed his weapon at Matt's crotch. "Any way you want it, you're coming here."

Walt lowered his weapon and shoved it into his underarm holster. Matt stepped toward Hound, his hands up beseechingly.

"I...I'm sorry about your friend," Matt started. "He slipped..."

Hound swung a powerful left fist into Matt's stomach, taking Matt's wind and doubling him over. Matt staggered forward, and Hound swung his sledge-like gun hand down against the back of Matt's head. Matt crashed to the floor.

"Here he is," Hound barked at Walt. "Have your talk."

———

MATT WAS A dead man. That much he knew. He was groggy, unable to form clear thoughts as he lay in a heap between Hound and Walt, yet he knew they would kill him. The only certainty beyond death was that Walt needed something from him.

"Where is it, Mr. Carter?" Walt asked calmly.

Matt pushed himself up to his hands and knees, struggling for breath and clarity.

"What?" he croaked hoarsely. "What do you want?"

Walt glanced at Hound who drove his tree trunk left leg into Matt's exposed side, then yelped in pain from the use of his wounded leg. Matt sprawled to his back as Hound staggered slightly away.

"Don't play games with us, Mr. Carter," Walt said. "I want the parchment."

"I don't have it." Matt whispered and tried to roll to his side.

Walt smiled.

"I expect you don't have it with you. I want to know where you have it."

"No. I don't have it. I gave it away," Matt said.

Walt stared. "To whom did you give it?"

"To the priests...the priests at the Cathedral." Matt stammered. He pushed himself up on an elbow. Hound stepped toward him. Matt flinched, bringing his hand up to ward off a blow. When none came, he turned back to Walt.

"I can get it back and give it to Mr. Christian, if he wants it. They're keeping it for me."

Walt glanced at Hound, hesitated, and then reached into his pocket for his cell phone. He moved a few steps away.

———————

PETER CHRISTIAN HAD instructed Walt to call if they found Carter in the building. He'd waited in the back seat of the limousine until his patience, short by any rational measure, was gone. Thus, after only a few minutes, he'd stepped out and followed his men through the fence at the back of the project and into the structure. By the time Walt dialed his number, Christian was following the sound of voices to the fourth floor.

"I'm here, Walt," he said as his phone rang. He jogged up the final few steps, his phone lighting his way.

Walt met him at the top. Christian stopped in shadow. His eyes found Mathew Carter prone at Hound's feet.

"He said he gave the parchment to the priests," Walt whispered.

"Do you believe him?"

"He's trying to save himself," Walt said, glancing over his shoulder at Matt. "He's scared; definitely trying to buy time, but I believe him."

Christian watched Carter.

"It makes sense," Walt continued. "We saw him at the Cathedral yesterday. What other reason would he have had to be there?"

Christian silently assessed Walt's analysis. It was the only plausible explanation. A smugly satisfied smile spread across his face.

"Looks like he did our work for us." He stepped past his bodyguard to Matt.

CHAPTER SIXTY-FIVE

MATT HEARD CHRISTIAN. He tried to sit up, but was shoved back to his side by Hound, whose wall-like body loomed up from powerful legs that straddled Matt's feet. Hound turned his hate-filled eyes to Christian who stepped into the dim light.

"Well, Matt," Christian said, condescension dripping from him. He crouched down. "Looks like you've saved us some time by delivering your sacred parchment to exactly the right place. Thank you."

"What do you mean?"

"Let's just say it will end up right where it should have when the dear Professor met his untimely fate."

Matt stared, dumbfounded.

"It would have been better," Christian continued, "if you'd just given the damn thing to Detective Gutierrez in Tucson. He's one of us, you know. If you'd given it to him, none of us would be here now. You'd be living your trifling little life, and my friends and I would be going about our business running this world of ours."

His face lit up in a comical smile—eyes large, head tilted to the side, grin maniacally wide as if he'd revealed some long-held secret. He loved this stuff. He loved the control; but most of all, he loved the impact his presence and words had. He held the smile for only a few seconds before letting it fall away then leaned closer to Matt.

"But you had to be a hero, didn't you; you and your girlfriend? You had to protect your family's honor," he said sarcastically, pausing to revel in Matt's discomfort.

"Did you think you could beat me?" His face hardened. "Me?" he shouted and slammed both palms against his chest.

"I wasn't trying to beat anyone," Matt whispered, his head shaking.

"What? What was that, Matt?" Christian demanded, leaning closer.

"I wasn't trying to beat you…or anyone. I was just trying to protect my grandfather's parchment; that's all."

Christian nodded, brightening again. "Well, thanks for clearing that up. I feel much better." He chuckled mirthlessly as he glanced at Hound and turned to Walt. A puzzled look crossed his face. "Where's Mr. Sprigs?"

"Sprigsy went over the side," Hound blurted, pointing toward the ledge. "This piece of shit killed him."

Christian's eyes widened.

"Did he now? Well, Matt, that's a surprise. Mr. Sprigs was one of my best men. I guess you'll have to suffer a bit at the hands of our good friend Hound here for that. You see, they were buddies. He's not happy."

Christian hesitated, expecting a response. He leaned in, cupped a hand to his ear.

"Nothing?" he asked. "Well, that's okay. And, since I have other business today, I'm going to have to say good-bye. Oh, by the way, you would never have made it in my world. You gotta be tough and motivated up where I play; you know, killer instinct, attitude? You've got to want to destroy the other guy; not just win. You've got to destroy him. You're not cut out for that."

Christian smiled, clapped his hands lightly on his knees, and began to rise.

Matt tensed, stole a glance at Hound, who eyed Christian. Matt's mind raced. He needed time…anything to give him more time.

"Why," he croaked, his mouth dry, his mind riven. "Why," he tried again, louder. Christian glanced down. "Why are you doing this?"

Christian let out a short laugh.

"Of course," he chirped. "You don't know, do you? You have no clue what this is all about."

He crouched again, picked up a length of splintered wood and began tearing it.

"You live in your little world of tits, booze, and pointless work thinking your existence has some meaning. You actually believe you might be important in some way; that you might be contributing." He shrugged. "Actually, you're no different than all the other hangers-on who gorge at the government trough and suck-up to their crazy religious leaders." He lazily chucked the wood-splinter away and extended his index finger at Matt. "Let me make something clear to you, Missss-ter Carter," he drew out Matt's name in mock respect. "You. Are. Nobody! This world you live in dies without the hope I bring to it. Without me, there is nothing—no government trough, no religion, no world. You might say I'm the reason you're alive. But you don't get that do you? You can't possibly understand that your world ends if I'm not here to keep it going. So, you ask why, Mr. Carter? You ask why I'm going to destroy your granddaddy's parchment, and why you're going to suffer here today? I'll tell you.

"That worthless parchment you're so damn protective of actually has a chance of setting us back a ways. Not because it has any real meaning...no, not that at all. It's because people are so damn gullible, they'll believe any new thought that comes along. And if they believe the crap your professor was about to put out, the crap your parchment seems to support, it'll—let me put it this way—it'll cause us problems we'd really rather not deal with. The bottom line is that if you'd turned that damn thing over when we asked for it, there'd be no problem. But you forced me to pay attention. Well, we're going to end it all today. It's really as simple as that."

He smiled and threw his hands out, palms up, and shrugged.

Matt's next words came without thought.

"You're afraid, aren't you?" he stammered.

Christian's smile disappeared.

"You're afraid someone's going to show you you're wrong." Matt's voice strengthened at Christian's discomfort. "You're afraid this life isn't about you and your wealth and power." He grunted a short laugh, shocked at his own temerity. He pushed himself higher on his palms. "You're afraid there might really be something that doesn't revolve around your almighty buck; that maybe there is a god other than the dollar bill. And you don't want anyone to know about it, do you? Because you're not the boss in a world where people know about God, are you? You're afraid your whole life is a lie."

Christian's entire being stiffened. He glared blankly, his jaw twitching. Without a word, without warning, he swung his right arm and drove his fist into the side of Matt's head. Matt crashed to the floor, rolled to his back, his legs pulled up at the knees, hands clutching the side of his head, desperate to maintain consciousness.

Christian glared at Matt's writhing form before he stood abruptly, shaking out his hand. He turned away and glared at Walt.

"Do as you will with him," he said.

Matt heard the instruction. He acted instinctively. He lifted his feet, drawing both knees to his chest, and thrust them at Hound's left knee. They struck with a resounding crunch that hyper-extended the man's leg. Hound stumbled forward, screeching in pain. Matt pulled his legs back again and drove them again into the knee. Bones cracked as one leg hit dead center and the other slid up to scrape the still bleeding wound in Hound's upper thigh.

Hound howled, hobbled backward, his left hand scrabbling for the wounded leg while his right flailed for balance. He tumbled to the ground, falling hard on the knuckles of his right hand, scraping them against wood and steel, breaking his grip on his gun.

Matt rolled to his knees, still groggy but desperate for life. He watched Hound tumble, and saw the gun skitter away. He dove for the weapon at the same instant Hound reached to re-grip it. Their bodies smashed into each other and Hound screamed louder.

Christian turned sharply, but his forward motion propelled him into Walt, who was reaching for his holstered gun. The bump pushed the big man off balance, causing his weapon to catch on fabric and leather under his arm. He yanked harder as he struggled to disentangle himself from Christian.

Matt kicked and thrashed. Fear that the next moment would be his last, knowing Walt was aiming at his back, prickled his nerves, driving his animal instincts.

Hound fought maniacally through mind-numbing pain, his weight and bulk providing only slight protection from Matt's relentless thrashing, speed, and athleticism.

Walt shoved Christian aside as his holster finally gave up his weapon, and he swung it toward the grappling bodies.

Matt gripped Hound's gun and tried to roll away, but Hound lurched atop him, grabbing Matt's throat in a vice-like claw.

At the same instant, Walt's gun thwipped and was followed immediately by a muffled grunt as the slug caught Hound just as he covered Matt's body.

"Sonuvabitch!" Hound growled through gritted teeth, tears, saliva, and sweat now pouring from him. He gripped Matt's throat tighter, trying to tear through muscle and tendon with his bare hands.

Matt was frantic, his strength fading, his speed and agility useless beneath Hound's staggering weight. But Hound's strength ebbed, his eyes glazed, and the secretions running onto Matt turned warm and red. Matt's bile surged as blood ran from Hound whose grip on his throat loosened. Matt closed his eyes against his nausea, heaved the man-block to the side, and rolled away wiping blood from his eyes.

Another thwip pinged off the steel crossbeam just behind Matt's rolling body. Matt leapt to his feet. A quick glance through the haze of Hound's blood found Walt standing spread-legged, square to him, ten feet away. To Walt's right, Christian cowered. Walt's gun arm followed Matt to his feet; a flash accompanied another thwip.

A searing pain tore through Matt's side and wobbled him, but only for an instant. His fear, anger, and disgust coalesced into a rage and insane scream that thrust him at Walt. He took two steps and dove, catching Walt in a chest high tackle that staggered the big man, sending him stumbling backward with Matt clinging to him.

Walt grabbed at Matt, fought him, tried to pummel him; but Matt's legs pumped, pounding the floor, driving the man backward. They stumbled together until Walt hit a steel girder. Walt's head struck with a resounding crack followed immediately by the sucking thud of something penetrating his body and a blast of air from his mouth. Resistance ended instantly; Walt's body jerked and convulsed, until his hands slid away to his sides and his gun fell to the floor.

Matt held on, maintaining forward pressure until he realized he had no resistance. He pushed away slowly and stared, tensed for another attack. Walt's head lolled to the side; blood ran from his mouth, nose, and eyes. But he remained erect, pinned against the girder. Matt pulled back and inched to the side whence he saw the bolts.

Ten-inch steel wall-bolts, spaced twelve inches on center, protruded from the girder up its entire height. At least two bolts were embedded in Walt's back, but it was the fifth bolt from the floor that entered at the junction of his neck and skull that killed him.

Matt stood motionless, in shock...until he heard movement. He whirled around.

Peter Christian was standing wide-eyed and open-mouthed staring at his man, dead against the girder.

Christian's eyes moved to Matt's in stunned slow motion. Matt saw Walt's dropped weapon just as Christian dove for it. Matt was closer. He fell to the ground, scooped up the gun, and rolled away from Christian. A second later Matt was on his feet, gripping the gun and aiming it at his tormentor.

CHAPTER SIXTY-SIX

"WAIT!" PETER CHRISTIAN screamed. "Wait…wait, Matt. Wait!" He cowered behind hands extended as shields.

Matt seethed, his breath coming in tight spasms, his arms shaking uncontrollably as he jammed them at the groveling blob, the gun gripped tightly in his hands.

"Don't shoot, Matt! Don't do it!" Christian screeched. "This isn't you… we can talk this out. Please, Matt!"

Matt stared at the evil creature begging for mercy as it skittered away from him until it bumped a steel upright and stopped.

Each man held his position in silence: Matt's rigid, tightly focused, internal voice demanding that he squeeze the trigger; and Christian's cowering, eyes downcast behind the useless protection of his hands.

Squeeze, Matt's mind said. End the nightmare. You know how to do this. You've done it, before. You've killed a man. It's easy. Squeeze the trigger and it ends forever.

Yet, as he stared, the human being before him came into sharper focus, and suddenly the demands to fire the weapon dissolved, the shaking of his arms slowed, and rational thought returned. As he began to breathe again, another sensation struck him. He felt light-headed—a sudden sense of unbalance. He stumbled back.

Christian sensed the movement and stole a glance from beneath his hand-shield. He noticed Matt looking down to his left side where a black glob was spreading.

Matt eyed the tear in his shirt just above his waist on the left side. He looked closer. The sight of blood soaking through the shirt and running onto his jeans unnerved him. He grew dizzy, teetered, and began to swoon. He stumbled back, bumped into Walt's still pinned body and reached to right himself, but the spinning didn't abate. He jammed his gun hand against Walt's girder, scraping his knuckles, trying to steady himself. He wobbled, struggled to maintain his feet, lifted his head skyward, and closed his eyes. He sucked in deep draughts of rain-infused air.

Peter Christian saw his chance. He stood in a crouch, arms spread, and stepped toward Matt. But Matt's head dropped and his eyes squinted open the instant Christian moved.

Matt's eyes bulged. He swung the gun away from the girder, fell back hard against Walt's body, and aimed the weapon at Christian's head.

"Stop!" he shouted, the weapon unsteady.

"Okay…okay…" Christian hunched back, raised a protective hand, and spoke quickly. "You're hurt, Matt. You're bleeding. I'm just trying to help."

"Stop, damnit!" Matt shouted.

Christian did, but he held a tight eye on Matt's floundering stability.

"Get on the ground!" Matt waived the gun. "Right where you are. Down!"

Christian kept his hands high.

"You need a doct…" he started.

"Down!" Matt shouted. "Right where you are. Get down damnit!"

Christian raised his hands higher and nodded capitulation. He dropped to the floor.

"Okay," he said calmly. He sat with his knees and calves tucked under his haunches, his hands atop his thighs. "Okay, I'm down."

Matt grimaced, the wound's pain coming in waves. He pushed himself upright; eyes and gun glued to Christian. He breathed deeply, steeling himself for another look at his side. Finally, he looked down. He touched the shirt gently at the tear and felt his blood's sticky moisture. He applied slightly more pressure, kneading his side beneath the tear, and although there was pain, it was mostly numbness that he felt. As he increased pressure, a shock wave and spot-filled semi-consciousness bolted through him. He grunted, clenched his teeth and closed his eyes—but only for an instant. When they squinted open again, Christian sat still.

"You need a doctor, Matt. I can take you if you'll let me."

Matt didn't respond. He glared at Christian, took several deep breaths, and again glanced down. He placed his free hand back over the tear, carefully traced a straight line around his side, to the back of his shirt. The thick, sticky moisture disappeared for a space, and then returned again just before his fingers found a second tear at the small of his back, just above his left buttocks.

It went through, he thought.

Bleary-eyed, rain-soaked, and in pain, Matt's mind sharpened with the knowledge that Walt's bullet passed through him. It wasn't lurking inside his body.

He again glanced up. His grimace morphed into a labored smile.

"It'll get infected, Matt. We've got to get you some…"

"Shut up!" Matt growled. "Just shut up."

His eyes swiveled to Christian's right, to the construction box next to a high table upon which several sets of rolled plans lay. The box was the large wooden enclosure upon which Hound had plopped after dragging his wounded leg up the steps. Matt stared at it, Christian's words biting him. The box had to have some purpose. Perhaps it contained a first aid kit.

"Stay there," he ordered through gritted teeth.

He shambled unsteadily to the box, eyes and gun trained on Christian. He reached down, clenching away pain, and tried to lift the lid. It was locked. He stepped away, aimed the gun at the locking mechanism, and squeezed the trigger. The mechanism exploded, and the lid popped open. He turned quickly and noticed that Christian had kneed slightly closer.

"Don't think about it," Matt said. "I'm not passing out yet." But he was exhausted, dazed. He needed to stop the bleeding and rest if he was going to survive.

Christian said nothing. He nodded calmly and glared at Matt.

Matt lifted the lid. Sitting neatly on a shelf to the right of the enclosure was a large white metal box bearing a red cross on top. He tucked it under his gun arm and dropped the box's lid back in place. He then sat atop it, rested the first aid box on his lap and opened it.

"I can help you," Christian offered.

Matt nodded slowly, eyes hooded.

"Stay where you are." His voice though labored, was calm, in control.

It took Matt fifteen minutes to remove his shirt, open and apply gut-stinging iodine to the entry and exit wounds, haphazardly goop on an antibiotic salve, and apply large self-stick antiseptic bandage pads to the wounds. Blood flow was slow but continuous during the entire effort, and he grew lightheaded again; but the grip on the gun and the direction of its aim never wavered. Finally, he tied his shirt tightly around himself by its sleeves, ensuring continuous pressure to both wounds. When he was done, he sat quietly, head and shoulders slumped, breathing slow and ragged.

Christian said nothing during Matt's ministrations. While he remained tautly primed to spring if the man faltered, it became clear that Matt's constitution was stronger than Christian had credited him with. So he waited, his mind racing with options, until Matt rested.

"Now what, Matt?" Christian asked calmly, no threat in his tone or demeanor. "You're not going to kill me. You know that. That's not who you are. Don't get me wrong; I appreciate that about you. I really do. I saw that humanness in you the first time we met. That's why I thought you'd be a good fit for us."

Matt sat quietly as Christian spoke.

"I'll tell you," Christian shook his head. "Even though you've done a good job of fixing yourself up there, you need to get to a hospital. Trust me, I know what the loss of blood will do to a man. I can help you. Look, my car is out back. I'll drive you."

Matt smiled wearily.

"Yeah, you can drive me." His voice was weak. His mind, however, had regained sharpness; fatigued still, but able to respond with purpose. "But not to the hospital. We're going to the police."

Christian didn't flinch; his face didn't drop. He smiled, as if he anticipated the move.

"Okay, if that's what you want," he said.

Matt, surprised, was suddenly unsure of his decision.

"Let's go to the police, Matt. And what are we going to tell them? You're going to say I tried to kill you? That I ordered these three gentlemen lying dead here to kill you? Yet you're the one with the gun. Your fingerprints are on it, not mine. The bullet from your gun killed Hound over there, and it sure doesn't look like my guys got the better of their encounter with you."

Matt's mind raced. No one would believe he was the aggressor here. It was Christian who...

"And who are they going to believe, Matt?" Christian continued. "A part-time waiter who tells some cockamamie story that Peter Christian is part of some conspiracy against God; that you're the guy who figured it out? I don't mean any disrespect here, but c'mon, who's going to believe that? Especially when I tell them what's really going on. When I tell them you were blackmailing me, in cahoots with the Hound over there and Mr. Sprigs, two of my trusted associates who turned against me? How you managed to kill Walt here and then take his gun after he fought off Hound and Sprigs?"

Christian babbled on as Matt tried to make sense of his words. They weren't right, but he couldn't form the thoughts that explained why. Surely the police wouldn't believe Christian. He started to speak, but Christian continued louder, more forcefully.

"I know you're thinking they can't possibly believe me. But, look at it, Matt. Is your story any more believable than mine? And do you think you have a chance against my connections in this city? You tell me who they're going to want to believe, then you tell me who they're going to believe."

Matt struggled for clarity. Maybe Christian was right. He, Hannah, and Corny believed the police were part of the conspiracy for his parchment. And what were the chances they would believe Matt even if they weren't part of Christian's web? Who would believe such a story in a cynical world geared only to the realities of the secular senses?

He wasn't thinking straight. He knew it, but he couldn't figure how to change it. He braced his empty hand atop the box and pushed himself to his feet. He wobbled, caught himself, and finally stood firmly. Christian eyed him expectantly. Matt lifted the gun and aimed it at Christian's head.

"What do I do then to get you to leave me alone, Mr. Christian?" His voice cracked, weak again, now from lack of direction in addition to fatigue. "Do I shoot you here; leave you with your friends?"

"They'd catch you, Matt," Christian responded without hesitation, but with great calm. His voice was soft, soothing, unhurried. "You'd be made out to look like some crazed killer; someone who'd reacted insanely to a perceived employment slight. That'd destroy your family. Besides, Matt, that's not you." His confidence grew with each word, but he continued to sit, still at Matt's mercy.

Matt's arm wavered and the weapon dropped slightly.

"Look, I have a way we can solve this thing," Christian said. "We both come out looking good. But you'll have to promise me something."

"What's that?" Matt whispered.

"I'll get to that. First, I think the best way to handle this is that we go to the police. But we go together, on the same side. We give them the story that you saved my life. You came in today for a job interview, we've got evidence of that, right?"

Matt nodded absently.

"We explain how Hound and Sprigs, along with Walt, were blackmailing me, and that you saved the day by fighting them off, much the way you actually did."

Matt frowned, shook his head.

"It'll work. I'll make it work." Christian said. "Look, do you mind if I get up? This cold floor is killing me."

Matt nodded, but followed Christian up with the gun. Christian raised his hands and nodded, making no move toward Matt. He began bending his knees and lifting his legs to work out the stiffness. He smiled.

"The joints get creaky with age." Christian eyed Matt closely. "So, the thing I need from you? It's that parchment."

Matt flinched, suddenly awake, confused but alert.

"I want you to promise me you'll get it to me sometime in the next week. Bring it to my office. When I have it in my hands, I'll hand you a cashier's check for five million dollars."

Matt's eyes bulged. He stepped back, gun poised, but hanging lower.

Christian clucked a short laugh.

"Let's say I'd like to help you get on your feet as a reward for saving my life." He stopped bending, stood straight, hands on his hips, confident. "What do you say? Does that work for you?"

Matt's mind again tried to work thoughts moving in directions that made no sense.

"Why?" Matt croaked.

It was Christian's turn for surprise. His confident smile morphed quickly into confusion.

"Why do you want the parchment so badly?" Matt continued.

"Oh." Christian smiled awkwardly. "Let's just say I'm a collector of antiquities. I like old stuff."

No, Matt thought. That makes no sense. That couldn't be what this was all about. Christian wanted to destroy the parchment…didn't he?

Though Matt's eyes were aimed at Christian, his gaze was distant, pensive, his mind working through Christian's words. Slowly his thoughts coalesced around the parchment, something to which he could cling, as if Christian had opened a door and reminded Matt of the real issue. He spoke slowly, deliberately, thinking through every word.

"You said the parchment was already where you wanted it. Why would you need me to get it for you?"

Christian was nonplussed for a second, but again quickly recovered, shook his head, and smiled lightly.

"Sure, it's at the cathedral. I know I could buy it from the priests there, but I thought the money should go to you and your family."

That's bullshit, Matt thought. He wants to destroy it. That's what he's always wanted.

The discussions with Corny came back to Matt and he remembered there was more. There was Professor Rosen's murder and the murders of others who'd made the mistake of getting in Christian's way; there was the attack on his father's dog, and there were the attacks on Hannah, Corny, and himself. And what of the steely-eyed Arab—the killer who'd bowed before Christian a short time ago? He'd worn the same Cornerstone Security uniform Matt had seen at the Cathedral—the uniform of Peter Christian's own private security forces. What was that all about?

And before Matt completed the question, he knew the answer.

CHAPTER SIXTY-SEVEN

"SO, DO WE have a deal?" Christian asked expectantly.

Matt nodded, staring at Christian, this time not with hatred, anger, or vengeance, but rather absently as he assessed a plan taking shape in his mind.

"Give me your jacket," Matt said, his voice strengthening with new understanding.

Christian's smile dissolved. He didn't respond, and didn't move to comply. He simply stood, peering from beneath a brow creased with questions.

"I'm cold Mr. Christian. I can't go anywhere without covering myself. You're about my size."

Christian smiled again, tentatively this time, his prior confidence replaced by doubt and hesitation. He nodded, removed the jacket and heaved it underhanded to Matt. Matt slipped into it, grimacing as he favored his wounds.

"Now give me your keys and cell phone."

Christian shook his head. The smile disappeared.

"I'll drive, Matt. I know the way. You're injured. I can handle this," he said.

"I'll take the keys and cell phone, Mr. Christian."

Christian was silent, tense, trying to understand. His moment was slipping away.

"No, Matt," he said firmly. "I'm not going to give them to you. You're not right in the head. I told you I'd drive. I'll drive."

Matt leveled the gun at him.

"What? Are you going to shoot me now...over car keys and a cell phone?"

Matt squeezed the trigger. The bullet cut a perfect hole in Christian's left shirtsleeve before it entered and exited his forearm. Christian screamed as his arm flew backward, spinning him around, and staggering him nearly to the floor. Shock gripped him. He turned sharply in a crouch to Matt.

"The next one hits a leg, Mr. Christian," Matt said without emotion. "And the one after that, a knee. Give me the keys and cell phone."

Blood oozed through Christian's fingers gripping his left forearm. His face was clouded, the arrogant, self-assured smile gone, replaced by a stunned, dark anger.

"Now!" Matt growled.

Christian reached into his right pant pocket and extracted the cell phone and keys, both covered in his blood.

"Put them on the floor right there, and step away," Matt instructed.

He did.

Matt bent gingerly to the first aid box atop the construction box. He removed the tube of antiseptic salve, a gauze bandage roll, and tape, and flipped it all to the ground at Christian's feet.

"Take care of your wound," he said. "I'll drive."

CHAPTER SIXTY-EIGHT

ASSIM RAHMAN WAITED patiently in a janitor closet along the corridor between the cathedral's parking structure and its bottom level mausoleum. The long concrete corridor provided a workmanlike bunker feel that served no purpose other than as direct access to the cathedral's lower level from the garage. The mausoleum itself was a magnificent blend of marble and stained glass that housed the treasures and relics of the Church's Southern California history as well as the final resting place of St. Vibiana, the cathedral's patron saint, and other private personages in a warren of steel-reinforced crypts. Assim Rahman wasn't interested in any of the mausoleum's elegant beauty however. He waited in the closet for his moment.

The fifteen-minute drive from the Cornerstone building to the cathedral had taken him nearly an hour through the rain-slogged traffic of L.A.'s streets. But he'd anticipated delay. His time would not come until three quarters of an hour past noon, during the mass's Bible readings. So he waited, tightly prepared, but patient in the knowledge that his time drew near.

Ever since Assim had left the Master, he'd been at peace. He'd exited the parking structure in the black rental truck with opaque side-windows, through the employee gate, the same way he'd entered: without notice.

He'd flashed his Cornerstone Security badge at the cathedral's structure without providing a clear view of his face, and he'd walked directly to the closet—just another security guard doing his job beneath the cathedral's main thoroughfares. All would have been perfect had a plain-clothed member of the Swiss Guard patrolling the crypts not happened to open the garage-access corridor door just as Assim Rahman was entering the closet. The rules were that Cornerstone security-people were only to pass through the corridor without dawdling. Certainly there was no need for any to enter the janitor closet and close the door behind him.

"Hey!" the guard shouted as Assim stepped in, pretending he hadn't heard.

Seconds later the door flew open, and the stone-faced Swiss Guardsman stepped into the doorframe shouting in heavily accented English.

"What the hell are y..."

Assim met the man at the entry with a knife-thrust into the neck and an arm around his shoulders that spun him around. He dragged the stunned man into the room. Not a drop of blood fell until Assim completed the killing by turning him to the side and dragging the blade across his throat. The blood geyser shot at the sidewall. Assim dropped the body to the floor. He then stepped past, scanned the corridor, and pulled the door closed.

Now, an hour later, the iron smell of blood mixed with the body's other releases would have been suffocating to anyone else. But Assim Rahman was unfazed. Several times since the encounter, he'd heard voices, some asking about "Andre," presumably the man who'd bled out at his feet. But no one tried the door of his hideaway, and he'd not been challenged again. So, he'd sat quietly, alert to the sounds of life outside, yet deep within himself in a trance of clarity. Here was the very purpose, from the beginning of time, for which he was born.

When his watch's timer beeped, he stood. He allowed himself several seconds of deep stretching to ensure his every muscle was ready for the task; then he pushed open the door and scanned the corridor. After he stepped out, he secured the door behind him and started toward the mausoleum of the Cathedral of our Lady of the Angels.

CHAPTER SIXTY-NINE

PETER CHRISTIAN DIDN'T utter a word as he and Matt followed the cell phone's light down four flights of steps, through the structure's first floor, and out the back to Christian's limousine. He said nothing as Matt held the front passenger door open, the gun aimed low at Christian's mid-section; he slid gingerly into the seat. He said nothing as he bandaged his wound, dripping blood over himself and the car's upholstery, and tried to find a comfortable position in which to hold his throbbing arm. His thoughts were of dark-hearted vengeance. Not once did he anticipate the day ending with anything other than his complete victory. Not once did he believe he could be outdone, even when he noticed that Matt was missing the turn to the Los Angeles Police Department's office on West 1st Street.

"The station's to the right," he said.

Matt nodded grimly, but did not respond.

"Matt, the station is that way."

Again Matt said nothing.

Christian peered out the windshield at rain soaked structures now touched by rays of sunlight through breaking cloud cover. Traffic was heavy on soggy streets whose slick going slowed their progress. Then, in a moment of perfect understanding he knew that Matt Carter, the waiter who'd been such an irritant for the past two weeks, wasn't going to the police station. He knew that Matt Carter intended to take them to their deaths.

AFTER CHRISTIAN WAS buckled into the passenger seat of the limousine, Matt had stepped gingerly around the front of the vehicle to the driver door. There, he stood and dialed a phone number he read from the soggy, blood-stained card he'd taken from his jean pocket. He prayed for an answer, but it rang without response and ultimately went to the message voice.

Matt didn't leave a message. He ended the call and dialed again, hoping persistence might help, even as anxiety surged in him. Again there were several rings. Matt silently pleaded for a response.

"Hello," came a whispered voice.

"Cardinal Metzinger?" Matt was at once relieved yet anxious, as he turned his back to the limo.

"Yes," Metzinger responded haltingly.

"It's Mathew Carter, Father. I…I need your help, Sir. I think something is going to happen to the Shroud today. We need to stop it."

Silence.

"Cardinal Metzinger? Are you there?"

"Wait, Mathew. I have to step away."

Matt waited, his stomach churning, light-headedness returning in subtle waves. When Metzinger's voice returned, it did so with volume.

"What is going to happen?"

"I don't know…it won't make sense if I try to explain over the phone. But I feel it, Father. No, I know it. I know something is coming."

"Take your time," Metzinger soothed. "Tell me what you…"

"We don't have time, Father. It's going to happen soon. It might even be happening now."

"Mass will be starting soon. I stepped away from the pre-processional activities to take your call. Nothing appears out of the ordinary. What is going to happen?"

"It'll happen during the mass," Matt mused softly before he again spoke to Metzinger. "I don't know what it is, but it will be during mass. Please, meet me at the garage entry. I'll get there as soon as I can. Please."

"I'll meet you, but give me something…something to watch for."

"I have Peter Christian with me. I think one of his security people intends to do something to the Shroud. I think they intend to steal it...or destroy it."

"Which security person?"

"I don't know his name. He's Arabic, dark skin, thick black hair, but he has blue eyes. They're almost a silvery blue...like steel. He's dangerous, Father."

"WHAT ARE YOU doing?" Christian screamed as the limo approached West Temple. "Where are we going?"

Matt didn't answer. He didn't turn to Christian. He maneuvered the vehicle to the right and braked to a stop, right turn-indicator clicking.

Christian stared ahead wide-eyed. He shook his head, fear surging. He needed to stop this idiot.

"Don't do this, Matt," he said.

"Don't do what?" Matt asked softly. He glanced at Christian, his face giving no sense of his thoughts, his right hand resting comfortably with Walt's silenced weapon aimed at Christian's mid-section.

The vehicle completed the turn onto Temple; Christian's eyes bulged wider, panic bubbling.

"You crazy bastard," he shouted. "Don't do this! You can't go to the cathedral!"

"Why?" Matt shouted. "Why can't I go to the cathedral?"

Christian's head swiveled to the scene out the windshield, back to Matt again, and then to the growing hulk of the Cathedral of Our Lady of the Angels several blocks away.

"No!" Christian shouted again.

He lurched left and grabbed the steering wheel in his left hand, as his right reached but was constrained by his seat belt. He jerked the wheel to the right, pain from his wounded forearm tearing at him; yet he held firm, the pain and an auto accident being preferable to what awaited them at the cathedral.

Matt's right hand shot up, still clutching the gun, and it joined his left at the wheel, gripping to hold the car steady; but it swerved right. Horns blared, brakes shrieked, and a battered light pickup struck a glancing blow to Christian's side door causing the pickup to spin to the right and the limo to lurch left. Christian's grip waivered, but only for an instant, and he re-gripped and yanked again. Matt's foot was off the gas, covering the brake, as he fought for control. He tugged and pushed against the constant pressure, but he couldn't wrestle control away from Christian's panicked grip. Matt reflexively lifted his gun hand and slammed it down on Christian's forearm. Christian screamed, released the wheel, and immediately tried to re-grip.

Christian kept coming, Matt fighting, until Matt finally backhanded the gun to the point of Christian's nose. Christian slammed backward and gurgled a shocked cry. Both hands came to his nose. Blood poured through his fingers.

The car continued to swerve as Matt struggled to steady it, continually watchful for a new move by Christian. But Christian made none. His head leaned back against the headrest, blood trickling under his protecting hands down his jaw and onto his shirt.

Traffic around the limo had stopped until Matt had it again rolling straight in its own lane. Vehicles began to slip past as quickly as they could, their drivers craning to see through the opaque side windows. The light pickup driver, a man carrying construction materials in the bed of his battered truck, also stole a look, but appeared content that the limo made no move to pull over. Matt drove on, taking sidelong glances at Christian, who appeared subdued...until the limo pulled into the left turn lane at Hill Street. The cathedral grounds and parking structure were on their left.

"I'll pay you ten million dollars," Christian mumbled, his voice scratchy and muffled through hands cupped over his nose.

Matt said nothing. He looked to the garage entry in search of Cardinal Metzinger as he pulled into the intersection and waited for cross-traffic to clear.

"Matt," Christian begged, his voice quavering. "Do you hear me? I'll pay you anything you want...enough for you and your family to live the rest of your lives without having to work. Don't do this."

"What's happening here?" Matt demanded. He turned to Christian. "What's your guy going to do?"

Christian didn't look at Matt. He stared out the windshield, beaten. The intersection cleared; Matt started his turn.

"It's…a bomb," Christian whispered.

CHAPTER SEVENTY

CARDINAL METZINGER, CEREMONIAL vestments flowing, reached the mausoleum level and started along the mausoleum's main corridor through the private chapels and crypts to the garage access corridor. Assim Rahman stepped into the same corridor from the other end. The young Afghan's every sense had been sharply alert, his mind completely focused. He was acutely aware of every crypt, every surface shaping his path's way, and every sound reflecting from the mausoleum's walls, yet he was surprised when he turned into the corridor and noticed the big man lumbering heavily toward him. He hesitated an instant, and then lowered his eyes and turned quickly down the nearest row of crypts just as the cardinal raised his head.

Assim knew the cleric had seen him because he could hear that the big man's pace had slackened. Assim quickened his. He reached the end of the row, turned and scuttled noiselessly along the mausoleum's north wall using the crypt rows as shields, his hearing now attuned exclusively to the movements of the cleric. He waited at the end of one of the crypt rows until he heard the rustle of the cardinal's vestments suddenly quicken and pass his row. He then continued on and only turned up the final row of crypts to the main corridor when the cardinal's steps muffled sufficiently to confirm that he was far enough away and heading toward the garage. Assim waited to hear the garage corridor door open before he stepped fully back into the main mausoleum corridor.

Assim took the steps to the main level slowly, one at a time, as if he were in no hurry. When he reached the landing, he turned down the north ambulatory and shifted his focus.

The corridor was sporadically spotted with people; a few milling absently about the hall, but most focused inward, either staring into or moving to seats in the nave. Security guards were spread about, some with the Cornerstone Security insignia prominently displayed, others wearing the uniforms of the Vatican's Swiss Guard, and others still, plain-clothed, like the man who lay dead in the janitor closet in the basement. All eyes were focused inside the nave, out of which came the sonorous notes of the pipe organ diverting the enormous crowd before the start of the procession of clerics down the church's long central aisle from the baptistery to the sanctuary.

Assim Rahman walked slowly down the ambulatory toward the exit. About mid-way down, on his right, was an alcove containing a kneeler before a dimly lit painting of the Virgin Mary of Guadalupe. Beyond that was an access aisle between wood-paneled confessionals and the sand-colored stone block of the wall. He stepped through the access into a long narrow room. Chairs for those awaiting confession lined the stone wall beneath two small paintings, one of the crucified Christ, and the other of ancient clerics unknown to Assim. No one was in the waiting area, just as Assim had anticipated. So, he stood alone. He listened to the sounds from the nave, and he waited for the beginning of mass.

———

CARDINAL METZINGER SAW the Cornerstone Security Guard within seconds after reaching the cathedral's mausoleum level. His immediate reaction was to wonder why a Cornerstone guard was on this level at this time, particularly in view of Matt's warning that some evil was coming from just such a person. Metzinger slowed as the guard turned down one of the crypt rows; the cardinal moved slowly past glancing down each row, intent on questioning the guard. But he didn't see the guard again, and as he thought about Matt's description of "thick black hair," his mind's eye revealed to him that there was no hair poking out of his cap. In fact, the only thing he noticed in his distant glimpse was a thin white fringe that protruded just below the back of the hat's crown. He wondered another moment whether he should call to the guard, but thought better of it as he remembered Matt's urgency.

Metzinger waited at the garage's entry for ten minutes before a black Mercedes limousine turned left from West Temple to Hill and then waited for traffic to clear a path to the garage entry. But the limousine didn't turn in—even after cross-traffic cleared.

CHAPTER SEVENTY-ONE

A BOMB! THIS lunatic is going to blow the Cathedral to destroy the Shroud?

Matt's mind froze.

"You're going to kill us both if you enter that structure," Christian mumbled flatly.

The cross traffic cleared, but Matt did not turn.

His head swiveled to Christian, who rolled his head sideways, and eyed Matt through bloodshot eyes. Matt shook his head, wanting to scream something, but he had no words.

Christian's promise of unimaginable wealth was irrelevant; still, things had suddenly changed for Matt. No longer was he on a mission to save the Shroud and his parchment from theft, damage, or destruction. No longer was he going to put the perpetrator of numerous evils behind bars, and in so doing, end the horror of the past weeks. Those thoughts disappeared with the shocking change in stakes. While the danger inherent in what he was doing had played at the fringes of his mind from the moment he'd decided to go to the cathedral instead of the police, the reality that death was possible—no, probable—had not struck him until this moment. And suddenly his decision had become one to sacrifice his life for something only weeks before he'd not even known.

He sat in stunned silence as his focus turned absently away from Christian.

Was he willing to die?

For what?

Was he willing to sacrifice his life and everything he knew for this… this cloth?

Could he give his life? Even if it was to save the only tangible proof of God's existence: the first gospel of the death and resurrection of Jesus Christ?

Matt knew what Peter Christian and his man intended. He was the only person who knew, the only one who could do anything to stop it.

Did he have a choice?

Christian's sidelong look bore into him. Outside, Cardinal Metzinger shrugged, questioning Matt's delay.

Matt turned to Christian, smiled resignedly, and started his turn into the garage.

———————

"IT'S A BOMB."

Mathew Carter's simple statement as he rolled down the window and maneuvered the Mercedes into the garage shocked Cardinal Metzinger. But it was the sight of the bloodied Peter Christian and the immediate understanding of his involvement that made the shock a reality.

The cardinal directed Matt to move the limo to the far side of the garage, and hesitated only a second before he trotted through parked vehicles to meet them at the access door to the cathedral's basement. While hesitation in the face of such a threat would have been justified for thoughts of personal safety, Metzinger's hesitation was only for prayer. He prayed for strength to do what was necessary to save the three thousand souls sitting hopefully as mass unfolded in the cathedral above.

———————

"THIS IS SUICIDE you crazy sons-of-bitches," Christian screamed when the big cardinal opened the passenger door to pull him from the car.

"I'm not getting out! Kill me here if you want," Christian spewed. "I'm not going up there!" And he rooted himself in his seat, entangling his arms tightly over the seat belt, and holding himself rigid against attempts to remove him from the car.

The cardinal didn't hesitate. He pulled his left arm back, balled his enormous hand, and drove his sledge-like fist into the right side of Christian's face. The businessman grunted as blood spurted onto the cardinal's vestments; Christian fell into semi-consciousness long enough for Metzinger and Matt to unhook the seat belt and drag him from the vehicle.

Matt stumbled under the groggy Christian's weight as he and the cardinal supported him through the basement corridor and mausoleum level to the first floor elevator. Metzinger had noted Matt's rain-soaked, blood stained, haggard appearance as the two pulled Christian from the car. He'd seen the open jacket that matched Christian's pants, and the flannel shirt tied inside just above Matt's waist. He'd said nothing in the initial rush, both he and Matt knowing what they had to do. But, now, as they entered the elevator and Matt leaned heavily against one wall, Metzinger looked at him.

"Can you do this, Mathew?" he asked.

Matt nodded, eyes down, exhausted again.

"Are you wounded?"

Again, Matt nodded.

"He needs a doctor," Christian gurgled, coughed.

Metzinger extracted a handkerchief from inside his vestments and handed it to the bloodied Christian. "Wipe your face and hold it to your nose," he ordered. He then turned back to Matt.

"Mathew?" Metzinger eyed him closely.

"I'm good, Father," Matt croaked. "I lost some blood…gunshot. I'm okay, just a little weak. I can do this." He glanced at Christian and then stood up straight. He returned his attention to Metzinger as the elevator door opened. "Let's go."

MOMENTS EARLIER THE music accompanying the procession into the church stopped. The churchmen had attained their places in the sanctuary, behind the altar. Assim Rahman stepped from the confession alcove, walked up the north ambulatory, and turned into the first point of access to the nave. He paused to hear Archbishop Parra greet the crowd. Then he stepped into the nave and pressed his back against the nearest wall.

Although the cathedral grounds and interior corridors were thick with Cornerstone Security, the church interior was off limits once the mass started. Security during the service was in the hands of plain-clothes and ceremonial-garbed Swiss Guard. But, with the tightly packed crowd standing in their pews and in the aisles at the beginning of mass, Assim was able to slide inconspicuously along the sidewall toward the front of the church. Once there, he stopped and surveyed the sanctuary.

His eyes found the wall behind the altar. There, hanging horizontally, was the object of his mission—the icon to which such reverence had been given, the only hard evidence to which the deluded could point to justify their belief in their god. Its destruction would free them and bring them to the light the Master sought for them. Shortly, it would be over. Shortly, his new life would begin.

His eyes next scanned the closest worshippers for signs of interest in him. When he noticed none, he reached with his left hand into the interior cuff of his right sleeve. He grasped the end of the detonator and pulled it into the palm of his right hand. He gripped the device firmly, flipped up the protective covering, and laid his thumb lightly atop the tiny plunger. He waited for the crowd to sit and the Bible readings to begin.

MATT AND METZINGER entered the nave with Peter Christian held firmly between them. They made their entry through the same tiny corridor through which the Afghan stepped less than two minutes before. Unlike his entrance, however, theirs was quickly observed, and immediately met with stares. The bedraggled appearance and the blood with which each was spattered drew much of the attention, but it was the recognition of the battered Peter Christian that drew shock.

A plain-clothes guard with obvious concern for the cardinal quickly intercepted them. As Matt stretched to see over the assemblage, Metzinger whispered to the guard.

"There is a bomb in the church," he said calmly.

The guard's mouth dropped. Metzinger grabbed an arm and pulled him close.

"We must act now, young man. Please have your guards quietly escort people out through the back exits. When the bomber makes his appearance, there will be panic. Make sure you are prepared to deal with it."

The guard nodded numbly as Metzinger released him with a slight shove. But the guard didn't move.

"Go now!" Metzinger growled.

He did.

MATT SPOTTED THE bomber. He picked off the black-with-red-side-panel Cornerstone Security uniform almost as soon as he stepped away from the wall and peered down the side aisle toward the front of the church. He wasn't sure it was the killer, however, until the young man leaned forward, away from the wall, and fidgeted with his right sleeve. That's when Matt noticed the white fringe of bandage extending below the cap and behind his right ear; and that's when he saw his right hand close around whatever had dropped into his palm from his sleeve.

Matt's stomach lurched. He knew it was the detonator. His mind screamed for him to run. But he stood rooted, breath constricted again as fear heaved through his chest to his brain.

The crowd sat in unison, with those closest to Matt still eyeing him and his companions. The bomber stepped forward. Matt closed his eyes.

"Oh God," he mumbled.

When he opened his eyes only a blink later, the killer had not moved further. His eyes were fixed on the priest approaching the lectern for the first reading. Matt's eyes followed the killer's gaze to Father Roberts and in the next instant he caught sight of the killer's objective.

On the wall behind the altar, now visible over the heads of the seated throng was the Shroud of Turin. The 14-foot long linen hung horizontally above its protective casket. It was encased in a thick glass-like, air-controlled sleeve. The image, normally faint up close, was clearly visible, and, to Matt's eye, appeared to radiate an aura of peace. Matt nodded grimly.

"I see him," Matt whispered over his shoulder. He pointed. "He's up front, along the wall."

Christian squirmed, tried to wrench out of their grasp. Metzinger's grip tightened; his other hand took the front of Christian's bloodied shirt and pulled him close. Christian stared pleadingly into the big man's eyes.

"You can stop this," Metzinger whispered. Christian shook his head, began to speak, but was cut off when Metzinger leaned closer and snarled, "You will try!"

Matt tugged Christian's arm, and the three shuffle-stepped past others standing in the aisle. They were within five feet of the killer when Father Roberts stepped to the lectern and opened the book for the first reading.

Assim Rahman moved quickly.

CHAPTER SEVENTY-TWO

THE AFGHAN TORE open his outer vest and shirt exposing the inner vest, visibly wired for detonation. He held his right hand high, the control mechanism firmly gripped, his thumb pressed down tightly on the plunger. Release of the thumb would cause detonation.

"I have a bomb," he shouted, his voice echoing in the dead silence that preceded the first reading.

An instant of bewildered silence took the crowd. Eyes moved to the black-clad killer. He leered, wild-eyed and crazed at the assemblage, and pandemonium erupted.

People leapt from their seats, screamed for escape, climbed over one another, and clambered for distance. But the chaos formed blocks of frenzied congestion over which no one could climb and through which no one could squeeze. While some were able to trickle through side access ways, most were simply caught in the roiling cauldron of panicked humanity. The killer's eyes bulged with excitement.

Archbishop Parra stood behind the altar, his mouth agape, eyes wide. He saw the "Cornerstone Security" lettering on the back of the bomber who twirled in a tight circle as he admired the chaos. The archbishop nonsensically wondered how this could be happening. He glanced around at the 15 other priests, bishops, and auxiliary bishops seated about the sanctuary. None had yet moved. All stared at the young man wired with explosives. The archbishop next looked for escape, but saw immediately that no path existed. He stood in stunned silence.

"Please!" came a shout nearby.

Assim Rahman whirled, a manic smile on his face. Father Roberts stood in front of the lectern, hands held out beseechingly, mouth working with words the killer did not hear. Assim lowered his head, eyed the priest malevolently, and strode deliberately toward him. Roberts stood tall at the approach; he did not flinch or cower away, but stepped forward as if to meet the young Afghan—to help him—to talk him down. But Assim smiled; and, as he reached the priest, he drew his left fist back and drove it into the priest's stomach, bending him over in a whoosh of lost air. When Assim withdrew his fist and continued past Roberts, the priest toppled, struggling for breath.

Assim turned to the other clerics in the sanctuary. They were on their feet, running about the altar and into the roiling crowd, scrabbling, like the rest, for the safety that was impossible to attain.

CARDINAL METZINGER RELEASED Peter Christian and leapt to Father Roberts' side. He crouched to aid the priest.

Matt's grasp of Christian tightened. He dragged him to a point five feet in front of the altar, directly in line with the encased Shroud. There they stopped, Matt firmly committed, Christian shaking uncontrollably.

From this place, they would be the first to die; Christian would have no choice but to act.

"Call him," Matt ordered.

Christian's eyes were glazed, his stance wobbly.

Matt re-gripped him, held him upright, stepped into his face.

"You can stop this! Do it, now!"

Christian looked at Matt, eyes pleading, still glazed but slowly clearing. Matt glared at him, turned him to the altar. Christian stared at Assim Rahman, who pranced maniacally beneath the Shroud's encasement.

"Assim," Christian croaked, barely above a whisper.

The bomber turned and stood with his back to the Shroud's velvet draped casket. He glared wild-eyed, at the swirling chaos of panic, and his smile widened.

Matt shook Christian, pushed him closer to the altar.

"Assim!" Christian shouted.

———

THE AFGHAN HEARD the Master's voice. His smile wavered as he scanned the faceless creatures crushing one another in their attempts to escape. And then he saw the Master, raising his hands and shouting his name, and Assim's smile broadened.

The Master will join me in our final victory.

———

CARDINAL METZINGER SAW the bomber's reaction to Christian's shout. He noted the initial hesitation followed by the widening smile, not this time of insanity, but of…excitement? And he knew Christian's presence would change nothing.

"Protect yourself," Metzinger whispered to Father Roberts.

As the priest scrabbled away, the big cardinal stood.

———

MATT SAW THE change in the bomber's expression. He immediately understood that Christian's words would have no effect. He instinctively pulled Christian back and pushed him away, behind him to a safety that didn't exist.

Christian stumbled and fell to the floor.

Matt's eye caught Cardinal Metzinger's massive frame hurtling toward the bomber just as Matt threw himself to the ground. When he glanced up, Metzinger had reached the startled killer and thrown one arm around him as the other reached for the detonator wielding hand. The force of the cardinal's attack took them both to the ground and the bomber's thumb slid off the detonator.

CHAPTER SEVENTY-THREE

THE EXPLOSION GOUGED a crater in the four-foot thick steel-reinforced floor of the sanctuary and sent missiles of debris on concussive waves through the church. The bomber and Cardinal Metzinger were obliterated instantly, not a molecule of either ever to be distinguished from the blast's other detritus. But it was the cardinal's body, many said, wrapped around that of the killer that absorbed the detonation's major killing force and saved the others...all except two.

As the other priests and bishops ran past Archbishop Parra, heads down, frantically seeking distance, he stood dumbfounded and stared, the events unfolding in seeming slow motion. He saw the bomber leering maniacally at the frenzied mass of churning humanity, raising his right hand firmly over his head, ready to remove his thumb and detonate the bomb. And then he saw Cardinal Metzinger lunge at the killer, take him to the floor in a powerful hug, and strain to reach the detonator.

That's when Archbishop Parra turned to run, but the blast took him with a force that dismembered and disbursed his parts before he'd taken a single step.

THE BLAST'S SONIC wave tore the altar's six-ton red marble slab from its base. It lifted it high and flipped it over the prone bodies cowering on the

THE FIRST GOSPEL

floor between the sanctuary and the pews. The wave then threw the slab atop three just vacated rows of wooden pews, crushing them to the ground.

The altar's heavy marble base withstood the blast, holding in place and providing Matt a funnel of protection from the full force of the blast's first wave. But the wave tore at him, shredding his coat and jeans, searing exposed flesh, and driving him to slide into the solid wood front wall of the first pew. His head struck with a resounding crack that was lost in the still echoing din of the blast, and he lost consciousness.

While the wave destroyed hanging light fixtures, tore the magnificent tapestries, and crumpled pews, the human damage was in broken bones, gashes, concussions, and gaping wounds. No one other than the two at the point of detonation and the Archbishop of Los Angeles were killed in those first seconds. It was the ricochet wave that claimed the final victim.

The walls along the back of the sanctuary absorbed much of the blast's force with a strength for which its architects would be commended for years to come. But the magnificent alabaster windows high above the sanctuary shattered and the pipes of the organ were destroyed.

When the wave hit, the entire structure shook and what wasn't immediately absorbed in the stone ricocheted back into the nave, taking with it the casket of the Shroud, which tumbled end over end and crashed into the first rows of pews on the nave's north side.

The ricochet-wave also took the Shroud, fully encased in its one-ton protective sleeve. Hanging from the back wall, the sleeve was ripped from its anchors and lifted. It cartwheeled over the altar's base before it landed with a deadly crash.

In the nanoseconds between the shock wave's first pass and the coming of its ricochet, Peter Christian flipped over to his back and noticed the body of Mathew Carter splayed unmoving to his right. His immediate thought was that he had survived and that his young nemesis hadn't; but then he saw the Shroud's massive sleeve flip high in the air in a lopsided arc. His initial relief morphed into complete understanding, the instant before the Shroud's encasement struck him chest high, and drove its corner into him, pinning him dead to the marble floor of the nave.

The Shroud's sleeve teetered on its point before it toppled and crushed the remains of Peter Christian.

CHAPTER SEVENTY-FOUR

WHEN MATHEW CARTER woke the afternoon sun shone a funnel of warmth through his room's window. On the credenza beneath the window sat dozens of flowers in motley hues. He eyed the cheery sprays, absently wondering where he was.

When he rolled his head away from the window to the other side of his room, he saw Hannah standing in a doorway.

"Matt?" she whispered.

"Hi," he responded weakly.

"Matt; you're awake!" A broad smile covered her face as she stepped to the bed.

Matt nodded, hesitated, and then reached for her hand. She squeezed it. He smiled.

"How are you?" She sat, placing her other hand atop his, softly caressing it.

"I'm good, I think." He nodded. Violent flashes of events in the cathedral began to come to him. "Where are we?"

"You're at UCLA's trauma center. The ambulance brought you straight here after the explosion. People were taken to a number of hospitals…there were a lot of injuries. They brought you here."

"How long have I been here?"

"Two days. I flew in yesterday as soon as I heard." She dropped her head as tears came to her eyes. She lifted a hand to wipe them away.

"Am…am I going to be okay?" he asked.

She looked up with a relieved smile as she continued to wipe away tears.

"You've got cracked ribs, some other injuries…your head was cut badly and you have a concussion. All of that is in addition to the gunshot wound." She shrugged as if asking how that happened? He shook his head and waved the query aside. "The doctors said you're going to be okay, though."

Matt smiled at her, taking in her steady gaze, moist, but happy. Neither one spoke. They stared at each other. Finally, Hannah smiled awkwardly.

"Your father's here," she said, motioning to the door. "Your sisters, too. They're getting lunch."

Matt squeezed her hand.

"How's Corny?" he asked.

"He's a tough old guy. He's going to be fine."

"How about you, Hannah? Are you okay?"

She nodded, dropped her head again, fighting tears.

"Yes," she stammered. "I…I was worried about you, Matt. When we heard about the explosion, the injuries, the damage, and the deaths, I…I didn't know. But you're okay."

"How many deaths?" Matt asked.

"Four. But they're saying there should have been more. People are calling it a miracle, Matt. They're calling you a hero…you and the cardinal from Rome."

"What? Why?"

"Father Roberts, the one you gave the parchment to? He was somewhere up front. He wasn't hurt. He's talking to the press, telling them you and the cardinal were part of the miracle."

"I didn't do…" Matt started, shaking his head. "Is Cardinal Metzinger okay?"

"No. He didn't make it. He grabbed the bomber; he died instantly; they said his body absorbed a lot of the blast's impact…and saved lives. The Archbishop died, too."

Matt nodded.

"There was one more?" he asked.

"A famous business man was the fourth. His name was Peter Christian." Father Roberts said he was there with you and the cardinal."

Matt nodded, surprised.

"What happened to him?" he asked.

"The Shroud," she said. "Father Roberts said the Shroud was in some protective case?" Matt nodded. "The explosion tore it from the wall and threw it toward Christian." She shook her head. "He didn't say toward Christian, he said at him. Father Roberts said it looked as if the Shroud went after him—purposely chose him."

Matt's eyes moved from Hannah; his thoughts drifted.

"Was he there with you, Matt? Christian?" Hannah asked.

"He was," he answered flatly. "Christian was behind all of it. He's the one who had Rosen killed. He was crazy…"

Hannah took his hand again. He stopped and looked at her.

"It's over, Matt," she whispered. "It's over."

He nodded, hoping it was; yet he wondered. Could it all just end with Peter Christian's death? Was it that simple?

Deep down he knew it wasn't.

He knew that while Peter Christian was responsible for the deaths that began with Professor Rosen's murder, there were others of Christian's ilk who would not rest until their own misplaced beliefs in the sanctity of wealth and station were the only guiding lights of the world.

It wasn't over…but for Mathew Carter, he could no longer reflect on what might yet come. He could not fathom the extent of the dangers that lurked in a world run by the Peter Christians of this life.

He smiled wearily. He reached for Hannah; she leaned into him, taking him in a hug, and he wrapped his arms around her.

———————

IN A PLACE far from Los Angeles's Cathedral of Our Lady of the Angels, a very old man of incalculable brilliance stared out the window of his darkened study. Before him stretched the rolling grounds of his estate, from perfectly manicured lawns to a surrounding fringe of forest, all now bathed in the eerie light of a full moon. From behind him came the padded footfall of his aide. The brilliant man, head now bowed, turned slowly. The aide stopped short and awaited permission to speak. The brilliant man raised his head, a glint of pale moonlight catching a red flicker from his hooded, ancient eyes.

"Have you his name?" the brilliant man asked, his voice fractured by age, but firm, calm, and menacing in its demand.

"Yes, Mr. Warden," the aide said, nodding sharply. "His name is Mathew Carter."

EPILOGUE

THERE WAS MUCH talk in the Vatican of cancelling the tour of the Shroud of Turin, but Father Roberts, with the now passionate support of the American Catholic clergy, was compelling in his argument. He spoke of the Shroud's "miraculous" survival despite its presence at the very epicenter of the blast. He told of his survival, completely unscathed despite his proximity to that epicenter, and he described the Shroud's protective aura that saved the lives of the thousands of people inside the cathedral. Most compelling however was his recounting of the martyr's death of Cardinal Metzinger.

Roberts told of the powerful American businessman bent on destroying the Church's most holy relic because he believed faith in God was a cancer to be stamped out in favor of worldly wealth. He told of how that man's evil had been thwarted by the cardinal's sacrifice; how Metzinger had chosen to do the Lord's work and give his life for the love and protection of God's children.

"How can we now turn and run? How can we hide?" Roberts had asked the council of Vatican prelates who sat with the Pope in rapt attention. "Our brother, Cardinal Andrew Metzinger, while opposed to the tour from the beginning, came to understand the great gift left to us by our Lord. He came to understand that we have no greater evangelical tool at our disposal than that gift, and he came to know it had to be shared with all who would know our Lord. A man of the devil tried to stop this tour. A man of God saved it. Let us not give victory to the evil by cancelling this tour. Let us honor the man who gave his life for it, and let us honor our Lord who gives us all the gift of eternal life."

HISTORICAL NOTE

GENERAL JOHN KOURKOUAS, referred to in the Prologue, is considered one of the greatest of early Christianity's military leaders. History notes his army's march across Mesopotamia, its siege of the city of Edessa, and his demand for the Cloth of Edessa in exchange for leaving the city in peace. When Edessa's Emir turned the cloth over, General Kourkouas and his 80,000-man army returned in triumph to Constantinople carrying the Christian faith's most holy relic.

The Cloth of Edessa, also sometimes referred to as the Mandylion, is described by some historians as a square or rectangle of cloth upon which the miraculous image of the face of Jesus is imprinted. These historians say that "Christian tradition" is that the cloth bore Christ's facial image, as if there were no evidence of the true nature of the cloth and the scope of the actual image thereon. Yet, with a simple review of the historical record, it will become clear to even the most skeptical of observers that evidence of the cloth's true nature and scope abounds.

While the "Carter Parchment" is a fictitious document, the events and characters related in it are historically accurate:

- There was a King Abgar in Edessa who made Christianity the city-state's official religion. While the cure of his leprosy is attributed by "tradition" to his viewing of the image of Jesus Christ on the cloth, the fact remains that he accepted Christianity in a world that was exclusively pagan before the cure.

317

- General Kourkouas did besiege Edessa in 943 A.D. and he accepted Christendom's most holy relic in exchange for sparing the city.

- Archdeacon Gregory Referendarius did conduct a mass at Constantinople's Hagia Sophia cathedral within days after the cloth's delivery to the city. At that mass, he gave a sermon, a copy of which exists to this day in the Vatican Archives, in which he spoke of the image on the cloth as the likeness of a man, and he described bloodstains and the wound in the man's side—both references implying that the cloth portrayed a full body image.

In addition, considerable other evidence supports the proposition that the carbon dating done in 1988 was wrong. Consider the icons, religious artifacts, and relics that predate the earliest of the carbon test dates of 1260. Among them was a letter written by a knight in 1204 A.D, almost 6 decades before the earliest of the carbon dates. In that letter, Robert de Clari, a knight of the Fourth Crusade, describes entering the Church of St. Mary at Blachernae in Constantinople and seeing "the sydoines in which our Lord had been wrapped" adding "on every Friday this raised itself upright so that one could see the figure of our Lord on it."

The two sources I found most helpful in my research and study of the Cloth of Edessa/Shroud of Turin are:

- A book titled *The Blood and the Shroud*, by Ian Wilson, an historian and prolific writer currently residing in Brisbane, Australia. In this highly literate and wonderfully entertaining book, Mr. Wilson compiles the historical, scientific, and analytical history of the Shroud of Turin, addressing each theory of the possible origins and authenticity of the cloth and its image.

- The Shroud of Turin Website found at www.Shroud.com. This site was created by Barrie Schwortz, the official documenting photographer for the Shroud of Turin Research Project, Inc. (STURP) in 1978. STURP performed the first extensive scientific examination of the Shroud of Turin, and included among its members the leading scientists of the day in the various fields involved in the testing.

Mr. Schwortz, who was raised an orthodox Jew, and still practices the faith, came to believe that the "Shroud of Turin is the cloth that wrapped the man Jesus after he was crucified." His statement of this fact "is not meant as a religious statement, but one based on [his] privileged position of direct involvement with many of the serious Shroud researchers in the world, and a thorough knowledge of the scientific data, unclouded by media exaggeration and hype."

Mr. Schwortz goes on to state, "The only reason I am still involved with the Shroud of Turin is because knowing the unbiased facts continues to convince me of its authenticity. And I believe only a handful of people have really ever had access to all the unbiased facts. Most of the public has had to depend on the media, who always seem to sensationalize the story or reduce the facts to two-minute sound bites from so-called experts who have 'solved the mystery.' Very few of these 'experts' ever took the time to research the subject, perhaps in part because so much of the information was hard to find."

Thus, he created the site to bring together all evidence and information available about the Shroud and present it in an easy to use format that will enable you to make your own decision of the Shroud's authenticity.

Visit the site to learn the truth about the cloth that bears the one true image of Jesus Christ, a man who lived, died, and rose again 2000 years ago.

OTHER BOOKS BY DARRYL NYZNYK

The Third Term

... masterful plot of terror, faith, deception, and conviction. Readers will be drawn immediately into a carefully and splendidly crafted vortex of memorable characters and unpredictable events.
MIDWEST BOOK REVIEW

Keep your eye on Darryl Nyznyk. ... He is on a par with the best – already better than Grisham, Forsyth, and Harris.
JOHN ANTHONY MILLER,
PHANTOM BOOKSHOP

Mary's Son

Winner of the Mom's Choice Gold Award for Fiction and Inspiration

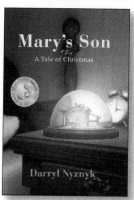

... a wonderful and poignant story ... an inspiring read that reinvents the real Christmas story and crowns it with a modern twist.
LAUREN SMITH, EZINE BOOK REVIEW

Aimed at readers of any age, it's a book for all seasons.
ROGER ZOTTI, RESIDENT BOOK REVIEW

"... a timely, inspirational novel" that has the "hallmarks of a new Christmas classic."
CARL ANDERSON, SUPREME KNIGHT
OF THE KNIGHTS OF COLUMBUS

The Condor Song

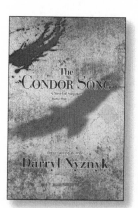

The legal expertise of John Grisham meets the environmental activism of Barbara Kingsolver in this thriller by veteran author Darryl Nyznyk.
SHEILA TRASK,
FORWORD BOOK REVIEWS

... intriguing ... fast-paced narrative ... takes you from the depths of sorrow ... to the triumphant ... overcoming [of] evil ... [The] descriptive detail [made me feel] I was actually present in the [Sierra Nevada Mountains] enjoying the beautiful scenery.
VALERIE ROUSE
FOR READER'S FAVORITE